Delderfield, Ronald
    Charlie, come home.

Charlie, Come Home

R. F. DELDERFIELD

SIMON AND SCHUSTER

NEW YORK

Copyright © 1969 by R. F. Delderfield
All rights reserved
including the right of reproduction
in whole or in part in any form
Published by Simon and Schuster
A Gulf+Western Company
Rockefeller Center, 630 Fifth Avenue
New York, New York 10020
Designed by Edith Fowler
Manufactured in the United States of America
1   2   3   4   5   6   7   8   9   10

Library of Congress Cataloging in Publication Data

Delderfield, Ronald Frederick, 1912–1972.
    Charlie, come home.

    First published in Great Britain in 1969 under title:
Come home Charlie and face them.
        I. Title.
PZ3.D37618Cf3   [PR6007.E36]   823'.9'12   76-10600

ISBN 0-671-22325-9

For my old friend
Tom Salmon,
acknowledging so much encouragement
over the years

Chapter One

They didn't hang people anymore.

That was my first thought when I saw them digging, and after that another thought. They would scarcely have time to run down the truth if, as I thought unlikely, the trail went full circle once again and came back to Charlie. They hadn't been able to make a breakthrough when the trail was fresh, so why should they achieve one now, after nearly forty years?

It was this feeling of security, of course, that enabled me to toddle up here day after day and watch the earth-moving machines at work.

I could look on with indifference, wearing that slightly superior expression people with nothing to do wear whenever they watch others at work. A stooping, graying, used-up man taking his morning constitutional. Without a wisp of guilt or a tremor of fear. I had survived after all.

I didn't have all that long to enjoy the victory but at least I had lived to see it through to a finish. And that was something I had never expected.

Behind my natural curiosity I still wondered how I would react when it actually occurred. What I might say and do if, against all probability, the trail did lead back to me and they stood around firing questions at me as they had all that time ago. Would I be scared? Would I contradict and condemn myself? Or would I lie as coolly and consistently as I had lied then? Now that it was all on private record would I care enough to lie?

I didn't know now and I realized, standing there, that I never had known. What had once happened on that spot and back in the town was too improbable, too far removed from the mainstream of everyday life. It always had been and it still was. Not like something out of a book, a film, a Sunday newspaper, or one of the currently popular TV plays in which people lied and quarreled and killed, but more like a thread that ran a haphazard course through a nightmare. But even the worst nightmares have no power to terrify by day. They can even become absorbing if the dreamer recalls a sufficient number of figments in the morning. And I could recall every detail of this one.

Chapter Two

1

I could begin almost anywhere. With the moment when Ida made a man of me. Or with the moment when Delphine, her opposite number, converted me into a big-time crook. Or I could begin much further back, at the moment my father, himself a refugee from the pits, decided that I should be given the passport to the good life and enter Cadwallader's Mercantile Bank where, as a junior on a starting salary of twenty-five shillings a week, I paid out four-fifths of the money for board and lodging.

In a story like mine there are a thousand starting places. For the real motive wasn't love and it wasn't greed. It was not prompted by a thirst for adventure, or a desire to be rich and idle. It rose to the surface out of a gray pit of boredom and burst, very softly, in my face, like a sewer bubble. It happened at precisely four-thirty P.M., as the Chester–Holyhead train began to brake and run in along the straight coastal approach to Penmadoc Bay. Appropriately the date was April 1st, 1929.

I wasn't the first April Fool to carry my grips out onto that down platform overlooking the town filling the half-moon of the bay. I had done my homework on Penmadoc after learning that I was due for promotion from fourth man at a five-man branch to fifth man at a six-man establishment. I knew, for instance, that Penmadoc had had three starts in life to my one but we had a kinship, the town and I. Every time either of us fired a challenge shot at the century we both went off at half cock. From where I stood, with my back to the sea, I could recognize Penmadoc's three separate bids for an identity. The thin factory belt lay on the level land between the outer rim of the town and the jagged, grape-blue line of the nearest mountains. It was working at half-time then and the gauze veil of chimney smoke was not so dense as to screen the view of an older, less ambitious Wales. Its presence there established Penmadoc's attempt to convert itself into an industrial community, and failure in this respect came round about the last decade of the nineteenth century, when the Penmadoc fathers had another bright idea. They covered the area between factory belt and coast with streets of tall, narrow, granite houses and then launched a campaign to attract permanent residents. This almost succeeded and the population doubled itself in twenty years. But then the 1914–18 war broke out, and the kind of people who might have retired to Penmadoc made more money in four years than they had in forty and decided to move out of earshot of factory whistles. They migrated south or farther west, and soon all those narrow houses were hanging out "Board and Lodging" signs.

In the first year of the peace Penmadoc tried again, this time launching itself as a seaside resort and awarding itself a title, "Queen of the Cambrian Riviera." It extended its promenade and built a Baghdad-type pier pavilion. The attempt failed, of course, for it was made a generation too late. Colwyn Bay, Rhyl and Llandudno were well established by then, and entertainers like Clara Butt and Peter Dawson were not tempted by the Byzantine glitter of the onion dome that crowned the pier pavilion. Some visitors came, of course, but in relatively small numbers and rarely more than once, and by the time I arrived Penmadoc had settled for an uneasy compromise. It was neither an industrial town, a market town, a fishing town nor a resort, but a bewildering compound of all four, depending upon which part of the town you happened to be in. By 1929 there were about twenty thousand April Fools down there. I was just one more.

It wasn't my idea to make a career of banking and I never did think of Cadwallader's as my father and mother and all my uncles, aunts and cousins thought of it, a citadel against the sallies of the mining recruitment officer and the assaults of poverty, insecurity and industrial strife. I didn't think of it at all although I should have done, for I had grown up in the most wretched era of the coal industry and had seen dole queues a hundred yards long in towns with a smaller population than Penmadoc. But I didn't, and the reason I didn't derived from my father's own escape a generation before when he had fled the pits at nineteen and taken a teacher training course financed by a relation. His own relative security had buttressed me against his terrors. I didn't shrink from the pit for the very simple reason that I had never been down one and never wanted to go down one.

It didn't take me long, however, to realize I was going in the wrong direction. A position in a bank, any bank at that time, was regarded as a spectacular hoist up the social ladder and this not only in Wales, where unemployment was always high, but anywhere in the Western world. To get a footing in Caddie's, however, was something else for a Welshman because Cadwallader's was a national institution. It was one of those archaic demonstrations the Welsh have been making against English absorption for seven centuries, rather on a par with the Eisteddfod or the preservation of the Welsh language. Frantic efforts had been made by the Big Five to gobble it up but inside Offa's Dyke these attempts had met with small success, largely because Caddie's directors preferred to recruit staff from native-born Welshmen. As an institution it was very proud of its survival, so proud indeed that it paid its junior clerks a shilling a week higher starting salary than its rivals. To offset this singular advantage, however, it had the built-in feuds and jealousies of most family businesses. Its administration, based as it was on tribalism, was narrow even for these days and sometimes smacked of nepotism. The overall atmosphere of its smaller branches was as close and prescribed as a convent but this, of course, was not new to me. I had been raised in a strict, Nonconformist circle and could have taken the prohibitions of Caddie's in my stride had I been interested in banking as a career, or the least bit grateful for the limited security it offered. Unfortunately this wasn't so. All the time

I was progressing through the stages from inkwell filler and blotting-pad renewer to junior ledger clerk I developed a claustrophobia that was not the less oppressive for being subconscious. I didn't know what I did want to do with my life but I knew it wasn't this. I could not admit to such a heresy to my father. He was getting on for sixty then. The shock could have brought on a seizure.

Take a good look at me then, as I stood gazing down on the town on that mild April afternoon, an imitation leather suitcase in one hand, a canvas grip in the other—Charlie Pritchard, changing jails after a seven-year stretch; only another forty-odd to do before collecting his presentation clock and walking out into the world a free man; Charlie Pritchard, five-foot-five inches, nine-stone-two in his dark gray double breaster and square-toed shoes. He thinks of himself as no more or no less of a catch than the next man, despite his horn-rimmed spectacles and lack of inches, although the latter bothers him a little, and he has to remind himself now and again that Napoleon was a little man. He has brown eyes that rove as far and as speculatively as any young Welshman's and is secretly vain about his long lashes, good complexion and the breadth of his shoulders. For all that he doesn't qualify as a Don Juan, or the kind of young man whose intellect enables him to make light of Don Juans. He is still virginal, certainly not from choice but because of lack of cash, lack of opportunity and the heavy hangover of a Chapel upbringing. For the same reasons he can't dance and doesn't frequent bar-parlors but perhaps the Almighty had Charlie's long-range interests at heart when He did His handicapping. With these built-in limitations Charlie is ideal ledger fodder for Cadwallader's. After all, what else can he do of an evening but go home to his digs, read romantic fiction, and cram for Bankers' Institute?

2

I was in no hurry to present myself at the digs. I had a letter for my landlord, Evan Rhys-Jones, who was also manager of the branch. Dad's first miracle had been to land me a job with Caddie's. His second was to fix me up with unimpeachable digs through Evan's second cousin, who was one of his school managers. Evan's wife, Gladys, supplemented the family income by letting one room. The old Dad was delighted about this because he was nervous about the company I might keep so far from home. At all my previous branches he had been breathing down my neck. "How much have you got in your account now, Boyo? Do the clerks there smoke when the doors shut at three? Exchange dirty jokes, do they? Well, you don't have to listen, do you, Boyo?" It comforted him to know I was up here not only working with Cadwallader's but going to bed with them.

The air was very still that afternoon. The thin columns of smoke from the tin-plate factory went straight up and behind them the hazy outline of the mountains seemed to tremble. Not much stirred down these, just a car or two, and a few shoppers in the High Street, and then a two-stroke motor-cycle stuttering up the gradient of one of the cavernous roads behind the town center that ended in the tree-lined fringe of the Craigwen estate.

Suddenly but very decidedly I made up my mind. I would give it a go for a month or maybe two but by midsummer, if it wasn't a spectacular improvement on previous billets, I would run for my life. I didn't know in which direction but at that time this didn't seem important. All I knew with certainty was that inside the Cadwallader's Charlie was a Charlie who was bold, brash and a great deal more expectant and experimental than the yes-sir-no-sir-three-bags-full-sir Charlie Pritchard. The slow processes of economic and social conditioning were beginning to lose their impact. The obstinate hangover of a Bethel Chapel upbringing was beginning to lift. Out there, somewhere beyond the rim of the mountains, was a rainbow end and within walking distance of it were unimaginable rewards, not least among them personal independence, something more than a subsistence wage and, above all, a soft-skinned woman who would tremble when I touched her on the breast. Internal as well as external pressures were at were at work on me and the former were beginning to domi- work on me and the former were beginning to dominate. I had, by then, about eight years' post-puberty dreaming behind me and you can't go on dreaming forever. Dream backlogs have to be tackled just as resolutely as biannual accounts and mine had been building at a prodigious rate lately.

Rhys-Jones's home was one of those tall, narrow, graystone houses built during the middle period of Penmadoc's development in a steep road leading up to the wooded edge of the Craigwen estate, family seat of the only gentry we had left in the town. The house was called, for some inscrutable reason, "St. Ninian's," and was one of the few houses in that section that didn't have a board-residence sign clamped on it somewhere.

Evan Rhys-Jones had left the bank an hour earlier than usual, not to welcome me but to assess my possibilities as a replacement for the clerk who had moved on and had also been a lodger in the house.

He was one of those chubby, scrubbed-looking Welshmen you often meet in the north, the kind who grow to look like Pickwick round about the fifty mark and then trade on it, so that overdraft-seekers part with them feeling they would have been more successful if only they had told them the truth. He had an almost round head, a clipped mustache, thin, graying hair and a gravity that you could mistake for dignity until you adjusted to the maddening deliberation of his movements.

It was this characteristic that fascinated me on that first occasion, so that I found myself wondering how long it would take him to select a stick of celery, bring it up to his chubby jaws and produce the soft, carefully modulated snap, in contrast to his wife's regular volleys from across the table. You had the feeling that if you asked him to pass the salt the meal would falter to an uncertain halt; so in the end I compromised, watching him but listening to his wife's coy exploration of my nonexistent lovelife. They had a daughter, Ida, who sauntered in to be introduced about halfway through the meal and it didn't take me long to realize the significance of Gladys Rhys-Jones's persistent line of inquiry. Ida, a pinkish, generously-built, carroty-haired woman of about twenty-seven, was still on their hands and marriage prospects in Penmadoc were not bright for girls younger and more personable than Ida. I gathered that this was the reason why they let one of their bedrooms and although the grilling Gladys gave me did not bother me because I had no secrets to keep, I felt embarrassed for Ida, who made any number of attempts to head her mother in another direction. Once or twice she looked hopelessly at her father but he stuck to commercial subjects and in any case his attention was pretty well engaged cutting squares of bread and butter and adding sugar to his tea with tongs he handled like a surgeon's probe.

Gladys Rhys-Jones was a sallow, slab-sided woman and her appetite did a good deal to explain her sagging bulk, but demolition of a plate of paste sandwiches, a jar of celery, four cups of tea and two or three shop pastries did not prevent her from extracting a vast amount of trivia concerning my family background.

"There now," she sighed, "twenty-three and no *cariad bach*! We'll have to find him one, won't we, Ida? A young man with a steady job shouldn't have any trouble about *that* in Penmadoc, should he now?" and she went off into a series of soft wheezes that passed for laughter.

Evan, folding his napkin with the deliberation of a one-armed man striking a large marquee, came in with "Hold your chatter, Gladys, and show Mr. Pritchard to his room now!"

She didn't like the way he said that and the look she directed at him was the first hint I had that his air of authority was spurious.

"Ida can do it," she said, "everything's ready up there. Saw to it personally I did," and she sailed out into the hall and disappeared into the rear of the house.

I went up the narrow stairs behind Ida, noticing that her legs were far shapelier than her build would have led me to believe. I also noticed that she wore lisle stockings and not the art silk most girls favored in those pre-nylon days. My room was on the top floor with a single sash window facing southwest but in spite of a view of the sunset that flooded the shoulder of the Craigwen estate it looked as cheerless as the previous bed-sitters I had occupied. The narrow iron bedstead had brass knobs tarnished the color of sand. There was a deal chest of drawers with a spotted swing mirror, a basket chair with a badly-fitting cretonne cover and a wool rug that looked like a tiny tropical island in a sea of green linoleum. On the wall opposite the window was a steel engraving of the Prince of Wales's investiture at Caernarvon, in 1911, and over the bed a framed needlework text worked in red on a saffron ground. It announced, noncommittally, "Hallowed Be Thy Name." The first thing Ida did was to unhook the text and put it away in the bottom drawer of the deal chest and while she was doing this I got my first real look at her.

She was about two inches taller than me and weighed half as much again, with a rounded bust and heavy hips of a woman approaching middle age, but her face offset this maturity. It had a smooth and cheerful innocence that I found reassuring after the grilling that had done duty for a welcome downstairs. She wasn't pretty but she wasn't plain either, in spite of a long nose and a rather weak chin that made her nose look even longer. She had blue eyes with tolerance in them, and wore her rust-colored hair in a long bob, with a carefully-brushed fringe across the forehead. Her best feature was her mouth. It wasn't pursey, like her father's, or slack and gossipy like her mother's, but full and well-shaped, with humorous puckers at the corners where faint traces of lipstick showed, as though she had wiped it clean before joining us at the table. She said, slamming the drawer on the text, "Not be needing that, will you now?" and I said I could get along without it so that she giggled and the giggle gave me an opening for a remark that set the tone on our relationship all the time we lived together under that roof.

"You don't have to worry about all those questions your mother asked me," I said. "All mothers carry on that way when a single man shows up. It's happened to me before, in digs down south."

It was inviting a snub, I suppose. All her mother had done, when you came to peel away the hints, was to express satisfaction that I lacked a "cariad bach," the term North Walesians of her type invariably use for "sweetheart." Yet I knew, and Ida knew that I knew, that the confrontation downstairs needed justification. She didn't say anything for a moment but then, turning away from the chest and facing me with a kind of exasperated cheerfulness, she said, "That was on account of Wally. Mam took a nasty knock over Wally."

"Was Wally the clerk who had this room ahead of me?"

"Yes. He's gone to the Sanatorium with TB. Mam got it into her head something might come of me and Wally, but I never did. I was just sorry for him. TB runs in families, doesn't it?"

I said I had heard it did but she wasn't listening. She went on, vaguely, "Hear him coughing up here, I would. Mam and Dadda pretended it was just a bad cold. He didn't tell anybody, see, except me, that is. He was that afraid of losing his place at the bank. I'd say to him sometimes, 'Who gives a damn about the ole bank? Do they give a damn about you, now?' "

I asked if Wally had been a religious chap, the text over the bed having planted the idea.

"No," she said, "Wally never went near Chapel. Didn't believe in it. He always said he was a communist. You're not, are you?"

I said I wasn't anything. I had had a bellyful of politics growing up in the south during a wave of strikes and lockouts but I thought Evan Rhys-Jones must have been relieved to see the back of Wally. A communist son-in-law, with or without TB, would be a liability to a branch manager of Cadwallader's.

She heaved herself off the chest and walked over to the window looking out across the Craigwen estate. The sun put a torch to her hair so that it turned from rust to furnace red and was the better for it. I got the impression that she was trying to make up her mind to say something important and I was right.

"You don't *have* to stay here," she said suddenly, staring me down in a way that reminded me of her mother, "there are people in town who need the money and would be damn glad of a lodger with a steady job. Might even find a place where there were young people, if you was lucky."

"You mean you'd like me to make some excuse? Say I don't like the room perhaps?"

She thought this over, her strong teeth clamping down on her lip and making it redder than the smear of lipstick at the corner of her mouth. Then she took a deep breath and said, "No. Play it that way and Mam would be right after you, the way she was with the others. And Dadda will have to back her and that might make things sticky for you down at the bank. Mam gets a hot flush every time she thinks I'll die an old maid but it doesn't bother me. Like old Miss Evans used to say, 'It's not so bad, once you've got over the disgrace.' "

I laughed at that. You had to because she said it seriously. "What is she getting in such a sweat about?" I asked, "you can't be more than a year or so older than I am."

"Thanks for the benefit of the doubt," she said. "Mam'll let slip tomorrow I'm twenty-five but I could give you more than that. I'll be twenty-nine next birthday."

"Well all right," I said, "but that doesn't mean I have to decamp because your Mam is out fishing for a husband. Your father isn't so crazy he thinks a man could get married on what I earn."

"Mam's got money of her own. Not much but enough to help out. She even told Wally as much."

Suddenly I didn't like the way this conversation was going and asked if the lodger who preceded Wally was yet another bank clerk.

"No," she said, "the one before last was Mr. Waring. He'd just lost his wife. I was sorry for him, too."

The only thing to do was to make a joke of it.

"Is there anyone you aren't sorry for?"

"Not many," she said, calmly. "Dam' silly of me, it is, but you can't help the way you're made, can you? I'm sorry for stray cats too." Her head came up and she gave me that frank, steady look again. "Bit of a stray yourself, aren't you? Tell you something else while we're at it. You hate Caddie's, don't you? You'd be dam' glad if the bank went bust, closed its doors and showed you the street! That's true, isn't it?"

Considering that less than two hours had elapsed since I had faced up to this decision the accuracy of the statement took my breath away. I just stood there gaping and at the same time I experienced a curious shrinking sensation that had to do with some indefinable crisis, or series of crises, that lay ahead, perhaps for everyone in that house but centering on me and on my arrival in Penmadoc. I found my tongue at last and said, irritably, "Are you telling me to walk out of my job as well as my digs just because the chaps here ahead of me had bad luck?"

She said, slowly, "It's not ghosts I'm talking about. You're not getting old, like Mr. Waring, and you aren't dying, like poor old Wally. It's up to you I reckon."

"Damn it, *what's* up to me? To walk out on a safe job into the unemployment queue?"

"Ah, 'safe,'" she said, "that's a word we use a lot around here, Mr. Pritchard. Dadda's safe. Safe as Cadwallader's bank he is, but look at him." Then, directly, "It's not a cushy branch, Mr. Pritchard; if there is such a thing I mean. You'll find out soon enough. Bloody awful it is and not only on account of Dadda being a worrier. That's just the part of it he brings home." She had me thoroughly interested now, but before I could comment she said, abruptly, "Leave you to unpack," as though we had just concluded the most formal conversation imaginable. "Biscuits and cocoa at nine-thirty. No extra charge," and she went out onto the landing and down the stairs.

I sat on the bed trying to get my thoughts in some kind of order and Ida's contribution to them wasn't the only reason why I felt disturbed and confused. Mainly it was the persistent malignity of the room so that presently, emptying the contents of my case and grip onto the bed, I picked up my raincoat and went down to the hall and out into the blue dusk of Craigwen Terrace. I had a fancy to take an objective look at Penmadoc and study the outside of the bank on the way home.

Chapter Three

1

Cadwallader's Penmadoc branch was a squat, brown, two-story building, occupying a site two-thirds of the way down Station Road that led to an open space in front of the railway embankment. It was about five minutes' walk from the digs and two minutes from the promenade. At the bottom of Station Road, one of Penmadoc's main shopping centers, the road forked and both branches took you to the seafront, east or west of the pier.

The grilled lower windows were emblazoned with the golden dragon, Caddie's insignia, and the fabric looked better cared for than all the other business premises in the block. The floor above was called "Overbank" and was a largish flat. Evan Rhys-Jones had told me that this was occupied by Powell, the chief cashier, a man with an English wife and two boys at the local grammar school. As a place to work in it looked more comfortable and commodious than any of the other branches I had served down south. It had a clean and dependable aspect, the kind of place where your money would not only be well guarded but taken out and dusted off once a week.

You couldn't say the same of the premises on either side of it. Nearer the station was Corwen's, stationers and newsagents, its double-fronted windows pasted over with flyblown notices hand-written by people who wanted to buy or sell something, mostly sell. The shop front was starred with tin advertisements wooing passersby to smoke this brand or that and Corwen, the proprietor, who was still open when I called in for a packet of Player's, was a paunched, defeated man, who looked as if he shaved every other day. He asked me if I was a visitor down for Easter and when I told him I was the new clerk at Caddie's my stock at once shot up several points.

That was the curious thing about Caddie's in those days. All over Wales it lent prestige to anyone who worked for it, as though even the junior clerks were handpicked and only rejects moved on to hammer at the doors of the Big Five. This may have had to do with the intense nationalism of the Welsh, who thought of Cadwallader's in the way an Englishman might think of the Bank of England. The newsagent said, "My, but that's good! That's a safe job!" so that I remembered Ida's parting remark about the popularity of this word in Penmadoc. Already I was half persuaded that I was one of the few survivors of a catastrophic wreck and ought to be down on my knees thanking God for breath and a weekly wage. It didn't do much to inspire confidence in the town's economy.

Immediately above Caddie's was a draper's, called Thos. Cook & Son, its window full of garments hung on coat hangers surrounded by bolts of muslin and curtain material piled in untidy pyramids of blue, green, gray and brown. The place looked almost as seedy as the newsagent's and that was saying a good deal.

Beyond the draper's was a narrow-fronted café called "The Rainbow" and its garish colors, together with the amount of business it seemed to be doing, made it the odd man out in that moribund street. From across the road it looked like a single rowdy drunk, lost among a cluster of Chapel deacons with Cadwallader's as their pastor. The café's fascia boards and window ledges were picked out in mauve, crimson and primrose, and somewhere inside a honkytonk or electric piano was blaring a popular dance-tune. It made a sound like children running hoopsticks along rows of iron railings.

The incongruity of The Rainbow fascinated me. I watched a crowd of youths emerge and collect their bicycles stacked against the curb, and then two stringy girls went in giggling and nudging one another, as the boys made some pointed remarks. It was obviously the unofficial mating center of Penmadoc and catered for the rising generation. When the honkytonk stopped I heard the long hiss of the milkshake or coffee machine. It sounded like the laughter of a powerful man tormented by catarrh.

I crossed the road and went in, taking a seat at a yellow-topped table at the back. The surface was stained with a predecessor's red-currant drink, sticky to the touch. In here the noise of the restarted honkytonk, an automatic machine that looked like a pregnant robot, was deafening. Customers on both sides of the café were talking and I could see their mouths open and close but although the shop was not more than twenty feet across and thirty deep I was unable to hear a word any one of them exchanged. My glasses steamed up and I had to take them off and polish them.

It was not until I replaced them that I noticed the girl collecting dirty glasses and cups just across the aisle. Behind the counter, operating the machine, I half saw a man but I paid him no attention and for a good reason. It was the girl who caught and held my glance and I only had to look at her once through unmisted lenses to learn one reason why The Rainbow was popular with all the local lads. She was stunning. No other word describes the double impact she made upon my senses, two distinct blows hitting with a force that literally knocked the breath from my body. That is the only way I can convey my reaction to the first glimpse I ever had of the Rainbow Queen and it has taken me all of forty years to absorb the recoil.

I had been looking at women speculatively, hopefully and hopelessly for years but this was something altogether different because a glance was enough to establish her unattainability and I came to terms with that in a matter of seconds. From then on I watched her as a man saving up for a second-hand motorbike might gaze at a streamlined sports car that had set its owner back a couple of thousand pounds.

I find it very difficult at this distance in time to convey the overall impression she made upon me and one reason for this is that it was both aesthetic and sensual, in proportions of about one to two. She had good features and unusually light blue, dark-ringed eyes that set her apart as a more than ordinarily pretty girl, and her figure, well-formed and a little unfashionable in those far-off, flat-chested days, was mature and pleasing, but neither face nor figure was more than moderately arresting. What held the eye after it had been caught was something much more singular, and sex appeal is far too tame a phrase to describe it. So are words like sensuality and voluptuosity, because Delphine's appeal was more basic than that and reached further back in time. It was a kind of animal vitality that showed in her every movement and posture and had about it tremendous promise tempered by what I can only describe as a wary aggressiveness. As she drifted about, gathering a trayful of cups and plates soiled with lipstick and traces of ice cream and fruit juice, you had the impression that she was half poised for a spring at your throat or your genitals or both, and this is not to say that she employed any of the recognizable artifices in the armory of provocation. She didn't, either then or later. She was just herself, with a slender waist, a pair of hard, aggressive breasts under a tight lilac overall and a pair of hips that indulged in a slow, deliberate dance every time she reached over a customer's shoulder to add to the load of crocks on her tray. Her expression was that of a slightly bored woman performing a casual chore and for some reason you knew that the leering glances and inconsequent chatter her arrival at each table provoked made absolutely no impression on her. It was just part of a day's work in a noisy, sleazy backwater and could be dismissed with a yawn when the time came to pull down the blinds and count the day's takings.

When she arrived at the table across the aisle I had a closer look at her face. Her eyes, slightly upslanting, were her most arresting feature, a shade of blue I never recalled seeing before, midway between the underside of a periwinkle petal and the heart of a violet, but her hair was pretty too, smooth, dark brown, and worn in a long bob that made the most of its prodigality. Her mouth, considered in isolation, was a

24

booby trap. It looked submissive and generous until you set it against the short, straight nose and the small, resolute chin. Her complexion was pale and should have been moist in that close atmosphere but the texture of the skin resisted the temperature in the way its owner, as a person, was able to divorce herself from the steamy conviviality of the room. The only thing about her that brought you down to earth was her voice. It was husky and matter-of-fact, with a very definite transatlantic drawl of the kind we were only beginning to adjust to with the very first of the talking pictures. Somehow it had no business at all issuing from that mouth. I would have been ready to bet a month's salary she would speak with a Latin accent and I don't think I would have been much surprised if she had addressed me in French or Italian. She said, in reply to my subdued request for a coffee, "You serve yourself, Bub. Over there," and said it without looking at me. I wasn't deflated so much as chastened by her casual unconcern.

I got up and went over to the counter to give my order and while the machine was blowing off steam I had an opportunity to study the man. If she hadn't been there he would have impressed me more than he did at that time. He was a broad-shouldered, good-looking man in his mid-thirties and there was no doubt at all about him being a Latin, almost certainly an Italian. He was very swarthy, his hair was jet black and oiled, and he had blunt fingers that reinforced an overall impression of strength and agility. He was more civil than the girl and served the coffee with a swift, meaningless smile and an almost amiable nod. I took the cup back to my table and found myself wondering about them both to the total exclusion of everything else in Penmadoc. When she was at the other end of the café and he was masked in steam I had a few seconds' leisure to think about the clientele. I came to three conclusions about them. The men were mostly hooked on the girl, the girls were resigned to being wallflowers at a hop as long as she was around, and nobody in Penmadoc would make the Rainbow Queen even if she wasn't married to the good-looking Wop behind the counter.

I had another coffee, dreamed a few extravagant dreams and went out into the April twilight. The honkytonk, now grinding out "Horsey, Keep Your Tail Up," speeded me on my way up Station Road and I could still hear it when I crossed over into Craigwen Terrace. In the hall I met Ida who gave me a quizzical look.

"Well?" she said.

"I've worked in worse places."

"Oh no you haven't, Boyo," she said, but kept smiling. "You want that cocoa? We have it about now."

I said I didn't and went up the steep stairs to bed. It bothered me to bandy words with Ida after an hour in the presence of the Rainbow Queen.

2

Ida was right and I realized that in less than a week. The course I shaped in Penmadoc was my own but the pressures surrounding me, and the circumstances dictating that choice, were closely involved in what happened. The most important of these was a terrible tension within the branch created by the clash of personalities among the staff.

Judged solely on physical conditions and, to a degree, prospects of promotion, the posting was good. One of the first things to astonish me, for instance, was the tremendous volume of business we did there, but this increased rather than diminished tensions between members of the staff. There were external as well as internal reasons for this. At that time Caddie's was fighting a tremendous holding action against the Big Five and it was a gallant, forlorn struggle, doomed to ultimate failure, but the real reason for the explosive atmosphere in that big, first-floor room could be traced to the assembly of that team in that place at that particular time.

To begin with Evan Rhys-Jones wasn't up to his job as manager. Men who are bullied at home, as he certainly was, usually take it out on juniors at their place of work, but all Evan Rhys-Jones did when he hung up his hat every morning was to exchange the mild tyranny of a stupid wife for a more positive intimidation on the part of an arrogant chief cashier. In addition he was a born worrier, and anyone who has worked under a worrier can tell you that a bully or a sluggard is preferable as a boss. Evan Rhys-Jones worried about his overdrafts, his security, and things like the amount of office sugar we put in the tea we brewed when we stayed late balancing the cash. But mostly he worried about his cashier, Nicholas Powell.

Socially, Powell was a cut above the rest of us. He was that extremely rare phenomenon, a Welsh-based snob, who thought of his superior as a hobbledehoy whose local connections had got him a managership that should have come to Powell when the vacancy occurred. Powell's wife, a London woman, looked upon everyone in the Principality as a white coolie. She had money of her own, and their two boys were entered for an English public school. She dressed smartly but extravagantly, drove a little red sports car, and talked with a plum balanced on her tongue. It was clear they had long regarded this branch as their personal province, especially since they lived on the premises, and Rhys-Jones just wasn't man enough to force Powell to toe the line. One of the more justifiable sources of Powell's contempt was the manager's anxiety neurosis that often led to all of us working overtime in order to satisfy Rhys-Jones that the locking up and key-dispersal drill had been carried out in a manner as to ensure him a good night's sleep. Another was the manager's tendency to mark an overdraft higher than a customer rated if he spoke Welsh, was a regular chapelgoer, and had some connection with the current Eisteddfod. Rhys-Jones wasn't a nationalist in the way that Griffiths, our second cashier, was, but he never let Powell forget that he had been born of Welsh parents in Chester and thus had no real claim on a Caddie's managership. It was his only way of getting back at Powell for the cashier's insufferable interference and occasional insolence.

Griffiths, the second cashier, wasn't a bad sort once you adapted to his obsession with Celtic mythology and all the blether this type of Welshman uses to offset the fact that Wales was conquered by the English in the thirteenth century. He was a solemn, industrious man, a bachelor supporting an elderly mother and easier to work with than either Rhys-Jones or the sneering, saturnine Powell, with his English airs and graces. He was also far less patronizing than my immediate superior, an Englishman called Porsen, who was first ledger clerk. Below me, a person who plays little part in this story, was Gregg, the dogsbody junior. The only singular thing about Gregg was that he had a permanent sniffling cold and was liberal with germs that had taken permanent residence in his septum.

Because I worked behind the barrier and only occasionally took a turn at the counter, I associated with Porsen more than any of the others. He was a hearty, pink-cheeked type, who worked tremendously hard at being masculine but when in the company of superiors he liked to ape the English gentleman. With a junior he reverted to what he was, a coarse-minded, bumptious cad. He owned a Brough Superior motorcycle and its pillion seat was fitted with a leopardskin cover awaiting the next victim of a revved-up courtship. It was fascinating to watch him set out on one of his hunting expeditions. He wore goggles and leather gauntlets and sat the machine in such a manner that his fat arse stuck out in a curiously challenging manner. I don't know how many local girls he codded with his act but if it was half as many as he claimed he was going to need monkey-gland treatment before he was thirty.

Not long after I had joined the staff I was fool enough, in the presence of the sober Griffiths, to ask Porsen for information concerning the people at the café next door but one.

"Aha," he gloated, in his egregiously superior manner, "so you've already been smitten by Lickerish Lil the Wanton Wop, have you? We'll have to watch you, Pritchard! We can't have you drooling after our Delphine like those bounders from the tin-plate works whenever they can spare time from the dole queue!"

Griffiths said, sourly, "For God's sake, stop making every-

28

thing you say sound as if you were reading aloud from a lavatory wall!"

Nobody had ever succeeded in snubbing Porsen so he accepted the rebuke without comment. "Strictly out of bounds, kid," he said. "Better men than you have tried, me included!" It was the only time I ever heard Porsen admit to a failure in this field.

Later on, when I could approach Griffiths alone, I repeated the question. He told me that the Italians—he wasn't even sure they were Italians—had come there about a year ago from San Francisco or Los Angeles. They were, he said, stepbrother and stepsister, their father having married twice, and there was talk of the father joining them as soon as he had disposed of business interests in the States. In the meantime they kept themselves very much to themselves. The only people who knew anything about them were the dozen or so Catholics in the town and it was from a Catholic customer that Griffiths had this limited information. They didn't bank with us, he added, and probably didn't bank at all. The man, Beppo as the customers called him, appeared to speak very little English and although she was much younger than her stepbrother the girl seemed to manage the business. The general idea was they would work it up, sell it, and disappear overnight. "Most foreigners do," said Griffiths, "including the English who try their hand here."

Griffiths, as I later discovered, knew as much as anyone about them but Porsen was right about every young man in town (and some who were not so young) trying to make the girl. I often went in there for a coffee on my way home, or after an evening potter along the seafront, and always there was a table of men or youths skylarking around the blaring honkytonk. She shrugged them all off, with her aggressive hips, her absentminded smile or, just occasionally, a flat, deflating stare. One way and another Delphine didn't go out of her way to encourage business, but as there was no late-night competition in Penmadoc, The Rainbow café seemed to show a profit judging by the number of customers it attracted.

As for me, I never escaped from the spell the girl's latent promise had cast over me that first night but I never tried to compete with the local Romeos. For the time being I was content to sip coffee and watch her supple, effortless drift about the room. I could never see her stacking crockery without thinking of a ballerina, perhaps a ballerina promoted to the position of favorite in the court of a dissolute king. Her expression was always the same, one of self-satisfied abstraction, with the faintest tincture of boredom. And yet, behind this was promise, high life and bedroom promise on certain terms and the terms, of course, would be prohibitive. When she addressed Beppo she used Italian and then, for a few brief seconds, she seemed to crackle and become one of us. But then she would subside again so that mostly it was like watching a film with the sound turned off. The only variation about Delphine's performance was the color of her overall. Sometimes it was lilac, sometimes primrose, sometimes cherry and sometimes white, but whatever the color it helped to create an impression that it was part of a flower that should have wilted in the steamy atmosphere but didn't because it bloomed by celestial decree.

I took to calling in at The Rainbow as a true believer might seek solace in church. I was never a person to make friends easily, lacking the gregariousness of the Welsh and having, notwithstanding extravagant dreams, more than my share of shyness when it came to making a direct approach. I couldn't make a friend of any of the men at the branch. All but Porsen were too old and Gregg, the sniffler, was generally under the weather with one of his heavy colds. I was always grateful to escape from the bank but going home meant hobnobbing with Rhys-Jones, his honking wife Gladys, or his daughter Ida. I didn't go out of my way to avoid Ida. As a matter of fact, her frankness on the night I arrived in town interested me but she made no physical appeal to me and when I failed to respond to her half-hearted approaches she left me alone. I thought then that she had written me off as a dull dog, lacking the romantic mantle of Wally's TB and

Mr. Waring's tragic bereavement. So always, when I was tired of walking, or fed up with the isolation of the room I shared with two ghosts, I ended up at The Rainbow drinking two and sometimes three coffees and watching Delphine prowl. Both palliatives helped to keep me awake into the small hours.

I see now that it was the unattainable Delphine that helped to damp down the fires of rebellion that had been smoldering long before I arrived in Penmadoc and had burst through the crust of apathy for a brief moment when I looked down on the town for the first time and decided to give Caddie's one more chance. Notwithstanding this I soon grew to hate the branch and the town, and I loathed the sight of Powell, who was a bully, a pedant and a snob, together with the sound of Porsen's voice. Griffiths, the nationalist, bored me and I began to share some of Powell's contempt for the manager but for different reasons. What irritated me most about Rhys-Jones was his deification of the men who had worked him so ruthlessly from the day he bought his first celluloid collar and went to work for Cadwallader's. Like my father he thought of the bank as a temple and the directors, smug on princely incomes in Cardiff, as its archpriests. Even his wife Gladys made no secret of the fact that she thought him a fidget and a dullard. She had outside interests but he had none, except ritual attendance at Chapel every Sunday. My state of turpitude, however, notwithstanding my silent absorption with Delphine, was to end very soon.

By July, when the holiday season was in full swing, we were about as busy as we could be, particularly toward the fag end of the week when all the bed-and-breakfasts came in to bank their takings and the local tradesmen's turnover was nearing its peak. With the rush of business, feuds exploded into hatreds. Rhys-Jones and Powell were sparring all day long and the battle was beginning to tell on both of them. Griffiths and Porsen were constantly snarling at one another over fancied insults and sometimes made a point of communicating with each other through me. Then, seeing how things were, Rhys-Jones teamed up with Griffiths and the Chester-born Powell made a junior ally of Porsen. Partisanship on this scale didn't make for efficiency and every hitch in routine touched off a minor explosion. Finally Gregg went sick and I was left with the four of them and Gregg's duties into the bargain.

One of the major social advances of post-war decades has been the introduction of women into every field of commercial activity. With women about their place of work men might be facetious or goatish but mostly they stop short of puerility. In the absence of women as safety valves men in authority can out-bitch any woman alive. This was precisely how it was at Caddie's that summer and by the end of July I was nearing the end of my tether. Even the prospect of sacking myself, condemning my parents to nervous breakdowns and myself to tramp the roads and sleep in haystacks, seemed preferable to staying on as a buffer between two warring factions, both of whom I was beginning to loathe. The terrible predictability of my life beat in on my senses like a knell. It was as though I stood at the bottom of a gigantic staircase with the years marked off on every tread, facing a climb of forty years in the company of men like Rhys-Jones, Powell, Griffiths and the leery, fat-arsed Porsen, and there were no breaks in that staircase. It stretched out of sight, every stair identical, with no alternative but to climb and climb, regulating one's stride to the jostlings of the others and getting buffeted every inch of the way. There was no short cut to the top and there was no taking two stairs at a time. The only prospect of escape, and it seemed to me then and now a desperate course, was to back down and start again in another direction. By the last Saturday of July, the weekend of August Bank Holiday, I had made up my mind to do just this.

3

God knows, I was ill equipped even for flight to nowhere. In my account was nineteen pounds ten and in my pocket the balance of my weekly pay packet after lodgings and insurance had been deducted, a matter of about sixteen shillings. I had two suits, one of them nicely polished by Cadwallader's ledger rests, a supply of socks and handkerchiefs, and three shirts, two of them ready for the Monday wash. It was probably acknowledgment of the sheer desperation of my plight that checked a half-hearted attempt to pack and caused me to sit on the bed, hands on knees, staring at the picture of the Prince of Wales's investiture, on the wall. Then, with a sense of shock that returns to me even now, I felt a tear spill over my cheek and run down past the corner of my mouth so that I tasted the brine and thought, with a kind of savage shame, "Christ, this is what it's come to! Charlie Pritchard, who once believed he could see them all off, sitting here crying like a kid in the dark!" and as I jumped up and dashed my hand across my face I heard a tap on the door and Ida's voice saying, "You there, Boyo? Can I come in a minute?"

I was glad to see anyone at that moment and after blowing my nose I called to her to come in. I knew she would query the stuff piled on the bed and I welcomed a chance of unloading some of my wretchedness on her. She at least didn't disappoint me but said, opening her eyes in a way that advertised her lack of eyebrows, "Going away for the weekend, are you? You never said you were!" It was an invitation to dramatize the situation.

"I'm going all right," I said, with counterfeit bravado, "but not for the weekend, for bloody good!"

She didn't seem as shocked as she should have been. After a polite pause she said, carefully, "You in some kind of trouble, Charlie? At the bank, I mean?"

"I'm in every kind of trouble there is," I said.

She went back onto the landing, cocked an ear for her

mother, came in again and sat down in the wicker chair. I noticed then that she had dressed herself up and wondered if it was for my benefit. She had on a navy-blue two-piece I hadn't seen before and instead of the lisle stockings and the sloppy, flat-heeled shoes she wore she had silk stockings and patent leather shoes with two-inch heels. Her long nose still glowed but the glow had been subdued by a heavy dusting of powder and she had traced a fashionable Cupid's bow with her lipstick. I couldn't help comparing her pathetic attempts to improve on Nature with Delphine's sexy presence after a day spent in that steaming café. She said, "If you're walking out on Caddie's then there must have been a bust-up. Dadda hasn't said a word about it!"

"How could he?" I said, brutally, "he'd have to get Mr. Powell's okay before he mentioned it, even to your mother."

She said, with restraint, "All right, tell me about it. I warned you what it would be like but tell me how you're involved."

I told her something of the furious bickering and nagging that was going on down there, but much more concerning my own status and wretched prospects. I told her how my father felt about me having a job with Caddie's, and how that job had come to look to me in the last year or so. I told her pretty well everything except of my devotionary visits to The Rainbow. She was a good listener and let me talk myself out before saying, "You can't go home then. Have you got some other job lined up?"

"I thought I'd try for a steward's job at Liverpool."

"That's mad," she said, "that's just fool's talk! They're laying ships up and besides, you'd need a good reference. I can't see you getting one from Caddie's if you go in this mood."

"Right, but I'm not spending my entire life as a Caddie's pen pusher," I said, "I'd sooner walk off the end of the pier."

"A thing like this needs thinking about," she said. "You've got to give yourself the benefit of every chance that does exist. There aren't so many as you can throw one away."

This was a different Ida from the one I thought I knew, the rather drab nonentity I had seen used by her bell-toothed mother as a glorified skivvy. She had authority. She conveyed the impression of having contemplated flight herself and given the possibilities a good deal of thought.

"I'm not saying it would be easy," she went on, guessing what was passing through my mind, "but it's easier for a man than a woman. That is, if he doesn't panic the way you are now. The first thing is to believe you're somebody worth employing." She looked at me steadily, without blinking her sandy lashes. "Your trouble is that, deep down, you don't and never have, Boyo. You spend your time dreaming instead of doing." Then, but still without taking her eyes off me, "You're still a virgin to start with."

"We're talking about jobs not pastimes," I said.

"In your case they go together. A man of your age who has never had fun with a woman wouldn't make much of a fist at walking out on a safe job. It's got to do with pride. Did you know Zulus weren't allowed to marry until they had bloodied their spears?"

For some reason this remark introduced a gleam of humor into the situation. It also reminded me of Ida's compulsive need to dispense sympathy to every star-crossed man she met. Perhaps this was what she meant by "being sorry" for the two previous occupants of this room.

Suddenly I decided that I not only liked but respected her as someone who insisted on being a person instead of a unit in a mindless universe. Her very presence there in the squeaking chair, waiting for me to react to what was clearly an invitation, warmed and excited me and not merely in the sexual sense. Just as Delphine represented the ideal and unattainable, so Ida was her complement, a woman who was prepared to dispense courage and comfort with no prospect of reward other than the satisfaction of helping a fellow human being over a hump. Acknowledgment of this, however, had a disastrous effect upon my emotions. Suddenly, but this time entirely without shame, I began to cry again, and as I bowed my head I heard her say, "Wait, Charlie! Wait a minute, Boyo!"

She jumped up and went out to the stairhead leaving the

door open. Without understanding what she was doing I saw her descend the stairs and heard her open the front door. She called, loudly, "Going to Chapel, Mam!" and the door slammed. A moment later she was ascending the stairs carrying her shoes. She came in, locked the door and stood looking down at me where I sat on the edge of the bed among the clothes tumbled from the chest of drawers.

"By God, Charlie," she said, softly, "you really are in a bad way, aren't you now?"

She said it like a doctor addressing himself to the task of patching up a child with a grazed knee. Methodically she reached behind me, lifted my grip and clothes from the bed and put them back in the chest of drawers. Then, without haste, she took my face between her hands and kissed me softly on the mouth. She might have been saying, "Now this isn't going to hurt one little bit, Charlie. It'll be over before you realize it!"

It was too, or so it seemed to me. The way she went about it, with a kind of joyful gusto, made it as uncomplicated as falling off a wall. To Ida the act of loving a man was a welcome chore, something that had to be achieved before settling down to the serious business of the day, but I don't mean by that that she failed to derive pleasure from it. She did, but it wasn't a simple physical gratification of the kind she was able to bestow in such good measure. You had the impression that what she really enjoyed was the ability to distract a man so quickly and effortlessly and that she was standing outside her body and congratulating it for fulfilling such a practical purpose. I suppose this was partly why I experienced no guilt and absolutely no fear. In a few breathless moments I learned more about sex than I had learned since puberty. And this in itself was a kind of miracle, for growing up in a small Welsh town and having, like everyone else, to rely upon dirty jokes, books passed from hand to hand, and the speculations of equally baffled associates, I had been taught to associate sex with sin and the blackest kind of sin at that. In a community of this kind almost everything is black or white and even sex within marriage is a dingy gray. It came as a very pleasant surprise to find I didn't have to square my conscience with the act or Ida.

We lay there for an hour or so, watching the setting sun turn the underside of the clouds coral pink and bronze, and the shadows cast by the bulk of the Craigwen hillside creep across the floor. She was right about that link she had mentioned. I was a different Charlie Pritchard already. The secret, cocksure Charlie of fantasy had taken on flesh, bones and bounce, and understanding this I had the impulse to thank her and might have found the right words if she hadn't sat up, swung her long legs down to the floor and made some kind of shift to tidy herself in the oval mirror. She said, "Didn't tell you why I came up here in the first place, did I now? It was about tomorrow. Evans-the-Tours gave us two free passes for the Llanberis–Bettws-y-Coed trip. We get them every year for sticking a bill on the back gate and Mam thought you might like the odd one. She's still hoping, you see."

"Were you going anyway?"

"Yes, but I've been times enough. You don't have to go, or if you'd rather go alone I can change mine for the Anglesey tour. Might do you good. You could start making a plan. A proper one, I mean."

"I'll go if you'll come along. I'd far sooner that than go on my own, Ida."

She swung round in the act of fastening her suspender clip and looked at me as if what I said had exasperated her.

"Listen, Boyo, that's not the little gentleman's way of saying thank you, is it? If it is it's like as giving me a pound note for obliging!"

Her terrible honesty was something you had to get used to and learn to live with, a bit at a time.

"I'd like a chance to talk things out," I mumbled. "We wouldn't have to stay with the party all the time, would we?"

"No," she said, looking relieved, "and I know the place. We can skip lunch at Bettws-y-Coed and take sandwiches." She hitched her skirt as high as her fat rump, winked at herself in the mirror, and unlocked the door. I guessed that she would creep down, open and close the front door as noisily as possible and give Mam a breezy "Here I am" hail from the hall. It was probably a drill perfected after desperate attempts to solace Wally and Mr. Waring.

"See you then," she said. "They start out at nine, so it's breakfast at the usual time."

I turned in early and enjoyed the best night's sleep I had had in a month.

Chapter Four

1

Ida's "right place" was a shallow dell on a bracken-covered hillside downstream of the falls. The roar of tumbling water was muted here and the woods were sown with boulders arrested in their passage down the slopes a thousand years ago.

It was the best kind of country up here, the kind of landscape you see advertised on railway posters but rarely find in season because so many people are out looking for it. Harebells grew in the crevices and when you turned your face toward the falls you could feel the spray on your cheeks and temples.

It was a spot where you could get your problems into focus by raising your eyes and looking over the woods at peaks, wreathed in mist trailers but the lower slopes clearly seen, and picking up the glitter of quartz or last night's raindrops in the bright sunlight. What had happened and would happen to you, was insignificant. The hills had seen worse troubles and had survived them.

The mountains, and the weight of water going over the falls, must have had this effect on Ida. She was so subdued that it was difficult to imagine how briskly she had gone about the business of seducing me less than twenty-four hours ago. She hadn't forgotten why we had come here, however, and after disposing of the sandwiches the gleeful Gladys had cut for us, said, "You wouldn't care to be a hill farmer, I suppose?

They don't make any money, but they get by, and always seem to me more cheerful than people in towns."

I said I had known hill farmers back home who were anything but cheerful, and at least one who had cut his throat. She was philosophical about this. "Well, it's a battle from the cradle to the grave for ninety-five percent of us. You have to make up your mind to that from the start. What is it you really *want?*"

I almost said I could get along comfortably with her for the time being. That was another discovery I made in her company, that sex is like the temperance advocate's definition of drink and creates its own appetite. Already I had a broader and far less inhibited outlook. I can't say that I felt capable of punching Porsen's nose when he shouted "Hey, kid!" or telling Powell to jump off Snowdon but at least I had repossessed myself of a few rags of human dignity. I said, "After last night I can think of something better to do," and I rolled over and kissed her, at the same time letting my hand stray down the front of her dress.

She told me, laughing, that I was making good progress but that as we were due to rejoin the coach in a few minutes I had better confine myself to the business that had brought us here, namely my chances of sidestepping a life sentence behind Caddie's counter. "Get involved with me, or anyone else for that matter, and you'll have no option. Fun and games are one thing, Charlie, but courtship and marriage, that's slow death to what you have in mind."

She asked me how much money I had and when I told her less than twenty pounds she said the first step was to make it a hundred.

"You need a float," she said, "and a hundred can give you freedom of action for six months if you're careful. Without that there's not even any point in paying lunchtime visits to the library to look through the 'Situations Vacant.'"

Her practical approach impressed me. In all the time I had been rebelling against the confines of the cul-de-sac it had never once occurred to me to go to the library and look for an alternative in the daily papers in the reading room.

"Does anyone ever land a worthwhile job that way nowadays?"

"They get ideas. There are possibilities you've never even heard about in those 'wanted' columns. The thing is to find something you *think* you might like and might even be good at, and then contact someone local in that particular field and go to work on him."

"Does this someone local provide training?"

"Gosh no! He's probably holding on to his own job by his fingernails but if you butter him up he gives you what you need, the technical information. After that it's the Workers' Education Association for an evening course, or maybe a small county grant if you're lucky. A lot of firms whose accounts you've been handling for years have students' grants and students' courses. They all go to someone, so why not you?"

My opinion of Ida Rhys-Jones's initiative began to enlarge in direct proportion to my assessment of my own feebleness. The very predictability of a job with Cadwallader's was the padlock that kept you clamped to the treadmill.

"You might even branch out on your own once you feel your feet," she said. "Making money for yourself, and watching it grow, that can be fun. So can being your own boss, in spite of the headaches that go along with it."

"Where did you find out all this?" I demanded, and she looked at my slyly.

"I could say by keeping my eyes open, and using the common sense I was born with but that wouldn't be the whole truth. Mr. Waring, the commercial, taught me some of it. He'd been around, you see, and worked all over. Forty-five he was, when he came to us."

"Were you in love with him? Him or Wally?"

"No, Boyo, neither one of them, not for a minute."

"Was there someone else, someone before them?"

She said, cheerfully, "I could never love any one man. I found that out at fourteen."

"Did something happen about that time?"

"Nothing sensational, except that it was then I discovered men never grow up. Just get randier, they do."

She sat up and looked serious for a moment. "That's a funny thing about the Welsh now! Nothing they enjoy better than rough and tumble, but there's a part of them that keeps rumbling and grumbling what a wicked sin it is, so that after falling over one another to get into bed they can't look one another in the face in the morning. That's not me, though. I thought about it first time I had a man and decided it wasn't a sin at all. No, Boyo, maybe it's the one way someone like me is any use in the world. I'd found out by then I wasn't clever and no one could call me beautiful, could they? I can do a bit of cooking and dusting and make over the bed but most men can do that for themselves. So why should they marry and go through their lives without twopence to call their own when anyone can get a good lodge for twenty-two-and-six a week?"

"Then what is important? What's the most important thing in the world to you? It isn't just sex, is it? I mean . . . we all think a lot and hope a lot about it but the way you look at it it's just a physical process."

I thought she was going to laugh at me again and she almost did but checked herself and kept her face straight, saying, "For a man it is, Charlie. You've found that out already, haven't you?"

"But damn it, Ida, for a woman too the way you go about it."

She looked resigned then and I thought I had irritated her and began to qualify what I'd said but she cut me short, scrambling up and brushing the bits of bracken from her skirt.

"I haven't got through to you, Charlie. Maybe I will but it'll take time. And you've wasted enough time already haven't you?"

"What do you mean by that?"

"That you've never had any *fun*! Damn it, man, Dadda had more than you at your age. 'What's important?' you ask. 'What's the most important thing about being alive?' I can tell you that, Charlie. For a man it's being someone he can look in the face at fifty and say, 'There then, Boyo! Stood on your own feet you have! Got by without hanging on the coattails of some bloody great corporation like Caddie's you have, or that stinking tin-plate factory that has half the men in Penmadoc queuing for a work ticket with their hands up like little boys asking to go to the privy!' If I ever did love a man it would be someone who could do that, but there's not so many around, I can tell you!"

"All right, all right, but for a woman?"

"There's no such choice, not the way things are at the moment. They'll change, I daresay, but not quickly enough to be much use to me. You think you're underpaid and so you are, but do you know what shop girls pick up in a place like Toynbee and Williams', in the High Street? Ten bob a week and a half-crown bonus at Christmas if old Mr. Williams can pinch their bottoms in the stock cupboard.

"There's the chara horn sounding for us. Come on!"

We set off down the rock path to the car park and all the way I kept thinking of other questions I wanted to ask her and wishing we had taken a picnic into the Craigwen estate where we might have done something other than talk all the time. I said breathlessly, as we hurried round the last bend, "Come up again tonight, Ida?"

And she said, grimly, "I'll come up whenever I'm needed."

The charabanc driver grumbled at us for keeping the party waiting but the passengers, mostly elderly trippers, exchanged smirks in a way that would have brought the color to my cheeks a day or so ago. Ida didn't bat an eyelid, in spite of the bits of fern she hadn't bothered to remove from her ample behind, but she was silent all the way home. Maybe she was still assessing my chances of profiting from her impulsive generosity against those of other men she had championed in the past.

2

Looking back, with all the benefit of hindsight, I often wonder if I would have ever taken those first bemused steps onto the new plane if I had had the advantages of Ida's common sense and the solace of her generous body. I doubt it very much. Ida might have been fascinated by the enormity of hitting Caddie's where it hurts most, in its strongroom and prestige, but the idea would never have enlarged itself into reality. It would have remained a rich and private joke between us, a might-have-been source of amusement capable of sustaining us for the rest of our lives. And that is the only possible way it could have shown us a profit.

Throughout the whole of this period our relationship was not merely close but mutually rewarding. Not only did we console one another's loneliness but thoroughly enjoyed the excitement of carrying on a clandestine love affair under the alerted noses of Evan and Gladys. I continued to pay my devotional calls at The Rainbow café and generate daydreams at the shrine of the sulky goddess in the lilac overall. For having access to Ida did nothing to moderate the homage I paid Delphine as an ideal. A man who enjoys a deep, inherited faith finds no great difficulty in reconciling moral shortcomings with spiritual aspirations. The good Catholic knows that he will sin again but that does not prohibit the passage of some between the Mass and the whorehouse. It is, of course, more difficult to maintain this balance on the fulcrum of a Nonconformist conscience, but I did. Delphine, notwithstanding her stridently sensual appeal and magnetism, was both unattainable and sacrosanct. She was a symbol that possessed tremendous allure but yet remained in the realm of fantasy. To watch her drift here and there among the tables, swinging her hips and turning her bold, impersonal profile this way and that as she spirited stained crocks from shop to counter, was a kind of quittance for all the ordinariness and ugliness of the world I knew, compensating for the joylessness of so many narrow articles of faith of the dispossessed. She was the one person in that sterile town who had not only triumphed over her own sleazy background but transformed it by her presence. I didn't see her as a woman but as a pledge that beauty could still exist and be seen to exist. In her presence I could think the thoughts that Griffiths, the nationalist, ascribed to the heroes of his sagas. But Ida had a function in this complicated process. It was left to her to siphon off my lust. The one belonged in the waking hours of workaday life. The other walked in dignity across the astral plane of dreams.

Gladys Rhys-Jones did not take long to adjust to the fact that there existed, as she herself would have put it, "an understanding" between Ida and me, but past failures had made her cautious. She put a modest price tag on it and went on hoping for a bargain sale. When we sat at table together she employed her full repertoire of ogles, bridles and knowing nods as though it was essential to advertise her approval of our association. Mam's caution, however, owed something to Evan's restraining hand. He was like a punter who had backed so many losers that, understandably, he hesitated to plunge on the most promising colt the stable had so far produced. His attitude operated in my favor at the branch. His nagging toward me moderated a little and, for good or evil, this obliged me to wear the colors of the Rhys-Jones—Griffiths faction, to the unspeakable chagrin of the Powell—Porsen alliance.

I had another small advantage. I was the only one among them who could use a typewriter with more than one finger and they all liked to make use of me in this respect, so I made a point of giving the manager's demands marked preference over matters within Powell's orbit, and it wasn't long before Powell and Porsen looked upon me as teacher's pet. I could endure this, for I had now come to regard my servitude as temporary. I had taken Ida's advice both as regards hoarding every copper I could spare, and making a regular scrutiny of the wanted ads in the newspapers and technical journals at the library. I even replied to one or two of them but nothing promising emerged, although I soon discovered she was right about there being a range of possibilities. I toyed with the prospect of becoming a chef, a nitrate inspector in Chile, and even a soap exporter in West Africa, but I can't pretend that I was obsessed by the prospect of changing course and facing the risks involved. Somehow, after that August Bank Holiday incident, what she had hinted at began to occur. The urgency ebbed from my desire to remove the inkstains of Cadwallader's from my fingers, and this was partially due to the strategic position I now occupied at the bank. It wasn't every two-penny-halfpenny clerk who went to bed with the manager's daughter twice a week and, to that extent at least, all the nagging and pettymindedness that went on down there could be viewed objectively if we kept our secret. It not only added piquancy to my responses to Evan's petulant bell, it also enabled me to listen to accounts of Porsen's pillion conquests with a certain superiority. His exploits cost him money and the exertions demanded of a stealthy and often unsuccessful stalk in the heather. Mine were free, with success guaranteed in advance.

In roughly the same way I could measure my lot with that of Powell and Griffiths and Gregg the junior, sometimes striking a modest credit balance. Powell was saddled with his bile, an expensive wife, and two spoiled children, Griffiths with a widowed mother, and Gregg the junior couldn't hold hands with a girl without giving her a head cold. I wouldn't have changed places with any one of them so long as things drifted along as they did in the weeks leading up to Christmas, but I never had that kind of luck and I ought not to have been surprised when my life took another sharp turn, the impetus coming from a quarter where it was least expected. Ida Rhys-Jones, who could be said to have reoriented my entire outlook and made my life tolerable, suddenly went sour on me.

Chapter Five

1

The storm came up out of a clear sky, on a day when we could have relaxed completely in one another's company in a way we had never been able to do when she went through the pretense of leaving the house and slipping up to my room in her stockinged feet.

Up there I had a cast-iron alibi. I was studying for the foreign exchange section of Bankers' Institute and although, as long as I lived in that house, I never opened a textbook on the subject, talk of it was enough to keep Gladys and Evan at bay if they were in the living room down two flights of stairs. I even chalked up a good mark for taking my profession so seriously.

Occasionally, very occasionally, they would both go out to a Chapel function, leaving us alone in the house, and we naturally took advantage of this. Another time—it must have been one of the rare occasions when I took the initiative—I crept down to Ida's room in the small hours, but this was to court unnecessary risks for had I been seen a shotgun wedding would have followed as a matter of course, notwithstanding opposition on Ida's part. Economic pressures would have been applied and in the end we should have been obliged to capitulate.

Toward the middle of December we had a small slice of luck. Gladys's aged mother in Anglesey was taken ill in the absence of her younger daughter, who took care of her, and Evan had to drive Gladys over in his bull-nosed Morris. It was early on Saturday afternoon when they got the news and about seven that evening they phoned a neighbor, asking her to tell Ida they were staying the night and wouldn't be back until after lunch on Sunday. They asked Ida to cook my meals and she did. She also decided we would spend the entire night together.

We went to the pictures that night and saw one of the early talkies that had just arrived in Penmadoc. The apparatus broke down a dozen times but I didn't care. My mind was fixed on more homely entertainment. We had some fish and chips and I had an uncomfortable moment when Ida suggested we should go on to The Rainbow for coffee. This didn't suit my book at all. I had never exchanged a word with Delphine, apart from ordering coffee, but I preferred her not to know that I sometimes descended from Olympus.

So I steered Ida past the café, saying it was a rackety place full of louts, and we went straight home. When I suggested tea she said she had a better idea and produced a bottle of port. Evan was a teetotaler but, like most teetotalers, he kept a bottle of something tucked away for emergencies.

The port produced in me a mild glow but it made Ida reckless. She said, "Look, Charlie, why do we have to squeeze into your single bed? Let's treat ourselves, let's take over their room for the night and I'll change it in the morning."

The prospect of spending the night in Evan's double bed made us laugh so much that we almost overset the port, but when she produced her father's long white nightshirt from under the pillow I almost split my sides. It was that kind of evening. Everything conspired to make us laugh uproariously, especially the twin of the text that had once hung over my bed. The one in their room read "If It Be Thy Will" and this had me helpless for several minutes.

We took the port and glasses upstairs and had another drink in front of the gas-fire. I had never been inside this room before and it was all I would have expected of a bedroom shared by Evan and Gladys. The furniture was dark and heavy and the interior of the wardrobe reeked of mothballs. Under the night table Ida showed me a square cavity with a sliding shutter. It was the place, she said, where Evan deposited his keys every night, among them the key I had seen him use to open the inner grille of the vault. The key to the outer grille and the keys giving access to the safe and the premises were in Powell's charge, who always opened the bank in the morning, but nobody could get money out of the vault until he and Evan had gone below and opened up.

The odd thing was, now that we were here alone in the house, I felt almost married to her so that there was no urgency about climbing into Evan's substantial double bed. We sat sipping our port and it made me feel vainglorious rather than goatish. I said that one day I would give Caddie's something of a jolt and go out with a flourish. She said, seriously, "Don't get any ideas on those lines, Charlie. When you leave you leave quietly, with handshakes all round. That's an essential part of the plan, providing you've got a plan. How is that hundred-pound float coming along?"

"I've got close on forty pounds," I told her.

"Then what do you mean, 'go out with a flourish'? Publish a letter in the paper about downtrodden bank clerks and the need of a more militant union to watch their interests?"

"That's not a bad idea, Ida."

She gave a snort, and with that long nose of hers she could snort very emphatically.

"It's a damn silly idea," she said. "Why? Because it would single you out as a rabble-rouser wherever you happened to go and no firm, big or small, wants a troublemaker on its payroll. Next thing you know you'd be earmarked as a Bolshie and besides, you'll want a spotless reference to account for the seven years you've been employed by Caddie's." When I went on to try and explain that a gesture of some kind would give me a lot of satisfaction, she said, "Gesture my foot! Don't you make your precious gesture every time I go to bed with you? Aren't you making your gesture right now? Leave the gesturing to me, Boyo, who put you up to it in the first place. As a matter of fact . . ." and then she stopped.

"Well?"

She changed her mind about something. "Skip it for tonight. Let's turn in before this port makes us too sleepy," she said, corking the bottle, "I'll top it up with homemade cherry wine in the morning. Mam'll never notice the difference."

Casually, as if she did it in front of an audience every night, she began to undress. In the late nineteen-twenties fashions didn't do very much for a woman's figure. Skirts were as short as they became in the sixties but the overall effect of the jumper-suits Ida usually wore was to flatten. I watched her with a kind of Satanic glee as she pulled off her clothes. She had never undressed on the previous occasions and this was an entirely new experience for me. When she was nude, and still as indifferent as an artist's model, I decided she was far more attractive than I had deduced from earlier encounters. She was an exceptionally hefty woman, with what they would now call an Edwardian figure, and this is an accurate description because she did somehow recall illustrations of principal girls of that period I had seen in bound copies of magazines at the library. Her breasts and thighs, although formidable, were well-proportioned, and if her waist was half as big again as that of the average girl in Penmadoc it couldn't have sacrificed much without making her look like a pink balloon tied in the middle. She was the kind of girl Victorian painters used as models for Danae or Clytemnestra.

Amused by my fascinated scrutiny, she said, switching off the light, "Well, there you are, Charlie. Curtain up, Boyo. I fetched your pyjamas down. On the stool they are, by the dressing table."

She climbed into bed then and turned her back on me. Somehow she knew I didn't want to be seen undressing. I had the working-class shame of peeling off clothes in front of an audience, male or female. Reticence departed, however, once I had turned off the fire and surrendered to her vast embrace and after an interval she said, with a lazy chuckle, "Tell you something, Boyo. Beginning to believe in you, I am, in a way I didn't at first. That business about being sorry for you was true, but I can't honestly say I fancied you much as a man, or not then. I was wrong though. About as wrong as I could be. All you needed was a bit of a nudge, lad. You'll do something one day and it'll be me that started you off. Nice thought to go to sleep on, that is."

2

We were there until nine the next morning and she handed me a cup of tea when she drew the curtains. I felt relaxed and secure lying there watching her move about in a pink dressing gown she didn't bother to fasten. Everything about her was warm, cozy and uncomplicated, and it may have been this that made me feel more tolerant of my life and prospects than I had ever been, certainly since going out to work. As I watched her dress I thought, theoretically, that I might even be able to settle for life with Ida. It would require no effort providing one could meet the physical demands her positive energy would make on a man, and, I thought, as I rose in Caddie's hierarchy and brought home more money, there might be something to be said for predictability after all. My error on that occasion was giving expression to these thoughts.

We both took a bath and made up the bed with clean sheets taken from the airing-cupboard and then went down to breakfast in the kitchen. Something of my newfound smugness must have showed in my face for she said, looking at me curiously, "You look different, Charlie. A bit subdued. No, not subdued but 'married.' Almost as if we'll soon be on our way to Chapel and then home to a Sunday roast."

"And what's so terrible about that?" I asked, innocently.

She slammed down the teapot so hard that I was surprised it didn't break.

"You're not getting any ideas are you? Of you and me settling down in a place like this?"

I wasn't, not really, but it amused me to kid her along a little, so I said, "Well, I don't know. I've enjoyed the last twenty-four hours like nobody's business and don't tell me you haven't because I wouldn't believe you."

She looked quite startled then but got control of herself in a moment and reached behind her for her handbag. She flipped it open and took out a folded paper clipped to some foolscap sheets.

"Wish now I'd got this out of the way before we started playing mothers and fathers. No, wait a minute"—as I reached out for it—"I'll have to explain first. A week or so ago I had an idea. I wrote to Mr. Waring and asked if there was an opening in Atlas Products as a trainee manager on one of their source plantations in India. Well there is, or there soon will be, because they've just started a home-based course and I think you might stand a chance of getting one of the first vacancies. They like someone trained in basic accountancy and on paper you could satisfy them. There's the medical, of course, but actual physique doesn't come into it. You've nothing like poor old Wally to disqualify you."

"Did you go job hunting for Wally too?" I asked, and she made the gesture of dismissal she always made when I fished for information about her previous lovers, or the two she admitted to.

"Leave Wally out of this," she snapped, "and just listen. This brochure Mr. Waring sent along is about their new scheme. If you pass the initial interview—and he says that's a formality at this stage—you get a three months' course at their London headquarters. Then you take an exam and have another interview and if you pass that you get an assistant managership on one of their Madras plantations, where they grow the stuff they put into their products."

"What happens if you don't pass?"

"You're given a further three months' training and a guaranteed six months on the road. Here, go over it carefully while I clear away."

I took Waring's letter and the papers and it was all just as she said. The subsistence grant they offered during the training period was a few shillings in excess of the weekly salary I was getting from Caddie's but the starting salary, once you signed on and took ship for India for a minimum of three years, was more than twice as much, plus an overseas living allowance. On the face of it it seemed just the kind of opening I had been looking for since she sent me to the public library. The prospect of an actual plunge, however, daunted me and I began to hedge.

"I can't see myself trailing from town to town selling pickles," I said. "And suppose I passed out first time and did sign on. Three years is a hell of a long time and suppose they didn't like me, or I didn't like them?"

I don't think I've ever seen anyone look as exasperated as she did when she swung round from the sink. Her long nose glowed with indignation.

"Suppose! Suppose!" she jeered, sounding like her mother in a fury, "Is that all you can do? Look for the snags and pitfalls? 'Three years is a long time!' So it is, but it would be three years in a new country even if you were out on your ear at the end of it. And why should you be? You've held down a pen-pusher's job for seven, haven't you? My God, if it were me . . . !"

"Oh, it's easy enough to talk like that, Ida," I said, trying to justify my lack of guts, "but it isn't you that has to make a decision that big. It's me, and I'd want time to think it over."

She dried her soapy hands and sat down facing me.

"Listen, Boyo," she said, "and don't chip in until I've finished. When I thought of this it seemed a shot in the dark and when those papers arrived, proving it wasn't, I took my time over them, considering all the 'ifs' and 'buts.' Certain as I'm sitting here this is a marvelous break, the best you're ever like to get, especially as Waring, who has been with the firm twenty years, has promised to recommend you. Of course there are risks but show me any worthwhile job where there aren't. Look at Evan, after nearly forty years, and Powell after more than twenty! Look at the whole bloody lot of you down there and match any one of them against someone who would gamble on a chance like this. Then think what you'd rather be, someone like the best man in Caddie's or someone who had had a go, who had tried to break out and show people what he was made of!"

"But you can't expect me to make up my mind about a thing like this on the spot?"

"I can and I do," she said, without taking her eyes off me. "You wriggle out of this, Boyo, and it means that, deep down, you don't mind settling for Caddie's. Okay, I was the one who started all this, but I was honest with you, wasn't I, now? Told you what made me go to bed with you, didn't I, and I'll tell you something else, Boyo, why I went on with it once you'd perked up a bit. Seemed to me the only way to put a bit of guts into you there's a fool I was! Last night I thought I'd made it but I hadn't, had I? All you wanted was a pillow to cry on!"

In her indignation her accent thickened and she went red in the face. I let her have her full say, mainly because I was lost for words, or words that didn't sound like bleats. Maybe she was right, and that secretly I had cherished the security of Caddie's, or maybe she was only half right and seven years with the bank had drained off what initiative I possessed as starting-out capital. We sat there looking at one another across the table and then, mumbling something about taking a walk and thinking it over, I got up and went out taking the papers with me. I knew I wouldn't make the step and she knew it as well. I could see that by the crumpled look on her face and the way her almost nonexistent chin dropped as I passed her on the way to the hall. I thought about that chin as I made my way up the frosty slope of Craigwen Terrace. I thought it curious that so many people should regard weak chins as a sure sign of irresolution.

I took the path behind the town that led over the shoulder of the old Craigwen estate, the only part of the coast about here that had resisted the three attempts Penmadoc had made to achieve an identity. It was a tangle of beech, ash, laurel and rhododendron, a pleasant place in summer or winter. Today, with temperatures hovering around freezing point, it sparkled with rime and was magically still. The only sound was the rasp of dead leaves under my feet and the rustle of puffed-out robins flitting about in the undergrowth. I tried to think about India and the prospect of making a new life there but it was a hopeless task for someone who had never been outside the Principality in his life, not even to London on a football excursion. I had read Kipling but all I could summon up from memories of *Kim* was a picture of heat, dust and an alien loneliness more frightening than the loneliness of digs in Penmadoc, especially with Ida in the offing.

I walked about for three hours that day but the tramp didn't solve anything. You never do resolve important problems by thinking them over, by weighing all the pros and cons. All the big decisions have to be made on impulse. Ida was right about that too.

When I got back, tired and more irresolute than when I had set out, Evan and Gladys were home and Ida made a point of keeping me at bay. I didn't exchange a word with her all day, although I kept listening for her foot on the stairs. I think that if she had come to me in a friendly mood and made one more appeal I might have signed that blasted application but she didn't. She had had her say and now it was up to me.

I saw her briefly at breakfast and Gladys must have sensed we had quarreled while they were away for she made one or two clumsy attempts to patch things up, but without success. Ida wasn't having any and I got the impression that both Gladys and Evan suspected the rift had been caused by an attempt on my part to take liberties in their absence. He was particularly testy all day at the bank and we were kept late.

Ida appeared in my room about cocoa-time that evening but she made a point of not coming in. She asked me for Waring's letter, saying she wanted to answer it. I was strung up to a high pitch after my grueling stint at the branch and this was all I needed, an unfriendly approach on her part. "Why does everything have to be decided in such a flaming hurry?" I demanded. "Why can't I sleep on it and make up my own mind?"

"You have slept on it," she said, "and the hurry was to be first in the queue—your name at the top of the list, with Mr. Waring's recommendation."

I said something very churlish then. "Is Waring doing this on the strength of past favors or future ones?"

She held out her hand for the papers.

"Hopeless you are, Charlie," she said, "and for my money you can go bald at Caddie's. Give me the papers and forget the whole thing. Wrong as I could be about you I was. You're hooked, Boyo, that's what you are, hooked!"

I gave her the papers and she went out. Apart from civilities those were the last words I had with her until I was launched on a career of quite another kind.

3

I didn't relish the project of a long winter evening in that dreary little room so I got my coat and scarf and gravitated to The Rainbow. At least it was warm and noisy, and at least I could sit and watch Delphine's lazy hip-hoists and speculate about her in the role of a man of experience. By now, probably by reason of the impetus given me by Ida, my dreams about Delphine were lit by a less ethereal glow. I never saw her as I had seen Ida, nude and jovial, but I had got as far as wandering down a wooded path beside her in the Avalon Griffiths used as a backdrop for his Celtic lovers in the early morning of the world. I was floating along on the magic carpet of some such dream when the incident occurred that set all the others in train.

I was sitting near the door of the café because, when I had entered it, the room was nearly full and another regular, a big tin-plate worker, was across the aisle, directly opposite. He had one or two of his mates with him and they had all been drinking. They talked in loud voices and pushed one another about, advertising their high spirits by guffaws of laughter and mild horseplay. This was nothing new to the Rainbow clientele and Delphine ignored it. Beppo, her silent stepbrother, was behind the counter and she was moving up and down the tables filling a big tray with coffee glasses and sundae-smeared plates.

About nine-thirty the café began emptying. There was a dance at the Institute in the main road and most of the young people were attending it. Soon I was the only customer except for the convivial group opposite, and Delphine drifted down to our end of the premises and began to clear their table.

The big man said something I didn't catch and the others laughed. It was probably some broad comment on Delphine along the lines of Porsen's frequent remarks concerning her inviolability. Whatever it was, her only response was a vague, humor-the-customer smile that was hardly more than a bored twitch of the lips. I was taking it all in without noticing as much, and as she leaned across the table to reach crockery nearer the wall the tin-plate worker gave her a playful smack on the behind. It was nothing to make a scene about, a boisterous gesture on the part of a man with just enough liquor inside him to make him eager to caper and clown in front of his cronies, but it showed me a Delphine far removed from the cool, impersonal creature I had gloated over for the past eight months. She spat something at him, a single word that sounded like a foreign oath and then she let go of the tray and swung her open palm across his grinning face with tremendous force.

The smack rang out like a whipcrack and was delivered with sufficient force to jerk his head back against the wooden partition in a way that produced another, more satisfying crack. The clout across his jowls didn't hurt him but the crack on the head did. One hand shot to the point of impact and the other, instinctively, closed over her wrist and jerked her forward so that she fell face downward on the table creating a vast clatter among the crockery there. At the same time the loaded tray hit the floor, contributing to the general uproar.

I acted without any understanding of what I was doing. If I had stopped to think, the limit of my intervention would have been to cross over and reason with the man, perhaps advising his mates to take him out before there was more trouble. As it was, this never occurred to me. Almost before Delphine's tray had hit the ground I had grabbed a heavy vinegar bottle on my table and brought it crashing down on his head. It was thick glass, made to withstand frequent contact with the floor, and it did not break. His cloth cap deadened the impact to a great extent but for all that it knocked him cold. He slumped back against the partition and was only saved from sliding under the table by the knees of the men opposite.

I stood there with the vinegar bottle in my hand gaping down at him, conscious of a swirl of people about me and, behind them, Delphine's face, serene again once more but almost expressionless. Then I saw Beppo hustling them all into the street, two men half-carrying their semiconscious comrade who looked like a large, gray sack. The next minute the door was shut, the bolts were drawn and the blinds were down. Beppo, Delphine and I were standing in a welter of broken crockery and the honkytonk was still playing "The Wedding of the Painted Doll."

Suddenly I felt a complete idiot standing there with the bottle in my hand and put it down on the table, mumbling something about being sorry for having acted so precipitately. Delphine said, addressing me for the first time as a person and not a customer, "What the hell have you got to be sorry about, Buddy? He's the guy who'll be sorry when he comes round. I was the fool to smack his face, I should have called Beppo and they would have gone without any trouble, the way they always do. But what you did was swell. It was real gentlemanly, that's what I'd call it. Thank *you*, Mr. . . . ?"

"Pritchard," I said hastily, "Charlie Pritchard," and I thought her somewhat naïve use of the word "gentlemanly" very misplaced in the circumstances.

She said, "Get Mr. Pritchard another coffee, Beppo. He likes it strong. Come round behind, Mr. Pritchard."

Still in a daze I followed her past the raised flap of the counter and into a passage that led to a room at the back of the premises. It was a very cheerful room, with a bright fire burning, easy chairs, and a Turkey carpet. There were pictures on the walls that you wouldn't expect to find in Penmadoc, framed reproductions of Rembrandt and Caravaggio. One was of a man in a gold helmet and the other was "Mercury Instructing Cupid Before Venus." Upended on the mantelshelf were two Dresden plates and between them a glass honey-jar. The place had an air of taste that was a great contrast to the garish décor of the café and went a little way toward explaining Delphine's immaculate appearance. I don't know how Beppo fitted into the background. When he came in with my coffee it occurred to me that, outwardly at least, he was as dim as the man I had just crowned with the vinegar bottle.

I sat down on one of the easy chairs and Delphine coiled herself in the other. Beppo, after an amiable nod in my direction, slouched out and I heard him sluicing down the café.

"Why *did* you do it?" she asked, "I didn't scream, did I?"

"No," I said, almost spilling my coffee in an attempt to adjust to the novel role of protector of the outraged, "you just shouted something in Italian."

"Ah," she said, smiling, "that wasn't Italian, Bub. It was a very rude Corsican word Beppo taught me."

"Well he asked for it," I said, "and that blip on the head, but I daresay he or his mates will be waiting to sort me out in the streets."

"Don't give it another thought," she said, "I'll have Beppo tail you home. He could handle those canteen cowboys and he'd get a kick out of doing it. He was a bouncer in a Los Angeles club before we crossed over."

"Are you Italians, Corsicans or Americans?" I asked her, and she said that they were a bit of each. Beppo had been born in Corsica but their father was a Neapolitan who had emigrated to the States via Bastia before the war.

"My mother was a Creole," she added, "and I was born in Chicago, so I guess I'm a little of everything."

I was stuck for conversation after that, finding it difficult to follow the sharp upward curve of my luck. I had entered the café less than an hour ago feeling every bit as ineffectual as Ida had implied and here I was not only talking to Delphine in private but being regarded by her as a chivalrous defender of the weak. She said, "You work at the bank, don't you?" and it gave me an additional lift to learn she had taken that much interest in me.

I said I did and that I had been a regular customer since

my first night in Penmadoc last April but added, hopefully, that I didn't expect her to single me out from so many regulars. She didn't disappoint me. "I've always known when you were in," she said, and then, drawing her neat brows together, "*why* do you come so often? Is it because you don't get fed at your lodgings?"

Her frankness and friendliness gave me an unexpected opening. I said, half jocularly, "I come mostly to watch you." Then shyness caught up with me and I began to stammer but she didn't seem impressed one way or the other.

She said, with a lazy smile, "I know. I guess I've always known. From the first week, that is. I thought it was strange but then, later on, very flattering."

"You never showed it. I didn't think you had noticed me, except as you would any regular."

"You didn't give me all that much encouragement, did you? Apart from looking me over, I mean."

There it was again! Charlie Pritchard the all-time onlooker; Charlie the touchline supporter, who could never quite convince people he was capable of joining in the game. Well, that was behind me. Now I had joined in. Now I had scored a try and been given free coffee in lieu of a medal.

"Your name," she said, "it's Welsh, isn't it? There are so few surnames about here a girl gets confused. All these Robertses, Joneses, Morgans, Evanses, Jenkinses and Pritchards."

I found I was getting to like her voice, the one thing about her that was without promise. In here, removed from the steamy racket of the café, she became a person with whom it was easy to communicate. The husky timbre and transatlantic idioms she used conveyed amiability so that she shed the wary attitude she used to keep all but drunks at bay. And with it went a good deal of her inviolability, not enough to encourage a man to approach close enough to touch, but sufficient to make her neighborly. She managed this, however, without sacrificing a tittle of her sensuality. Every time she moved a limb you breathed a little faster.

Then she asked three direct questions about the bank. "You like it here? Is that a good job? Do they pay well?"

"No, to all three," I said, surprised at feeling so much at ease with her. "It's a dead-end job, the pay is lousy and I always have thought the town stinks."

"Me too, brother," she said, "but I wouldn't have said so unless you had. The Welsh are supposed to be proud folk, or so I've heard."

"Not in places like this. Penmadoc isn't typical of Wales."

"No," she said, "I've noticed that, even as a foreigner. It's a town that tries real hard to be lots of things and ends up being nothing."

I couldn't have put it better myself. She was, I thought, unusually perceptive for a girl who possessed her kind of looks and figure.

"Of course," she went on, "there's dough to be made here but you'd know a whole heap more about that than me."

It flattered me to be regarded by her as a man of business so I told her that the branch was the busiest in my experience. I said I didn't know where some of our roughneck customers got their hands on so much money but they did, particularly at certain seasons of the year.

"You mean vacation trade?"

"Not specially. The farmers and butchers seem to do very well about now, with Christmas approaching, but our busiest time is early autumn, when they have that horse fair. People come here from all parts. We bank for the tin-plate works too. They're on half-time right now but they still have a heavy payroll."

It would have made Evan sweat to hear me say this to a stranger but she showed no more than a polite interest, like someone taking part in a casual conversation.

She said, nodding, "Sure, that's every Friday, isn't it? Friday is our hectic night."

I asked her something that had puzzled me for a long time.

"How did you and your stepbrother come to pick on a place like Penmadoc? I mean, having got as far as California why put up with our God-awful climate?"

"Family split," she said, laconically. "We had a swell little business back in LA but Poppa was a lush and a tightwad.

We figured we'd do better on our own and we have. We would have tried over there but rents come high and an uncle gave us free passage on his freighter. We saw these premises advertised and didn't have the dough to take a lease on a ritzier place."

"Will you stay now it's doing well?"

"No, we'll move on I guess, to Blackpool or some place else, where there's more doing after dark."

The prospect of passing The Rainbow and seeing a stranger loading trays of crockery gave me a pang. All the time I had worked in Penmadoc the café had been the focal point of my emotions, notwithstanding my involvement with Ida.

"I hope it won't be too soon," I said, and she smiled.

"Not for a year at least. Even here you need dough to get good premises in a popular seaside place. We might go back to the States if we did well enough."

"I've always fancied America," I told her, "it sounds exciting but I daresay I'd be disappointed once I got there."

"No you wouldn't," she said, with unexpected emphasis, "you'd love it! Sure it's exciting, and it's a young man's country. It's gay and things happen all the time. The pay is better too and people in banking don't have to be put off by the Depression. Why don't you go try your luck? Unless you're thinking of marrying and settling down."

"If I was in that line of business I wouldn't come here every night looking at you, would I?"

I heard myself saying this and it amazed me. I was getting to be quite a wag as well as a muscleman. She accepted the implied compliment but in the way she had admitted to noticing my solemn scrutiny over the last eight months. It interested her, mildly, but that was about all.

"Well, you don't have to just sit any longer, Mr. Pritchard. We can at least say hello, even when I'm busy. We don't get many customers of your class. And thank you for being so quick on the draw tonight." She got up, smoothing her overall down with the lazy, absentminded grace that characterized all her movements. "I'll have to help Beppo now. They always leave the place like an ash tip and there's that trayful of smashed crockery to sweep up." We went out into the café and while I was putting my coat on she addressed Beppo in Italian and he nodded.

"You go out and Beppo will tail you," she said. "I don't think those hoodlums will be out looking for more punishment. They've had plenty enough for one night."

I hoped she was right. In spite of the glow in which I had been basking for the last half hour I shuddered at the prospect of being worked over by a tin-plate gang.

Chapter Six

1

It was about a fortnight later that my life took another sharp twist.

One morning, early in the New Year, we discovered, to our amazement, that Ida had gone. Her bed had not been slept in and she left the traditional note propped up against the clock. She said she had landed a job down south and had gone like this because she knew they would try and talk her out of it. She would write later, as soon as she had found digs.

Evan and Gladys were dumbfounded, so much so that it was twenty-four hours before they got around to linking me with their daughter's flit. Evan, glowering like a big, pink-faced baby deprived of his rattle, took his hat and marched off to a deacons' meeting at the Chapel. No doubt he considered Gladys better equipped to conduct a third degree aimed at establishing what part, if any, I had played in Ida's disappearance. Gladys didn't waste time tackling me. She backed me into my room as I was on the point of escaping to The Rainbow.

"If you know where she is you'd best tell us and no old nonsense about it. There's a pretty thing it is I must say, after the way we treated the pair of you!"

I adopted an indignant attitude at first, denying all knowledge of Ida's whereabouts and saying, more or less truthfully, that I hadn't any idea why she had gone.

"There's a lie it is and you know it," shouted Gladys, "been very close you and our Ida have, ever since summer, right up to that night we had to leave you alone in the house about a month ago."

I had to think quickly and balance the risks. I didn't want to help put them on Ida's trail but I didn't want to rouse Evan's anger to the pitch where it would make things even more harassing for me at the branch. So I said, carefully, "Look, Mrs. Rhys-Jones, you've been wrong all along about me and Ida. We were always friendly but there was never anything romantic about that friendship. We never even held hands."

Technically this was true, but I was astonished at the amount of indignation generated by the disclaimer.

"You mean to stand there and tell me you were never our Ida's *cariad bach!*"

Christ, how I had come to hate those two words and the woman who kept using them! "*No,*" I said, "*never!* It was all in your mind, Mrs. Rhys-Jones, you just jumped to conclusions and went right on jumping to them until now."

She looked at me with her slack mouth agape and then shut it so suddenly that her false teeth hopped. Just to look at her made me feel sorry for Evan. He wasn't much of a catch but he deserved better than that. She said, at last, "You could have *told* me! One or other of you could have *told* me! All this time! All this time . . . *wasted!*"

I didn't follow her there but I let it go, hunching into my overcoat and clutching it to me as if it represented all that remained of my dignity.

"Where are you going now?"

"Out," I said, "do you mind?"

"Since you ask, I do. Dadda will have to be told."

"I don't think it will astonish him as much as it does you, Mrs. Rhys-Jones."

She choked at that and it gave me the opportunity to slip past her and down the stairs. She got in a final volley, however, before I reached the hall.

"You know where she is! Not sure I believe you either! She was up here times enough . . ."

I was on the step by then and slammed the door behind

me, so that I never did discover whether Ida's elaborate se-
crecy had been wasted or whether the old besom was bluffing.

After that, however, the pressure was on down at the branch.
Anxiety concerning his daughter's whereabouts, the attempt to
keep her disappearance from the others, and the effort of resigning himself to the fact that I was unlikely to marry into
the family, combined to isolate me from the Rhys-Jones—
Griffiths camp, but without enlisting me with the Powell—
Porsen faction. Instead they both used me as a buffer and as it
was a time of year when there was work enough for ten,
every working day became a succession of sharp explosions,
frantic spurts of overtime, and long sulky silences. I was
kicked about between Rhys-Jones and Powell like a soggy
football and sometimes had both of them storming at me from
either side of the typing table. Porsen extracted a good deal
of satisfaction from my sudden loss of favor with the manager
and soon divined the reason, losing no opportunity of taunting me out of Rhys-Jones's hearing.

"So poor old Dadda backed a loser after all, did he? Well,
now, isn't that a shame? Our Ida returned unopened, and
young Pritchard reduced to the ranks. You really have made
a hash of things, haven't you, kiddo? There you were, sitting
real pretty. All you had to do was stuff Ida, get her in the
family way, take her to Chapel, and make it up over Grandpa's
little dividend. Next thing you know I should have been on
my way and you would have been upgraded without a posting. I'm disappointed in you, Pritchard. I would have bet a
pound to a penny you could have pulled that one off without much trouble. Damn it, I know Ida's no Venus but they're
all the same in the dark, or didn't you know?"

I stood this kind of thing for a week or two and then, fortunately for me in Powell's absence, it reached a point where
I could stand it no longer and I punched Porsen on the nose
so hard that he spurted blood all over the ledgers. He would
have made mincemeat of me notwithstanding his temporary
handicap if Griffiths hadn't thrown himself between us and
then, hearing the uproar, Evan popped out of his hutch and

there was a dressing down for all of us, including the innocent junior, an absorbed witness to the occasion.

When the mess was cleared up Porsen and I were carpeted and Evan tried hard to discover the cause of the quarrel. When I refused to tell him I thought I detected a gleam of gratitude in Porsen's puffy face and that decided me to hit him again, this time below the belt. With a great show of reluctance I said, piously, "Well, sir, he will keep telling me his filthy jokes . . ." and then hung my head, as though contemplation of Porsen's mind shamed me beyond power of expression.

I don't think I have ever seen a man more outraged than Porsen at that moment. He glared at me as if I was a reptile he had discovered in his bed, but I left the office in a mood of quiet triumph while Rhys-Jones gave Porsen a further piece of advice, telling him to wash his mouth out three times a day. Later on Porsen found an opportunity of whispering, "Christ help me, I'll fix you for that, Pritchard! I'll fix you if it costs me my job, you see if I don't." His threats of violence didn't bother me much. He was taller and heavier than me but a blowhard in this as in every other sphere. He did go to Powell with his version of the incident, however, and that did nothing to improve overall relationships in the place. By the end of the month I think any one of us, Griffiths included, would have rejoiced to see the other five laid out on mortuary slabs.

Things were like this when Delphine made her first exploratory step. I didn't see it as that, of course, or not then. At the time it was little more than a playful gesture, somewhat out of character perhaps, but still something I could regard as a joke.

I had taken to going into The Rainbow almost every day and my new relationship with her, and the haven represented by the café, was the one thing that kept me from making another and possibly more resolute attempt to bolt. I had about forty-five pounds in my account then, enough to keep me from starving, or throwing myself on my father's charity for a few months, and if it hadn't been for Delphine's presence as an emotional safety valve I think I really would have taken the irrevocable step of walking out of the bank and trying my luck in London or Liverpool.

One night I took my troubles to Delphine after closing time, getting myself invited into the back room on the strength of saying I wanted to discuss a change of digs with her.

Since the night I had gone berserk with the vinegar bottle our relationship had mellowed to the point of making small talk every time she served me and once or twice, as the last customer, I volunteered to stay on and give them a hand clearing up. But we continued in our roles of love goddess and worshipper-from-afar. I still called her Miss Beppolini, and she continued to address me as Mr. Pritchard, and this despite a friendliness on her part that many young men might have regarded as encouragement. I was far too grateful for her availability after a day's servitude and dared not risk the consequences of a snub. Porsen was right about her deadly skill at fending off approaches, of which she had about a dozen a week. She was superb at doing this without humiliating and perhaps sacrificing a regular customer. Dozens of young men addressed remarks in her direction, hoping to draw her out, but she went right on pretending to be deaf and stupid, and when a few of the bolder ones tried to hold her hand, or slip an arm round her waist she just shrugged them off, said a transatlantic equivalent of "Stop fooling," and sidled out of reach. It was a technique that ought to be taught in every girls' school in the land.

She gave me an opening as soon as we were alone in the back room.

"Say, you look real peaky, Mr. Pritchard. Aren't you feelin' so good?"

"I'm all right physically," I said, "but I'm fed up to here with that damned bank and changing digs won't cure that. It might even make things worse but I've got to make some kind of move."

She looked surprised and mildly sympathetic.

"You mean scram? Clean out of this dump?"

"Out of banking altogether. That branch is worse than most but they're all much of a muchness for someone in my situation."

"What kind of situation is that?"

"Are you really interested, Miss Beppolini?"

"Sure I'm interested. I'm human aren't I? Wait, I'll fix you something stronger than coffee tonight. Try Beppo's tipple, four-star brandy, and I'll have a gin to keep you company."

Then I told her the whole story, not only about how things were at the branch but also a brief survey of my life up to that time. I even told her about Ida, although I said nothing about us having been lovers. I related Ida's efforts to persuade me to cut loose and try for the job in India, and the real reason I had let it pass, which I now saw as lack of confidence in myself. She was a good listener and didn't interrupt. I said, in conclusion, "Well, there you are, that's about the size of it."

She replied, thoughtfully, "You missed something. How much does that nine-to-five stint bring you in paydays?"

"Two-fifteen, after they've deducted insurance and pension contributions," I said. "Next year it's a bonanza. Chaps in my bracket get a rise to three pounds, two and sixpence."

She was clearly astonished. "You don't say! How long before you're in line for a pension?"

"In my case? Another thirty-six years at least."

"You mean you have to hang on until you're that old?"

"To have enough to live on, yes. Some don't make it."

"But that's slavery," she said. "How come more of them don't help themselves the way Come-Home-Charlie did?"

"Is he someone I should know about?"

"The bank clerk in Scotland who got away with eleven thousand plus a month or so back. They haven't caught up with him yet, or if they have it hasn't been in the headlines. I know because I kept looking. It made me laugh so much. As a matter of fact, knowing you were a Charlie, I cut out the picture. I guess I had some idea of kidding you about it."

She went to the little bureau she used for her accounts and rummaged in a drawer.

"Here it is. 'Come home, Charlie, and face them!' That killed me. I mean, as if Charlie would?"

It was a page from one of the Sunday tabloids, a picture of a lugubrious-looking housewife standing at the gate of a semidetached house in a featureless suburb. She was Charlie's wife and had presumably posed for newsmen in the forlorn hope that Charlie would see it, feel guilty, and backpedal. In a panel below they had printed a two-paragraph summary explaining why Charlie was missing. He was thought to have falsified his accounts over a longish period, skipped off and had last been seen awaiting the departure of the London express on a Glasgow platform. Judging from the picture it looked as if Charlie's trail was cold and he was unlikely, of his own volition, to respond to Mrs. Charlie's appeal.

The story was not entirely new to me. Now that I was reminded of it I remembered reading about it at the time but the picture made a deep impression, perhaps because it implied that Delphine had thought of me the moment she saw it. I had been unaware that she knew my Christian name. I said, "Well, it does happen now and again but not so often as you might imagine. Bank security is good and getting better all the time. My guess is that he found a new twist on the Liverpool Bank frauds but in those days anyone with enough nerve could get away with it for a time."

She wanted to know all about the Liverpool Bank frauds so I told her all I could recall of the macabre story of Goudie, the bank clerk who, in 1902, had embezzled a vast sum of money from Hudson's, the soap firm, by the relatively simple process of drawing cash on their account, making false entries in the ledger, and destroying the checks to which he had regular access. To my surprise she was fascinated by the story.

"Say, that's cute! Whatever happened to him?"

"He was caught, given ten years and died in jail."

"But at least he had the dough tucked away somewhere."

"No he didn't. Two gangs of bookies had it and one gang was never caught."

"You mean he spent it *all* on horses?"

"Every penny."

"Well this Charlie hasn't. Looks like he had an escape route worked out in advance and I'd sure like to know what happened to him."

"So would a good many other people. They'll catch up with him."

"Suppose they do, they still couldn't get him back here if he'd had the sense to go to a country without an extradition treaty."

Her interest in the case, and in bank robberies generally, puzzled me, possibly because it seemed uncharacteristic. She was not the kind of person I would have thought wasted much time reading crime reports and detective fiction. Until that night she had seemed so absorbed in her business and so uncomplaining about the long hours and hard grind the business demanded. My newspaper reading taught me that hard workers were never recruiting grounds for crooks.

"Big-time crime is always making news in the States," I said, "did you ever see any famous gangsters when you were over there?"

"Sure I did," she said, as if it was the most natural thing in the world, "they sometimes came to the Coast and Beppo pointed them out to me. Beppo served gangsters with drinks but not in our place, they always go to ritzy joints. I once saw Bugs Moran, the man whose gang was rubbed out in the St. Valentine's day massacre last February, and one day, at a city parade, I saw Dion O'Banion, who was later killed by the Capone mob."

Now she had me fascinated. At that time the Chicago gangsters were always making headlines in Britain and everybody was familiar with the St. Valentine's day massacre, and bootleggers like O'Banion and Bugs Moran. It was astonishing to think that I was talking to someone who had actually seen these men and could talk about them as if they were politicians, like Lloyd George and Stanley Baldwin.

"What were they like?" I asked, "to look at, I mean?"

She laughed. "Why, like anybody else. You figure they'd have two heads? Those I saw looked like top salesmen on a vacation."

"It always beats me," I said, "that they can walk around that way. Damn it, they've actually killed people, and yet they get film-star treatment everywhere they go."

"That's the States," she said. "I guess we've got a different attitude to crime over there. People of that kind, guys who have made a killing out of Prohibition, are like—well—Robin Hoods to most folks. Maybe they represent something."

"What, exactly? Adventure?"

She coiled her beautiful legs under her the way I had noticed the first night she invited me there. "They see all the big guys in so-called legit business getting away with it and working the little guys the way that bank works you—for peanuts that is. Then, when somebody like Capone shows up and throws custard pies at the law they root for him."

"But who the hell could admire a murderous Wop like Al Capone?"

"Anyone. Just anyone who hadn't made the grade, Bub."

She looked at me with a half-smile and I mean that literally. Her mouth smiled but there was no laughter in her eyes. Instead there was a kind of speculative blankness, the look a woman living on a small budget might direct at a bargain counter. "Honestly now, would you buck at walking out of that bank with a bag of money if you were certain sure you would never be caught?"

I considered this, for it was something I had never really thought about. Did I owe society and, more particularly, Caddie's any loyalty? Did I still believe to some extent in the Old Testament God with X-ray eyes standing behind a blind policeman? Or did any scruples I might have stem from the thought that the policeman was only pretending to be blind? I had to be honest, even if this was only a game so I said, "No, not really. Mind you, I don't think I could ever convince myself that I wouldn't be caught, but if I could I don't think morality would stop me."

The answer pleased her. "I'm glad you didn't duck that one, Charlee."

We were silent for a moment. Already I felt better for talking to her, and for being able to look at her without sharing the privilege with a café full of tin-plate louts and flappers, but she seemed abstracted now so that I wasn't able to decide whether she was bored with my company or just tired after twelve hours on her feet. I gulped down what was left of my brandy and handed her the newspaper cutting.

"Keep it," she said, "it might cheer you up when things get tough down the road."

"You keep it," I said, and then, in an attempt to sustain my role as a wag, "if we were ever short at the bank and they found this on me they'd send me up on suspicion." She didn't laugh, as I had hoped, but took the cutting, folded it carefully and put it back in the bureau drawer. On the way out I had to squeeze past Beppo who was stacking crockery on the shelves behind the coffee machine. He grinned and said goodnight. It was all he ever said to anyone except Delphine.

2

The bank could not have done a better job if its directors had been listening in to our conversation and had decided to mold me into a real Charlie just for the hell of it.

When I let myself in Evan called from the living room and I could tell by his tone that he was in one of his showdown moods. I went in thinking I was due for another inquest on the Porsen row but that was only a part of it. Gladys was there, squatting in the one comfortable chair they possessed and looking like a malevolent toad.

"We've heard from Ida," Evan said, "she's working in London."

He waited for me to comment but I didn't.

"She's got a job as a packer with a firm called Atlas, a pickle factory," he went on. He said "pickle factory" very slowly and with a kind of stunned solemnity, and when I still didn't comment he repeated it. "A *packer*! In a *pickle* factory!" I wanted to laugh then but only for a moment because Gladys chipped in saying, "Dadda wants you to get her back. It's important to us and could be important to you."

"How to me, Mrs. Rhys-Jones?"

She looked at him. For all her dominating disposition she wasn't much good at making people back down if an opponent was careful to deny her an opening. Evan said, with an attempt to sound more conciliatory, "It's ... er ... like this, Mr. Pritchard. We'll write, of course, but we don't think any appeal we make would succeed on its own. Mam thinks it would be a good idea if you wrote too and we enclosed your letter in ours."

So that was it. Come home Charlie and now come home Ida.

Their presumption irritated me. I said, "Honestly, Mr. Rhys-Jones, what earthly good would it be me writing? If you can't persuade her, how could I?"

"Mam is certain she's very fond of you," he said, turning to Gladys for corroboration but not getting anything more than a nod. "She sent her regards to you."

"But I've already explained to Mrs. Rhys-Jones that there was never anything between Ida and me."

"Don't believe it!" This from Mam, sinking an inch or so deeper in the leather chair, a toad half submerging in a brown pool.

"Well, I'm sorry about that but it happens to be true, and if you don't believe me you can ask Ida."

He made the fussy hand-chopping motion that I had seen him make so often when things displeased him at the branch. "True or not, I'm asking you to pretend it is until we get her back here. If you wrote saying you'd like her back, wanted her back, Mam thinks she'd give up this ridiculous nonsense and come home. Once that happened we could sort things out. We would have her here and wouldn't let her go again."

His proposal converted my irritation into anger, not only because they seemed to think of her as a prisoner on the run but also because I had now made up my mind that to

74

enter this triangle would be to invite suffocation. I could take Ida but not Ida plus Gladys and Evan. I said, desperately, "No, Mr. Rhys-Jones, it's none of my business! Ida's not a child. She's twenty-nine and if she wants to work as a packer in a pickle factory she damn well can!"

He looked at me then as if he could beat me about the head, but I knew this wasn't so much on account of a longing to have Ida home but because he knew Gladys wouldn't stop nagging him until she surrendered. There was a reason for this. With Ida out of range Gladys felt deprived. There was no one around to nag when Evan was at work.

"Is that final?" he asked.

"Yes it is. Like I say, it's none of my business."

"I can make it my business. You aren't shaping any too well at the branch. There was this unsavory scene with Porsen this afternoon . . ."

"What scene was that?" Gladys surfaced at once. It outraged her to learn there had been a scene at the bank and she hadn't heard about it, but by this time Evan was so steamed up that he made one of his chopping motions in her direction so that she subsided, at least for the moment.

"You wouldn't do this, to stop me and Mam worrying?"

"There's no need to worry, Ida's old enough to look after herself."

"Very well, we'll see," and he walked past me and flung open the door.

It occurred to me then to tell them what I believed to be the facts, that Ida had got that job by applying to Mr. Waring and, for all I knew, was now living with him as wife or mistress. I resisted the temptation and went out and up to my room, hearing the rumble of their conversation as I mounted the stairs. I knew what this small gesture of loyalty would cost and I was right. From then on I was the pariah of the branch and only someone who has worked in enclosed premises, after having incurred the enmity of his superiors, can appreciate my position.

One of the by-products of this final break with Evan was a comparative if temporary lull in the nonstop duel between the heavy artillery. Both factions now resorted to sniping and mostly they had me in their sights. I didn't imagine the contempt of Powell, the spite of Porsen, and the steady hostility of Evan that was whetted every night on the edge of his wife's tongue. Only Griffiths stood aside, and watching them he must have needed all his faith in a Celtic revival to buttress him against the irreconcilability of the real Welsh, represented by Evan, the border English represented by Powell and Porsen, and the half-alien Southerner represented by me. We detested one another with a dedication that took precedence over every other aspect of our lives and each of us, in our several ways, did our best to make the lives of the others as unbearable as possible.

My contribution to the general atmosphere was not impressive but I was not defenseless. Anticipating latter-day Trade Union tactics of working-to-rule I did my utmost to exacerbate the quarrel between the two main adversaries, and soon I had the sour satisfaction of seeing them at one another's throats again, although without either of them letting up on me. It was not an edifying spectacle, a handful of grown men behaving like thwarted, spiteful children.

3

I am not going into the details of everything that happened down there as winter drew to a close and spring came round again. Ida (who had withheld her address) did not write a second letter, and I failed to take the obvious step of shifting my digs. I know why I stayed on at St. Ninian's. It was one way of hitting back, particularly at Gladys, who found my presence hateful but somehow could not bring herself to take the irrevocable step of showing me the door.

I strengthened my contacts with Delphine and, because she seemed vaguely interested, I passed on everything that happened in the branch. I went to the café every night and it became home to me, but she never let it be seen by other customers that I was privileged and I was never invited into the back room, until the last of them had gone. Not even Porsen noticed the progress I had made toward establishing the theory that Lickerish Lil, as he still called her, could be wooed from the glacial isolation she had maintained up to this time.

I did make another friend about that time. This was Gwyn Morgan, a local police constable, who happened to come from my hometown. We had been at school together and Gwyn had joined the County Constabulary soon after I went to work for Caddie's. He was a bumbling, heavy-footed young man, with feet that might be said to have determined his choice of profession. "Gwyn-the-Boots" they called him at school, and even for a policeman he had enormous feet and a very ponderous way of moving, as if he was a looming barge forever seeking an anchorage among a shoal of dinghies. He hailed me one day when he was on traffic duty at the junction of Station Road and Llandudno Road, delighted to discover one person he knew on a beat peopled by strangers. After that we met often and once or twice he invited me back to his digs in a terraced house at the western end of the town. I was glad to see him, if only because I still had qualms about the tin-plate gang's intention to avenge the incident of the vinegar bottle.

The incident that put a match to the gigantic firecracker I ultimately detonated occurred in early May of that year, that is, about thirteen months after I had come to Penmadoc, and some four months after Ida had disappeared. The initial impulse sprang directly from the visit of one of Caddie's directors, who dropped in unannounced, bringing a bank examiner with him.

Their descent on us created a mild stir. Porsen got rapped over the knuckles for having failed to carry out instructions to mark down an overdraft, and Evan and Powell were reprimanded for small faults that the director picked on to justify his existence. Then the examiner gave the branch a clean bill of health and Evan set to work to repair his defenses, ringing for me in the absence of the junior and telling me to fetch coffee for his visitors.

"Don't make it," he added, as I was on the point of leaving, "buy it, from next door. Mr. Gibson and the examiner haven't got all day to waste," and he threw half-a-crown on the table. I picked it up and saw the director's glance hover over my inkstained fingers. He was a choleric little mandarin, with reddish hair, flashing prince-nez spectacles and a florid complexion. He wore an expensively cut suit and I knew that he and the examiner had arrived in a company Daimler, driven by a uniformed chauffeur. I didn't have any special feelings about him except that I welcomed his presence as an embarrassment to Evan and Powell.

I went next door but one and Beppo lent me a tray to carry three coffees to the bank. When I set them down on Evan's desk I did so without noticing a paper knife that lay there and the tray tilted slightly, slopping coffee into the saucers. It was too good an opportunity for Evan to miss.

"Careful, butterfingers!" he shouted. "Mr. Gibson doesn't want it in his lap!"

"Indeed not," said the director, with a thin smile, "and while we're at it, Mr. Rhys-Jones, might I ask if the toilet facilities are in working order?"

"Why certainly, Mr. Gibson," said Evan, completely off his guard, "I'll show you where they are, it didn't occur to me that you would be interested . . ."

"Oh, I don't want to inspect them," said Gibson, smiling, "that's a matter for Fabrics. I just wondered if they were working because this young man obviously hasn't had a chance to use them this morning. I daresay he's been too busy."

I understood then the hidden provocations that cause apparently motiveless murders. The insult, a studied attempt to draw Evan's attention to my ink-blotched fingers, was gratuitous, the casual flick of a whip administered by an exalted passenger being conducted on a tour of the galley slaves by an obsequious captain. Of all the humiliations I had endured in that place this was the most wounding, if only because it was so deliberately calculated. It could serve no purpose at all but to degrade, not only me but Evan also, and along with Evan all the people whose labor had gone to purchase that Savile Row suit and the Daimler that awaited him outside. It would have given me tremendous satisfaction at that moment to have picked up the heavy shell-case doorstop Evan used to prop open his door and batter Mr. Gibson's head to a pulp; it would have given me even more to explain to judge and jury what had prompted me to act in that way.

Evan said, in a stifled voice, "Go and wash your hands, Pritchard," and I went out. Gibson must have died a long time ago and this is a pity. I should have liked him to learn of the part he played in all that happened that summer at the Penmadoc branch of Cadwallader's Bank.

As soon as he had driven off, Evan read me an insulting lecture on the habits of personal cleanliness and it soon got round the branch that Charlie Pritchard was averse to washing. Porsen, of course, at once seized on this and during the remainder of the time we worked together would greet me with remarks like, "Do you stand your socks up in the corner when you go bedibyes, Pritchard?" or the old advertising tag, "Good morning! And have you used Pear's Soap?"

It was about a week later that I broached the subject of walking out to Delphine. I now had about seventy pounds saved and the knowledge that it was there comforted me to some extent. I remembered that she had once mentioned an uncle who plied a cargo boat between America and the Continent and I had some idea of exploring the possibility of working my passage across to Canada. That night I was explicit about what was happening to me at the branch, even admitting the truth concerning my involvement with Ida, and I went on to tell her about the incident of the inkstained fingers. As usual she gave me her sympathetic attention and then poured me a stiff brandy and soda.

"Sounds as if you need that, Charlee," she said, putting emphasis on the second syllable in a way that always intrigued me, "and while you're knocking it back I'll tell you something. I daresay it'll rock you, and maybe even stop you from coming here, but I'm going to say it. In your shoes I wouldn't want to run. I'd want to hit back and give the bastards something to remember me by."

I took it for granted she was advising me to repeat the punch on the nose I had given Porsen, only this time go for the manager and chief cashier, but this didn't recommend itself as a means of letting off steam.

"Wherever I go I'll need a reference," I told her, "and at the moment they couldn't give me anything other than a straightforward one. If they did I could appeal over their heads to headquarters. There's absolutely nothing against me on the official record."

"That's the idea," she said. "From where you stand you could drop the lot of them in pitch, then stand off and laugh at them for the rest of your life. Not only that creep of a manager and this Powell you were telling me about but the bank itself, all those guys like that vice-president who told you to go wash yourself this morning."

"How could I do that?"

She looked me straight in the eye. "Did I say you could? Yes I did, didn't I? What I really meant was that *some* guys would. I figure I might if I was standing in your shoes."

"You'd do what, exactly?"

"What Charlie-Come-Home did to this bank in Scotland."

I couldn't take this seriously. An overt suggestion that I should monkey with accounts simply in order to get my own back on Caddie's was so ridiculous that I came to the conclusion she was expertly pulling my leg.

"That's just crazy," I said, "and even if it wasn't I wouldn't have a clue how to set about it."

"Wouldn't you? Well, I would."

"*You would?*"

"Show you something, Charlee," she said, and heaving herself up led the way out into the passage, but instead of returning to the café, where Beppo was working, she went through the arched door that led to her cellar.

I followed, still shocked but now indulgently amused. It

was like playing a daring game and who wouldn't want to play daring games with her?

We went down a flight of stone steps and through an arch into the cellar. It was littered with cartons and wooden boxes that had once contained fruit drinks and the place smelled strongly of damp. I knew that all the buildings along this side of the street had big cellars, but ours at the bank had been merged into the strongroom and entirely rebuilt when the premises were converted from a shop more than thirty years before. The cellar of The Rainbow was intact. Its walls were of brick and its ceiling was plastered. The brick needed pointing and in the dim light of the 25-watt bulb they had down there I noticed something else, a two-foot square iron grating that could only connect with the cellar of Thos. Cook & Sons, the drapers between the café and the bank.

I said, "Good God, Delphine, you're not serious, are you?"

"Depends," she said. "Let's say I could be, if you were."

My impulse when she said this was to back up those steps and get the hell out of the place, and I did make a move in that direction but I only got as far as the bottom stair and then sat on it, quite involuntarily, so that she laughed.

It was the first time I had ever heard her laugh, although sometimes accounts of our antics at the bank had made her chuckle. The laugh, I discovered, was a little shrill but this did something to reassure me. It suggested that this game scared her as much as it scared me, and the breathless chortle was an expression of release.

"That's right," she said, "take your time. After all, there's no charge for trying to solve this puzzle."

"It's a dead-end puzzle," I told her, "and I can tell you that from here. That grating only leads into Cook's cellar and if it has a twin the far side it's blocked with two feet of reinforced concrete. Even then it would only lead to our washroom and that's on the wrong side of the grilles. And beyond the grilles there's a safe, half as big as a bus."

As I told her this I pictured the familiar layout of the below-street level of the bank premises. The section nearest us was a narrow piece of the original cellar walled off to make a lavatory with a handbasin. It was no more than a kind of passage, buttressed on one side by the wall dividing the draper's and the bank and on the other, the side farthest from where we stood, by the blank side of the vault, a wall of formidable thickness. If you turned left as you emerged from the washroom three steps brought you to the grille door, or rather doors, for there were two separated by a space of about a foot. Once, when we were locking up and Evan had his back turned, Porsen had slammed the outer door and imprisoned the junior between the two steel gratings. He pretended it was an accident and Powell had to return down the stairs to let him out. Evan kept the key of the inner grating and Powell the key to the outer. We all had occasional access to the safe key that was in the custody of Powell by night and Evan by day. Powell also kept the keys of the bank premises. His flat had no direct access to the bank but because he lived above it he always opened up about a quarter to nine, and locked up in his own time once the security drill below had been completed in the manager's presence.

I recounted this, or as much of it as was relevant, with the patronage of a clever Dick putting the damper on a silly woman's romantic fancy, but all she said when I had finished was: "Sure, but suppose, just suppose, you *had* keys to the grilles and the safe? Is there anything to stop anyone digging through into the washroom? Provided they had plenty of time, and providing they weren't disturbed?"

"Nothing but about two feet of concrete the far side of Cook's grating. And always supposing Cook has a grating like this."

"He has," Delphine said. "I know because I've been in there."

"Old Cook let you go rooting about in his cellar?"

"He didn't know I was there. I lifted that grating out and went to see for myself. He hardly ever uses his cellar. It's full of ratty old cartons and wrapping paper and about as filthy as it can be, but there is a grating on the far side exactly like ours. They must have put one in every building along here to keep the air circulating, but that would be long before the bank was built. It is blocked, just as you say, but it looks kind of crumbly to me. Care to take a look?"

I hadn't the slightest wish to but there were at least three reasons why I didn't admit this. One was an uncomfortable certainty that a crawl through that grating into Thos. Cook's cellar represented to Delphine what the Atlas project had represented to Ida. Secondly, she hypnotized me. The mere thought that she had got as far as contemplating the act of tunneling into Caddie's bank made her into a special kind of person, almost on a par with those gangsters she had talked about. I was terrified and horrified but I was also spellbound by her fantastic arrogance. Thirdly, and this is far more difficult to explain in retrospect, I was already half sold on the exhilarating prospect of solving her ridiculous puzzle, even if it meant demonstrating to her beyond all doubt that no solution existed or ever could exist. There was another element too. I think this tiptoe approach stemmed, at least in part, from a desire to protect her from a contemplated folly of tremendous magnitude, rather as a man might instinctively throw himself between a fused bomb and the blundering feet of a child. I said, wiping my palms on my trouser legs, "Okay, so long as you promise not to make a sound I'll prove what a crazy idea it is," and we crossed the littered cellar to the grating.

She lifted it out effortlessly so that I saw at once it had been detached from its frame, the rusty boltheads having been prized away at the corners. The wall here was about a foot thick and composed of old double brick. Beyond was complete darkness but I could smell the rotting cardboard she had mentioned.

The squarish hole now connecting the cellars was about eighteen inches by fifteen inches, enabling a person of my build to wriggle through with comparative ease, but as I stepped forward she said, giggling, "Wait, Charlee, I'll go first. I've got me a torch."

She had too and I hadn't even noticed she was carrying one. She switched it on and the beam fell on a jumble of crushed, decaying boxes. Beyond the hole in the cellar was a sea of cartons and pieces of wrapping paper to which a skein of tissue paper still adhered. I remembered then that the Cook family were misers, and the old man's habit of forgetting to give customers the farthing change on goods marked four and eleven-three was a Penmadoc joke that had probably originated with the first Thomas Cook who had set up business here in the eighteen-fifties. The rubbish was packing material that had been dumped until it was either used or rotted.

Delphine went down on her hands and knees and began to ease herself through the hole. She took her time, moving by inches; so that I had leisure, in the dim light cast by the naked bulb behind me, to see her from a very unconventional angle and the glimpse I got of her had a direct bearing on everything that happened from then on, inasmuch as it altered my conception of her and, because of this, changed our relationship. Up to that time I had always regarded her as a very desirable woman, but the aloofness she maintained toward the café Romeos extended to me, notwithstanding the friendliness she had shown me since the vinegar bottle episode. In a matter of seconds this was dispelled, for her skirt rucked up to her waist exposing a generous portion of her thighs above her stocking tops, and a shapely behind screened in a pair of pink panties. If that had been all, the aspect would have been no more than comic, encouraging me to think of what we were doing as a kind of romp with a girl like Ida, but the underpants she was wearing were open-legged, of the kind they called "French Legs" in those days, and she thus revealed a good deal more of herself than would have been the case in other circumstances. Moreover, I knew, somehow, that this was a deliberate act, both an invitation and preview on her part, and this converted the romp into a far more serious business. She went on pushing herself forward, her legs waving free, and I stood a yard or so back sweating like a man trying to rally enough moral courage to refuse a gigantic bribe. I knew then that it was a bribe and that if I accepted it I would be the first man in Penmadoc to make the Rainbow Queen. I didn't put up much of a fight. No sooner had her heels disappeared than I was more than half enlisted. One preliminary survey, as it were, encouraged me to embark on another.

I climbed through to find myself standing shin-deep in rubbish. The cellar was an exact replica of the one I had just left, and I crept across to the opposite wall. There was the grating, firmly embedded in its frame, but what surprised me more than I could say was that beyond it, with a clearance of less than an inch, was not the buttress of concrete I had expected but a brick wall. The bricks were in better condition than those on the Rainbow side of the cellar but they must have been there all of thirty years and probably much longer. I realized, looking at them, that entry into the bank washroom was practical to anyone prepared to remove them and chip through a layer of concrete on the far side.

"Well?" she said, standing back with her hands on hips.

"I was wrong," I admitted, "but it's solid concrete the other side of those bricks."

"Only as far as floor level. Look next time you're in there. I'll guarantee you'll find there's a brick floor to that washroom, with only a skin of concrete."

I said nothing. Breathing this fetid air and turning over the monstrous possibility of tunneling my way into Cadwallader's strongroom made my senses reel. I could feel the sweat striking cold under my arms and I know that my hands were shaking. She must have been aware of this for she said, in the matter-of-fact tone to which I had grown accustomed, "Okay, Charlee, we'll go home now."

Her tone of voice steadied me so that I thought, with relief, "The silly game is over. That view of her backside cost me nothing but a scare. We can go back to that room of hers now and stop playing with dynamite."

We returned across the cellar and through the hole, Delphine remaining a moment to replace the grating. The air on the top step was a joy to breathe. I dusted myself off and noticed that no sounds came from the café. Beppo must have finished cleaning up and gone to bed. He never seemed to use the back room and I had already begun to think of him as a handyman rather than a partner in the business.

She said, pouring me another brandy, "What now, Charlee? Home to bed?"

It might have been the glow produced by the second brandy or maybe the reassuring ordinariness of the room, but now that I was above ground I felt almost as indulgent as when the subject was broached.

"It's as daft as ever. Granted it might be possible to get into the washroom, taking frightful risks that is . . ."

"What risks?"

The words snapped out as she stood looking down at me in the slightly insolent stance I had seen her use so often in the café, feet astride, hands resting lightly midway along her thighs.

"Noise for one thing. Right above that cellar is Cook's shop. You couldn't remove the grating and bricks without making a hell of a noise and what guarantee would you ever have that Cook, his son or one of their assistants, didn't come down to investigate?"

"In the middle of the night? Or after closing time? That's a thousand to one again, Buddy. It would depend when you worked. They all sleep on the top floor and it's obvious no one uses that cellar except as a dump. They probably stand on the stairs and throw the junk down."

"All right, take the tunnel as read. What good would it be blistering your hands and choking half to death in that stinking place, in order to bob up in a washroom? The only thing to pinch in there is a toilet roll and a cake of soap. We even have to bring our own towels and keep them in a locker upstairs."

It had descended to this level, a jocular exchange of ideas, a couple of youngsters speculating what they might do if they won the Irish Sweep, but if it amused her and kept me in her company, I was prepared to speculate indefinitely.

"There are three things to consider," she said, coiling herself on the settee in that catlike way of hers. "First and most important is getting to the place where the money is. Second is picking a time when there is enough money there to make it worthwhile. Third is getting away. If you were inside man on a job like this, when would be the best time of the year to do it?"

"Mid-September," I said.

"Why?"

"The tail end of the season and the annual horse fair. That mightn't seem important to you but it brings a lot of extra money into the town and we have to cater for it in advance. I'd pick a Thursday night. The tin-plate works draw their pay on Friday mornings and the payout runs into four figures."

"Now about getting clear—that would be for me to figure, and there I'm sitting pretty. I've got Uncle Berni."

"The one who brought you and Beppo over here on his boat?"

"He makes several trips a year. I would have to check, of course, but I know one of them is in the fall. Suppose I wired saying Beppo and me were for going home again and couldn't raise the fare? He's a nice guy. He'd probably hang around in Queenstown, so long as it didn't mean too much delay."

"You mean you'd go to Ireland first?"

"Sure. And what's simpler? Boat train to Holyhead, overnight passage on the Irish Mail, and first train out of Dublin. We would be halfway to Queenstown before that guy Powell opened up and found nothing but small change in the vault!"

The prospect of Powell making this kind of discovery was enormously satisfying. Happily I pictured his stupefaction once he had headed Evan down those steps and opened the outer grille. And then, like a string of firecrackers, the entertainment enlarged itself to include Evan unlocking his grille and the two of them stepping into the strongroom to swing open the safe. They wouldn't find a thing amiss until then, providing we had tidied up and left things shipshape. They would stand there dumbfounded, like men who had died and been resurrected in a new century. For minutes, perhaps, they would gape and gasp and choke and stare and then, like raving madmen, they would begin to rummage among the safe documents and after these had been strewn about Evan would scream for help and everyone else would come tumbling down the steps. It was the most rewarding pipe dream I had ever had. Looked at like that it was almost worth doing seven years' hard labor to convert it into reality.

She said, "What's so funny, Charlee?"

"I'm thinking of all those bloody directors, chaps like that bastard Gibson, who made a scene about a few inkspots on my fingers."

"Well," she said, prosaically, "back to business. We've picked the time and I've figured a getaway but we still haven't got to the money."

"That's what I mean when I say it's just a lovely fable, Delphine. If I didn't know that I wouldn't even discuss it with you." It gave me an inward tremor, indeed, to reflect that I had already committed unforgivable sins in the eyes of Cadwallader's. I had not only familiarized an outsider with the layout of the strongroom, I had also told her the peak period of the year as regards our inflow of currency. I got up, feeling the effects of the brandy. "I'm tight, Delphine," I said, "I'll go home now. It's been fun."

She yawned. "Time you had some. God knows, someone should step in for Ida and raise a laugh once in a while." Then, thoughtfully, "You figure you were ever in love with her, Charlee?"

"No," I said, "Ida was just a damned good sport."

She thought about this for a moment and then she stood up, placed both hands on my shoulders, and kissed me full on the mouth.

"Poor old Charlee," she murmured. "Go home, Charlee, and face them."

I don't recall my feet taking me up Station Road, across the main road and on up Craigwen Terrace to Evan's place. I don't even remember letting myself in, climbing the stairs, and undressing in that narrow little room. Her kiss, so casually bestowed, and so entirely unexpected, had the power not only to banish Penmadoc, and everything that went with it, but also to convert me into a legendary hero who rode a white steed across the imagination of Griffiths. She had kissed me, uninvited and unsolicited, and half the young men in Penmadoc would envy me that if they knew about it. Charlie Pritchard had made a killing at last and would never be quite the same man again.

Chapter Seven

It happens to everyone, that trick of becoming aware of an object, a process or a person that has been around a long time before making a sudden impact, after which full recognition occurs over and over again in a matter of days, sometimes hours.

It was this way with the bank keys and bank security generally. I was aware of them without recognizing them as instruments or processes possessing an identity. Until then they had merged into the routine patterns of the weekly stint, but once I had discussed them with Delphine I could isolate them and think of them in an entirely new context. The three keys that opened the way to the cash detached themselves from all the other apparatus we used in the course of a working day, and the regulations surrounding them, in which their security reposed, took on a significance that they had not possessed up to that time. Without knowing it I became watchful and alert whenever keys were mentioned and handled, waiting for the slightest deviation in the drill that governed their use. Criminals in film and fiction never operated without a preliminary "casing." After that evening with Delphine I became, if unconsciously, a thoroughgoing caser.

I had already handled two of the three keys, Powell's key to the outer grille, and the larger key that unlocked the safe. The only key with which I was unfamiliar was the key that opened the inner grille and no junior ever got more than a glimpse of that one because it never left Evan's key ring. On the other hand all of us, at one time or another, had occasional access to the safe, a massive, old-fashioned single-lock structure, anchored in its concrete base opposite the grilles. Nowadays an institution holding large amounts of cash on the premises would put small faith in a repository of this clumsy design but in those days combination locks were all but unknown in small branches and none, so far as I knew, had been installed by Cadwallader's.

At Penmadoc we based our security on the double-grille system and each door possessed what we thought of as a relatively modern lock. The safe was a longstop, for access to it, even when it was open, was barred so long as one of the grilles was shut. We juniors, and I include Porsen in this group, rarely entered the strongroom unaccompanied. Usually either Evan or Powell was there, both when we opened and locked up morning and late afternoon, which were the only occasions when large amounts of cash were transferred to or from the tills.

Caddie's security was no better and no worse than the average small bank at that period. It differed from most only insofar as we placed too great a reliance on a single member of the staff as custodian, Powell being permanently resident on the premises. Some banks in those days did not go to much trouble to guard against entry of the actual premises. I have even known cleaning women entrusted with keys. They relied instead on the formidable double lock of a door barring the way to the vault, but for some reason we had no such door. Once you were actually inside the bank you could approach the grilles freely by passing through the counter-flap and descending the stairs, but here, to get at the cash, you had three independent barriers, two somewhat complicated locks on the grilles and one on the safe itself.

After our inspection of the Cook cellar, and our fanciful discussion upon the general practicality of a robbery, I found my mind returning to the subject every time I was below stairs at the branch, but I continued to ponder the problems academically, as one might chew one's pencil over a trio of crossword clues. It remained a game I played with myself, for, as the days passed, Delphine did not return to the subject and at no time during what I now recognize as the basic planning stage did I see myself as a bank robber in anything but an extravagant fantasy.

All the same, as time went on the fantasy became obsessive so that when I was not thinking about Delphine's lips and legs and availability I was thinking, consciously or subconsciously, about how an unauthorized person could enter that vault.

In some ways the two fantasies were fused inasmuch as I was sure that I could never dominate Delphine as Charlie Pritchard, bank clerk, but I might, if I was sufficiently bold and cunning, win her with brains and daring. Then my fantasies would move out into a far wider field and I would see the two of us sipping cool drinks on a Mediterranean terrace overlooking a bay bathed in golden sunshine.

I don't think I ever saw us as conventional man and wife. The idealized version of the girl who had preoccupied me as a bystander had been banished, not only by the stark proposition that I should partner her in a bank robbery, but also, I think, by that Peeping Tom glimpse of her scrambling through the grating into Cook's cellar. Our association had taken on a kind of desperate decadence, of the kind against which my mentors had been at pains to inoculate me since childhood. She represented the Scarlet Woman of the Old Testament who demanded, as her price, the soul as well as the flesh. And at that stage—that is before committal on my part—I was ready to pay the price and be damned to the consequences. It required opting out of civilized society and the shedding of all the values of the past, but this entailed small sacrifice on my part, at least in the imagination. What the hell would I care about abstracts like honor and honesty once I had acquired exclusive rights over those shifting hips, that soft mouth and the tremendously exciting animal vitality that instinct told me was concealed behind the negligence of her café pose? She wasn't like that at all and this I was prepared to swear. For the right man she could switch on an entirely different personality that would convert every erotic fantasy I had ever had about women into searing reality. Could respectability and a pension at sixty-plus match that?

And what had honesty and application brought me so far? A couple of pounds a week and a gruff command to go wash the inkstains from my hands. So I dreamed and so the days slipped by, Delphine crossing the floor of a luxury suite in a transparent negligée, Delphine emerging, laughing, from her bubble bath, Delphine stark naked on a bed panting for the man who had the guts and the brains to blast his way into the world of the privileged. In the meantime, of course, there was the real world to be faced.

The weekends were the worst time to live through, in spite of the dog's life I led at the bank. Sunday in Wales is a trying day for those who have a home and friends, but for someone like me, watching the hours pass in digs, it was endless. The Chapel bells tolled their monotonous single notes. Everybody wore black or dark gray. Traffic was very light and background noises were muted. There was absolutely nothing to do but dream, for The Rainbow was not permitted to open on Sundays and although I longed for an invitation to share a Sunday with Delphine I never received one.

After that evening when we solved part of what she had called her puzzle there was, I sensed, a slight cooling-off on her part. At first it was barely noticeable but within a fortnight it became obvious that I had exaggerated her interest in me as a person rather than a customer. We continued to exchange light conversation before closing time and once she asked me into the back room for a coffee but during the fifteen minutes or so we remained alone there she seemed bored and our conversation faltered so that I left feeling she was glad to see the back of me.

It was for want of a topic to reawaken even a passing interest in me that I deliberately revived the subject of bank robberies again on an evening when trade happened to be very slack and by ten o'clock I was the only remaining customer.

I said, "That 'puzzle' of yours, Delphine. I think I might have solved part two, an approach to the actual cash."

The change in her expression, from one of polite boredom to lively interest, should have alerted me at once but it didn't.

"Tell me about it," she said, and to Beppo, "Lock up,

Beppo! It's dead tonight. I guess it's that deadbeat circus on the front and the new Janet Gaynor movie at the Fleapit."

We went through and she poured me a drink. I said, by way of introducing the subject, "It's funny, but after our talk I couldn't get that nonsense out of my head. I've been trying to convince myself it was as crazy as it appeared."

"And did you?"

"Did I what?"

"Convince yourself?"

She wasn't smiling, or looking the way people look when they are talking nonsense. She might have been ordering a crate of soft drinks from a vanman.

"In a way I did. It would depend on one member of the gang being able to reproduce keys. Suppose the inside man of the gang, the Charlie-Come-Home type, could get impressions?"

As I said the word "impressions" I had a sense of making a deliberate step from fantasy to fact and the shift was almost physical, as if, after leaning for a long time on the parapet of a high bridge, I had suddenly vaulted it and projected myself into space. It was not in the least an unpleasant sensation. Rather it was exhilarating, and invested with zest and even a kind of relief of the kind I had found in Ida's company the night she had first addressed herself to the task of emancipating me.

"Give me another drink and I'll tell you," I said.

"Yes, Charlee," she said meekly, and took my glass.

"Those three keys," I said, relishing the almost dutiful way she handed me a recharged glass, "two would have to be cut from impressions."

"Why only two?"

"The Charlie-Come-Home type could get his hands on the other one if he watched his chance. The manager keeps it, and I know where. On his chain all day, and in a cavity under his night table all night."

She looked at me admiringly. "Not so fast, Buddy. If Charlie could borrow the keys why couldn't all three be duplicated?"

"For two reasons. Time is one. Rhys-Jones is never parted

from that key except when he takes his trousers off but Powell parts with his, just occasionally. The other reason is that Rhys-Jones's key, the one that opens the inner grille, is more complicated than Powell's. Of the two grilles Powell's has the simpler lock. Don't ask me why."

"How about burglar alarms?"

"You've been reading too many crime magazines. We don't have one, discounting the old clanger upstairs and that's a precaution against a holdup during the day. It isn't even wired to the vault."

"Wouldn't it be less effort all round to duplicate the key to the bank itself?"

"No, it wouldn't. Powell never lets that one out of his custody. I've never even had a close look at it because he opens and locks up every day. Besides, he sleeps right over the front porch. A tunnel is a much safer approach and you were right about the concrete skin. In the washroom the concrete looks as if it clothes the walls and then covers the floor surface. If you tackled it from below you could break through in a couple of hours. So there's your crazy puzzle solved, providing of course that the gang knows how to cut keys from impressions and they surely would."

I noticed that while I was talking her color had heightened and that her rate of breathing accelerated. This did spell something out to me, namely, that she was actually weighing the risks and the curious thing is that this did not shock me at all. Without really knowing it I had already passed that point after uttering the word "impressions" and then by describing the situation in detail, and now I was neither sweating nor trembling as I had sweated so freely while inspecting the cellar.

There followed a long silence between us. Outside in the mild spring evening, life ticked over. A passing car hooted and down at the siding a goods train moved off with a series of metallic coughs as buffer struck buffer. But in here were a man and woman at a crisis in their lives.

She said, at last, "*Would* you? Could you ever do more than talk about it, Charlee?"

"That depends."

"But how? Apart from operating from these premises?"

I said, deliberately, "It would be something that would bind us together. For the rest of our lives."

"You mean you hadn't taken that for granted?"

"No. Why should I? Why should it be worth doing if you went your way and I went mine?"

"You mean you would only do it if we married?"

The emergent Charlie could have laughed at this but he checked himself. "Not necessarily. We'd just have to stay together. What would marriage count for if we had done something as big as that and done it together?"

There was another silence. I had made up my mind that I wasn't going to give her any more help than was necessary.

"There's another thing I have to know, Charlee."

"Well?"

"How do you see our life together? Afterwards, years afterwards and in another country?"

I could have told her then about the Mediterranean terrace, the transparent negligée and all the rest of it but tonight these fantasies seemed as naïve and immature as they seem to me at this distance.

I said, "Like anyone else's. I've always had a theory about crime. That almost anyone with a clean record can commit one big one and stand a first-class chance of getting away with it. Crooks are caught on their second, third or tenth time round. Hardly any are nabbed the first time out."

"How would that figure in your case? Once the bank was hit you'd have to scram and having gone you'd be number one suspect."

"I wouldn't scram," I said, and I think this took her breath away. "You and Beppo would, and everyone would be looking for you. You would split and never meet again, but I'd stay around. I'd gape down at the hole in the floor and look as amazed as Powell and Porsen. I'd be grilled by the police, of course, and by Caddie's people from HQ but no more than any member of the staff. Then we'd all be posted to different branches. Bank staff always are after far more trivial affairs than this. And I'd have to stay on working for Caddie's for months, for more than a year even."

"And then?"

"Then I'd go sick and start botching things so badly one way and another that they would heave a sigh of relief when I gave in my notice. I'd even blame that on the robbery. A crack-up. 'The shock got him down.' That way I'd see all the fun and I wouldn't want to miss that."

"Does that mean you'd be doing it to square yourself with them?"

"I'd be doing it mainly so that I could have you to myself for good. I want that a hell of a sight more than I want money, or even freedom."

This couldn't have been much of a surprise to her and she took it calmly.

"Is *that* the whole truth, Charlee?"

I considered and realized that it wasn't. It was most of it but it wasn't all.

"I'm twenty-four," I said, "and I've had a bloody awful deal so far. I want to get out in the open and see as much as I can before I go bald and wheezy and grow a paunch like old Evan. I don't even care if it's a short run, so long as you're around to share it with me."

"You mean you're in love with me, Charlee?"

"Physically I am. I don't believe in the other kind."

The answer surprised me more than it did her. It was a very different answer to the one I would have given when I entered the room half-an-hour ago, but then I wasn't the same man and I never would be again. Now I was seeing everything in reverse, like a man standing on his head, and the thing that puzzled me was not that this should be so but the fact that I was able to adjust to it with so little effort and absolutely no distress.

"Well," she said, a little breathlessly, "you sure can surprise a girl, Charlee, and I figure you've been honest—if that's the right word. Okay, I'll come across too at the risk of you backing down. I've been working on you one way or another ever since I found that loose grating, but I'd about given up."

"What stopped you? Most people give up after a week or two."

"I don't know. Maybe it was a hunch, or maybe it had something to do with that girl you told me about, the bank manager's daughter."

"Ida?"

"Sure, Ida." She got up, rummaged in the bureau drawer for a packet of cigarettes and lit two, sticking one between my lips on her way back to the couch. It was the first time a girl had ever performed that service for me and she did it unconsciously. She was still assessing the influence Ida had had upon me. "Ida," she repeated thoughtfully, "the name sure fits your description of her. Cozy and comfortable, especially flat on her back. But not your type."

I came to Ida's rescue.

"Ida wasn't all that to look at but I'm damned grateful to her."

"So am I, brother, because if it hadn't been for her you wouldn't be sitting there planning how to get into that bank. Was she the first woman you ever had?"

"Yes, she was."

"Why so long, Charlee?"

"Partly I didn't want to get landed, the way most chaps around here do, but mostly it was lack of opportunity. Girls round here aren't so dim as they seem guzzling ice cream at your tables."

"I'm not talking about them," she said, with a slow smile, "I'm talking about you. It wasn't just what Ida had to offer. It was the fun you got out of her being who she was and where she was. That's true, isn't it?"

"What of it?"

She hitched her skirt, shot out her legs and looked at them speculatively.

"After that you started asking yourself where keeping in line was going to get you and now, I guess, you've come up with the answer. You'd never make it legitimately, any more than I would or Beppo would. We could all three work all the hours God sends without getting within spitting distance of the jackpot."

I said, guardedly, "Where does Beppo fit into this? I realize he'll have to clear out, and that you'll have to stake him for a time, but I don't see him playing a big part in it. I'm not even sure I'd trust him."

"You'll have to," she said, "and not simply because we can't dig through into your washroom without him knowing, dim as he seems to you and to most other people around here. Point one, he isn't dim but just likes to pretend he is. Point two, he'll do anything I say without a second thought and has done since I was so high. But point three is more important. Beppo can make any keys we need in that workshop he has upstairs. From where I'm standing that means a three-way split."

"And afterwards?"

"Afterwards we'll part company. That's only common sense. Even out of here we'll travel different routes. Beppo's a big boy. He can find his own way home providing that's where he intends going. No, Charlee, it isn't trusting Beppo you have to worry about, it's trusting me. About a year you say? Well, if I were you I'd be asking, 'Will she be there when the time has run out?'"

"I think you will."

"I've got my share and I'm at sea before they get around to asking you a single question. What's to stop me kissing you goodbye right here? Loyalty?"

"People like us can't bank on that. It's just that I already know too much and you'd never feel safe if you went back on me."

"What do you know that's so important?"

"About your uncle's boat and all the things you've told me about yourself and family. If they got to me they'd get to you eventually and I think you weighed that up in advance."

"What you're saying is if I didn't play it straight you wouldn't?"

"Would anybody?"

She laughed and got up, reaching out for the brandy bottle but I shook my head. "I don't want a thick head in the morning. I've got too many problems."

"There's one you've already overlooked," she said. "From now on you stop making sheep's eyes at me in the café six times a week. If you want that alibi of yours to make sense you and I will have to have a big row. In public. And as soon as possible."

She sat thinking for a few moments, then she said, "The old sue-and-be-damned routine. That ought to cause quite a stir and people will remember it. Next time you order a sandwich bite into it carefully. If you have one hell of a surprise make it public. I'll play it from there but your line is injured innocence."

There didn't seem any more to be said at that stage so I told her I would get on home and to bed. She said I should start preparing the alibi at once by leaving via the yard and from now on, whenever I called, I was to use the back door but never in daylight hours.

I had never been to the rear of their premises but I knew they had access through high double gates to a broad alley that ran parellel with Station Road. There was no moon and the light shed by the street lamp at the far end of the alley was masked by the tall boundary wall. The wall had glass splinters on the top but there was a postern cut into one of the big doors and this was fitted with a Yale lock. Before we left the room she gave me a spare key but warned me not to use it until after we had staged the demonstration in the café. She would try and arrange it for the following night. Then she accompanied me across the yard and we stopped just inside the gates.

"How do you feel about it now, Charlee?" she asked, and I said I felt slightly tipsy. I noticed, however, that she didn't seem at all eager to be rid of me and it occurred to me to wonder how far, even now, she really trusted me. Then, it seems, she made up her mind to resolve any doubts she had.

"Charlee," she said, in little above a whisper, "you'd best understand things fully. You're not hooked yet but you will be the moment you come in through that gate with one of those impressions. If you want to cry off do it right now because I wouldn't want to go on toying with something this big." A thought seemed to strike her. "It couldn't be that you're kidding me along for the fun of it, could it? The way you did down in the cellar?"

"No," I said, "I'm past the kidding stage. But how about something on account," and I grabbed her and kissed her on the mouth, as if I had been treating all the girls that way since I was fifteen.

We embraced for a moment, the new Charlie exultant, the old one standing off, dumb with admiration. Then she began kissing me back and I knew that, whether or not she was committed, I certainly was, and that she knew this and it gave her the assurance she needed. It wasn't until I began to run my hands over her that she ended the kiss with, "Not here, Charlee, but soon, I promise you. Go home, Charlee," and she chuckled and reached over my shoulder to open the door.

Chapter Eight

1

The charade staged to inform Penmadoc at large that I was disenchanted with The Rainbow was a riot. It couldn't have been more successful if we had rehearsed it for weeks.

I went in there about eight-thirty the following evening to find the place full of the usual type of customer, leggy girls, strident youths and half-tipsy tin-plate workers. I asked at the counter for a coffee and when Delphine served it she pushed a plate containing a cheese sandwich toward me. I took the coffee and sandwich back to my seat, waited until some other customers had approached the counter, and then took a large bite at the sandwich. I wish I had taken her warning literally. Buried in the cheese was a broad-headed tack and my front teeth, slipping on it, bit into my tongue so that I did not have to simulate pain but jumped up with an oath, clapping my hand to my mouth and holding up the tack for general inspection.

"It was in the sandwich," I yelled, "I've broken my tooth."

Delphine looked at me steadily and Beppo, who had been collecting dishes near the door, sidled down the aisle, his hands hanging loosely at his sides like a Western gunman itching to draw.

"Don't you know better than to try that one?" she asked. "Every hash slinger in the country has that trick played on him once a week."

The disclaimer was made so coolly that it came near to convincing me in spite of myself.

"But there it is," I protested, "I've just taken it out of my mouth, it was in the sandwich. . . ."

Beppo was close beside me now. He didn't say anything, he just stood there looking attentive and expectant. When he flexed his fingers my ears tingled. I never met anyone who could look so polite and so menacing at the same time.

Delphine said, addressing the customers at the counter, "The next thing he'll say is the bit about his dental bill, and after that he'll get around to his goddam lawyer. Later on he'll try and collect your names as witnesses."

The customers chortled, settling themselves to await what would happen next but nothing did for a moment. Delphine went back to work on the coffee machine, Beppo continued to breathe down my neck, and the honkytonk played "Meet Me in My Dreams Tonight."

"But it's damned scandalous!" I shouted, "I demand an apology and my money back!"

Delphine chuckled at this. "That's a new routine," she said amiably, still not addressing me directly, "they usually want their money back but they don't often ask for a 'so-sorry-sir' thrown in."

This amused the customers very much. They guffawed, pushing one another and slapping their thighs, and then one of them, a tin-plate worker who had been present when I hit his colleague with the bottle, said, "Going to sue, Dai? Go on, man, serve the summons on Beppo. He's about your weight!" and they all laughed, including Delphine.

I remembered her cue about dignified disdain so I took out my handkerchief, wrapped the tack in it, tucked it back in my breast pocket and said, "You'll hear more of this!"

Cue notwithstanding, I wasn't prepared for Delphine's reaction. She spun round in a fury, spitting out a string of Italian expletives and sailing out from behind the counter to take up a position on the far side of me. When she ran out of Italian swearwords she screamed, "I'm sick of these tricky little bastards. Sick to death of them! Coming here trying to show a thousand percent profit on ten cents invested in coffee and a snack! You going to leave or does Beppo have to throw you out?"

"I'm not going to leave before I get satisfaction!" I said.

"Satisfaction, is it? Well, here's your sixpence for the sandwich. There was no sawdust in your coffee, was there?"

She flung down the coin and I left it lying there. We now had the undivided attention of everyone in the café. A free show like this in out-of-season Penmadoc wasn't to be missed.

"It's not just the question of the money," I said, "there's my broken tooth. This gentleman was a witness, weren't you, sir?"

I picked on the tin-plate worker and he looked surprised and then foxy. "Never saw a thing, bach," he said, "had me bloody back to you, same as everyone down this end!" He said it in a way that implied that anyone who backed my story would have to reckon with him as well as Beppo.

Delphine knew when to stop. She jerked her head at Beppo and he reached out casually, took me by the collar and the seat of my pants and frogmarched me the length of the café. He must have been a very good bouncer back in LA for he did it smoothly and effortlessly. In five seconds flat I was sailing through a door that somebody had obligingly opened. I didn't even have an opportunity to shout the bit I had thought up about the Inspector of Public Health, I was too busy clutching at a lamp post to check my progress beyond the curb. I caught it but the swing around brought me to my knees. The door closed on a roar of laughter and that, it would seem, was that. From now on The Rainbow was out of bounds to Charlie Pritchard. As soon as it got around that I had made no official protest every witness would assume it had been a try-on, just as Delphine had suggested.

It didn't take long to get around either, for Porsen had wind of it by the following day. News that I had been publicly ejected from The Rainbow entranced him. He said, in Griffiths' hearing, "So Lickerish Lil has decided to cut down on her genteel clientele? Well, I can't say I'm that surprised and you shouldn't be either. If you eat alongside tin-plate yobs you have to adapt to their table manners, don't you?

104

Otherwise they feel inferior and they won't stand for that. After all, their normal diet is tin-tacks. If there *was* a tin-tack!"

Griffiths, who usually opted out of this kind of exchange, was interested and when I pretended to sulk he asked Porsen to tell him what happened. He had it fairly accurate, probably from the tobacconist's assistant who had been a witness. Then I gave my version and Griffiths, taking my story at face value, was sympathetic.

"No future in making an official complaint," he said, "none of those tin-plate people would back you up. They think of people like us as members of the capitalist class and besides, Owen, the Council MO, is a lazy devil and would never follow it up. If I was you I wouldn't go near the place again."

"Do you imagine I would? Those Wops are crooks. No one but a crook would assume that a customer would manufacture an incident like that. I've a damned good mind to charge him with assault and battery."

"Don't do anything so crazy," said Porsen, seriously for once. "That plug-ugly brother of hers would put you in hospital for a month if the court found against him."

"But if I don't report it everyone will assume I really was trying for damages," I argued, more than satisfied with the way things were shaping.

"Who the hell cares what the Primitives think? Forget it, and do like Griff says. Keep clear of the place and if His Nibs sends you in there for coffee in the future tell him why you won't go."

We left it there and soon, I imagine, they forgot the incident, to be reminded of it in my time and not theirs.

It was late March then and dusk came about eight o'clock. That night I waited until ten-thirty before I slipped down the alley and let myself in with the key Delphine had given me, having first made sure that the café blinds were down. Delphine was waiting for me in the back and seemed in high spirits.

"Splendid, Charlee!" she said, "you looked so pompous that I had my work cut out to keep a straight face. Beppo is in the cellar giving it the once-over. He says to leave the digging to him. He's clever with his hands as you'll see. You haven't got an impression yet, I suppose?"

"Good God, no, give me time! We've got months in hand, haven't we?"

"Five months and a bit," she said, "I've done some checking. That fair ends September fifth. That means we move in the night of September third. Thursday, you said, didn't you?"

"I've been thinking," I told her, "wouldn't it be better on a Saturday, leaving all day Sunday to get clear? Nobody would discover it until Monday at about eight-forty-five."

"It would if we decided to play for smaller stakes but not only will the tin-plate wages he paid out, so will everyone else's wage bill."

It was true and I had overlooked it. Friday was our busiest paying-out day, not only throughout the season and the week of the fair but all the year round. It was not often we kept a great deal of cash on the premises over the weekend.

"There's another thing," she went on, "we can't start until the lights in Powell's flat have gone out. If we left it until Saturday we would have to catch a Sunday train to Holyhead. The first train out of here Sunday is the one that leaves for Bangor, the nine-fifteen, summer service."

"You could go to Bangor in your van and catch the Saturday night mail there."

"And leave the truck as a clue to our jumping-off place? No, Charlee, leave the getaway to me. You concentrate on the keys. I've written to Uncle Berni to get the likeliest date he'll be in Queenstown. Would you like to go below and hear what Beppo makes of it?"

I said I would. I wish it was possible to convey the curious effect this kind of discussion had upon me but it isn't. The thing was so big that it numbed my brains so that I could address myself to the mechanics of the task without any trouble and put the thing itself in mental quarantine. Besides, I was curious to discover what effect the enterprise had upon Beppo. I had learned almost nothing about him during the year I had spent in the town. He was always there, but we had never exchanged more than a word or so.

"How did he take it?" I asked, and she said just like an instruction from her to sweep out the shop but that didn't mean his reliability was in question. "He takes his cue from me over here and that's on account of the language mostly. He was pretty well grown when he arrived in the States and has never learned to get his tongue round some English words. He's got it into his head folk laugh at him every time he tries."

We went on down and as we approached the grating I saw the thin pencil of Beppo's torch moving along the wall on the far side of Cook's cellar. Presently he came back, negotiating the narrow aperture with surprising ease for a man of his build. He was supple as well as beefy and the control he exercised over his muscles suggested that he had been other things as well as a hash slinger and a bouncer, perhaps a small-time wrestler or acrobat of some kind.

"Pushover," he said, and it was the first English word I had ever heard him utter. Brother and sister then exchanged a word or two in Italian and he nodded at me, using his amiable grin.

"Beppo says he hopes he didn't overdo it last night," Delphine said.

"Not at all," I said, "he only came within inches of smearing my brains on that lamp post. Tell him any time at all and that goes for what you did to my gums."

At that stage I used to stand off and listen to myself talking tough in this way. It was part of my new character role. Charlie, the inside man of the Rainbow Gang. Charlie, the dark horse, who played Bob Cratchit all day and Romeo and Al Capone by night. In her ears it must have sounded ridiculous. We returned to the ground floor together and Beppo, with a nod in my direction, went upstairs to his room.

"He's going to look over his tools," she said, and when I expressed surprise that he didn't want to discuss details with me, she said, "Oh, Beppo doesn't talk much," as if I didn't know that already.

I thought then that she might be prepared to fulfill her promise of the previous evening but we had some way to go before we reached that milestone. All I got that night was a kiss and a fumble the yard side of the gate. She did allow my hands to stray but not beyond the perimeter of any back-gate embrace of that period.

2

I see the passage of the early part of that spring as a pro-longed saunter across a wide delta on a series of short bridges approaching two principal arms of a river. I saw the three earliest approaches as the broaching of the project itself, the initial investigation of Cook's cellar, and the manufacture of my alibi. There were two others, Delphine's plans to rendez-vous with Uncle Berni at Queenstown, and Beppo's prelimi-nary work on the tunnel but neither of these concerned me. My business was to reach the first of the main crossings represented by one or other of the keys. The acquisition of the third key, Evan's, required entirely separate planning and at that time I had no idea how it could be achieved. It was something that didn't need thinking about, however, until I had impressions of the keys of the outer grille and the safe.

For a long time after the farce involving my expulsion from The Rainbow I made no progress at all and this was due more to my lack of resolution than lack of an opportunity. I handled the safe key three times and the grille key once but on three of those four occasions one or other of the staff was present in the vault. I had decided to use putty as an agent and kept a kneaded lump in a tobacco tin in my jacket pocket, but there it stayed. I had no faith in my ability to make an impression while any of them was within a yard of me. Once, when I was alone there for a few seconds while Griffiths went ahead of me up the stairs, I took out my tin but then Powell flushed the lavatory next door and his sud-den exit from the washroom startled me so much that I dropped my tin with a clatter. I looked so shaken when I went upstairs that Griffiths asked me if I was ill.

The difficulty of contacting Delphine did nothing to boost my sagging morale. I could never approach the café except by the yard, and only then after dark and having first made sure no one saw me turn into the alley. Even this simple operation was not without risk. I had to watch both southern and northern exits, as well as the curtains of the Cook bedrooms on the first and second floors, and once a period of nine days passed without my being able to approach her in ideal conditions.

It was on the tenth day that I saw her standing in the window of the café when I left the bank about five o'clock and she looked, I thought, glum and exasperated. As our eyes met she jerked her head toward the rear of the café and I interpreted this as a command to call that night.

Luckily it came on to rain about eight, the seeping, springtime rain of North Wales that is usually accompanied by mist. As soon as it was dark I put on my mackintosh and slipped out without either of the Rhys-Joneses noticing and this was just as well. A ready-made excuse of going out to post a letter might not have justified a downtown walk at ten o'clock on a filthy night but I could always return easily enough. They invariably went to bed about ten-thirty.

There was no one about at the northern end of the alley and I was inside the yard in a matter of seconds, approaching the window and tapping four times, our prearranged signal. She came to the scullery door at once and practically pulled me into the scullery.

"What the hell is going on?" she demanded, as soon as the door was shut. "It's close on a fortnight since you were here."

I explained that it wasn't just a matter of popping into the yard whenever I felt like it and reminded her of the window-peeping Cooks next door. She was only half convinced and said, grudgingly, "Well, you're right to be careful but this dump shuts down at dusk. You aren't likely to be spotted by anyone interested."

"Except Gwyn-the-Boots," I said.

"Gwyn who?"

"A local bobby I know. We were at school together."

She was amazed. "You mean you actually went to school with one of the local cops?"

I explained about Gwyn Morgan and how we passed the time of day whenever we met.

"But, for Heaven's sakes, don't you see that could be important?"

"How? Except that I have to make damned sure he doesn't see me come in here!"

"Didn't it occur to you to check his beat?"

It hadn't and the admission depressed her.

"I would have thought that was obvious," she said, and then, rather sourly, "It's no use asking if you've got an impression."

I tried to convince her I was trying, describing my tin of putty and the one occasion when I had had a chance to use it. She said, "Putty is wrong anyway. It'll leave traces and so would soap or wax. The surefire way is to get an outline and draw them."

"*Draw* them? You mean with a pencil?"

"With a mapping pen so that Beppo can make a trial key. The first two or three wouldn't work anyway. Look, Charlee, we just aren't getting anywhere are we? It's no use fixing a rendezvous with Uncle Berni until we've got trial keys."

"How will they help? When we came to use them they wouldn't open either lock."

"Of course they wouldn't. You would have to test them, find out where they rubbed, and then bring them back to Beppo for filing. It might have to be done a dozen times before we got it right."

This methodical approach hadn't occurred to me and my first thought was that it might simplify my work, despite all the to-ing and fro-ing involved. I had supposed, up to that time, that any impression I obtained would have to be extremely accurate, but if I could find some way of committing the outline to paper, and then test the dummy Beppo produced, we could at least make a start. In reply to my eager questions she said that every test on the soft metal Beppo would use would show scratches and indentations and in this way a workable key would eventually evolve.

"We've got less than a hundred days left if we allow a

fortnight for the tunnel," she said, "and even that doesn't allow for getting the manager's key. I'll have to start thinking about that but in the meantime at least give us something to work on." She stood thinking a minute, her teeth clamped over her lower lip. Then she said, amiably, "You're not really sold on the idea, not all the way that is. I don't think it's nerve. I think it's about me coming across. What do I have to do to convince you? Sure I could go to bed with you but what would that prove? Ida went to bed with you but you backed down on her the first time she came up with a proposition. There comes a point in everything the wrong side of the law when associates have to take something on trust."

I said, "You don't trust me. I daresay you've got perfectly reasonable grounds for doubt, but the fact is you don't."

"Oh, I do in a way," she said, cheerfully. "I'm not absolutely sure you've got the nerve but how can I be until you bring in an impression? The fact is, I don't think you would have gotten this far if you hadn't satisfied yourself on three separate counts. First, you hate that bank and everybody in it. You'd still want to square the account if they made you the president. Then there's conscience, but that wouldn't hold you up any. Some guys, but not you, Charlee. Your conscience doesn't stretch to bank money. It might jib at lifting pennies from a blind man's tin but it could be put to sleep by anything you took from that vault."

What she said sparked off a memory and the recollection made me laugh, the first real laugh I had had in weeks.

"What's funny? It's true, isn't it?"

"Yes, it's true and it reminded me of something. At my last branch we came up with a dud half crown. We do that every so often."

"What happened to it?"

"It was bent double, the way we bend all base coins."

"But it didn't stay bent?"

"No, I straightened it out and palmed it on a tram conductor. It showed me a profit of two-and-fivepence. But you said three points. What's the last one?"

"Boredom, frustration, call it what the hell you like. You

think I got you into this but I didn't, Charlee. I just happened to be standing on the touchline."

"How long are you going to stand there?"

"Until I'm good and ready to prove I mean business," she said. "Like this, maybe."

She heaved herself up, moved across to where I was standing near the fireplace, and put her arms round me and her mouth to mine. I recognized it was a calculated maneuver unlikely to convey anything more than the promise she held in reserve, but that didn't make it less welcome. She kissed me in a way Ida never had, or anyone else for that matter, and while we hung there together she let her hand do some aimless exploring. I think that was about as far as she intended to go at that time but in any case I was out of luck. Beppo's footsteps sounded on the uncarpeted stairs and we separated, Delphine leading the way into the scullery just as he came round the turn of the staircase. Once in the yard she said, with the object of heading off any renewal of the encounter on my part, "Not here. Somewhere in comfort, and with him out of the way. Just trust me, and Charlee—stay with it! Just stay right with it!"

I went out of there with mixed feelings. We had a rude word for that particular routine and I still couldn't make up my mind if it was applicable to Delphine.

3

Soon after opening up the next morning we ran short of silver in the till and as there was a small queue of depositors at Griffiths's counter Powell called across to me to bring up a bag from below. Usually at least one grille door was shut but either Evan or Powell had left them both open on this occasion, probably anticipating an immediate return for more cash. Powell handed me the safe key and down I went, feeling as though I was descending a dozen floors in a runaway lift.

The first thing I did was to study the pattern of the key,

something I had never done before, despite the fact that my attention had now been directed on it for weeks.

It was a relatively simple pattern but its grooves were deep and it was heavy and rather cumbersome, almost twice as large as the grille keys and surprisingly little worn for all the years it must have been in use. This time I didn't hesitate. First I measured the length and thickness of the key with a six-inch ruler and made a mental note of the readings. After that I whipped out a letter I had received from my father that morning written on the flimsy paper he always used, opened the safe, placed the key on the metal surface of a shelf and pressed the last sheet of my father's letter down on it. Then I folded the sheet, replaced it in the envelope, grabbed the silver, locked up, and hurried upstairs. I had not been absent more than two minutes and Powell noted as much with a lift of his eyebrows.

"My stars!" he said. "Somebody must have been dosing you with Kruschen, Pritchard! We're beginning to wake up a little, aren't we, and not before time, I must say." It never mattered how busy Powell was, he always had time for a crack of this kind.

When I got home that night I locked my door and went to work on the tracing, using a mapping pen and some graph paper I had bought at W. H. Smith's on the way through town. The impression was a good one, revealing the outlines of the key quite sharply except in the center where my palm had exerted rather less pressure than the ball of my thumb. I made three copies before I was satisfied and then burned the drafts and the original in the ashtray. Delphine had said the point of no return would steady my nerves and she was right. Slowly the old, devil-may-care mood came creeping back again. I saw the tracing in my hand as a tray of custard pies to throw in the faces of Caddie's board, with a specially juicy one reserved for the director who had drawn attention to my inky fingers. I was so pleased with myself that I thought I would take advantage of the mood and reconnoiter the cavity where Evan kept his keys at night.

I listened at the top of the stairs and could hear the murmur of the nine o'clock news bulletin on the living room radio. They always listened to that religiously, so I slipped out of my shoes and went down one flight to their bedroom.

I hadn't been there since the night I had shared their double bed with Ida and now I thought fleetingly of her, wondering how she was and what she was doing. If they had heard from her again they hadn't passed the news to me for my relationship with them had reverted to that of lodger and landlord. Evan rarely spoke to me in the house and Gladys glowered whenever we came face to face. She had taken to feeding me in the dining room and they took their meals in the back room where there was a fire.

I inspected Evan's shuttered wall-niche under the bedside table. It was empty, of course, and I still couldn't see how I was going to borrow his key (much less return it) when the time came but that was still a problem that could be shelved. As I went out I saw the wall text we had laughed at, "If It Be Thy Will." For the second time it made me laugh.

I found I couldn't wait until darkness for Delphine's nightcap so I went down to the "Maltster's Arms" and bought a pint of draft. As soon as it was dusk I dawdled along the main road to the northern end of the alley, entering it without the usual hesitation. After all, it was a public thoroughfare and lots of people this end of town used it as a short cut to the station. A few minutes later I was in their yard. I hadn't even checked to see if the café was closed.

It wasn't, but as I stood there I heard the rumble of the shop blind out in front so I let myself into the scullery to wait until Delphine came through. It wasn't Delphine who appeared, however, but Beppo and he was in an unusually relaxed mood for he was singing something in Italian and he had a good tenor voice. He went into the living room still singing and I heard him pour himself a drink. I wasn't going to give my news to him so I stayed where I was and a moment later he called, "Honey! The usual, honey?" just as Delphine came into the passage. I don't know which jarred the most, his uncharacteristic sociability, or the discovery that he could speak English with almost no trace of an

Italian accent. Neither fitted my conception of him up to that time and both contributed a little to the sum total of suspicion with which I was beginning to regard him, although I could not have said why. Then I bobbed out and Delphine was so startled that she let out a yelp and would almost certainly have cursed me if she hadn't read my expression. She forgot her fright at once.

"Charlee—you've got them!"

"Have a heart," I protested, "I've only got one and it's the easiest, the safe," and I spread the tracing on the table. A lover presenting a woman with a mink coat could not have done it with more panache.

Beppo prowled over and studied it and while he was looking down, his weight resting on his hands, she winked at me. "Take it up to your workroom and find out if it's good enough for a trial run," she said. "Charlee deserves a drink. A double."

He picked it up, rubbed his chin and wandered off. "That'll keep him happy for hours," she said, pouring the drink, and I said he seemed happy enough when I arrived. She said, offhandedly, "We've had a good day. There's nearly twenty pounds in the till. Here's your drink, now tell me how you came by the impression."

I was glad enough to do that and made the most of the opportunity. There was a part of me, however, that wasn't in the room but standing a way off, listening with amazement to Charlie Pritchard boasting of his prowess as an inside man on a bank robbery. I kept this aspect of me out in the cold. She looked prettier than ever with her cheeks pink with excitement. After I had gone over every detail of the exploit, and answered one or two shrewd questions she asked, she said she would go up to the workroom and find out if the tracing was as practical as it looked.

"Can't I come?" I said, and she said "no" because Beppo would be noncommittal if I did.

"I'll find out what he really thinks," she said, and then, reluctantly, "Charlee—honey—don't *ever* come in without signaling. You gave me a real scare just now. Help yourself to another drink if you need one."

115

I carried my drink over to the divan and when I heard her go up the uncarpeted stairs to the top story I made a curious discovery about myself. I was jealous of Beppo's intimacy with her, and the way he was always around to inhibit her. He smoked a brand of rank Continental cigars and the whiff of them was heavy in the room. I found myself hating not only his presence but his unavoidable involvement in our plan, if we had a plan outside of fantasy that is. Somehow it made rationalization of the scheme that much more difficult. He got between me and the clarity of purpose she could always inject into me when he was out of the way. Then I came to terms with the real reason why I disliked him. I was afraid of him, not as a beefy ex-bouncer but as Delphine's brother and I knew why. He was born a Corsican and I had read somewhere that Corsicans were extremely sensitive about the honor of their womenfolk and had been known to knife men who transgressed their code. It was something I would have to set straight with Delphine as soon as possible.

She was gone a long time and when she came downstairs she had exchanged her overall for an exotic-looking kimono. She had also washed away all traces of her stint in the café and looked fresh and sparkling, the way she had looked the first time I saw her more than a year ago.

"Is it as good as we think?"

"He says it'll do fine for a start. He'll make a dummy and then you can test it. Where it shows scratches he'll make adjustments and you can try it again. You can manage that easily enough, can't you?"

I told her I could but it was likely to prove more difficult to do the same with grille keys when we got our hands on a similar tracing. "When will that one be ready?"

"In a day or two. We'll probably post it to save time. They don't peek at your mail, do they?"

"No," I said, "I'm always down first but make a small enough parcel to go through the letter-box."

She wandered over to the window and stood there indecisively, as though turning something over in her mind.

Finally she said, "All right. Lock the door, Charlee," and plucked at the loop of the cord fastening her kimono.

Years later I read a short story by H. E. Bates called "The Kimono" and not only the title but the first encounter between the two main characters took me back to this particular evening. In Bates's story a man goes into a sleazy city café on a sultry night and sees a girl behind the counter wearing a kimono. He knows somehow that this is all she is wearing and from that moment he is enslaved by her. In a way it was like that with me and Delphine but there was a difference. Feverish as I was to take advantage of her invitation there were two things that held me back. One was undoubtedly Beppo's presence in the house but the other a less positive reason, an uncomfortable awareness of the blatant link between the tracing I had given them and her availability. It was a combination of these factors that made me hesitate and I saw by her baffled expression that I had at last succeeded in astonishing her. She said, her hand still on the cord, "What is it, Charlee? You figure it's your turn to play hard to get?"

"It's him," I said. "Suppose he comes down again and finds the door locked. . . ."

"To hell with him," she said, briefly, "he's in this as deep as we are and from here on I play this any way I like." And then, looking hard at me, "That's not all, is it? You think I'm using myself as a lollipop for a good boy. . . ."

"Well, aren't you?"

She smiled and drifted over to me where I sat tense on the divan.

"You don't know all that much about women, Charlee. Maybe it's because Ida didn't get a chance to finish what she started." She reached out and cupped my face in her hands. "You never figured I could want a guy for reasons of my own?"

"Not this guy," I said, but I stayed where I was, with her cool hands cradling my cheeks. I liked it that way. It made it easier to believe that the lollipop theory wasn't all there was to be said about the situation. She said, quietly and reasonably, "Why not? You think I don't get bored and lonesome in this stinking place, with no one but Beppo and all those pawing tin-plate Romeos around?"

"You could have anyone. You know that."

"Sure. As a tumble and done with it. But what's wrong with a girl waiting around for a guy who is prepared to take big risks for the privilege? Wouldn't that make it more of an occasion for her?"

Suddenly she enlarged her hold on me and tilted my face, bending swiftly and kissing me at first softly and gently but then as though she meant it, so that all the reservations I had flew out the window to stick like burrs on the onlooking Charlie Pritchard in the grandstand. He wasn't looking so astounded now. He was out there rooting for me. I grabbed hold of her and saved her the trouble of fiddling with that girdle knot. She wasn't naked after all. She had on a short pink slip but that didn't bother me. I ran my hands over her and she had to force herself free for a moment to turn the key in the lock. Then she was back, without the kimono and half out of the slip. I didn't give her a chance to pull it off, I couldn't wait that long, but her impatience was as great as mine and it was this, more than anything else, that produced in me a sense of achievement far greater than anything I had experienced getting that impression. She launched herself at me and it was all over in a matter of minutes. Nothing remotely like this had happened to me in Ida's maternal embrace. There was no conscious giving or taking, just an impetuous use of one another, rough on my part, expert on hers. We sprawled there on the divan for a few minutes coming to terms with the new situation. For me it was a kind of embarkation but, even at this distance in time, I don't know what it was for her except that I am pretty well convinced that nobody could simulate that kind of enthusiasm and that I was as necessary to her at that moment as she was to me. Maybe, on that first occasion, I was the means of releasing in her the same kind of tensions that had been building up in me ever since that first visit to the Cooks' cellar. I was convinced of this at the time and it made me want to go out and bray my triumph across the width of Penmadoc Bay.

Chapter Nine

1

The parcel arrived forty-eight hours later wrapped in packaging used by one of the mail-order firms that did a brisk business in places like Penmadoc.

I retrieved it before Gladys could get her hands on it and carried it up to my room, burning the wrappings in the water tray set in front of my tiny gas-fire. The key looked workable and I found myself looking forward to testing it. If nothing else it represented a visit to Delphine that night. I found an opportunity during the lunch hour when alone with Griffiths and left him on the pretense of going down to the washroom.

The practice of leaving the strongroom open on occasions like this, when there were only two or three of us on the premises, was in direct contradiction with the solemn ceremonial of opening the vault in the morning and locking it at night but I suppose it had developed out of necessity. With two grilles that could only be opened by keys held by two members of the staff, we could not forever be descending in a body, and hanging about getting in one another's way while we opened up. The safe was always kept locked, and theoretically no one was allowed to open it without a witness, and this was deemed to provide sufficient security during working hours. Even then it was a very old-fashioned routine and has long been dispensed with, but at that time no branch of Caddie's had ever been raided and I imagine they preened themselves on having found a system that combined convenience with prudence.

Beppo's key went into the slot easily enough but it wouldn't turn. When I drew it out there, sure enough, were the scratches and dents she had told me to expect, three or four of them almost in the center of the flange. I wrapped the key in my handkerchief, flushed the pan in the washroom and hurried upstairs. I was tapping at Delphine's window about eleven o'clock that night.

This time I saw Beppo, who produced a jeweler's glass to study the scratches. He looked sinister with a glass screwed into his eye but his only comment was a couple of grunts, after which he went up to his workshop to make adjustments, telling Delphine he wouldn't be long. This ruled out all prospects of romance even had she been so disposed, so we sat talking and drinking. She told me something of their life in Los Angeles, and the frantic bustle of that rapidly growing city. She also described Hollywood and some of the stars whose fabulous homes, complete with the then almost unheard of luxury of private swimming pools, had been pointed out to her at one time or another. I recall that Harold Lloyd's was one and Gloria Swanson's was another.

"Have you got a yen to live like that?" I asked her, and she said no, that kind of thing wasn't for her. All she wanted was a cozy apartment within easy driving distance of the Pacific and guaranteed sunshine all the year round. She hated the heavy mists and thin rain of North Wales, indeed, of all Northern Europe. She said she couldn't imagine how such places had ever become thickly populated for they were only habitable by savages.

I mentioned the mountains but she said, "Who needs mountains? They make a person feel insignificant. Besides, look what you've done to your towns. There isn't one cozy building in the whole goddam community."

The incident of two nights ago had eased our approach to one another. She was more relaxed and I was far more sure of myself. She said, hearing Beppo's step on the stairs, "Just you wait, Charlee, you haven't seen a goddam thing yet. You'll live to thank me for showing you the way out of here."

Beppo gave me the modified key and she saw me as far as

the gate. With their van between us and the windows of the Cook family we kissed, this time lightheartedly. "I'll expect you tomorrow or the day after," she said, "but don't risk calling unless you got a reason. No sense in pushing our luck."

In the event, three days passed before I was there again and this time I had two reasons for calling. I had not only tested the safe key and discovered, to my amazement, that it half turned the lock, but I also had an impression of Powell's key to the outer grille.

I read somewhere, I believe in a book about First World War escapes from the Germans, that a would-be escaper's best chance was to take immediate advantage of any minute alteration in the established routine of the guards and also that, no matter how strong were the walls and locks of a jail, there was always a flaw if you had the time and the patience to spot it. To exploit any such flaw, however, it was necessary to have one's apparatus to hand in order to be ready for the opportunity at any time. I followed this advice, having assembled my modest apparatus after finding the flaw in Powell's method of opening the outer grille.

I noticed that when we opened up in the morning Powell, having used his key, stood aside to allow Evan to use his, and then both of them marched into the vault followed by an underling who was on hand to help carry up the cash. The flaw here was that sometimes, if Evan was brisk about opening the inner grille, Powell left his key in the lock, collecting it on the way out. He didn't always do this but only when the inner grille was opened in a matter of seconds. If I was close behind them I could slip the key out of the lock while their backs were turned and make some kind of impression in the interval it took them to open the safe and take out the trays. It wasn't all that risky either, or not if I didn't fumble. All I had to do if Powell turned was to hand the key back to him.

To make an impression in a matter of ten or twenty seconds, however, I had to have the means concealed in my pocket and they had to be less amateurish than the sheet of writing paper I had used for the safe. I gave the matter a great deal of thought and finally decided upon a small wooden block about half as big again as the key, mounted with a pad composed of several carefully-cut sheets of tracing paper. I manufactured this in an hour or so, using a thin paste to fasten the paper to the oblong block. The first morning I took it to work I was the one summoned to carry up the cash and Evan opened his grille with a single action so that Powell moved forward at once, leaving his key in the lock.

Without realizing it I must have rehearsed the trick in my mind a hundred times. It worked perfectly and in rather less than the fifteen seconds or so it took them to cross the vault and open the safe. With my right hand I whipped out the key, transferred it to my pocket, held it firmly against the block and pressed my side hard against the angle of the aperture. Then I took it out, and, as neither of them had turned, slipped it back in the slot and walked forward to take the tin box Evan had lifted from the safe. I was first out of the vault and Powell retrieved the key as he followed in my wake.

The impression, when I had a chance to look at it, was sharp but I thought Beppo would have his work cut out to make a usable dummy in two runs. It would more likely require five or six, and my opportunities for testing would be limited, for the grille was more exposed than the safe. However, I had reason to congratulate myself for that same afternoon I had a chance to try the safe key. It was stiff, but it worked. I didn't actually open the door but both heard and felt the steel tongues snap back into the recesses. I thought I would double-check when I got a better opportunity.

Delphine was elated by my double coup and after she had given Beppo the new impression and the safe key, which he said needed a touch or two here and there to ensure against the possibility of it breaking in the lock, she made her proposition.

"Why don't we celebrate?" she said. "Have you got any plans for Sunday?"

"I never have plans for a Sunday," I told her, "I just get through it like everybody else up here, but how could we possibly celebrate together?"

"That would depend where we went," she said. "If it was a city, and far enough away, there wouldn't be any risk. I figure you need to relax, Charlee. We don't want you over-trained on the night."

Every time she referred to "the night" I had qualms. It may sound ridiculous but even now, with one key nearly perfected, another in the process of being made, and plans for the tunnel well advanced, I was still able to remove the actual com- mission of the robbery to a great distance, something prob- lematic like Armageddon. It might eventually occur, and we were now working toward a specific date in September, but September was still months away and any number of things might happen in between. I might be posted. We might find no practical method of getting Evan's key. Or I might die. Now and again, in between short bouts of recklessness, I rather hoped I would. Only frequent injections of her brand of confidence, spiced with the exhilaration I derived from actual operations, had brought me this far and reaction to the double triumph of the day was already setting in. She must have realized I was faltering and put a bold face on it.

"Well," she said, when I hesitated, "you sure don't seem all that enthusiastic about it and that isn't very flattering to a girl. What I had in mind was to book Saturday night at an hotel, strike up a nodding acquaintance at dinner and go on the town somewhere."

I think I understood her real motive in putting forward this proposal but it did nothing to make it less attractive. After all, I was in need of more positive encouragement and the prospect of having Delphine at my disposal for forty-eight hours was very exciting. To have her in bed, miles away from that cat-footed enigmatic brother of hers, was a bonus I hadn't looked for until we had that vault open. I said, weak- ening, "Look, you don't have to sell me an idea like that but is it really a hundred-percent safe? If we were seen to- gether..."

"Nothing in this world is that safe, Charlee, but we'd have to be unlucky to slip up, providing you did what I said. Don't think I haven't realized that you've been under one hell of a strain, a far bigger one than me or Beppo, and now I'm telling you you need a break. Do any of those people at the bank go to Manchester?"

"Not that I've heard. Powell sometimes goes to Chester and Porsen to London occasionally. The others never go farther than Llandudno or Colwyn Bay, or maybe take a chara trip round about here."

"Are any of them on vacation this weekend?"

"No."

"Well, we can guard against Powell taking it into his head to go to Chester tomorrow by using different trains. You can go on the two-thirty and I can follow at around four. That'll get you there in time for tea and I'll arrive around six."

"I've never been near Manchester," I told her, "where do we meet?"

She went over to the bureau and poked around until she found a grubby little card advertising a private hotel called "The Randolph," at a suburb called Swallowfield. She said that she and Beppo had stayed there when they had been looking for premises soon after arriving in the country. "We won't even have to book. Everyone pours out of Manchester at the weekend, especially Whit Week. They all come here and the place is half empty. Somewhere a bit more lively would be better but we don't have too much choice and my guess is we're more likely to bump into someone in London."

We checked the timetable, decided to travel light, worked out the approaches we would make to one another with me in the role of a fresh young man making a pickup, and various other details. The only snag I could see was how to cover her absence at one of the busiest weekends of the year, but she said she could find a substitute for Saturday night and Monday morning and she would be back in time for the rush on Monday night.

"How about Beppo?" I asked, "how is he likely to regard you going off like that?"

She said, with exasperation, "You can be so goddamed stupid, Charlee! How is Beppo to know you're coming along? As for me, I've already told him I'm taking my first weekend off in over a year and when I want to go places I don't have to wait for Beppo's nod."

2

The next day, Saturday, dawned fine and clear and by the time half the morning had gone the temperature was building up into the seventies. I was so preoccupied with the prospect of the weekend that I was more than ordinarily useless as a ledger clerk and my vagueness earned the usual spate of rebukes from Rhys-Jones and Powell.

At twelve sharp, seeing that it was a Bank Holiday weekend, we locked up and dispersed. I had found out that Powell was staying at home and that Porsen was going away, presumably on his motorbike, but I was glad we had arranged to travel separately. Our branch had plenty of local customers who knew me by sight and some must have known Delphine. It was an even bet that several among that number would be on one or other of the afternoon trains to Chester or Crewe.

When I had my bag packed I told Gladys I was going away for the weekend and wouldn't be back until Monday night. She asked me where I was going and I said to stay with a friend in Ross-on-Wye. She said I should have told her in advance and she wouldn't have got so much food in, as if she had prepared a banquet on my account. I didn't want a row with her then so I apologized and asked if they had heard from Ida recently. "Not since early April," she said, glumly, "she's got a secretarial post with that firm now. I suppose we should be thankful for small mercies. Think of it, a girl of mine, working as a packer!" and she stumped off into the kitchen. I forgot both her and Ida as soon as I was clear of the house.

The train pulled away and I settled in a corner with a daily paper. The front page was devoted to the Duchess of Bedford, who had just flown to and from the Cape in twenty-one days but I found the story impossible to concentrate on. Instead I thought about Delphine's enthusiastic approach on the divan and wondered if her anxiety about my nerve would encourage her to repeat it in the blessed anonymity of a strange hotel. I didn't think beyond that, certainly not as far as September.

At London Road, Manchester, I took a taxi and rattled south over the setts toward Swallowfield. I booked in at The Randolph under the name of Powell, a prearranged joke on our part, and was shown up to Number Twelve overlooking a small park. There were children playing cricket below and their cries reached me when one sent a ball bounding toward the pond, where smaller children were sailing toy boats and throwing bread crumbs to the ducks. Everything looked extraordinarily peaceful and innocent and I had a sudden awareness of having cut myself off from this safe, humdrum world. The reflection dulled the sparkle of the afternoon and I found myself wishing that Delphine would come.

I had two hours to kill so I walked across the park, standing by the pond and watching a little girl having tantrums after her toy boat had drifted out of reach. Her mother tried to console her but couldn't and presently a park keeper arrived carrying a long pole with a net attached to it for scooping up dead leaves. He set about retrieving the boat, mother and daughter looking on as though they were witnessing the sinking of the *Titanic*.

Then it happened. A policeman sauntered up, a chunky, broad-shouldered, heavy-booted specimen to stand listlessly beside the group watching. I didn't see his actual approach but suddenly found myself looking at squared shoulders and big hands, clasped behind a broad back. And then I had the kind of sensation a pedestrian has when he raises his eyes, sees a five-ton truck bearing down on him, and has nowhere to run. The shoulders and hands were those of Gwyn-the-Boots, the Penmadoc constable from my home town.

I was sure of it. There was not, at that moment, the least doubt in my mind and I wanted not merely to run but also to scream. Fortunately, I was powerless to do either. My legs were paralyzed and all that emerged in the way of sound was a kind of rattle like a nervous tenor clearing his throat. It didn't occur to me to ask myself what Gwyn was doing there in the uniform of the Manchester City police when, only a few days or so ago, I had spoken to him in Caerleon Road, Penmadoc. Neither did I reflect that, even if it was him he would be unaware that I was the inside man of a gang planning to hit Cadwallader's branch for everything in the safe. The only factor that emerged with clarity was that any moment I would feel his great hand on my shoulder, and at the touch of it would crumple to the asphalt path circling the pond. Then he turned and moved on and I saw that it wasn't Gwyn at all but a much older man with a graying mustache and humorous eyes. He sauntered away without a glance in my direction just as the park keeper netted the boat and the whimpering of its little owner was shut off, as by a door.

My relief was so great that I wanted to be sick. I tottered back to the hotel and flopped out on the bed. My watch said it was four-forty-five, an hour and a quarter before Delphine was due. I lay still, letting the waves of shock recede, and trying to assess the meaning of the incident in terms of a warning. Then my common sense, returning at a gallop after so long an absence, told me it was profound and that all this time, ever since I had first agreed to explore that damned cellar, I had been living out a crazy, self-destroying dream. I knew then that I just hadn't the nerve to rob a piggy bank much less a strongroom, that I never would have the nerve, and that I must have been mad or bewitched to have set foot on that long span of bridges in the first place. But it was not too late to draw back. I had, it was true, already committed a crime that could get me sent to prison by passing impressions of keys to people I knew to be capable of breaking into the bank, but it comforted me a particle to realize that, so far, there was no proof of my complicity. My retreat was still open. I could walk out of that hotel and break off all contact with Delphine and her brother and there wasn't a thing they could do about it except make threatening gestures at me through the window of The Rainbow. And within days, I decided, I wouldn't be there to face even that, for I now had a far better idea than helping to rob a bank. I would not only drop the entire crazy enterprise but would sever connections with its originators. I would leave the district at once, and the quickest and safest way of doing this was to throw myself on the mercy of Ida and beg her to find me a job. It didn't matter what I did or where I went so long as I put distance between myself, Penmadoc and The Rainbow café. Ida appeared to me then as the only possible sanctuary. Her broad, freckled face represented not only safety but sanity and the need to communicate with her became so imperative that I leaped from the bed and almost dived at the little table where sheets of headed writing paper peeped from the stationery rack.

I did not reach the table. Halfway across the room I was checked in my stride by a tap on the door and almost immediately it opened to reveal a Delphine I had never seen before, a stunningly attractive girl in a flowered-silk frock, high-heeled red shoes of patent leather, flesh-colored silk stockings and, most improbably, a little red hat shaped like a French kepi. A light coat was slung over her arm, and she marched gaily over the threshold.

"Why, Mr. Powell!" she exclaimed, "*what* a coincidence! And *what* a perfect day to run into an old friend!"

She shut the door, threw her coat and bag on the bed and kissed me soundly on both cheeks.

"Don't look so amazed, Charlee. I know I'm an hour early but I didn't come by rail. I drove myself here in the truck, leaving an hour or so after you and here I am, at Number Nine, just along the corridor. And what do you know? Ten and Eleven aren't occupied."

I didn't utter a word of greeting, but if she noticed the change in me she didn't comment but moved over to the window and looked down on the scene of my recent encounter with Gwyn's double.

"This is nice," she said, "I've been looking forward to it. I needed the break as well as you, that awful town was getting me down."

I said, at last, "I had a terrible shock in the park. I thought I saw Gwyn-the-Boots, that copper back at Penmadoc," and as her smile faded, "It's all right, it wasn't him. I...I...just thought it was. The fact is I'm as jittery as hell, Delphine."

She said, quietly, "Sure you are, Charlee, that's why we're here. Now listen, Charlee, forget Penmadoc and everything about it for a few hours. Let's relax and enjoy ourselves for once. There's just the two of us and nothing else matters a damn."

It was her no-nonsense approach that planted an idea of what I then thought of as Machiavellian. Why not do what she asked and put Penmadoc, Caddie's keys and Caddie's cash right out of mind? I could take my cue from her, enjoy the change of surroundings, and enjoy her as any normal young man would enjoy taking a dish like Delphine out on the town and home to bed. Then, when we were on the point of going our separate ways, I would simply admit that I wasn't man enough for the job and if she tried to argue I wouldn't listen, I would take my bag and go.

And that, more or less, was how it turned out. The few hours that followed my private renunciation of crime were among the most pleasant I have ever spent.

We had our tea and went downtown to the Opera House, where a London company was playing *The Barretts of Wimpole Street*. I had never visited a theater of such opulence before and the play certainly succeeded in sustaining the mood of exhilaration that followed my decision. She enjoyed it tremendously and from my new citadel of rectitude I could even patronize her a little.

The lordly mood grew on me, investing me with a kind of paternalism after we moved on to Belle Vue where she threw hoops for trumpery prizes, shot down a row of wooden ducks that I couldn't hit, and rolled pennies down grooves to win more pennies and protract the game for a few minutes. Then we took a trip on the Big Dipper and she pretended to be scared and pressed herself close to me as the car zoomed down the gradients and rushed up the opposite slopes. One way and another it was an uproarious evening but the best was yet to come.

We exchanged a public good night at the foot of the stairs, watched by a drowsy porter and the girl at the reception desk. I don't know whether they were fooled or whether they cared two straws who spent the night with whom, but Delphine made a decorous withdrawal and I drank a night-cap in the little lounge. Then, yawning in heedless faces, I went upstairs and along to Number Twelve to find that she hadn't wasted much time. She was already there, sitting up in bed and smoking a cigarette stuck in an amber holder.

She had done something original with her hair. The bob was still in fashion but she seemed to have grown ringlets in the time it had taken her to get undressed. Their silky texture trapped the gleam of the bedside light, emphasizing the un-usual paleness of her skin. She was wearing a nightdress decked out with bows and little hedges of lace at the neck and wrists. It was lilac color. I might have known.

"Don't worry about the hotel's reputation," she said. "I've decided it hasn't got one. Something tells me the Manchester businessmen bring their secretaries here, but not Whit Week. Then they take their wives to Rhyl."

I could match her mood. "It's too near home for Manchester lads," I said, "the regulars are probably pawnbrokers and bookies from Bolton and Rochdale."

She watched carefully while I laid out my keys and small change on the dressing table. "You're different here," she said, suddenly, "I'm not sure I can figure you." Then, stubbing out her cigarette, "You're not still beefing about that cop, are you?" and when I made no reply, "Come over here, Charlee-boy."

I went over reluctantly and sat on the edge of the bed. Her fragrance had me wavering for a moment but no longer. I had time to think, "Why the hell can't something like this happen to me on the straight? What would a lifetime at Caddie's matter if I had a girl like this to come home to? Eight hours a day with Rhys-Jones, Powell and Porsen wouldn't matter a damn if I could slam the door on them at five every weekday and midday on Saturdays!" Then I re-minded myself she wouldn't be here at all if I hadn't involved myself so deeply in their crazy scheme that I could only escape by the skin of my teeth. She was, by now, beginning to get an inkling that I was deeply disturbed and that her prescription for releasing the tensions of the last few weeks fell short of a cure-all. It was this doubt that prompted her to double the dose. She skipped out of bed and pranced across to the window, getting between me and the bedside light. "I bought this specially," she said, spreading the folds of the nightdress, "like it?"

I didn't have to parry that question. I said it was as pretty and provocative as everything else about her, and the sight of her standing there, parading her charms like a conscientious whore, reinforced my determination to escape notwithstanding the fact that she made me tremble with impatience. She said, smiling, "Know something, Charlee? I figure that conscience of yours is still around. Not about the job but about little me. It's that way with all you Bible Belt kids. So long as it happens on the front porch it's okay, but take them inside an hotel room and they get qualms. You got qualms, Charlee?"

I had them all right but they weren't the qualms she was talking about. I made a conscious effort to pull myself together. Whatever happened I had made up my mind to have this one night with her. She owed me something to remember her by.

"You don't have to stoke me up," I growled, "you know better than that. Take that damned thing off and get back into bed."

It was the first time I had ever employed this tone of voice with her and it made her laugh, perhaps with relief.

"Why, Charlee," she said, putting more than her usual emphasis on the second syllable, "I declare you could come across with the rough stuff if I teased you hard enough." The kittenish mood did not suit her but it was my opportunity and I took it. I went across to her, gathered her up, put everything I had into a kiss that must have hurt her mouth, and dropped her so hard on the rumpled bed that she bounced. She put on a good show of enjoying it and from then on I didn't have to pretend to dominance because, simmering just below ruttishness, was a smoldering rage that involved not only her and the manner in which she was using me, but all she and that money she wanted so badly represented in terms of unattainability. I knew then that there was no substance at all in the dreams she had encouraged in me and that Caddie's, and not the Riviera, would always be my terminus, and it touched off a kind of fury that surprised the pair of us. I didn't stop to get into bed or finish undressing and I didn't so much as extinguish the bedside light. I just went for her like a tormented bull and after a stifled plea for patience she went right along with me, almost surely as the likeliest method of keeping me in line. When we were still and lying in the dark I expected some kind of protest from her but all she said, before we drifted off to sleep, was, "You're a queer one, Charlee, and no mistake! How come you got this far without busting out?" I let that one go. I was already busy rehearsing my abdication speech.

It must have been about five when I woke up to a chorus of birds twittering in the park below. I knew that she too was awake and that her mind was turning and turning on the problem of how to prevent Charlie from going home at a run. She never solved the problem. In the event it was I who broached it for it seemed to me I would never have a better opportunity.

"I love you, Delphine," I said, solemnly. "You're the most exciting thing that's ever happened or ever will happen to me. I could work hard for the rest of my life for you, and think myself damned lucky to have the chance, but I can't help you and Beppo break into that vault. I simply haven't the guts and I think you know that by now."

I suppose I expected some kind of outcry, even if it was muted. At all events, I expected her to sit up and throw aside the arm that encircled her shoulder and breast but she didn't move. She lay quite still, looking up at the blue, distempered ceiling, and half a minute might have passed before she said, "Sure I knew it, Charlee," and then, as to herself, "what I can't figure is how you got this far. It wasn't for what I could give you, that's for sure. You're as randy as the next man and better at it than some, but pussy was incidental. There was a reason I don't know about."

"There are dozens of reasons and most of them I can't even explain to myself. Call it a kind of hypnotism if you like. I dreamed myself into this and it was the copper in the park who woke me up."

"There's Beppo," she said, slowly, "he's going to be real sore about it."

"I don't give a damn about Beppo. He's nothing to me and I never got the impression he's all that to you."

"I would have made it up to you. You believe that, don't you?"

"Yes, I believe it, but I'm still not the man for the job. God knows, I've tried hard enough to tell myself I am but I'm not and I know I'm not, and that's as important to you as it is to me. In the end I would have botched it and that would have meant curtains for all of us. I'm the wrong material. You can't breed a man-eating tiger from rabbits."

"You want to stay a rabbit, Charlee?"

"I've got no choice."

She climbed out of bed then and shrugged herself into her kimono.

"I'll drive on back now," she said.

"Couldn't we go back together?"

She looked down at me. "That wouldn't be very bright. You'll be hightailing it out of Penmadoc, I imagine. I can't see you staying long after this, and Beppo and me will do our own flit as soon as the season's over. We may owe money around town. So it had better be goodbye from here, Charlee." She stood by the bed for a moment and then, with what might have been a genuine impulse, she bent over and kissed me on the cheek. "Thanks for trying, anyway!" The door closed very softly. Outside, around the duck pond, the birds sounded as though they had stopped talking and started quarreling. I was amazed that I was out of it so cheaply.

Chapter Ten

1

The period that followed, bringing us into June, was the I-Could-Have-Been season. I got up, went to work, came home, ate a high tea in solitary state, went out, milled around with the holiday crowds, returned home and went to bed again. On Sundays I stayed in bed until noon, walked inland during the afternoon, returned home and went to bed about ten. And all this time, at the branch and away from it, I played I-Could-Have-Been.

I could have been the most notorious bank clerk on Caddie's payroll, my fame dwarfing that of the founder, who opened his first penny bank swindle in 1816. I could have been Flash Charlie, the Taffy who made it and had it made, and was currently sunning himself in California. I could have been the Welsh lover of Lickerish Lil the Lecherous Wop and maybe, if I had felt inclined, the father to her children. I could have been Penmadoc's sole maker of headlines, the Charlie who never came home to face them. I could have been all these things but I wasn't one of them. I was still Charlie Pritchard, fifth man of a six-man branch, playing games with himself day and night. Especially at night.

Not that I had any regrets. On the contrary, I thought of myself as fortunate, for how many fifth men in six-man branches had had their heads inside a lion's mouth and escaped with nothing worse than a whiff of bad breath? It lasted nearly a month, did this period. Twenty-four days to be precise and I can remember that without reference to a diary.

I gave up keeping diaries the week I signed on with Caddie's. There was too much space to be filled between lines marking off the days.

Then the letter arrived. An ordinary envelope enclosing an ordinary sheet of notepaper, half covered with Delphine's neat handwriting, that might have been that of a precise little man. Evan's kind of hand, with all the *i*'s dotted and all the *t*'s squarely crossed. I wasn't expecting any mail but I saw it on the mat when I went downstairs to breakfast. I pocketed it and waited until Gladys came in with my tray, and when she went out again I let her thin sausage and slab of fried bread go cold.

It was a simple, straightforward letter but not even I-Could-Have-Been-Charlie could miss the menace of the final sentence. It said, "Dear Charlie, I have to see you. Things are very difficult for me and you'll have to explain them to Beppo yourself. Come the same time you used to. Delphine."

I managed a cup of tea but I couldn't face Gladys's sausage and fried bread. Gladys didn't like things left on the plate so I wrapped the congealed mess in the inside sheet of an old *Liverpool Echo* and stuffed it in my jacket pocket. Then I went to work, the first to arrive. Powell was on the point of opening up when I passed the drawn blinds of The Rainbow but there was no clue to Delphine's difficulties there. The place was alseep.

Fragments of the letter kept recurring in my mind between every entry I made in the ledgers. "Things are very difficult . . ." What things? And what did she mean about explaining to Beppo when she had always treated Beppo as a half-witted handyman? What was there to explain that she couldn't make clear to him? And why was my presence needed? I made a hundred guesses but only one of them offered a possible explanation. Beppo, despite her denials, was even more dimwitted than his customers believed him to be. He intended to go ahead on his own, without further help from me. It was a very disturbing thought and helped me to decide to keep the rendezvous.

It was getting toward high season then and we were busy all

day at the counter. Twice I had to give a hand there and the second occasion, working alongside Porsen, I saw him wrinkle his nose, as though my presence offended him. "There's a stink of fried fat around here," he announced, during a brief lull, "it must be *you*, Pritchard." Like an idiot I put my hand in my pocket and brought out the crumpled page of the *Liverpool Echo*, containing the remains of my breakfast. He gazed at it, too surprised for a moment to comment. Then he backed away, holding his nose. "I always did think you were a scruffy bastard, Pritchard," he said, "but I'm damned if I realized you ate your lunch out of a newspaper!"

I got rid of the soggy mash before the next rush but the story was all round the branch by the time we had closed and Rhys-Jones asked me if it was true. I said it was, adding that his wife regarded plate-leavings as a personal insult. He said, pettishly, "But good heavens, man, what was the *matter* with it? Wasn't bad, was it?" No, I said, it was all right but it so happened I was late that morning and had no time to eat it. He was obliged to accept this but it was another score for Powell, Porsen saying in Powell's hearing that life must be hard at St. Ninian's when a lodger preferred going to work on an empty stomach to eating food Mrs. Rhys-Jones had bought at the Co-op.

"Do they shop there, Pritchard?" Powell asked, and when I said I didn't know where Gladys shopped he said he could believe it, for it had long been apparent that I didn't know the difference between a credit and a debit. I wished the whole lot of them roasting in hell. By the time I left at five there was nothing left of the smugness that had seen me through the last twenty-four days.

I had five hours to get through before I could approach The Rainbow and spent most of it trudging round the paths bordering the shrubbery of the old Craigwen estate. I walked back to the seafront as dusk was falling, passing some of the holidaymakers and envying a couple of lovers who had sought the extreme end of the pier for privacy they couldn't find in the town. One group, nearer the turnstile, were skylarking with the machines and pretending to throw some shrieking girls over the railing into the sea. Another couple, having worked up an appetite with this kind of horseplay, strolled off hand in hand and I watched them snuggle down into one of the shelter seats. Passing on the far side of it on my way back I saw the girl's bare arms go round the man's neck as their lips met in a long kiss and the simple incident deluged me in self-pity. I thought, desperately, "Why the hell can't something simple happen to me? All I get is Ida with Gladys and Dadda in tow, and Delphine on condition I help her rob a bank!" I recalled Ida's favorite dictum, "No strings!" but for me there had never been anything else. Either life was as featureless as a desert or it was a journey across a minefield. Extremes of this kind seemed to bypass people like that couple in the shelter but they never had any trouble finding me. Everybody had something. Evan had his bank. Powell had a wife with a private income. Porsen had his motorcycle and even Griffiths had his Celtic mysticism, but what did I have? On the one hand a dog's life in a bank, and on the other the kind of situation that faced me at this moment. There seemed to me no alternative now but to make my decision crystal clear to both Delphine and Beppo and then run for it, before it was too late. I didn't know where, exactly, unless it was to Ida in the hope that it was still in her power to whisk me as far away as Bombay or Madras. I had written to her via Atlas Products the day after I parted from Delphine in Manchester, but so far she hadn't answered and I doubted very much if she would. All I knew was I didn't want to be around if Beppo tried to hit Caddie's solo.

2

Delphine was alone when I tapped on the window and I saw one of the difficulties she had mentioned through the pane. She had a black eye, with bruising that spread as far as her cheekbone. She pointed to the scullery door and I let myself in, reflecting how crazy I must have been when I actually got a thrill out of arriving here. I had come prepared to bluster but the sight of that eye implied that bluster might not get me far. In fact, it revived those misgivings I had once had about her brother's Corsican prejudices. The black eye could have been the result of an accident but somehow I didn't think so. It was more likely to be a sample of what he had in store for me.

I said, breathlessly, "How did it happen?" and she replied, calmly, "Well, I didn't come by it walking into a door, Bub."

"You told me you gave the orders around here! You said that not once but a dozen times!"

"We all make the odd mistake," she said, and sat down, interlocking her fingers and letting her hands rest between her knees. She wasn't the Delphine I knew either before or since I had graduated from courtier to lover. She was just a tired, worried girl with a big black eye.

"Was it because he found out about us?"

"That wasn't the real reason," she said, "but it came in handy as an excuse."

"Then what was the real reason?"

"You mean you can't guess?"

"Damn it, I didn't come here to play guessing games, I came because you hinted you were in trouble."

She looked up, resigned and unsmiling. "No, you didn't, Charlee. You came because you were too damn scared not to and that was smart. Beppo dished this out when I tried to explain why you had chickened out. Writing that letter struck me as the only way to give you an even break."

I was still stuck with that Corsican nonsense. "You mean he wants me to marry you?"

Her head came up sharply and she laughed outright.

"*Marry me?*" She made it sound as if the idea was preposterous but then, in the succeeding moment, she looked puzzled, as though she found my reasoning incomprehensible.

"For God's sake, Beppo doesn't give a damn who takes me to bed. Get this into your head, you can lay me every night of the week so long as we stay in business."

I didn't absorb the full implication of this at once, but I understood enough to make the room swim a little so that when I took a step back, and my knees came into contact with the edge of a chair, I flopped into it the way I had against the cellar steps on my first visit there. Feeling the blood rush to my face I shouted, "I'm not going through with it! Okay, Beppo's disappointed, so he takes it out on you. Well, I'm sorry but I can't do anything about that either. He's a lot beefier than me so I can't beat him up and square things that way. But if he knocked me about I should go to the police."

"I don't think you would go near the police, Charlee."

"All right, I wouldn't, but he's not going to force me into going on with that crazy tunnel and neither are you, Delphine."

"Did I say I wanted to? Would I be looking this way if Beppo and I had agreed on that?"

"Look, it doesn't need genius to understand that you can't go ahead without my help. The keys you have got have to be tested and at least one of them needs a lot more work on it before it would open the outer grille. Then there's Evan's key. I could wait months without getting my hands on that."

"Beppo figures he knows a way around that."

"I don't care if he talked Rhys-Jones into lending him the bloody key, I'm having nothing more to do with it. I must have been mad to get myself this far involved but I've had plenty of time to think it over and it's no go. I see now we'd never get away with it and anyway, after this, how could either of us trust Beppo again?"

She said, surprisingly, "I never did, but I trusted you, Charlee."

"You mean you would still *want* to go on with it?"

"I still think it's feasible if we could all cool down and patch things up. That isn't the real point, however. The real point is you don't have a choice. You still stand to do about five years if Beppo does what he says he'll do."

She got up and drifted over to the window. I sat tight, feeling as though someone had stuffed my mouth with sawdust and was trying to siphon it out through my navel.

"What can he do without ditching all three of us?"

"Plenty. He can ditch you from a safe distance. He says he'll write a letter to Head Office after we leave here, enclosing the trial keys and your drawings."

I thought about this and it amazed me that I was able to do it, clearly and logically. It was possible, of course, and he might achieve it under conditions of almost perfect safety, providing he wrote from somewhere like Mexico or South America. A letter to Head Office. A little package, containing my drafts and the two dummy keys. I could see them being gaped at by a gaggle of directors. It would be fifteen minutes or more before one recovered sufficiently to pick up the telephone and ring Evan and the Penmadoc police. My imagination went further. I could almost hear the rising clamor down in Cardiff, the rush of men, like that ginger-haired bastard who had complained of my inky fingers, to be in at the kill and see the keys tested, and Charlie Pritchard, amateur cracksman, dragged away in handcuffs. It was all very plausible but, even so, there seemed to me an element of bluff about it, too much to make it credible.

"No one," I said, "could go to those lengths for spite. Not when his own sister was involved."

"Beppo could."

"Why Beppo more than the next man?"

"Because he thinks his honor is involved."

This struck me as quite ridiculous.

"If he doesn't give a damn about your honor how does his come into it?"

"You'd have to know Beppo as well as I do before you could understand that."

She was strung up, but I still couldn't make up my mind whether she was speaking as Beppo's advocate, a neutral, or someone preoccupied with her individual interests. Their relationship had always baffled me. Were they close? Were they on guardedly friendly terms? Or did they hate one another's guts? Was Beppo a sullen bully, or a thwarted idiot who had momentarily lost his temper and struck her? I realized he was the key to the new situation and I just had to know more about him. It was impossible to make any meaningful attempt to safeguard myself while Beppo remained what he had always been, a walking-on part who spoke in monosyllables.

"Okay," I said, "tell me about him."

"There's not much to tell. He's smalltime who has always figured he could move into the big league. This was his one chance to make the grade and when he saw it slipping away he went haywire. This eye of mine was just a starter but he can be real mean when the cards don't fall. He'll hold that evidence over your head until he's sure as he can be that you're ready to call his hand. Then he'll duck out of range and post that package just for the hell of it. How do I know this? Because I've been over it with him. There's something else you don't know. He's got a record. He's done time in state penitentiary for warehouse breaking and he's been up on charges of malicious wounding that didn't stick. Before he went inside he was just a layabout with a mean streak but in San Quentin he ran errands for big shots and I guess that made him ambitious."

It held together. Every piece fitted and the jigsaw picture revealed not only an implacable Beppo and a cowed Delphine, but Charlie Pritchard so far out on a limb that there was now no hope of crawling back. He could only go two ways, even farther out, or straight down, and once I had adjusted to this I was able to see the alternatives in much sharper outline than at any time since I set foot on that span of bridges.

"Where is he now?"

"In the workroom. But before you talk to him there's another thing you ought to know, something I decided before you cried off. The night we do it we all go, you and me in one direction, him in another."

"Was that your idea or his?"

"It was mine but he's agreed to it."

"He would have agreed to anything to get me back in line."

"It suited his book. You and I will go to Ireland and Uncle Berni, he'll go south and catch a cross-Channel boat. His passport will take him most places."

A month ago I might have accepted this startling modification without doubting her good faith. The question of passports had not been raised until then. I had taken it for granted that people who had put themselves in our position didn't bother with formalities of that kind.

"What about my passport?"

"Uncle Berni will see to that and you don't need one for Ireland."

"Suppose Uncle Berni takes Beppo's line with me?"

She said, patiently, "From now on you don't have to trust Beppo but you'll have to trust me, and there's at least one reason why you should."

"Well?"

"I've been stuck with Beppo for years. This is my way out too."

I had to be satisfied with that and I think I was, but even if I wasn't there was very little I could do about it. My chances of getting out of the country without her help were negligible. I said, "I'll go and talk to him. You stay here." It was some small satisfaction to be giving the orders at last.

I went up the steep stairs surprised to find that I wasn't dry in the mouth anymore. From that moment I don't think I had more than a few flickers of irresolution. Every half-ounce of nervous energy I possessed was channeled into the task of extricating myself with the least damage to my skin, while taking out what insurance was available on the future. Delphine was still in the picture but she no longer occupied a central or even an important position. From here on I was playing it strictly for Charlie. All this time I had been an amateur. Now I thought of myself as a professional and Beppo was the first one to get the professional treatment.

3

The Rainbow, like Cook's premises but unlike ours, had three floors. The second floor was occupied by bedrooms and a stockroom. Delphine's bedroom was the smaller room at the back, immediately above the living room. Beppo seemed to sleep at the front, over the café. On the floor above, reached by a shorter staircase, were two large attics. The rear one was full of cartons and crates of empty bottles. The one at the front was his workshop.

It had a long bench, a spread of tools and a vice clamped to the center of the bench under the window. The window had no curtain but it didn't need one. It hadn't been cleaned in years and you couldn't have seen through it in daylight. The room was lit by a single bulb that shed light directly on the bench. He was there in his shirt sleeves and what looked like a model of Powell's key was clamped in the vice, protected by wedges of felt. He was working on it with a thin, tapering file and when I came in he grinned, wiped his nose on the back of his hand and bent over the bench again. He didn't seem surprised to see me and probably wasn't. I said, standing just inside the threshold, "Put that thing down, Beppo. You and I are going to have a straight talk."

He laid aside the file and turned toward me, doing this with a shrug, as though he resented the interruption but politeness required him to pay attention to a visitor.

"It's almost finished," he said, mildly. "Tomorrow, or the day after. Then she'll come back two, maybe three times."

"To hell with the bloody key," I burst out, "there are more important things to discuss. So far you've let Delphine do your talking but from now on, if you have anything to say, say it to me. You can talk as well as anyone else. And you aren't deaf either!"

He looked slightly offended at this and showed it by rubbing his forefinger down the side of his nose but then, suddenly, he grinned again. I decided that I hated that superior grin more than any one thing about him.

"I'll go along with that," he said, finally, "you come up here whenever you want to talk."

"We don't have to like one another, Beppo. As a matter of fact I hate your guts, but it looks like I've got to go through with it in any case. That doesn't mean I'm ready to do it on my knees. You've always needed me but now I need you because the deeper you get into this the safer I'll feel. You could send me up but you'd have to be a long way off to do it and that would give me time to run. Just don't shove me, that's all. I've still got a card and I'll play it if I have to, and if I did my sentence would look like a weekend against the ones they'd dish out to you and your sister."

He said, still grinning, "What card is that, Bub?"

"I'm talking about a sniveling confession just before we hit the bank, when the tunnel is started and you've got all the keys in your pocket. Then I might lose my nerve again and tell them about the bloody Eyetie who caught me in bed with his sister, and threatened to kill me if I didn't help him rob a bank. That might cut a lot of ice with a judge and jury. They'd only have to look at us side by side in the dock to see that it was possible. A good lawyer could work wonders with that defense. He could say it was all a put-up job on the part of you and your little sister. And any Welsh jury would take a Welshman's word against a Wop's. I might even get off with six months."

The idea was one that only occurred to me at that moment and it brought with it a surge of confidence. Oddly enough, it also made an appeal to him and for a moment he looked almost benign. He was probably considering it from an aesthetic viewpoint. People like Beppo are fascinated by permutations involving the law and the way that law operates in given sets of circumstances. He said, emphatically, "That's damn good! That could work! It might even get you a suspended sentence, Bub!"

"That's what I thought."

"But wouldn't it be a lot smarter to get clear with the dough?"

"So it would, but just to make sure we do we're going to bring the date forward and hit it on a Saturday instead of a Friday."

"She said the date you picked would show the biggest take."

"I daresay, but it only gives us a few hours to get out of town and even when I wasn't coming along that was a part of it I never did like. My way we'll have thirty hours instead

144

of eight. We'll do it on the last Saturday in August. There won't be as much to split but there'll still be plenty."

"How much?"

"Just plenty."

"Used currency?"

"I'm only reckoning in used currency."

He considered and took his time about it. Finally, like me, he had to make the best of it and did so with a good grace.

"Okay," he said, "I'll go along with that if it keeps everybody happy."

"Right. Well, there's one other thing. We'll drive your van as far as Chester where Delphine and I can pick up the Holyhead train, the one that doesn't stop at Penmadoc. And that's where we part company."

He didn't object to this, in fact I got the impression he was expecting it. He said, "Okay. Now I got more work to do on this key. I think she's too fat. Take these along and get a real measurement. She's a lot trickier than the safe key."

He picked up a pair of calipers and showed me how to gauge the thickness of the key by passing it through the prongs at two points, one halfway along the stem, the other where the projections were deepest about an inch from the tip.

It was one thing watching him slip the calipers over the two points, but I thought it would be very difficult to perform a precise operation of this kind in the few seconds I was likely to have the master key in my possession. It might be done, I told him, but I would need two pairs of calipers and both would have to be much smaller, small enough to be concealed in the palm of my hand. Even with luck I was unlikely to get a chance to make two independent measurements.

"Okay," he said, "I make two sets. Pick them up when you come for the key."

We left it at that and he seemed to lose interest in me, replacing the key in the vice and picking up his file. After watching him at work for a moment I went downstairs. Delphine was standing in the hall, looking up.

"It's fixed," I said, "the last Saturday in August." She hadn't had time to adjust to my new role as senior partner so I added, "you had better start on that tunnel right away."

"Why, if we've got until late August?"

"He'll tell you why. It's a part of my insurance. You can hide keys but you can't hide a damned great hole in Cook's cellar. I'll look in and see how you're getting along when I call for the key."

"He didn't tell you his idea for getting the manager's key?"

"I didn't ask him."

"Don't you want to know?"

"Not specially, I'm working on an idea of my own."

We went across the yard and as I reached for the catch of the double doors she caught me by the arm.

"Has this gummed things up for you and me, Charlee?"

"It looks that way," I told her.

"Why?"

I couldn't say why specifically. Talking to Beppo I got the impression that she was the one who was pushed around and this in itself altered the entire balance of our relationship, but she was allied to him by blood and habit and so far nothing had given me the impression that I was much more than a tool manipulated by her at his direction. She guessed what was going through my mind and set out to change it. She knew me well enough by then to assess her value as an added inducement, and meant to use it to guard against a second attempt on my part to wriggle off the hook.

"Listen, Charlee," she said, earnestly, when I didn't reply to her question, "you can't have forgotten all I told you the night you showed up with that first key, and that still goes only more so. I've been dumb about you. I never figured you'd have the guts to stand up to Beppo and make a deal for yourself. So it's not just a matter of all that dough in the bank, not for me that is."

"What else?"

"Some women like a man who plays it rough!"

I couldn't be sure whether she was referring to the way I had handled Beppo or my uncompromising approach in the hotel bedroom the night before I backed out, but it didn't matter either way. The admission injected more warmth into the glow of self-satisfaction produced by the encounter in the workroom.

"I'd like to believe that, Delphine. Like hell I'd like to believe it."

"What's stopping you?"

She reached over my shoulder and pushed the door shut. When I put my arms round her she pushed her body against me with all her strength so that her legs parted and curled round one of mine. We stood like that for several minutes and it was worth all the misery and anxiety I had endured since I had opened her note. I thought for a moment of going back into the house, or even of taking her there right under Cook's windows but then caution caught up with me and I gently put her aside. Before she could say anything to reinforce the demonstration I said, breathlessly, "You know I'm going through with it because I've no choice, but if I could be sure of you I wouldn't have any bother about keeping my nerve. If you're stringing me along because of him for Christ's sake say so. I won't hold it against you but I've got to know the score. I can't go on indefinitely not knowing it and that puts all three of us on a tightrope."

"You know the score all right, Charlee," she chuckled, a small, gurgling sound at the back of her throat. "I never met anyone who knew it better." Her hand wandered over me the way it had when she was working overtime to keep me up to scratch. Then she slipped the catch of the door and eased it open an inch or two. "See you don't lose your latchkey," she said, with more laughter behind her voice, and we left it at that. When I went up the alley and across the main road to Craigwen Terrace I wasn't thinking about keys, hers or Cadwallader's.

147

Chapter Eleven

1

I collected the grille key and the calipers two days later, a Sunday. On the following Wednesday, when I was sent down for a bag of coppers in the lunch hour, I had a chance to try the key for size.

It was, as Beppo had feared, too thick and only penetrated halfway into the socket. For all that it looked like a twin, as I noted the following day when I returned the real key to Powell after he and Evan had opened up the safe. That same week, during a rush period about eleven-thirty on Saturday, I had a chance to try the safe key at my leisure. It opened the door as easily as the original.

The next problem was to use the calipers on the grille key and this presented all manner of difficulties and dangers. The only time I ever got my hands on it was when Powell left it in the lock, and I couldn't see myself finding an opportunity to measure its thickness at two points in their presence. If I was sharp it would only take a few seconds but even that was longer than they had their backs to me. I had, therefore, to devise some method of lengthening this period, that is, of artificially extending the moment between their advance to the safe and the moment Evan thrust the cash boxes toward me. For a long time, I couldn't hit upon a safe means of achieving this.

I had reckoned without Powell's annual holiday and it was his temporary absence that solved the problem, for Griffiths, who replaced Powell at the opening ceremony, invariably left the key in the lock when he followed Evan into the vault.

By the fifth day of Powell's holiday I had thoroughly rehearsed a plan. A few minutes after nine o'clock, when Evan was on the point of emerging from his office to summon us both and descend the stairs, I anticipated him by disappearing into the washroom and locking myself in the lavatory. I heard Griffiths call my name as soon as they had descended, and waited until I heard the double clang of the grilles. Then I slid back the bolt, pulled the chain, and used the noisy flush to cover the few steps from the washroom to the arch outside the grilles.

My luck was in. Griffiths, inexperienced at opening the heavy grating, had exerted far more strength than was necessary so that the grille swung back and came to rest against the washroom buttress. The key was not only in the lock but within three feet of the washroom door.

I didn't waste a split second. Before they had opened the safe I had reached out, yanked the grille key from the lock, used both sets of calipers at the required points, and replaced the key in the slot. I was even ready with an excuse had either of them turned. I was going to say the key had jumped out and fallen on the floor but neither of them did turn so I was able to retreat to the lavatory, re-lock the door and leave them to carry their own boxes up the stairs. The whole operation occupied about fifteen to twenty seconds.

As soon as I heard them go up (on this occasion, alive to his responsibilities, Griffiths shut and locked the outer grille) I took some squared geometry paper from my pocketbook and pricked down the two measurements, penciling a note to distinguish one from the other. Then I flushed the pan again and went upstairs, trying to look woebegone. Before Evan could complain I apologized for my absence, saying I was suffering from a stomach upset. I don't know whether he took this as a reflection on his wife's cooking but he only frowned, tut-tutted and disappeared into his office, where he remained for most of the morning. With Powell away he too could afford to take a holiday.

I went up to Beppo's workroom that same night and

watched him transfer my sketchy measurements to some drawings of his own. Our approach to one another since the showdown had been guarded but friendly. I said, casually, "Those sketches look professional. You had much practice at key duplicating?" I thought he would interpret this as an attempt to pry but he didn't. He only said, "There's damn all to key casing. I learned it in stir. Two cons got out of the block with a key I made in the workshop with the goddamned screws looking on. They didn't get clear of the can but that wasn't my fault." He concentrated on his work, comparing the dummy key with his tracings. "This time I make a good job of her. She'll go all the way in I promise you, though maybe she won't move all the tumblers in one. You look in soon, eh?"

"Sure," I said, "I can try it easily while Powell is away. Now I'm going down to see if Delphine's told me the truth about the tunnel." I was sure now that I had both Beppo and the bank over a barrel and I was becoming strangely dedicated to the enterprise. Years later, when I chanced on that famous dictum of Dr. Johnson, I rose to it at once. A man convinced that he is about to be hanged does have the ability to concentrate his mind; it is not knowing that makes concentration difficult. In addition, I was enjoying my first taste of power.

Delphine said, "Is he satisfied with those caliper measurements?" and I told her he must be because he had just admitted where he had served his apprenticeship.

"Are you going to stay on for a bit tonight?"

"Long enough to see how he's making out in the cellar."

Notwithstanding her declaration at the gate, or maybe because of it, I was beginning to enjoy giving her the same casual treatment I handed out to Beppo.

She got her torch and we went down the steps and removed their grating. She scrambled through and stood just inside Cook's cellar listening. There was no sound from above so she beckoned and I wriggled through, remembering the first time I had inhaled that nauseating stench of rotting cartons. It seemed a century ago.

I saw at once they had made a promising start. Not only

were the screwheads of the far grating sawn through so that the frame could be lifted out but one layer of bricks had been loosened at floor level and could be prized out by hand. Underneath was a hard core of rubble that might respond sympathetically to a vertical dig and would almost surely make excavating there less noisy than it might have been. I scratched the surface with a nail file and even this raised a little dust.

"How is he going to do it?" I asked her.

"He says he'll have to dig down about three feet before he goes forward. The bank is lower down the hill."

It was true and I could guess at the line the tunnel would be likely to take, down for a yard and then forward for six feet. That should bring us under a point about a yard away from the washbasin and altogether clear of the lavatory.

"He'll have to watch out for pipes," I warned her, "we don't want a flood and we don't want the waste blocked."

"You can leave that kind of worry to Beppo," she said. "Well, are you satisfied?"

I said I was and we re-crossed the cellar to the grating. I stood aside to let her wriggle through ahead of me. I was really feeling my feet that night and in no mood to miss another free show of the kind that had helped me in this desperate business. This time the show was better than ever. She wasn't even wearing pants under her slip and she took her time getting through. It was as though, clear across her buttocks, she had stenciled the tag "Instantly available in exchange for Caddie's keys" and the blatancy of her tactics made me want to laugh. I didn't, however, finding it more rewarding to pretend I was preoccupied with the tunnel, and when I joined her in The Rainbow cellar all I said was, "He'll have to work out a timetable for the noisy part of the digging. Maybe it would be safer in shop hours, with the Cook family out front and all the traffic passing up and down." Then I took a step toward the cellar steps but she caught me by the arm.

"I don't like what's happening to us, Charlee. You still don't trust me, do you? I guess it's hard to since Beppo put the bite on you but I'd sure like to convince you of one thing. It's changed for me as well. I was ready to fool around some to keep you interested—I've already admitted to that—but no man could use me the way you have if I didn't go for him in a big way."

That checked me. At last she sounded as if she was in earnest.

"You mean as a person?"

"Sure I do. When I started out the money was everything, but now I guess . . ."

"Now it's damn all? You really expect me to believe that?"

She turned on me, furiously, "You said it, I didn't! For Christ's sake, heave that chip off your shoulder. Sure the dough is important. Without it there's no future for either of us. But that doesn't mean you tag along, like I intended. You drew level with it before we got as far as that hotel room."

"When exactly?"

She drew a long, exasperated breath. "You won't take a damned thing on trust, will you, Charlee?"

"Not anymore."

"Okay. Here it is then. Ever since I ran my hands over you that night you showed up with the first drawing. Mind, you had me half sold on you by just showing up with it. I figured you'd taken one hell of a risk for my sake and nobody did anything that big for me before. Nobody! All the guys who crossed my path wanted it for a box of candy, or because they figured a girl would swoon the minute they pulled their pants off. Just having you hold me was enough. You don't really think I dreamed up that Manchester jag because I was sorry for you, do you?"

If she had sat down at a table with pencil and paper and sweated out the kind of appeal most likely to crumble the brittle arrogance I had been using to boost myself along ever since they cornered me, she couldn't have chosen a more telling approach. Here it was at last then, a beautiful girl rampaging for Charlie Pritchard, just like he had been imagining since he was fourteen. I believed every last word she uttered —I had to because, if I doubted it, I was stuck with all the

152

risks and no compensating factor. All the money represented at that moment was a means of keeping her interest in me up to concert pitch and getting Beppo off my back. I didn't give it another thought as money. To me it was no more than a one-way ticket in her direction.

We were standing together at the foot of the steps and she still had a detaining hand on my arm. I had a sense of being utterly cut off from the world outside, from all the people at street level and above, from the Cook family and the Powell family snoring away in their warm beds, and late wayfarers passing up and down Station Road. It was as though we occupied a few square yards of breathing space carved out of the bowels of the earth, with no prospect of ever surfacing, and it was this sense of isolation that prompted me to put my arms around her, draw her closer and stroke her hair. She gave a little shudder and the tremor excited me, not sexually but protectively. She raised her face so that the light of the low-powered bulb fell on it, and her expression came closer to tenderness than I had seen on the face of a woman with my arms about her. I kissed her hair and eyes and mouth gratefully and reverently but when I suggested we went upstairs she clung to me and said, "No, Charlee! As far away from him as possible!" Her saying that in that breathless way uplifted me, sealing me off from the dankness and dinginess of the place. I began caressing her in a manner that made all my previous approaches brutal or loutish. She wasn't just a lucky break any more. She was Charlie Pritchard's sole asset, in which he had invested his past, present and future. And presently, without haste and with a kind of solemn relish, I took her. In that setting and circumstance the act should have been grotesque or comic but it was neither. In a way it was a moment of fulfillment that has not been granted to me in all the years that followed.

2

I collected the new key three days later and was able to try it out the following lunch hour, when both grilles were locked and only Griffiths was on duty above. I waited until he was occupied with a dairyman's weekly deposit that necessitated a great deal of silver sorting and copper weighing and slipped downstairs, without him seeing me. He couldn't leave the counter unattended so there was no chance of me being interrupted.

The key slipped into place as easily as the real one. I took a deep breath and exerted gentle pressure to the left and to my astonishment it worked first time, and with the minimum of friction. I heard the snick of the tumblers and then, still holding the key, I shifted my weight and pulled. The grille swung gently outwards. It was a great moment. I closed the grille, taking great care to prevent a clang, extracted the key, wrapped it in my handkerchief and put it in my hip pocket, returning to find Griff still swimming through a sea of pennies and halfpennies.

That night, on my way to report progress at about ten o'clock, I had a fright. I was on the point of opening the front door when Evan emerged from the front room. I thought he had followed Gladys up to bed half an hour before but evidently he hadn't, but had been sitting in the semidarkness, smoking a quiet pipe. There was nothing particularly sinister about this but I felt alerted. I had the impression he had stationed himself there to waylay me and his first words proved this was so.

"This is getting to be a habit," he said, "where do you go this time of night? It can't be to meet the kind of girl a lad in your position would take up with." As I didn't reply to this he went on, "Not a barmaid, I hope, Pritchard?"

"I don't have a girl, Mr. Rhys-Jones."

"You don't?" He brightened up at this and his amiable tone relieved me somewhat. At least it implied he still had hopes of me as a son-in-law, and also that the reason behind the ambush had been to check on my love life, possibly at his wife's instance.

The duplicate key was beginning to burn a hole in my pocket. "I go for a walk when I've been swotting all the evening," I told him. "If I don't I can't get to sleep."

"Ah yes, yes," he purred, "that's a good idea. The trouble with our job is that it tires the mind but not the body. I'm a poor sleeper myself."

I was sorry to hear this. It made any attempt to steal his key that much more difficult.

Suddenly he hooked his Chapel-going hat from the hall stand. "I'll take a turn with you," he said, affably, "just as far as the main road."

Now that I was reassured as to his purpose I could smile at this, the manager himself escorting me on my way to report favorably upon a key that opened his vault. We went out, descending the hill in step and taking sedate sniffs of night air and he said, as we turned into the main road, "You've . . . er . . . not heard from our Ida, I suppose?"

"No," I said, "I wrote once but she didn't answer."

He seemed agreeably surprised that I had written and it encouraged him to pursue the subject. "You always seemed to get along very well," he said.

"We did. I always thought Ida was a very nice girl."

"I never will understand why she ran off like that," he said, shaking his head, "do you suppose she found Penmadoc too dull?"

I said I wouldn't be at all surprised and he said, "But why? You're happy enough here, aren't you?"

It amazed me that he could ask such a question. How was it possible for anyone to be happy in a branch that had him, Powell and Porsen on the staff? I decided to test him. "Mr. Powell doesn't like me and I can't get along with Porsen," I said, and waited for the usual pi-jaw about staff cooperation. It didn't come. Instead he said, thoughtfully, "I'm not surprised, I've been thinking of applying for Porsen's posting. Under different circumstances I might have done it months ago and that would have meant a quick step up for you."

I tried not to look surprised. He really was letting his hair down tonight and suddenly I saw the reason. He and Gladys must have arrived at some kind of compromise and he had been detailed to explore the ground in advance. At the price of helping him to reclaim Ida I could have Porsen's job, anticipating routine promotion by nearly two years. He didn't control staff appointments but his support was essential to a step of that kind, and as manager he was in a position not only to recommend me but also to denigrate Porsen and maybe get him posted to a country cul-de-sac. There might even be more in it than that. Porsen, if I knew him, would fight back, calling on Powell for help, and this would bring the feud into the open. I remembered now that Evan had been soft-pedaling and was obviously biding his time. As for me, I had nothing to lose and possibly something to gain. A closer relationship with Evan would improve my chances of getting hold of that key and it would be pleasant to see Porsen squirm and Powell humiliated before the mountain fell on the whole damned lot of them. I said, " 'Under different circumstances,' Mr. Rhys-Jones... Do you mean if Ida and I had been going together, as Mrs. Rhys-Jones imagined at the time?"

"I mean just that," he said. "It means a rare lot to Mother and me to see our Ida settled and naturally I'd be prepared to put my weight behind you if you and Ida . . ."

He couldn't quite bring himself to say "married" so I said it for him and he was grateful.

"If Ida wanted to marry me?"

"Splendid," he said, and then, artfully, "so there *was* something in it after all."

"Well, not as much as Mrs. Rhys-Jones thought," I said, "but that was my fault, not Ida's. We did talk about it but with the kind of money I earn there didn't seem much prospect . . ."

He seemed to grow an inch with every stride. All the time I had been in Penmadoc I had never seen him in this mood. By the time we emerged on to the seafront he was practically prancing and even took my arm, as though rehearsing his walk up the aisle when the time came.

"Leave that side of it to me, lad," he said, "and I'll tell you something else if you give me your word of honor it won't go any further. I've been looking for a chance to get rid of

Porsen. I never did care for him and there are times when he's been insolent. There are certain other changes..."

He trailed off, suddenly thinking better of admitting the source and inspiration of Porsen's insolence, but ended with a series of emphatic nods that were meant to convey a hint that flash point was not far away.

We had now reached the pier entrance and he stopped, saying, "You finish your walk, this is plenty far enough for me." He was obviously impatient to hurry back to Gladys with the news and wanted me out of the house when he broadcast it, but I didn't want to give him that much room to maneuver.

"Look, Mr. Rhys-Jones," I said, with what I hoped passed for desperate frankness, "you've been decent about this, and I'd like to tell you something else before it goes any further. Ida thought she was being rushed. By her mother, I mean, and I think the best thing you could do if you really want her back soon is to leave it all to me and let me handle it my way."

He beamed at me in the pinkish glare of the pierhead fairy-lights. "Handle it any way you like and as for Mother, leave her to me. As a matter of fact, and again between the two of us, Mother *is* inclined to rush things. I've told her so more than once, but I'll answer that she stays out of this until Ida comes back to us. As for everything else I've said, it'll remain our secret. Not a whisper of it at the branch, remember?"

"Naturally not, Mr. Rhys-Jones. It wouldn't do to let Mr. Powell know what was going to happen."

I couldn't resist getting that one in and it sobered him a little so that he tackled the station approach at his normal gait. I suppose I should have felt sorry for him and I did later on but not then, I was too full of a sense of triumph. One way and another, I told myself, Charlie was proving too much for everyone who tried to corner him. I now had Beppo tamed, Delphine at my feet, Porsen as good as banished, and the branch manager eating out of my hand. Given time I could add Caddie's directors to the list of people who had underestimated me. I was still rolling this on my tongue when I ran slap into Gwyn-the-Boots, who suddenly appeared from the shadow of the railway arch and clapped his enormous paw on my shoulder with a hearty *"Got you, Boyo!"*

It took me ten seconds to ride out that shock and he was delighted by the unexpected success of his pounce.

"Saw the Gaffer go by," he said, chuckling. "Didn't know you and he were buddies. You always said he was a right little bastard at work."

"He was," I said, still struggling for the breath knocked out of me by Gwyn's ambush, "but now he thinks I'm going to marry his daughter."

"My God, you're a crafty one, Charlie! Give you a bank of your own soon they will, if you play your cards right. I'm on until six A.M. Walk as far as my point with me."

First Evan and now Gwyn-the-Boots. It was fraternity night in Penmadoc.

"Where is your point?"

"Factory Lane, ten minutes from now."

Factory Lane was about half a mile east of Station Road. We fell into step and it occurred to me I might as well use this opportunity to discover all I could about nighttime police patrols. I asked him how often he was on nights, and if they had to patrol weekends. He said they had a seven-day rota system at the station, one shift from six A.M. until two P.M., another from two P.M. until ten, and the third the one he was doing now. This one lasted all night.

"Doesn't it get dull pounding a beat all night in a place like this, Gwyn?"

"It does if you let it," he said, with his booming laugh, "but I've got ports of call. They help pass the time, too quickly sometimes."

"You mean the odd cup of tea and a fag where people are still up and about?"

"Slap and tickle as well," he said.

I remembered then that Gwyn had always been popular with the girls, even when he was a boy. They liked his ponderous masculinity and there had been jokes about his potential in the schoolyard. I had heard him called Morgan the Organ.

"You haven't taken long fixing yourself up, Gwyn. Is it anyone I know?"

"Do you know Dilys Thomas, the milkman's daughter?"

I knew Dilys, a great strapping girl with a wide behind and thighs like the trunk of an ash. She had blue eyes, a laughing mouth and strong, freckled arms. Dilys was just about Gwyn's weight and I could imagine they would take to one another on sight.

"Her old man drives inland for his churns at five a.m.," Gwyn said, "and she comes down to the outhouse about the same time to get the cans ready. I usually look in about five-ten to help her water the milk. She's a good sport is Dilys. Now if I was the marrying type I'd look for someone like Dilys."

"How about the long night watch? I bet you don't spend all of it trying doors."

"No," he said, proudly, "only between two and four-thirty. The first door I try is the Aberavon Guest House, in Bryn Mawr Terrace. Mrs. Hughes there never can remember to shoot her kitchen bolt."

I knew Mavis Hughes too, because she banked with us. She was a trim little widow about forty, always well dressed and rumored to have dyed her hair the color of ripe barley. Her association with Gwyn might be important to me because her boarding house was on the far side of town, close on a mile west of Station Road. If he called there regularly it would be early in his beat, about the time we hoped to break out of the tunnel, and if Mavis kept him entertained for an hour or so we could be clear of the town before he wandered down to the shopping center to help Dilys Thomas water her father's milk. In other words, if the last Saturday in August happened to be a night when the citizenry was in Gwyn's keeping we had an excellent chance of a clear run out of town, and could be in Chester long before he signed off. A lot of "ifs" perhaps but all of them worth taking into account.

"How about your mates, Gwyn," I asked, "are they filled in as well as you when they're doing nights?"

"One is," he said, "Ted Evans, the senior constable. As a matter of fact it was Ted who put me on to Mavis, but Riggs, the young one, makes do with a crafty Woodbine and a mug of cocoa at the tin-plate works. I like it here," he concluded and I could understand why. It looked as if we wouldn't have much to fear from the Penmadoc Constabulary.

We reached the junction of the main road and the lane leading up to the tin-plate foundry where Gwyn posted himself conspicuously, ready for his sergeant's point.

"So long then, Gwyn," I said, "time I was home in bed. If Dilys Thomas ever wants a change tell her I'm an early riser too, will you?"

"Ah, Boyo," he said, letting his tolerant glance travel up and down my five feet five inches, "a nipper like you wouldn't know what to do with either of 'em, not if I staked 'em out for you. Stick to banking, Charlie, you're doing fine as you are."

I was glad he said that although he didn't mean to sound so disparaging. I liked Gwyn, and if I could I would have spared him the blistering he was likely to get if he was on duty the night Delphine and I turned our backs on Penmadoc. As it was, his name went down on the list of people who had failed to take the measure of Charlie Pritchard. I could have told him you had to pay for the fun you had in this world.

3

I slipped into The Rainbow yard about eleven o'clock. They were closed and Delphine said Beppo was below, digging up the second layer of bricks. This made me uneasy and I asked her if it wasn't a little early to start digging the actual shaft, but she said she had gone to a lot of trouble to check the movements of the Cook family next door and had satisfied herself that their lights were always out by ten.

"Don't they ever use that cellar of theirs?" I asked, and she said they went down there about once a fortnight, usually on a Monday when their deliveries arrived from the Manchester wholesalers. She had taken to watching their movements during business hours as well as at night, and said that Beppo had moved the rubbish at the foot of the steps a yard nearer the center of the cellar so that they could now find space to dump fresh packing paper without actually descending the last stair. He had also removed their light bulb and replaced it with a dud, and this was clever of him because Cook senior was a skinflint and it would be months before he could brace himself to replace the bulb. As it was he used 25-watt bulbs all over the house.

I told her about the key and said she had better call Beppo up for a conference. He joined us a few moments later and Delphine poured us both a drink. I found I could use mine. It had been an eventful day.

"The grille key is a real honey," I told him, "it works like a charm." I told them what I had found out about the movements of the police at night, and we got out a calendar to check whether the last Saturday in August would be Gwyn's night on. We were lucky again. The number of days before the big night was divisible by three. Barring accidents, or maybe a leave period, it was likely that Gwyn would be a mile away solacing Mavis Hughes's widowhood about the time we set out for Chester.

Delphine's eyes shone that night, mostly on me.

"You're terrific, honey!" she said, when I had finished, "you don't miss a trick, does he, Beppo?" Beppo grinned but didn't corroborate.

"There's one trick I've still got to take," I said, "and that's a really safe way to get Rhys-Jones's key when we need it."

"I've been figuring that myself," Beppo said. "You hang around and signal us at the back after they've turned in. I heave a rock through the front window and you lift the key when they run downstairs to check who's busting into the place."

"How about that, Charlee?" asked Delphine.

"It's the most hamfisted idea he's ever had," I said.

"Come up with something better." This from Beppo, but he wasn't offended.

"Gladys Rhys-Jones would almost certainly stay put if he goes down and Evan wouldn't go farther than the landing before shouting up to me to lead the way downstairs. Apart from that the shock alone would keep him awake all night, nursing his key ring. I know Rhys-Jones. If something scared him the first thing he'd do on coming back to his bedroom would be to check his keys and if the grille key was missing you would hear him scream a mile out to sea. The police would be up at our place as soon as he could get to a phone. Is that enough or do you want more?"

"Okay," he said, "so you tell me how we're going to open that other grille."

"The whole key ring will have to be lifted while he's asleep," I said. "How I don't know, and won't until I've given it a lot more thought."

"Can't you possibly get an impression of it, Charlee?" asked Delphine.

"He never parts with them from the moment he gets up until the moment he gets into bed. All day the ring is attached to his braces by a watch chain and he doesn't take it off when he opens and shuts the grille. Do you think I haven't checked time and again?"

We were silent for a long time. I had thought about getting at the cavity from the outside wall by using a ladder and boring a hole in the bedroom wall but the scheme was so idiotic that I didn't even mention it to them.

"If we don't find a way soon the whole damn thing falls through," Beppo said, without taking his eyes off me.

I decided then that they both needed a little encouragement, especially Beppo. Chipping away on his own in that stinking cellar had made him very edgy.

"Rhys-Jones and I have come to an understanding," I said.

That startled the pair of them and I let them goggle for a moment before adding, "He thinks I'm going to marry his daughter. He offered me a deal tonight."

"What kind of deal?"

"If I get his daughter back home he'll give me first ledger clerk's job and the pound a week rise in salary that goes with it."

Delphine saw the funny side of this but Beppo didn't.

"How does that figure? Does he throw in his key ring as dowry?"

"You could put it that way," I said. "I've been in the dog-house ever since his daughter ran off, and we've not been on speaking terms. But now it'll be different, and if there is a way to get the key I'll be inside the family circle to take advantage of it. As a matter of fact I have got an idea but I'd like time to work on it."

"For Christ's sake, you don't have all that time," Beppo said, irritably, but Delphine flew to my rescue.

"Take it easy, Beppo. Everything Charlee said he'd do he's done, hasn't he?"

She got up then, signifying that the conference was at an end. She was never happy acting as referee between two associates who trusted one another as little as we did. He shrugged and padded off up to his workroom and when I said I had better go, because the Rhys-Joneses might be waiting up for me, she walked me down to the yard gate. Before I unlatched the gate she said, "Go right on standing up to him, Charlee. It's the only kind of talk his kind understand."

I crossed the main road into Craigwen Terrace just as St. Budolph's church clock struck twelve. Evan wasn't waiting up for me but had pushed a note under my door. It read, "I told Mother and she is relieved and happy. She will be laying breakfast for you in the kitchen with us but don't refer to our conversation yet. E.R.-J."

So I was out of the doghouse in one jump.

4

Porsen was the first to notice this, indeed, he could hardly have missed it, for within an hour of our arrival at the branch next morning managerial brickbats were flying in his direction. He was indignant at first and then took refuge in sullen wariness. With Powell on holiday he had to watch points, and plugged away at his work avoiding all unnecessary contact with me.

For my part I was too preoccupied to bother with him. I had two interrelated problems on my mind and each needed careful thought. The immediate one was what to do about Ida. The other concerned an experiment I had decided to make on Saturday night.

As regards Ida some gesture on my part seemed necessary, if only to head off complications that might follow correspondence between her and her parents. Finally I hit on a stalling technique that would give things a chance to settle down a little. I didn't believe that anything I wrote or they wrote would bring Ida flying back to Penmadoc, but there was no point in taking the risk of this happening and I knew Gladys Rhys-Jones couldn't keep her mouth shut indefinitely, notwithstanding any pledge she had made to Evan. So I went upstairs after tea and wrote two letters to Ida, one to show Evan and the other I intended to post.

I wrote the real one first, not much more than a friendly note saying that I intended to give notice in September and chance my luck in London. I said I'd like to know how she was going on and that I would meet her in town if she felt inclined, but there were still no strings as far as I was concerned.

It cost me a qualm or two to write to her in that strain when I knew that by September my face would be in every newspaper, and everyone she knew at Caddie's would be under pressure or scattered, including her father, but the time for scruples of this kind was long past. I was now not only a prisoner of Beppo but of my own conceit, that was rapidly assuming the status of megalomania. Since I had faced the two facts that I had no alternative but to rob the bank and that Delphine was stuck on me, I had made up my mind to bring everything I had to the task. I didn't even let my mind dwell on another change of direction. The last of my reservations had disappeared the moment I discovered how easily Beppo's duplicate opened the outer grille. That, plus the tremendous fillip given to my ego by Delphine's words and behavior in the cellar, swept me along on a tide of excitement and suspense.

The second letter, a decoy for Evan, occupied me for an hour or more and after several drafts I settled on the following:

Ida, dear,

This week I had a long talk about "us" to your father and promised I would write. The fact is, both he and your mother are terribly fed up at you staying away and, for that matter, so am I but for the present I'm writing more on their behalf than mine. They worry a lot about you and that was how your father came to ask me if I still felt about you in a special way. I had to tell him the truth—that I did, but that when you were here any understanding between us was blocked by my prospects at the bank. You remember we did discuss this at the time and agreed that they were pretty dismal. The point is, Ida, they aren't anymore. I'm right in line for a step I didn't anticipate for another two years, and if I get it it will be due entirely to your father. In view of this couldn't you come home, at least for a week's holiday so that we could discuss it with him? Your mother has promised to keep out of it if you do and I believe she will. Of course, none of this will apply if you're going steady with someone else. In that case, throw this letter in the fire and don't bother to answer it but if not write me at the bank, and let me know how things are with you.

As ever,
Charlie

I read it over and it seemed to me as expert a forgery as Beppo's key.

The next morning I showed Evan this letter and he was delighted. He said if that didn't fetch her back nothing would and whether it succeeded or not I had done my part and he was grateful for my help. This was another way of saying that Porsen was for the chop so I settled down to watch the fun. Evan led him a lively dance that morning and I looked forward to Monday when Powell was due back.

That same night I carried out my experiment, that meant dosing myself with two of half-a-dozen sleeping pills left over from a prescription my hometown doctor had given me more than a year before, when I was suffering from a skin infection that kept me awake at night. I don't know why I still had the little phial containing the leftovers, but I came across it when I was searching my drawer for indigestion powder. I couldn't even recall how they had worked at the time and it occurred to me that they might have deteriorated over the period, so I decided to try them out on myself when I had no occasion to be up early in the morning.

I swallowed them with water about ten-thirty and within twenty minutes I was seeing double and felt as though I had several pints of draft beer under my belt. I pulled off my clothes and tumbled into bed and the next thing I remember was Evan hammering on the door and telling me he had a cup of tea and it was past ten o'clock. I struggled out of bed, rubbing my eyes and still unsteady on my feet. Evan said, "We called you several times. By George, I wish I could sleep like that! Come down and eat your breakfast in your dressing gown, Mother wants to clear."

I said I had been reading until after one A.M. and thanked him for the tea, reflecting that he could expect at least one good night's sleep at the end of the month. I felt drowsy until after lunch. I don't know what Dr. Llewelyn had put in those tablets but one of them would have put an elephant to sleep.

I was satisfied now that I had the answer to the last key and late that night went down to The Rainbow and outlined my plan to Delphine. She insisted on fetching Beppo to hear about it and he seemed satisfied too, and asked me if I would like to look at the tunnel. I said I would so we all went down and through the grating into Cook's cellar.

He had made considerable progress in the last few days.

Both rows of bricks had been expertly removed and he had dug down about three feet, level with the party wall. He had a couple of buckets for removing the rubble and had fitted them with felt handles to stop them rattling when he carried them into his own cellar. He used a bradawl to chip away the mortar and a short-handled mattock to scrape away the hard core and packed earth underneath. He had also used planks to shore up the sides of the shaft and was now ready to push forward under the washroom floor. We left him working there and went upstairs to have a drink on it.

We settled ourselves on the divan and she was in a lively, teasing mood. She said, giving my ear a playful twist, "Know something, Charlee? I figure nothing would stop you hitting that bank now. I guess you'd give it a whirl solo."

I wondered about this and decided she was probably right. Nothing so stimulating as this had come my way in the past and, aside from the gigantic conceit promoted by her interest in me as a lover rather than an accomplice, I was already looking across at the old Charlie Pritchard as someone who deserved nothing better than a life sentence behind Caddie's counter. Maybe I had convinced myself that they couldn't give me that long if I was caught and even in the event I would be revealed as a man with a thousand times more guts and drive than the rest of Caddie's staff in line.

I said, kissing the nape of her neck where the hair grew to a blunt point, "Maybe I'd watch for a chance to skip off with a sackful but it would take years and I can't wait that long with you around. There's the practical side, too. I'm not such a bloody fool as to think I could stay at large long in a strange country without your help. Sooner or later I'd make some kind of slip and then it would be curtains. Anyway, daydreaming about all the fun we'll have when we're out of here keeps me up to scratch."

We talked gaily about the prospects of Uncle Berni changing some of the cash into dollars and fixing me up with papers that would pass muster where he put us ashore, and then I asked about Beppo's plans after the shareout. I still had a nagging suspicion that he might prove hard to lose. She said, in what I thought of as too casual a tone, "Don't give it a thought. Beppo can watch out for himself."

"What will he do when he gets the money? Has he said?" My persistence seemed to bother her. "Do you have to know?"

"I want to get things straight. We're a team, aren't we?"

"Sure, a kinda team," and she smiled up at me with an expression half-candid, half-mischievous. "Well, let's see. He's mentioned traveling openly on the Harwich ferry. I guess he'll make for Rotterdam or some such place. Then south for some sun. He speaks French and Italian like a native so he'll get by. And that's enough about Beppo, honey. Beppo is his business."

I suppose I was satisfied with that but even if I wasn't she soon put him out of mind, saying casually, "You want for us to go up to my room?"

The odd thing was that I didn't, or not at that particular moment, and I was ready to tell her why. "I'm sick to death of this hole-in-the-corner lark, Delphine," I said. "Since that night in the cellar, and thinking over what you said, I'd rather wait until we're on our way, or at least somewhere where he isn't likely to snoop on us. Does that make sense to you?"

She thought it over. Then she said, seriously, "Sure it does. You feel differently about me. It's not just a matter of using me like a tramp."

"It's a lot more complicated than that."

She wriggled herself into a more relaxed position, kicking off her shoes and resting her stockinged feet on the arm of the divan. She was using a different perfume from the rather blatant one I associated her with. It was subdued and played its part in the subtle transformation of my feelings about her. She wasn't a goddess anymore and she wasn't an explosive target for lust. She was my woman and I wanted, most desperately, to convey to her the difference that represented.

"Keep talking," she said, "I'm listening."

"After we're clear away and settled somewhere I'd like us to get married and have a place of our own."

"What kind of place, Charlee?"

"Any kind of place, so long as it was ours and fixed up nice, with decent furniture and plenty of sun. It would depend on how much we got. An hotel, that might be an idea."

She looked almost pained. "You figure we got to all this trouble to wash more dishes?"

"We'll have to invest in something. We'd be a couple of idiots to have that much capital and not make it work for us."

She giggled. "My God, Charlee. You really are a banker! I never thought of it that way. I just thought of it as—well, as dough, I guess. An hotel, with a sign out and a night clerk? You figure on me running the kitchen?"

"If I said so. You've forgotten something."

"What's that?"

"You started out with a tame inside man detailed to collect key impressions. You've got yourself a boss."

She seemed to consider this, and nodded her head twice. Then her arms shot up and her hands locked behind my head, pulling me down so that our faces were jammed together. She forced her mouth against mine so violently that our teeth jarred and I remember thinking, behind the purely physical manifestation her frenzied kissing produced, "That's the treatment, Charlie Boy! You've been looking for the right approach half a lifetime and here it is, a bloody bullseye, man!" and my hand slipped under the hem of her skirt searching and finding a purchase on her bare behind so that I could lift her clear of the couch, dump her down and consolidate my triumph.

I didn't hear Beppo's foot in the passage but she did, and his action in shutting and locking the cellar door gave us a moment to sort ourselves out. She seemed more dispossessed than her previous dismissal of him warranted, for she said, breathlessly, "You're damn right, Charlee. It's no fun at all like this," and hoisted herself out of range and began to tidy herself in the mirror. As it happened he didn't come in, but went into the café where I heard the tap gush. I didn't feel as deflated as I should have been. I had said and done what was important and with Beppo above ground I saw no profit in hanging around until he went up to bed. We went through the scullery and into the starlit yard. It seemed we had been whispering goodbyes under the Cooks' windows since time began. "I love you, Delphine," I said, as she slipped the catch and eased open the door, and when she made no comment, "It's not just a case of wanting you like hell every time I come within touching distance. I want you in all kinds of ways, every way there is."

She came halfway out into the alley. "You said you could wait. Say it again, Charlee."

"I can wait. Not too long but until we're out of the wood."

"It makes more sense than kiss and run with Beppo coming and going. I'll go along with that but don't get any silly ideas if I look like going off the boil from here on. It's not for long enough to bother about."

She kissed me lightly on the cheek, withdrew into the yard and gently shut the door.

Chapter Twelve

1

About halfway through August I ran into what proved to be my last major snag.

Evan called me into his office soon after we had opened on Monday morning and handed me a letter from Ida that had come in with the weekend mail.

It was addressed to me and marked personal but I realized he expected me to open it on the spot and read it to him. For a moment I was at a loss. I hadn't asked her to write care of the bank in my letter—the real one that is—because I was always down first now and collected the mail. The letter with this instruction was the one I had destroyed as soon as Evan had approved it. I wished then I hadn't been so confoundedly clever as to send a cover note in case she wrote to her parents independently.

However, here it was, and there was nothing to do but bluff. I stuffed it in my pocket and thanked him for giving it to me so promptly. He looked disappointed but he couldn't very well ask me to pass it over, although Gladys would have done just that. Probably it was with this in mind that Ida had sent it to the bank in the first place.

As soon as I had a chance I went down to the washroom to read it and the first paragraph made me nervous. She apologized for not answering before, saying that she had been waiting for information promised her by the Atlas Products personnel manager regarding a vacancy. The trainee list was filled, she said, but there was a vacancy coming up in the clerical department at head office, and she had learned that not only was the pay better than I was getting, but the post would qualify me for a Continental traveling course they intended to set up the following year. The important thing, she went on, was to get a foot in the door and she hoped I would show a bit more gumption in this respect than I had eight months ago.

Good old Ida. She was still in there gunning for me, blast her. I turned the page and read the next paragraph.

I wouldn't have lifted a finger if you hadn't written right out of the blue soon after Whitsun, telling me you were still keen to make the break. The letter took a longish time to get to me as it went to the Acton plant where I used to work and was sent on here to Croydon, where they shifted me. I can't say I understood it properly. You sounded worked up I thought, like you were that time I found you blubbing in your room. Then I thought, poor old Charlie, going through another of his no-future upsets and me not there to put a bit of backbone into him, so I asked around a bit with the above result. You'll still have to come up for an interview in October, and better have your application in before that, Boyo, say early September, but I wouldn't trust Charlie Pritchard to cope without someone to lean on so that's why I made up my mind to come home for a weekend and fill you in all I can. You see, the clerical job is a kind of tryout post for the course vacancies and I want to be certain sure you get off on the right foot this time.

I'm pretty fit although things haven't been all that easy, but I'm glad I went before I took root and wish I'd done it years ago. Got a bed-sit in a suburb called Lewisham, nice people and only a pound a week for digs and one meal. With piecework rates plus basic I'm now picking up more than three pounds a week and that's more than level pegs with Caddie's, ha-ha!

Then the mine blew up. At the bottom of the second page there was a postscript marked "Later." It was obviously writ-

172

ten just before she sealed the letter and put it in the post, and it said:

> Just heard can pick up day they owe me and will come Friday 29th, 2:50 from Euston. Better tell the folks. Break it gently and don't mention job. Leave that to me. You still need that character reference and I'll get a good one out of Dadda if I have to twist his arm.
>
> Lots of love,
Ida

There were five scrawled crosses too. They were a big help.

I sat behind the locked closet door cursing Ida, cursing my luck, and cursing the day I had ever got involved with Atlas Products. Just when everything was going so well she had to throw a spanner into the works by promising to arrive on the doorstep within twenty-four hours of zero hour. Her presence in the house would prove disastrous and I didn't see how it could do anything less than stall the entire operation. It would make the theft of Evan's key next to impossible and almost certainly hamper all my movements both inside and outside the house on Saturday night. It would also, if I knew Ida, result in raising the alarm first thing Sunday morning and I dared not imagine what complications would arise from that. I had estimated that Evan and Gladys wouldn't wake up until about eleven o'clock and even then he would be muzzy and probably wouldn't check his keys for an hour or so but potter around in his dressing gown wondering what had hit him. That would give us eleven hours' start and it was even possible he wouldn't notice the key was missing until he arrived at the bank on Monday. This couldn't happen if Ida was around. Even if she didn't slip up to my room on Saturday night, as I thought very likely, she would bring in the Sunday morning cup of tea about eight-thirty and when she found I wasn't there she would almost surely tell Evan and her mother. If she had difficulty rousing them she would suspect something unusual had happened. Taken all round, her presence was courting a terrible risk and somehow she had to be headed off. She had to be made to stop feeling so damned sorry for people.

This wasn't the only problem either. As soon as I was alone with Evan he was sure to ask for a digest of the letter and what could I tell him? I went glumly upstairs, and it was just as well I was back under Evan's wing because I couldn't give my undivided attention to anything but Ida's postscript for the rest of the day.

I nipped out ahead of Evan and went the long way home. By the time I reached there I had a story, some sort of story and it was just as well. They were both waiting tea for me and I could tell by Gladys's face that he had passed on the news about the letter.

"Well," he said, gaily, "what's the news, Charlie?" He had taken to calling me by my Christian name in private and this was the only occasion it helped.

"I'm not sure how you're going to take this, Mr. Rhys-Jones," I said, chipping at my boiled egg. "There was ... er ... something I didn't care to tell you when we had that talk. Somehow it seemed ... well, ungrateful on my part."

He looked surprised but not overwhelmed. Gladys started to say "Well, I'm sure ..." but he cut her short with one of his hand-chopping gestures.

"Then tell me now," he said, "we've all got to know where we stand in this matter."

I said, diffidently, "When she was here I talked to Ida about changing my job and trying for something with more money and better prospects."

He looked amazed and so did Gladys, two people witnessing a momentous act of renunciation like the abdication of a throne.

"*Leave Caddie's?*" he said, in an awed voice. "You mean ... take up with some *other* firm?"

"Atlas Products," I said, "the outfit she's working with. It was the firm that your lodger Mr. Waring worked for, and it's my belief she got the job through him."

They couldn't find words to comment on this so I went on,

"We saw an advert in the paper asking for young men with clerical experience to train as assistant export managers for their warehouses overseas. The pay they offered sounded good and there were prospects of quick promotion, a lot quicker than in a bank, any kind of bank. This was before I could see any chance of getting a step up until I was about twenty-six or seven. After all, it never occurred to me that you would recommend me for Porsen's job."

He was reasonable about that. "No," he said, "it wouldn't, but *leaving Caddie's*..." The enormity of this slurred his tongue and he couldn't get any further. It was Gladys who took the practical view. "What happened?" she wanted to know.

"Well, I was doubtful from the start. That was the real reason we quarreled."

She looked at me almost tenderly. "You mean Ida *wanted* you to take that job?"

"Well, yes. I admit I'd been grousing about the pace of promotion and she was only trying to help."

They digested this slowly. It put things in an entirely different light. In Evan's estimation it hoisted me several rungs up the ladder of loyalty but it confirmed Gladys in her original belief that Ida had been desperate to marry me. Evan said, "What's happened now?"

"She's written to say there is another vacancy in October and she can get me an interview."

"I see. How do you feel about that?"

"Quite differently. I think I'd be an idiot to exchange certainty for a jump in the dark like that."

"Very proper," he said, "and very sensible! Did she suggest talking it over with you?"

I said, taking the plunge, "She wants to come home on a long weekend, the first weekend in September."

Instinctively I put the date forward a week. I was getting to be a very accomplished liar. "She said I'd need references and that you would want to hear from her what kind of job it was. So that you could advise me," I added piously.

"Well, I never!" said Gladys and left it at that.

He cut his toast into fingers, preparatory to dipping them into his egg. The operation took him about ninety seconds by the kitchen clock.

"That's too short a time for consideration, for you at all events," he said. "The first week in September? A Saturday, I presume?"

"A Friday. She has a day owing to her."

"Did she say what she was doing?"

"Invoicing. She gets more than three pounds a week."

This did impress them. Evan's wage at that time was only six-ten.

"Aren't you going to read us the letter?" asked Gladys, but I was ready for this and even managed a blush. "I . . . I'd sooner not," I stammered, "there were lots of other things in it."

"Of course," she said, triumphantly, and I was over that hurdle.

"Things are sorting themselves out a little," said Evan. "When she comes, of course, I'll explain everything to her and a job with a pickle firm won't seem as attractive as it does now. Maybe it would be as well if she kept her job for a year or two. My stars! Three pounds a week! She could save half of that for her bottom drawer."

Coziness stole into the room and I began to feel more relaxed. There was only one safety catch left to latch. "I'd still sooner handle this on my own," I said, "but if you wanted you could give me a note to put in with my reply, just saying she'd be welcome if she did pop back for the weekend."

"I'll write it now," he said, getting up and dabbing his mouth with a paper napkin.

I said I would do the same and slipped out with a sickly grin in Gladys's direction.

When I was in my room I shot the bolt and got out my writing pad. It wasn't going to be a long reply and I wasn't going to be any more explicit than I had to be.

"Dear Ida," I wrote, "Thanks for your letter, and the job sounds just what I'm looking for but *don't on any account* come on the 29th or before. Leave it until the next weekend. I've just had a talk with your people and got as far as mentioning I might be leaving Caddie's. You can imagine how this shook both of them and I must have time to talk them round before you show up." I stopped there and read it over twice but even with the underlining it seemed to lack the necessary urgency, so I added, "In any case, I won't be here that weekend. My father is retiring and they're making him a presentation and I've promised him I'll go home to attend." I thought of that as a neat touch. It didn't matter whether she turned up after zero hour. A good many people would be making their way to Penmadoc in the days that followed and I had no doubt that Ida would be among them. I filled the rest of the page with chitchat and went down to collect Evan's note, putting it in the envelope and saying I would go out and post it right away. I was careful to lick only the tip of the flap so that I could open it on the way to the pillar-box. It was just a few words saying they were looking forward to seeing her. I tore it up, sealed the envelope and posted it at the GPO. The moment I heard it rustle into the box I began to breathe freely again, and by the time I had reached home I had persuaded myself there wasn't anything I couldn't do if I put my mind to it.

2

It seemed necessary to keep Beppo and Delphine informed on developments so, as soon as it was dark, I made my way along the main road and watched for an opportunity to duck into the alley. It had occurred to me more than once since the showdown that there was no real point in continuing to conceal my association with them. If we were leaving together, and warrants for arrest were to be issued for all three of us within an hour or so of them finding that hole in the floor, then the charade mounted when I was ejected from The Rainbow had lost its significance. By that time, however, I was like an athlete preparing for a big event and any variation of routine was a breach of training. So as far as Penmadoc was concerned I was still the customer who had made a scene over a tack in his sandwich and had been thrown out. Other customers, including Porsen, remembered the incident and this was how I wanted it. So I never turned into that alley without a careful glance left and right, and I always made certain I entered the yard when Cook's windows were dark.

They were dark now as I passed between the wall and the parked van to approach the living room window, but as I was raising my hand to give the signal I heard the rumble of Beppo's voice raised as though in argument, and then, unaccountably, I heard him laugh.

The sound stopped me dead. Beppo grinned now and again but I had never heard him laugh. For some reason I had assumed he rarely did and when it happened it would mean trouble for someone. Then I had another, more disturbing, thought. There was trouble between them over me and although the sounds I heard did not suggest he was giving her another going over, there was something in that neighing laugh that implied contempt, as though he was taunting her on my account. I stayed quite still listening for the first signs of a real quarrel and my heart was beating as fast as when I was collecting impressions and testing keys at the bank. If he laid a hand on her again, I decided, he would have to reckon with me, and remembering his muscles I looked around for some kind of equalizer. There was nothing to hand so I crept over to the ashcan behind the scullery and found a short length of lead piping that had broken away from a raintub that had been there. It wasn't ideal but it was better than facing up to a man who could give me six inches in reach and about two stones in weight. Holding this I rapped sharply on the door. Delphine had it open in a matter of seconds and at first glance I thought I was right. She looked as scared as I had ever seen her look and when she saw the piece of piping I was holding her jaw dropped.

"What the hell have you got there?" she demanded, as soon as I stepped inside.

"I heard Beppo carrying on and I thought . . . well, I don't have to tell you how tough he can get, do I?"

She looked at me, then at the pipe and then at me again.

"For God's sake!" she said, with a little yelp of laughter, "I'm not having that kind of trouble with him. He's had a drink or two but he sure needed them. Put that silly thing down and come and have one yourself." The laughter went out of her voice. "We didn't expect you tonight. Nothing's gone wrong, has it?"

"Something nearly did but I coped with it." I put the pipe aside feeling a little foolish. "Has the tunnel caved in?"

"No," she said, composed again now or almost so, "Cook's elder son, the holy one, is frigging one of the shop girls, that redheaded one who shows a lot of leg when she's dressing the store window. Did you know about that?"

"No," I said, "I didn't, but what the hell did it have to do with us?"

She said, "Plenty. They came down into the cellar to finish what they started in the stock cupboard. Luckily Beppo saw them from the far side of the grating, their grating. He had to sit it out in the tunnel."

This was alarming news and not the kind I would have thought anyone in Beppo's situation could afford to regard as a joke. So far we hadn't been disturbed once down there and now that the tunnel was almost completed the last thing we wanted was a complication of this kind.

"You mean that's what he was laughing about?"

"Sure. Don't *you* think it's kinda funny? After all, he's the preacher type isn't he and married into the bargain? Beppo said it looked and sounded as if they've had plenty practice."

"But why should they suddenly start using the cellar?"

"Maybe because his wife is wise to it and they've come looking for a fresh perch, but don't worry about it. The store closes at seven on Saturdays and the girl doesn't live in."

"Then how comes it she is there now?"

"I can tell you that. His wife and the old man are both at a Chapel do, I saw them leave."

This seemed logical and so, when I thought about it, did Cook's involvement with a girl, Marion Skilly. I didn't know Cook well but he was reckoned a Holy Joe up at the Union Street Chapel and my experience with men of his type had taught me not to be surprised when one of them blew a gasket. Sooner or later half of them did. Some went on a prolonged bender, and others stayed on after prayer meetings trying to make the lady organist. As for the girl, she was one of Porsen's conquests, and he had remarked that Mrs. Cook must have been looking the other way when she was taken on. I could see that the circumstances added up to a mild joke but they didn't go all the way toward explaining Beppo's raucous laughter. However, I let it go at that, followed her into the living room and told them about Ida's letter and what I had done about it. Delphine said I had handled it neatly and Beppo, who looked to me as if he had been drinking more than his nightly knocking-off ration, added that if Ida did show up on the night I had better make sure she had her quota of sleeping tablets. I didn't tell him I had no more than four tablets and would need them all if Evan and Gladys were to get the double dose that had worked so effectively on me.

Something constructive did emerge from that uneasy meeting, covering a point I had overlooked up to that time. I had reckoned on a ten-hour start as a minimum, representing the period that would elapse between the time we actually headed for Chester and the time Evan woke up. Under ideal circumstances this period might lengthen itself into as long as thirty-two hours, that is, from the moment we drove off until 9 A.M. Monday morning, when Evan fumbled for his key ring to unlock the inner grille; ideally, I say, for it was difficult to visualize him getting through the whole of Sunday without missing the key. The best I hoped for was that he wouldn't discover the loss until he undressed at night and put the key ring in the niche. That would give us about twenty-four hours, but we couldn't really count on more and had, in fact, settled for less. This was cutting it fine but I couldn't see a promising way to add to it. It was Beppo who found one, the idea emerging from a fresh discussion of the time element touched off by my misgivings about what could happen if Ida was on the premises. He said, suddenly, "This key of his, is it about the same size and weight as the key to the outer grille?"

"No," I said, "it's smaller and flatter. The two locks aren't similar in any way."

"Like a Yale key?"

"No, not a bit like a Yale key. It's round at the end and the projections run more than halfway up the stem."

"Could you draw it? Maybe an outline?"

"Any drawing I could make wouldn't be the slightest use to you. It's a complicated-looking key, and I've never seen it off his watch chain. Neither has anyone else except Powell, who takes charge of it when Rhys-Jones is away. I've told you over and over again, you can forget that key until the night."

"I aim to make him forget it."

"How do you mean?"

"Draw the goddam thing," he said, "rough it out the best you can remember it."

To humor him I took a pad from the bureau and drew the outline from memory. My sketch made it about three inches long, just under an inch wide at its broadest projection, and about the same at the end where it hung on the chain.

He looked at the drawing for about a minute and then he took a pair of scissors from the workbasket and cut it out, holding the cutout in the flat of his hand. He had us both interested now. Delphine said, "What are you figuring, Beppo?"

He groped in his pocket and handed me the calipers I had used for gauging the thickness of Powell's key.

"How thick?"

I adjusted the calipers until the points were about seven millimeters apart and he studied that for a time. Finally he said, "Weigh around three ounces. I'll make me one to this scale and you can hang it on his ring once you've slipped the real one off. Chances are he won't notice the switch until he uses it."

I thought about this and what it meant in terms of risk. On the strength of a couple of superannuated sleeping tablets I was already committed to crawl into Evan's bedroom, slip the key from his ring and crawl out again. But if I took this chance of increasing our start I had now to slip the dummy key onto the ring. Knowing Evan's ring, a smooth steel coil from which keys were seldom removed, this promised to be a tricky operation, especially as it would have to be performed in darkness and complete silence. Both of them watched me weigh the doubts. Before I had resolved them Beppo said, sourly, "You figure you need something stronger than those pills to keep the old bandicoot quiet?"

"No, I bloody well don't," I said, not relishing the prospect of dosing them with anything he might give me, "they worked well enough on me and Mrs. Rhys-Jones is a heavy sleeper anyway."

He said nothing to this but addressed Delphine as though I wasn't present. "I figure I've gone in as far as I can without some kinda checkup from his end. Maybe he'd better come and take a look. We can get a fix by tapping." Then he finished his drink, hoisted his slacks and padded off leaving us alone. I thought she looked apologetic and ill at ease. "You noticed he's been knocking it back tonight?" she said.

"Yes. All we need now is for him to work up that kind of thirst on the night."

"I'll make certain he doesn't," she said.

Her general manner, half listless and half wary, left me with two uneasy impressions. One was that she was concealing something about Beppo, the other that her nerve was beginning to crack.

"Sometimes," I said, "I think that plug-ugly brother of yours is a bit cracked," and for a moment she looked almost outraged.

"He packs a nasty temper," she said, "but he won't let you down. His keys work, don't they?"

"I'm not worried about his keys," I told her, but she was clearly disinclined to discuss the matter further and said she was going up for a bath. I said I would go down and see what he wanted and give her a shout when I was back.

I went along the passage and down the steps, stopping to listen their side of the party wall. If he was at work he was being discreet about it. There was no sound and from where I stood near the grating I could detect the faintest glow of light spreading upward from the bottom of the shaft but no one who wasn't looking for it would have seen it and it would have been invisible from Cook's stairway. I stepped over the accumulation of rubbish and looked through the hole where Cook's grating had been. From here I could just see his up-turned heels, and then his right hand as it reached behind him to tip a trowelful of earth into the bucket. He did everything in slow motion and it was pretty to watch. I called, softly, "Beppo!" and the torch went out at once.

"I'm coming down," I whispered and went through the hole feet first, lowering myself into the shaft until I was within touching distance of him. He switched on his torch and I saw that he had progressed about seven feet forward from the foot of the shaft, and that the little tunnel, carefully revetted, was about four feet high. His work was like his movements, neat and deliberate. Shaft and tunnel were scrupulously clean and the smell of freshly turned soil mingled with the stench from all that mildewed cardboard in Cook's cellar. He worked stripped to the waist and the muscles of his torso glistened as he reached forward to scoop out about two ounces of fresh soil, empty it into the bucket and smooth the surface like a conscientious plasterer. I had the impression that manual work brought him satisfaction.

"How much earth will you have to cut through to come out in the washroom?" I whispered.

He handed me a length of brass stair rod, with one end flattened to a blunt point and nodded toward the roof. I in-serted the rod between two pieces of planking and pushed upward until the point jarred on something solid. "Is that the concrete skin?"

"Maybe," he said, "or maybe a piece of slate or a steel joist. I don't give a damn what it is. We don't come at her that way."

"Then what way? If you go on burrowing you'll bypass the bank and come up in the tobacconist's."

The small joke failed to amuse him. He directed the beam of the torch over my left shoulder and where it struck the top of the last piece of revetting I saw a small, lateral excavation about five inches square.

"Put your hand in," he said, "far as it'll go."

It wasn't pleasant cooped up down here with a man for whom I was beginning to feel fear and disgust. His breath reeked of brandy and his body of sweat and this, combined with the rank smell of the cellar, made me want to retch. I pulled myself together, however, and reached into the hole until my fingers touched a brick, or rather a brace of bricks with mortar in between. I hadn't reckoned on finding a wall there and neither, I imagined, had he until he stumbled on it. I was wrong. It wasn't a wall and he hadn't found it by chance. He had sat down and worked it out, the way anyone with regular access to the washroom could have done.

"It's a brick pier," he said. "I figured the floor couldn't just rest on slate or rubble. What I got to know right now is which pier it is and how far along this side the washroom floor."

"Why do you have to know that?"

"Because that's where I start to go up. That way we don't find no more than an inch of concrete if we come out where the pier finds floor level. We don't need to scrape a big hole, we just take out the bricks, same as we did on top."

I could follow him more or less. Once the supporting pier was laid bare to its base, it should be a relatively simple matter to chip away the mortar and move the bricks one by one, precisely as he had removed those below Cook's grille at the head of the shaft. It was safer and less noisy than chipping through concrete and trusting to luck where we emerged. In addition it ruled out any risk of cutting through a pipe and flooding the tunnel.

"Won't it bring the floor down on top of you?"

"With a row of piers intact? I'll chance that, brother, just so long as you give me a fix next time you're alone up there."

"It would have to be during a lunch hour, between twelve-thirty and one-thirty. What exactly do you want me to do?"

He rummaged in his tool bag and took out a light hammer. "Tap along the full length of the wall," he said, "just tap, bang, bang, bang. Start by the door. I'll be down here listening, and when I tap back mark the spot. If it's where I think it is we won't have no trouble at all."

I pocketed the hammer and told him to be in position between twelve-thirty and one-thirty every day from tomorrow onwards. Then I backed into the shaft and climbed out. Before I had one foot through the grating aperture he was at work again, carefully enlarging the hole that reached back to the brick pier.

I re-crossed the cellar and climbed through into The Rainbow premises with some of the bounce knocked out of me. As regards Beppo that is. I still felt perky as far as Delphine was concerned, climbing the stairs to the hall and making some attempt to dust myself off. She had a radio wired to her bedroom and I could hear one of the Northern dance orchestras playing "Happy Days Are Here Again," the hit tune of that summer. I listened for a minute and then went upstairs and along the passage to her bedroom at the back.

The light was on but she wasn't there. Her clothes lay on the chair beside the bed, every garment neatly folded. The chintz curtains were drawn and there wasn't a breath of air in the room. I was still spattered with brick dust and the smell of Cook's cellar clung to my clothes. I wondered whether to take them off, climb into her bed and wait for her to emerge from the bathroom. Then I thought of Beppo again and the implicit warning she had given me at the gate. That kind of thing would have to wait from here on. Leaving the radio playing I went out into the passage and tapped on the bathroom door.

"How long are you likely to be?" I called, and the door opened and she was standing there in a small cloud of steam, a towel draped round her shoulders and a turban over her hair.

"Nearly through, how did you two get along down there?"

"Like buddies," I said. "He stinks but there's nothing wrong with his digging." I told her what he wanted me to do and she asked if it would be risky to go hammering along the washroom floor in working hours.

"Not as risky as standing here looking at you starkers," I said and stepped forward, deciding I couldn't wait to get her to the bedroom, but she said, with a smile, "No, honey. We

185

agreed on that. Besides, I've got a better idea. I need fresh air so why don't we meet somewhere outside, clear of this stuffy place? It's late and if we go out separately there's no chance of being seen together. You know someplace?"

I was surprised but pleased. Apart from that one evening in Manchester we had never exchanged a word outside of those premises and even in our most relaxed moments I was always conscious of Beppo's brooding presence.

"There's the old Craigwen estate at the back of the town," I said. "No one is likely to be there at this time of night and if there is anyone they'll have other things in mind. It'll take you about fifteen minutes. I'll go ahead and wait."

"You do that," she said, and when I hesitated, "go on, I won't stand you up. About twenty minutes from now, but be careful when you go out, the moon is rising."

I went down and tiptoed across the yard, as usual keeping the van between me and Cook's windows.

4

I slipped into the alleyway and walked briskly up to the main road. It was quite deserted, with widely-spaced street lamps turned down to half pressure, so I kept to the pavement on the south side and it was here, outside W. H. Smith's, that I ran slap against Gwyn-the-Boots, smoking a furtive Woodbine in the porch. This time the encounter unnerved me so much that my knees would have sagged if I hadn't grabbed the bracket of Smith's shop blind.

"For God's sake don't *do* that to me, Gwyn!" I shouted. "Every time I run across you at night you make me feel like a bloody convict on the loose! Why can't you just say hello to a fellow, like anyone else?"

"Sorry, Boyo, just my fun," he said, complaisantly. "There's no fun for me tonight. Too early for Dilys and Mavis is away. It's not my turn on, see, I'm standing in for Roberts. He's had a bad time at the dentist's today. Do the same for me he would."

"When is your real turn?" I asked. "Next week?"

"Week after," he said. "Mavis will be back then. I only came off nights last Friday. You're late tonight, Charlie. Fixed yourself up at last, have you?"

I thought it was time I went part way toward explaining the hours I kept and told him that I had a bit of stuff who worked as a cinema usherette in Llandudno. There was a train just in from along the coast and he would know that an usherette was unlikely to be off duty until at least halfway through the second house.

"Hell of a long way to go for crumpet," he mused, sadly. "Expensive too. Three-and-six return, isn't it, now?"

"She's worth it," I said, "or she was tonight. Look, Gwyn, I'm flaked out and I'm going home to bed."

"You do that, Charlie," he said, genially, "I've got a point at Tin-plate Lane so I can't walk you so far. Be seeing you, Boyo," and he gave me a slap on the shoulders that was meant to convey his enthusiastic approval of my nightlife but was still heavy enough to boost me halfway across the main road.

It took me the length of Craigwen Terrace to recover from the shock of meeting him, but when I did I thought I had gained something from the encounter. If Gwyn came off night duty last Friday he would be on again on Saturday week. And if, as he had indicated, the little widow was back in circulation by then she would probably keep him entertained east of Station Road at the crucial time.

The street lighting stopped halfway up the terrace but by the time I reached the top the moon was riding over the bay and playing catch-as-catch-can with banks of cloud scudding seaward from the mountains. It was very still up there and the scent of wallflowers reached me from the gardens of the big detached houses that marked the outer boundary of the town. Down below a few lights still twinkled as I took up a position in the clearing between the rhododendrons, a few yards beyond the path that wound its way across the shoulder of the estate. I remembered that a few months ago this strip of land had been a gift to the Council and workmen had already begun to cut back the bank to make room for an approach to the higher ground behind. They had placed trestle obstruction round the excavation and hung a couple of red lamps there. I noted this as I lit a cigarette. It was a casual observation that was to save my life.

I sat down to listen for Delphine's footsteps ascending the hill, glad that Gwyn's point had taken him as far east as Tinplate Lane. It would have been awkward if he had seen her emerge from the alley in my wake. Before I finished the cigarette I heard her footsteps and she made straight for the glowing end as the moon slid in behind a cloud.

"Charlee? Phew, what a climb!" She settled herself on the seat beside me. "Did you come up here with Ida?"

"Never," I said, and slipped my arm round her so that her head rested on my shoulder. The scent of her bath salts or shampoo vied with the wallflowers. All my life the smell of wallflowers was to remind me sharply of her and of this particular spot. I asked her if she had passed anyone on the way up and when she said she hadn't I told her about the scare Gwyn had given me outside Smith's, adding that he would almost certainly be on duty on the night.

"Charlee," she said presently, "how much do you figure we shall get? Can't you make a guess on averages over the year?"

"Only within two or three thousand. It depends on so many things."

"What things?"

"Weather, what kind of week our customers have up to Saturday midday, and how much of it is in cash. It ought to be a sizable amount because the last week of August is the seasonal peak and there won't be many checks. We get a lot of checks in after each quarter day but very few at this time of the year. Then there's the branch float but that varies too. The amount is regulated by what we're likely to need on Monday but here again it should be one of the biggest of the year, barring Christmas week of course."

"*How* much?"

"The float? It could be four thousand but we'll have to leave the fivers behind, they keep a record of the numbers. It's a pity we don't have a night safe-deposit. We're getting one but it isn't installed yet. That would have bumped the total up because it would have included Saturday afternoon's takings from thirty shops."

"Know something, honey?" she said, in that teasing way of hers. "You better stop kidding yourself you're doing this for me."

"When did you decide that?"

"Oh, I've gotten around to it gradually. I was fooled by that stargazing routine of yours right up to the time you came close to raping me in that hotel room. And after you ducked out, the way you stood up to Beppo. Win or lose, no one will ever step on your face again, Charlee. I figure that's one thing I've been able to do for you."

Her assessment, and the way she arrived at it, interested me. For weeks now I had been learning about myself but my self-judgments were mostly guesses because I was finding it increasingly difficult to look back and get the original Charlie Pritchard into correct focus. It sometimes seemed to me that I had always been a key-stealer and an aggressive lover of bad, beautiful women. I found it hard to remember a time when I had not been a calculating liar, ready, if necessary, to reach out and pull the roof down on myself and everybody else. How much this change in me was due to her influence, and how much stemmed from frustrations dormant in me the first day I set foot in Penmadoc, I was unable to decide. It was something I might discover as time went on when we were isolated from everyone but each other.

She hitched onto my line of thought with her usual accuracy.

"Tell you something else, Charlee. You're not even scared any more and you know why? It's not because you're in so deep you can't get out. It's because you've already plastered that goddam bank of yours with custard pies and that's come to mean more to you than any amount of dough you fetch out of that vault."

She was right again. In a sense I had already routed them. Evan was an ally and Gladys was subdued. Powell, who had done his damnedest to make my life a misery, now had to tolerate the same brand of dumb insolence that he practiced on the manager. And Porsen was already a spent force. All that remained was to strike at people like that gingery bastard of a director, and remembering the occasion I had gone to her seeking comfort after the incident of the inky fingers I suddenly found myself wondering why, precisely why, she was out here sitting beside me trying, in her devious way, to shift the weight of my degeneration from her loins to my subconscious. There was a definite reason for it, for her presence and the line of conversation she was pursuing, and for the life of me I couldn't discover what it was except that somehow the thread ran down the hill, across the town and into that excavation where Beppo sweated and delved. I said, directly, "Why was it so important we should meet out here tonight?"

"I've got my problems too," she said.

"You mean Beppo?"

"He's only one of them." She hesitated a moment and then took a deep breath. "Listen, honey, don't get this wrong but— wouldn't it be safer for all of us if you went back to plan one and stayed put after we hit the bank?"

I was dumbfounded. She couldn't have said anything more calculated to feed the suspicion that had been gnawing at me ever since I paused outside that window of theirs and heard Beppo chortling.

"You mean hand over the key, bluff it out, and take my chance meeting up with you when the dust has settled?" I was almost incoherent with rage and a sense of betrayal. "What in hell makes you want that, at this stage?"

"I don't want it, honey. You got to believe that. But Beppo wants it. He's got it into his head we'll botch it if we scram together and they've got a line on you. Okay, it would mean waiting for both of us—but isn't there less actual risk for you if . . ."

I stood up and looked down on her. "That's my business. It isn't Beppo's and it isn't yours! The fact is I don't trust Beppo any farther that I could throw this park seat and it looks to me as if you're a damned sight more scared of him than I ever was. You don't have to be anymore but you are. It's in everything you've said and done tonight. Okay, I can understand that, but here's something you haven't had straight ever since we got into this. Beppo is a liability whichever way you look at it. He's a risk to us both on his own, and he's a risk if we travel farther than Chester as a trio, but the second risk is bigger than the first and as long as I'm with you and he isn't, you're my insurance. You tell him that. Tell him the deal we made in the workroom is still on or there is no deal, not even now. That's for him and this is for you. I've got just enough nerve to take me as far as that strongroom but it would be pushing my luck and yours if I had to face up to all the questions they'll fire at me on Black Monday at Caddie's Penmadoc branch."

"You're absolutely decided on that?"

"Absolutely."

She stood up. "Okay, Charlee. I'll go tell him, word for word."

I caught her arm. "Before you go—some things you still haven't told me, apart from all I'm expected to take on trust. First, you came up here tonight in the hope of persuading me to change my mind and your first impulse was to try it in bed. That accounts for the warming-up process at the bathroom door. I've got that one right, haven't I?"

"Something like that, I guess." Her tone was flat and impersonal, the voice she had used when she broke the news to me about Beppo's reaction to my backing down on them.

"Why did you change your mind and decide to say what you had to say out here, away from Beppo?"

She considered. "It seemed fairer. I've always tried to play straight with you. I guess that's something else you'll have to take on trust."

"I'll do that providing you'll give me straight answers to the other questions. This whole thing was Beppo's idea from the start. I mean, going to work on me, getting me hooked, and then bringing him in as an afterthought."

This time she answered directly. "Yes, it was Beppo's idea. He put it to me the night you hit that lout with the vinegar bottle. Anything else?"

"One little thing. What was the real joke when I arrived tonight? It wasn't Cook and that redhead smooching in the cellar. You were using that as cover."

"Something I said, I guess."

"Well?"

"I told him nobody could give Charlie Pritchard the run-around any more." She was still holding something back, but I had just about everything in focus now. Their relationship, my new status in her eyes, and her delicate position at point of balance between the two of us. But I still believed I could tip that balance in my favor. She wanted to be rid of him and she believed me capable of standing up to him. Maybe there was a chance that she could handle him after all but if she couldn't I could, so long as she stood behind me. I said, "Right, that's how it is then, my way or no way. Otherwise he can fill in the bloody tunnel, screw back the gratings and go back to serving coffees to tin-plate Romeos. You too for that matter."

"Will you come round tomorrow?"

"Only if I hear from you, not otherwise."

For a moment she seemed perplexed and it was a pleasure to anticipate how much of that uncertainty was likely to rub off on Beppo. But for all that she had the last word.

"Bigger and bigger, Charlee," she said. "You'll never come home now. Give me ten minutes' start and I'll write to you anyway."

She walked quickly down the slope to the top of Craigwen Terrace, and when she had passed beyond the red lamps that marked the cut in the bank I could hear her heel taps clacking along the first stretch of pavement. That might, conceivably, be the last I would ever see of her, except as a plate ballerina through the steamed-up window of the café, but somehow I didn't think so. I flattered myself I had convinced her and was capable, through her, of convincing Beppo. My way or no way, and frankly I didn't give a damn which. The real business of the new Charlie was not to rob banks but to influence people. Bank robbery was only incidental.

Chapter Thirteen

1

It was about one in the morning when I stood on the bank above the excavation listening to the tap of Delphine's heels descending the hill, and the period between then and what people now call "the moment of truth" remains in my memory more sharply and clearly than any corresponding period of my life. There is almost nothing that occurred during that span of days that has washed down the stream of the years with all the other flotsam of the seasons. I remember vividly deliberate acts, like making the washroom sound test, but also the small change of life, and in the greatest detail. My senses seemed to be tremendously alerted so that I moved about my hours of work and free time with the awareness of a sensitive child living in an atmosphere of crisis.

It was an interesting experience. I noticed things about the town and the people around me that had gone unnoticed all the time I had been part of that place. Tiny, irrelevant things. The intricate network of veins on the chubby cheeks of Evan Rhys-Jones. Porsen's habit of pursing his thick lips to whistle when he studied a bank statement taken from the sheaf at his elbow. Griffiths's air of irritated abstraction, as though every customer who walked into the bank got between him and his vision of Celtic twilight. The way the smart Mrs. Powell's bottom slid to and fro when she teetered up the stairs from street to flat after a shopping expedition. I noticed the weather, a succession of long, sun-bright days, when puff-clouds moved over the blue expanse of the bay. I noticed the gaiety of holidaymakers staying in the Shangri-La Guest House, at the junction of Caerleon Road and Llandudno Road, on my way to and from the branch; their arch poses on the steps for group photographs, their giggles and squawks as the fortnight's humorist made his inevitable sally. I smelled the soap Mrs. Hughes, our cleaner, left in the half-scrubbed corners of the bank, and the cheap perfume wafted by Cook's girlfriend as she pranced in and out of the shop to hang the day's display of dresses and blouses on racks at the entrance. And all these things contributed in some way to an overall serenity that settled over me like an insulating garment, as though I was no longer personally involved in what went on around me.

Only occasionally, when I had a specific purpose, would this mood resolve itself into one of deliberation, as when I carried out Beppo's assignment, or acted upon Delphine's brief note that arrived by first post on Wednesday morning, some thirty-odd hours after our moment of parting up on the Craigwen estate. The message did not surprise me but its brevity did. It said, "Back on course. Come Saturday, Sunday latest." It wasn't signed, not even with an initial, but I burned it just the same and with a thoroughness that was an act of ritual.

That lunch hour I was able to carry out the test to my entire satisfaction. Evan left after the morning stint to attend a fund-raising garden party in connection with his chapel. The only occasions he ever took an unofficial half-day coincided with a local event of this kind and even then he always looked in again in time for lockup. As soon as Powell went up to lunch, and Porsen went for his break, I slipped downstairs. We were not busy and I knew Griffiths could cope for five minutes. At twenty minutes to one I went into the washroom and took out the little hammer Beppo had given me, going down on my hands and knees and beginning to tap at the angle of the floor and wall nearest the stairs.

After the first two or three taps I heard Beppo's answering knock. It came from the right and I guessed his position at once. His estimate had been remarkably accurate. The small, lateral excavation on the left side of the tunnel obviously led to the last brick pier supporting the floor and the clarity of the sound, light as it was, told me there was no more than a foot of hard core and possibly an inch of concrete between where I now knelt and the highest brick he had exposed. I moved along the floor beating a light tattoo until I reached a point where I judged I was immediately above him. He answered and that was that. The tunnel would break about two feet from the wall and perhaps five feet on Cook's side of the lavatory cubicle. I put the hammer in my pocket and went upstairs to rejoin Griffiths.

On Saturday night I went round to The Rainbow about eleven o'clock, expecting Delphine to make some direct reference to the ultimatum as soon as I stepped inside the scullery door, but she didn't and there was no element of warmth in her greeting. I think it was this that alerted me so I bit back a question I was on the point of asking and said, in a matter-of-fact tone, "Is he down below?"

"Yes," she said "and near enough through, but before you go down he said to give you something."

She turned on her heel as though I had been one of her customers ordering a fruit drink and I followed her into the living room. She wasn't going to much trouble to hide from me the fact that she and Beppo were in one mind about me staying on, and the odd thing was that knowledge of this, which surely should have deflated me, brought me a certain satisfaction. I suppose, by then, I was getting used to calling the tune and learning to enjoy the privilege. For so long now I had been the one who jumped through the hoops, her hoops as well as everybody else's. Now even Delphine was numbered among those who made a cautious circuit around the new Charlie Pritchard.

The something she had to give me was the dummy key Beppo had made to hang on Evan's ring. She crossed to the bureau and rummaged among some papers enclosed in a thick, brown folder. I noticed that the folder was marked "Personal" in bold script, but this was not a conscious impression at the time. The key was in a sealed envelope and I took it out, weighing it in my hand. It looked very like Evan's key but brighter and newer, his key having become smooth with daily use. As regards weight it was difficult for me to judge, never having handled the original, but it looked about the same size and thickness. I told her this and mentioned the brightness and sharpness of outline.

"Beppo's going to do something about that," she said, "he says it needs rubbing down and stewing in cold tea for a day or so. He wanted you to see it first."

I returned the key to her and she resealed the envelope and put it back in the file. As she did this a snapshot slithered out of the bundle of documents and she picked it up and glanced at it.

"What's that?" I asked her and she passed it to me. It was a snap of her in a one-piece bathing costume, taken against the rail of a ship. She looked very slim and boyish.

"Is this your Uncle Berni's tub?" I asked, and she said it was and the snap had been taken during their voyage over here two years ago.

When I asked if I could keep it, however, she said, "No, it's crur......y. I had no kind of shape then. I can find you a much better one if you really want one."

She closed the bureau drawer and led the way into the hall. "Cook hasn't been down in the cellar again," she said. "Maybe his wife has rumbled what's going on."

"She couldn't have," I said, "the girl is still working there. I saw her this morning."

"Then watch your step," she said and I left her, descending into the cellar pondering the real source of her withdrawal and putting it down to a blistering, and maybe a thump or two, that Beppo had given her for failing to talk me into reverting to the original plan. It didn't bother me at all. The process of disenchantment had already begun although, at that moment, I don't think I had realized this. I was too full of my own conceit.

Beppo had made impressive progress. He had inserted shoring planks at the end of the tunnel and exposed the brick pier down to the level of the first excavation, so that the approach from the shaft was now a right-angled passage about nine feet in length. As a precaution against a cave-in he had roofed the new hole with the sides of a packing case and part of an iron bedstead. It was a professional-looking job and when I took his stair rod and probed the roof alongside the last brick of the pier the echo was hollow, indicating that no more than a few inches separated us from the washroom floor. I asked him how long it would take him to cut through and he said a few hours, perhaps less. "I won't touch her until the place is closed on Saturday," he said, "no point in weakening it until we have to." I agreed with this, saying that the estimated point of breakout was clear of the lavatory and the washbasin and no one was likely to go stamping along that side of the room.

"How about pipes?" he asked.

"They all run back to the branch sewer," I said, "you'll miss the nearest by five to six feet."

His manner, although more affable, was as enigmatic as his sister's. Again I waited for some direct reference to my ultimatum and again I was disappointed. I think I had expected one or both of them to make a final appeal to me and when they didn't but seemed ready to accept what couldn't be altered, it occurred to me that it was courting trouble to revive the issue. So I said nothing more and returned across the cellar and up the steps to their room.

She wasn't there and the fact that she wasn't gave me a few moments to weigh the situation. I tried to look at it from all three angles, hers, his and most of all, from mine. There was no doubt in my mind but that I would go, and I was equally resolved not to travel farther than Chester with him, but while I felt equal to standing up to Beppo I was still undecided how much influence he would exert over her if it came to a showdown between the three of us. It also struck me forcibly that none of us could afford to quarrel at this late stage and that if we did we were all in jeopardy. What I lacked, what I had to have in one way or another, was a more accurate estimate of their relationship and how they severally regarded me. She had made it fairly clear to me up on the Craigwen ridge that she was of the opinion their flight would be accomplished more safely without me, but did this opinion stem from misgivings of her own or fear of him? I was certain she preferred my company to his but not, perhaps, at the cost of additional risk represented by having a greenhorn in tow. Or was I wrong about this and all she really wanted was to get the hell out of there unencumbered by either of us?

It was a warmish night and the room was stuffy. I crossed to the window with the idea of lowering the top sash and getting some air and it was then, as I reached up to the frame, that I had an idea.

The catch of the window was rusted in. I remembered I had been unable to move it when I tried to lock the window on an occasion. They usually kept both sashes closed and they were closed now, with the heavy curtain pulled across. I went behind the curtain, lowered the top frame a bare inch and came out again, carefully replacing the curtain. They were unlikely to notice the gap even when they pulled the curtain back in the morning, and if they did they would be unlikely to remember whether the window had been open or shut. If I excused myself and left early I could creep back after an interval and, with any kind of luck, position myself under the window and overhear any conversation they exchanged when Beppo came up from the cellar for his usual drink. That, I reckoned, would be inside the hour. I made up my mind on the spot and went out to the foot of the stairs, calling up to her that I was dog-tired, had had a heavy day at the bank, and was going home to bed.

She came to the head of the stairs in the same jazzy kimono and seemed more than a little disconcerted by my abrupt decision to leave. "You could wait on a bit, Charlee," she said, "there's a lot to discuss."

"We've got another ten days to discuss technicalities," I said, "and the other subject is closed so far as I'm concerned. I'll look in about the same time tomorrow," and I yawned.

"Okay," she said, doubtfully, "but be sure you do."

I went out of there thinking I had handled that neatly. I wasn't much further on but then, neither were they.

2

I decided to give them forty-five minutes, long enough for him to come up and dust himself off but not long enough to separate and go to bed. She was already half undressed but I was absolutely sure they were to confer within the hour.

It was an ideal night for eavesdropping. The yard, cut off by the high wall from the half-power rays of the lamp in the alley, was dark as a bag. The only point of light about there was Delphine's window, where the curtains did not quite meet and a narrow beam traveled across the scullery roof to the raintub where it flattened itself on Cook's party wall. I let myself out, turned right toward the station and took the left hand fork to the seafront. It was coming up to midnight then and the esplanade was deserted.

I went along to the first shelter and sat there smoking and listening to the suck of the waves round the piles of the pier. I didn't feel smug anymore, but I didn't feel depressed. Just poised and reasonably confident that the next hour would give me a much clearer peep into the future and help me to readjust and settle down for the final stage of the adventure. After a second cigarette I ambled back, keeping a sharp lookout for Gwyn or one of his colleagues. There was mild activity at the station, where goods traffic was moving, but apart from that Penmadoc had gone to bed.

The first sensation I had on reentering the yard was one of keen disappointment. There was no glow behind the living room window and this meant that she hadn't come down and he was either in bed or still working on the tunnel. I thought I had left it too late but then I noticed that her bedroom light was still burning, and that the lower half of the window had been pushed up, because the curtains fluttered softly in the night breeze and the beam that ran down across the scullery roof to the garden wall was twice as broad as it had been less than an hour ago, indicating that the curtain chink had been enlarged.

I stood there by the bonnet of their van wondering what to do and then I heard the rumble of his voice, and after that her voice, replying in odd monosyllables. He had clearly looked in on his way to bed and if I was to learn anything to my advantage I would now have to eavesdrop under the bedroom window.

This wasn't easy to accomplish but it wasn't impossible so long as I moved carefully and faced up to the risks of exposing myself not only to him but to the Cook family next door. I went behind the raintub, felt cautiously for a foothold in the crumbling brickwork and hoisted myself onto the four-foot dividing wall. From here, steadying myself by the scullery guttering, I crept slowly and very cautiously along to where the wall went up in two steps to a height of about seven feet. When I placed my palms against the wall of the café I was only an inch or so below her windowsill and I could not only hear but see if I stood upright. I caught the tail end of a sentence he uttered, just the four words ". . . play it real cool," and she replied, casually, "Sure, unless he brings it up again."

This exchange, brief as it was, was enough to assure me of one thing. She was in partnership with him not me and from her tone I judged she wasn't stalling and playing a game of her own. Then she said, "To hell with taking a shower, honey, it's too damn late. I've been stuck here long enough. I thought you'd never show."

It was the impatience in her voice that made me forget everything, including caution. I just had to take a quick peep and see what was going on and I seized the edge of the sill and drew myself up to my full height. From here I could see about half of the room, but that half included the bed. I was so unprepared for what I saw that I came close to losing my balance, and clung there with my face against the brickwork. Then I looked again to make sure I wasn't dreaming.

She was sitting on but not in the rumpled bed, with her legs coiled under her and her back resting on an upended pillow. She had been wearing a nightdress but had half shrugged herself out of it so that she was naked from the waist. He was sprawled on his back with his head resting on her breasts and the only thing he was wearing was an undersized jockstrap.

It didn't need more than a second glance to absorb the situation. She was looking down at him with a kind of amused tenderness and her hand, thrown over his broad shoulder, was engaged in teasing the mass of dark hair that covered his chest. The first thing that registered, even before the realization that I was looking in on an incestuous relationship, was the almost perfect symmetry of his body, apparent even in that negligent pose. I had thought of him, until then, as a well-knit, muscular man, with flashy good looks if you liked the Dago type, but clothes did nothing for him and without them he looked like an athlete at the peak of training. He knew it too, that was evident in the smile that was playing about his lips and the arrogant sprawl of his limbs.

Luckily for me I now had a secure footing on the flat-topped wall. Had I been more precariously perched I should have slipped and crashed down into Cook's garden. I felt sick and perspiration struck cold under my arms. Then things began to happen. He said, lazily, "I'll go take that bath," and she, indulgently, "Forget it, you're not going anyplace, honey."

I took a grip on myself. Behind the shock that had me gasping and shuddering I could still estimate the tremendous importance of gleaning every last word of their conversation against the future, so I clung there like a fly on a wall, arms outstretched, fingers gripping both edges of the narrow sill.

Inside they began to romp and when I looked again he was struggling, halfheartedly, to escape from her embrace. He was chortling then but she wasn't, she looked like some predatory animal with a meal at stake and suddenly the banter went out of her voice.

"So you come in here and start what you can't finish! Take that goddam thing off!" and she lunged forward and grabbed at him but he half-rolled from the bed and she fell forward on her face, the discarded nightdress slipping to her knees. He said, between chuckles, "Take it easy, honey, that window's open," and as I ducked down again he made a move toward it but mercifully she caught him and I heard the sounds of a tussle and then a slap. I don't know which of them was on the receiving end but in their mood it was a bonus either way.

By now I was desperately concerned with getting clear and pushed myself off the wall, making a successful grab at the guttering. From here a quick scramble got me into the belt of shadow cast by the scullery roof, but I heard one or two more half-finished sentences, among them a pseudo protest beginning, "I'm no superman . . . ." and her quick comeback, "You figure you are . . . ." It was more than enough to speed me blindly down the length of the wall and over the raintub into the yard. Then the window closed with a soft thump and there was silence. I didn't have to ask myself who had won the contest, if it was a contest.

I don't remember letting myself out of the yard and have only the vaguest recollection of crossing the main road and passing St. Ninian's on my way up Craigwen Terrace. It was not until I barked my shin on the first of the workmen's obstructions at the top of the slope that I realized what had driven me there. I stumbled across to the seat we had occupied a few nights before and slumped down on it. I was as winded as a man who had just run a mile from a man-eating tiger, and about as distraught. I sat there with my head bowed between my knees repeating a single phrase over and over again, "Filthy bitch, filthy bitch, filthy bitch!" I said it like an incantation and somehow it helped me find my way back to an identity. It wasn't an identity I recognized. It had nothing at all in common with Charlie Pritchard the pen pusher, and very little with the debonair Charlie Pritchard who had recently come to terms with himself as a big shot and a Don Juan. It was a dry, brittle husk of a man, sensitive to the slightest touch outside but inside, where the kernel was, as hard as a bolthead.

Slowly, and with infinite deliberation, I went about the business of skinning myself until I could look right in on what was left. It astonished me to find that there was anything worth salvaging except a single crystal of implacability capable, perhaps, of resisting the fearful pressures to which it had been subjected by a woman who must have long since satisfied herself it did not exist. But it did. It was still there, half hidden in the rubble of dreams and conceits that had been accumulating at such a pace over the last sixteen months, ever since the night I bought my first coffee in The Rainbow and started the jag that had landed me right here, on a park seat in the middle of the night, and the certainty that it was there rallied me. I found I could look beyond the spectacle of Delphine slobbering after her stepbrother's phallus, and survey my own immediate prospects as someone so closely involved with each of them that escape was impossible.

I could see that at a glance. People who could behave like that while maintaining such a charade over so long a period would think no more of shopping a disloyal associate than swatting a fly in their café. Either I went along with them or I gave myself up and took my chances alongside them in the dock, and I dismissed this alternative at once because I saw it as yet another feather in her cap. Somehow I had to go through with it, right up to the moment of lifting that money and getting clear away with it, or half of it. That, I think, was my first real handhold to sanity, the claim to a half instead of a third. My advantage, as I saw it, lay in the fact that I knew the score and could keep the knowledge secret until the last possible moment. Then, in one way or another, she was going to repay all she had exacted from me to keep her gigolo happy all this time. For, even then, with the shock of that window peep still regulating the pace of my heartbeats, I was able to draw a tight circle of hate around her and leave him on the outside. I had no special feelings about him anymore. His absurd posturing and prancing at the foot of the bed had reduced his stature to that of an oaf, manipulated by her as surely as I had been, although he didn't know it and would probably never know it so long as she lusted after him. And as I thought this I began to feel confidence and courage seeping into me for I saw that, in a sense, the odds were now reduced from two to one to evens. Me against her and no holds barred. I remembered, with an added satisfaction, two

phrases I had heard when I had supposed them to be engaged in a laconic discussion of my refusal to change the
plan, his "play it real cool" and her "Sure, unless he brings it
up again." For this must mean that neither of them had yet
hit upon any practical plan for shaking me off and clearly my
line was to keep them guessing, right up to five minutes past
zero hour, and longer if it could be managed. They couldn't
do a damned thing about robbing that bank without me beside them every step of the way. Violence wouldn't help them
and I was armored against any resumption of the tactics she
had employed so successfully in the long zig-zag beginning
with her first shop-window display when she wriggled through
the cellar grating the first occasion we were down there together. But she wouldn't know this, and he would go on
relying on her and that left me holding not one trump but
two. Evan's key and the certainty that most men, knowing her
as I knew her, would prefer to bed down with an old whore.
I thought once more of her expression as she squirmed the
length of that bed and then I slammed the door on it, deciding that somehow, somewhere, she would squirm again
but for a different reason.

The luminous dial on my cheap wristwatch said it was ten
past two. I got up, stiffly, and walked down the steep slope
of the terrace.

3

The sureness and certainty with which I got hold of myself
during the next few days surprises me even at this distance. I turned my back on the cloud of shame, disgust and
humiliation like a man dragging himself out of a marsh and
when I touched the hard ground of self-interest I could look
not only at the immediate past but at the present, and with
a detachment that isolated me from everybody. It was as
though I was in the foyer of a busy hotel, watching the com-
ings and goings of staff and clientele. The clientele interested
me in a way they had never done over the seventeen months

I had spent getting to know their faces and characteristics. I was interested for the first time, in my career as a bank clerk, in the deposits they passed over the counter, for these now had relevance. At least some of those crumpled notes were likely to find their way into my pocket, and because Griffiths was on holiday, and I was often called upon to help out at the counter, I had a chance to guess what some of them would be likely to pay in between three P.M. Friday and twelve noon on Saturday, the peak period of the week for making deposits.

But watching the staff was even more absorbing. For the first time since I had joined it the tension had eased. Partly it was due to us being kept busy with a key man, Griffiths, away on holiday, and also because Porsen had been very subdued since learning that he was to get his marching orders in the near future. Then again, Powell had lost a good deal of his bossy arrogance. He and Evan still circled one another like a couple of gladiators but anyone who had watched them as I had over the past few months could detect that the ascendancy had passed to the manager. Perhaps he had lodged a formal complaint at headquarters, something he should have done a long time ago, and this had led to Powell being carpeted. Or perhaps Powell, buttressed by his wife's private income, was mounting a counterattack of some sort. I don't know and I never did find out.

One thing I was glad about. Griffiths, the only one of them who had shown me disinterested consideration, was unlikely to be involved to the extent he might have been. Prior to taking his fortnight's holiday he had been given a period of short time in order to nurse his sick mother, and there was a rumor of him resigning to join a relative's firm of solicitors at Llandudno. In a way this let him out for, apart from handling the safe key, as we all did from time to time, and taking Powell's place as grille janitor for that one spell when the cashier had been on holiday, he had no direct access to either key any more than Porsen or me. Porsen, however, stood badly with Evan and that wasn't going to help him when they accused him of carelessness, as they must accuse each and every one of them concerning their dealings with the missing Charlie Pritchard. Not that I lost sleep over any of them, Evan included. They were already receding figures in a crowd scene of a film.

I slipped into The Rainbow once that week but it was a business call. I collected the dummy key Beppo had rubbed down and aged by a two-day immersion in stewed tea, and he had made a good job of it. I thought it would probably fool Evan into believing he still had the original on his chain.

Before I left Delphine, arranging to call at about 11:20 P.M. on Saturday night, I reminded her to get the van serviced and its tank filled. I didn't want any last minute engine failure to delay our departure for Chester. It amazed me that I could outface them so calmly after what I had seen through that bedroom window, but it was all part of the protective shell I had grown now that I realized how things stood. I could give my undivided attention to anything that would help to convert an imponderable into a certainty. I might be an amateur but I was acquiring a professional touch.

Even on Saturday morning there was no way of estimating the amount of money that was likely to find its way to the safe for the weekend. We gathered in about ten times as much as we paid out, for nearly all our customers were trades-men or boarding-house proprietors, and even those who were not self-employed rarely drew out much money until October, when most of them took their holiday. The bank float, con-sisting mostly of new notes in unbroken bands, wasn't touched until Friday morning and then only a thousand or so was brought up for the tin-plate wage clerk. I estimated there was at least another three thousand five hundred in the float cash box on the lowest shelf of the safe. About a third of this would be in fivers and Beppo and I had already agreed not to touch them. It was a different matter with the odd fivers among the deposits. They were virtually untraceable but there wouldn't be all that number. Penmadoc was wary of high denomination notes.

By twelve-thirty everything was carried down and locked

away and I went up Station Road hands in pockets and whistling. I needed a drink but I wasn't going to have one, not even the odd half-pint. I wanted all my wits about me for the next twelve hours and had made up my mind in advance not to touch a drop until I was safely aboard the Irish Mail in the early hours of Sunday morning. Then, I told myself, I might buy a double brandy with Caddie's small change.

After lunch I went up to my room and packed my kit in the small grip. I left some of my things in the chest of drawers. A new life demanded new clothes. I came across a snap of Ida taken during one of our charabanc jaunts and wondered about her briefly. No word had reached me since our last exchange of letters. She had clearly taken the huff or, if she had not, had postponed her return until September. I slipped the snap into my wallet. It was all I would have to remember her by and I recalled her broad, freckled face with affection. After all, it was in this narrow room, still haunted by the ghosts of Wally the consumptive, and Mr. Waring the pickle traveler, that she had encouraged me to take the first positive step toward regeneration or degeneration according to how you regarded it.

It was a fine afternoon with a clear sky and a breeze ruffling the bay. There was nothing to do between now and round about ten, when Evan and Gladys went to bed, so I changed into slacks and sweater and went out and up Craigwen Terrace to the old estate, pushing through the rhododendron thickets until I came out on a shelf of tableland that overlooked the town from the southwest. It was high and windy up here. The pier looked about two inches long and the afternoon sun caught the underside of the Byzantine dome of the pavilion. I stood there looking down on the place a long time, thinking of all the people who would live out their lives in the granite semicircle that cluttered the rim of the bay and I didn't regret a thing, not even her atrocious perfidy. She was going to pay for that anyway and this I was already regarding as part of the prize money. I thought about Penmadoc as a community. There was a majority, resigned to drifting along a mainstream propelled by habit, and there was the rogue elephant who made an occasional stir by charting a course of his own. Such an opportunity had come my way and I had first taken and then rejected it. But Beppo's greed or her obsession with him had given me a second chance and now I was almost grateful to them. I turned my back on the town and walked inland in the direction of the mountains. I felt calm and free and as foreign to the few people I met as an Afghan brigand on his way to an ambush.

I had tea at a farm and began to wander back about six o'clock. By eight-thirty I was in my room again and this time I checked on the four sleeping tablets, taking them out and fragmenting them until they were small enough to hammer into powder. When this was done, and the grains were as small as pinheads, I divided the little heap into five parts, putting three parts on one sheet of paper and the remainder on another. The smaller dose was for Gladys, the heavier sleeper of the two, and my guess was that it would keep her quiet for fifteen hours. Then I found an envelope and cut both corners of it, making two triangular sachets into which I poured the powder, exercising the greatest care not to lose a grain in the process. After that I folded the unsealed edges of the sachets in a way that would keep the contents from spilling out and placed them in the open flap of my wallet. Then I went out onto the landing and listened.

The rumble of the nine o'clock news bulletin reached me from the kitchen so I went down the first flight to the landing and opened the door of Evan's bedroom. The hinges squeaked a little but I was prepared for this and took out an oil-squirt from a bicycle kit I had bought earlier in the week. I oiled both hinges and then the cradle of the doorcatch, working the knob and moving the door gently to and fro until it could be opened quite soundlessly if gradual pressure was exerted. I was back in my room again when Evan came out of the kitchen and called up to say it was cocoa time.

Here was the first real imponderable, how to empty the sachets into their cocoa mugs. I had two alternative plans, one taking preference over the other. It would be an obvious advantage to dose them individually but if this was impossible I was ready to fall back on the reserve plan and tip both sachets into the jug after I had helped myself. Luckily the tail end of the BBC news was still engaging their attention, and even more luckily Gladys had already placed their mugs and my cup on the draining board midway between the sink and the gas stove. I went across and glanced into jug and mugs. Gladys might have been a confederate. Not only was the cocoa made, and waiting to be poured out, but sugar had been placed in both their mugs. I said, "I'll pour it," lifted the jug and poured my own, at the same time slipping my left hand into my jacket pocket and groping under the flap of the wallet for the sachets.

I couldn't have picked a better night. Immediately after the news the announcer interviewed Amy Johnson, recently back from her epic solo flight to Australia. She had arrived by boat about a fortnight before and there had been a great deal about her in the papers. Evan and Gladys took an almost personal pride in her achievement and I thought this odd in view of their attitude to Ida's escapade. After all, Ida had only left home to take a job in a pickle factory, but here they were hanging on every word uttered by a girl who, so the papers hinted, had been the despair of her friends and family for years. I was glad of Amy's company at that moment, however, and without turning emptied the heavy dose into Evan's mug and the lighter one into Gladys's. I even had leisure to give the mugs a stir before passing them over. Man and wife sipped contentedly until Amy had had her say and a program of light music began. I watched them narrowly. Evan drained his mug, smacked his lips and turned off the set. He could never listen to a note of jazz without a grimace or a wry comment on the debased musical taste of the younger generation.

I set out to be pleasant and conversational, telling them where I had been that afternoon but keeping an eye cocked for their first yawns. They were not long in coming. First Gladys, and then Evan began to droop and each had difficulty following my detailed description of where I had had tea. Their eyes began to glaze and once Gladys almost dropped off but came to with a jerk and said she was more than ready for bed. Evan said, in the middle of a yammering yawn, "By George, me too! That dig in the garden must have taken it out of me. Are you staying up, Charlie?" I said no, I was tired after tramping eight miles that afternoon so we locked the back door, turned out the lights and all trooped up together. As I was tackling the second flight I heard one of them stumble. The tablets seemed to be taking effect earlier than I had anticipated. It was still only five minutes to ten.

I stretched myself out on my bed to wait until I judged it safe to creep down and listen outside their door for snores. I was prepared to give them the better part of an hour but the walk had tired me more than I realized and the next thing I remember was leaping up with my heart pounding like a steam hammer as I lunged for the light switch and looked at my watch. It was so quiet that I judged it to be the middle of the night and when I saw that it was only seven minutes past eleven I almost shouted with relief. I sloshed my face with cold water and opened my door. There was no cause for alarm. I could hear Gladys's snore from where I stood and when I crept down, to find they had not even latched their door in their haste to get into bed, I could hear Evan's tenor accompanying her alto. Here I paused to slip on a pair of worn kid gloves, something I had decided to use when I first made my plan about the sleeping tablets.

In all the detective fiction I had read, gloves were obligatory.

I had a bad moment just before I reached out to push the door open. This was it; in a couple of minutes from now there would be no going back. If anything went wrong while I was fumbling for that key no amount of explanation would open a way of retreat. Short of throwing myself on Evan's mercy (a bleak enough prospect), there would be no alternative to using main force and tying them down in bed. I realized, of course, that I could never steel myself to use violence on either of them, even if it meant me or them, but the moment of panic soon passed and exerting the minimum pressure on the door so that it opened wide enough to enable me to enter on hands and knees, I crawled into the shaft of light thrown across the floor by the landing bulb.

At this range the quavering snorts of Gladys were so emphatic that I wanted to giggle. He was putting up a better-than-average performance, but it was like a piccolo trying to compete with a French horn and the stark incongruity of our relative situations, they flat on their backs, me inching across the floor, struck me as farce rather than drama.

I took my time, advancing with one hand outstretched toward the wall cavity and I found it first time, my sleeve brushing his boots that had been placed side by side under the bedside table. I waited for a particularly resonant snort from Gladys before opening the shutter and letting my hand close over the bunch of assorted keys. Then I backed slowly across the floor to the sliver of light marking the door. Seconds later I was comparing the dummy key with the original on the key ring. My guesswork, Beppo's knowledge of keys, or both, had served us well. Judged on weight and approximate outline they might have been twins. Only if you looked at the detail of the indentations could you distinguish the genuine from the spurious.

It occupied me about a minute to switch them and then I was back listening at the door again. The unequal duet continued and this time I went in without hesitation, replacing the keys in the niche, closing the shutter and backing out again in about half the time it had taken me on the first occasion. On the way I stood up and softly closed the door. I knew it would worry him if he found it open and might even cause him to take a close look at his key ring.

I went up to my room, got my bag, hat and raincoat and took a last look round. It was a curious moment, half exhilarating and half nostalgic, but even then the ghosts of the former occupants, neither of whom I had ever seen, came forward to say their final lines. Mr. Waring said, "My God, you've done it now, Charlie. You've really done it now, Boyo!" but Wally, as a professed communist, was more encouraging.

He said, "Good luck, Charlie! Up the workers!" I closed the door on them and went down and out into the night. The breeze, blowing in from the sea, told me that I was sweating like a pig. It was as though someone had clapped one ice-pack on my forehead and another under each arm.

Chapter Fourteen

1

There had been no hitch, not even a minor one. What I had anticipated would be my most difficult and dangerous assignment had just been completed with the dispatch of a trained pickpocket. Evan and Gladys had snored on while I pocketed the key. And with them, as yet unaware of Charlie Pritchard's fantastic achievements, were all the other victims of my long-term planning and split-second decisions. The sarcastic-tongued Powell, the sneering, fat-arsed Porsen, the sandy-haired director who had drawn attention to my fingernails and was now approaching the shock of his privileged career. But there was more to it than that. Beppo and Delphine, both preening themselves on their adroit handling of Charlie Pritchard, were still on the defensive, looking this way and that for a way to ditch him and I knew that he wasn't going to be ditched. They were stuck with him for as long as he needed them. No wonder I felt equal to bluffing a more astute policeman than Gwyn-the-Boots if he interposed between me and that money in the time left to him.

For all that, caution did not desert me. I walked in the shadows as far as the head of the alley and when I saw a late wayfarer approaching I was careful to cross the road at a tangent and regain the south side opposite W. H. Smith's.

Delphine answered my signal with a speed that suggested she had been waiting with her hand on the scullery latch. She was wearing, most improbably, the same old kimono and I saw at once that she did not share my serenity. She looked almost haggard, as though the strain of waiting since closing time had been more than she could bear. I wondered if they had been arguing over what course to take or whether there was another, simpler reason for her tension. Maybe, obsessed with the job, he hadn't had time to slake her lust in the last twenty-four hours. When she spoke her voice, ordinarily so level, sounded clipped and brittle.

"Did you get it?"

"Of course I got it."

"My God, you've been time enough!"

I was indignant at this and snapped, "Take hold of yourself! It's only half-eleven."

The retort steadied her a little and she moved aside to let me cross the threshold, but halfway over I had a thought.

"I'll dump my grip in the van," I said and turned, but she shot out her hand and tore the grip from my grasp. "I'll do that, Charlee! Let me do it!" She shouldered her way past, ran to the van, threw open the door and tossed the bag inside. I noticed then that the vehicle, usually driven in, had been reversed so that its bonnet was within a yard of the gate. This was Beppo's preparation for a smooth getaway and I approved it, but her manner puzzled me very much. She had acted as though it was vitally important to keep me from crossing the yard and opening the van door.

"Why the hell are you so jittery? Has anything gone wrong?" I asked, as soon as she had returned and she said, briefly, "We have had trouble. Nothing serious and it's straightened out but Beppo was late starting. Cook and that girl of his decided to have fun and games in the cellar."

"When, exactly?"

"About teatime. Beppo was trapped down there."

"They didn't suspect anything?"

"No, they were too preoccupied, thank God, but it rattled Beppo and I haven't got over it yet."

"How long were they down there?"

"The better part of an hour."

The news didn't disturb me overmuch. After all, I had my own moment of panic outside Evan's door but had suppressed it without much trouble. "Good old Cook," I said, "this side of the street is really showing the rebel flag tonight."

She said nothing to this but led the way into the living room. I was surprised to see the remains of a fire in the grate and some charred fragments of papers they had been burning. The room itself looked as if it had been ransacked.

"What the hell has been going on in here?" I asked.

"We've been getting rid of things. There's no sense in leaving a lot of addresses and papers for the police to work on, is there?"

"You left that a bit late, didn't you?"

She flared up again, as temperamental as a prima donna. "For Christ's sake, Charlie! Stop sounding so bloody superior!"

I had never heard her swear like that before and it didn't suit her. I took the soft line. "Look, I daresay Cook's appearance down there gave you both a jolt but he isn't likely to repeat it. The girl is home in bed by now, and even if she wasn't, Cook couldn't manage two sessions that close together. Take it easy. Get yourself a drink."

She calmed a little but it required a visible effort. "Sorry," she said, and then, "I'll be all right once we start operating. It's all this hanging about. Beppo will show soon as he's through. He said he needed another hour but that was more than half-an-hour ago."

"Shall I go down and give him a hand?"

"No, there's only space for one to work and he isn't carting the trash away, just emptying it in the shaft. He said to tell you to stay here. Fix yourself a drink."

"No thanks," I said, "no drink for me until we get on that train."

She seemed to hesitate a moment, then she said, "Well, I guess I'll finish packing and get dressed. You wait here for Beppo," but instead of going to the door she sauntered past me to the bureau where I now saw the buff file marked "Personal" lying on the open flap. She gathered it up, turned swiftly, and skipped into the passage.

I don't know what it was about this movement that made me curious unless it was the way she worked at being casual and hugged that file to her breast. Both actions were at one with her eagerness to forestall me in stowing that bag in the van. I called, "I hope Beppo isn't as jittery as you are," and she said, over her shoulder, "Beppo's had more practice than me." Then she was gone and I heard her mules slip-slopping up the stairs.

I wasn't going to drink but I hadn't forsworn cigarettes so I went over to the fireplace, took out a packet of Player's, and stuck one in my mouth. I felt for a match and found that the box was empty except for a split stem. When this broke in my hand I went down on one knee and picked up a half-burned envelope to make a spill. I stuck it into the almost extinct fire, lit it, and then blew it out again, noticing some heavy black print on the flap that was scorched but still legible. The envelope was from HM Passport Office and when I straightened it out I could read the address and postmark. It was dated the twenty-eighth of August, the day before yesterday, and addressed to Mr. & Mrs. Giuseppe Beppolini, The Rainbow Café, Station Road, Penmadoc, N. Wales.

I sat down in the armchair and studied it for maybe a minute. At first it didn't arouse anything more than curiosity. I knew that Beppo's Christian name was Giuseppe, and that the name by which all The Rainbow customers knew him was a diminutive of their common surname. What caught and held my attention was the "Mrs." and after that, the date. As far as I knew Beppo wasn't married, and even if he was his wife certainly wasn't living in Penmadoc the day before yesterday. The envelope was substantially made. It had obviously contained a stiff-covered document and I could even read the words "Do not bend" where the flame had licked across the surface without consuming the join. Mr. Giuseppe Beppolini. *Mrs.* Giuseppe Beppolini. A joint passport? The kind of document married couples showed at customs barriers all over the world? *Man and wife!* It hit me between the eyes like a heavyweight's punch. For a couple of minutes I saw, not stars exactly, but a whole galaxy of factors and circumstances, winks and nods and nudges that lit up the path I had been following all these weeks, and I think the impact was even greater than that of watching them chase one another round the bedroom in the nude. I had thought of myself as being proof against further shocks and further disillusionment but I wasn't. The near-certainty that they were not stepbrother and stepsister, that they were not engaged in incest, and that the scene I had witnessed was really no more than a bit of horseplay between an over-sexed woman and a swaggering oaf should have moderated my disgust for them, but it did nothing of the kind. In a way it had the opposite effect because I now saw them not singly, a woman driven by some urge to debase every man she coveted and just another of her victims, but as a calculating team, a pair of slick commercial partners who had sat down in cold blood and conspired to use me for personal profit and no other motive at all. And this discredited them beyond the point reached when I had watched them from Cook's wall, two people with a common father gloating over one another's bodies. In the eyes of everyone else my latest discovery made them relatively respectable but in my eyes it made each of them far more dangerous.

It flashed across my mind then that this deceit had been practiced on Penmadoc as a whole for purely commercial motives. Once it got around that the Rainbow Queen was the wife of the stage heavy behind the bar the business in that place would be halved, for there was hardly a customer in town who, in his secret heart, did not dream about making Delphine and was not drawn into that noisy, sweaty room by the magnet of sexual fantasy. She knew that and he knew it, and all this time they had traded on it. Then I made yet another of my conscious efforts to stop moralizing and concentrate on the purely practical aspects of the tangle my life had become under their joint chaperonage. They were still far from certain of the course they meant to pursue. Everything that had happened so far proclaimed that.

There was that jumpiness of hers, revealed not only in her voice and expression but in her eagerness to stop me approaching the van. And this was linked to the way in which she had hung about until she could get her hands on that file, after which she couldn't get out of the room quickly enough.

There was the impression she left behind that, whereas the key was welcome, I was a terrible pain in the neck and they hadn't the least idea how they were going to shake me off without blocking their own escape route. I even had a curious conviction that, if I had handed over the key there and then, I could have got the hell out of there without stopping to say goodbye. And this set me thinking of the pressure, re-strained but very calculated, she had put upon me, allegedly at Beppo's insistence, to revert to the original plan and stay behind, maybe to help cover their tracks. She had done her best to persuade me to do that and the more I thought about it the more certain I was that here was a series of conspira-cies within a conspiracy. There was her black eye but anyone could fix a black eye. Self-inflicted black eyes were pennies when you were playing for thousands of pounds with a ten-year stretch in the offing. Other pieces fell into place to form a pattern. There was her apparently reluctant admission that Beppo had set her to work on me in the first instance, the Manchester trip to boost my flagging morale, the letter indi-cating that I had better resume partnership or else. There was their seemingly passive acceptance of my new terms—they would agree to anything at that stage to keep me in line—her pep talk at the gate, and later that burst of laughter I had overheard and her shifty attempts to explain it away, and all those questions she had plied me with up at the Craigwen estate ten days ago. Every act and every word on his part and hers began to assume a new and sinister signifi-cance and they all added up to the same thing. Keep Charlie on the ball. Keep him interested. Nourish his nerve. Feed him with promises and pledges and, when nothing else worked, with the only kind of bait that sends his brains to sleep so long as he clocks in. She had done just that and sometimes, judged on her impromptu performance with him, it must have seemed hard and distasteful work.

Mulling it over, the charred envelope still in my hand, cold, deadly fury took charge of me and it was rage, I think, that held panic in check. I can only suppose, looking back, that I had been under so great a strain over such a long period that

I had acquired the knack of absorbing any kind of shock. Charlie Pritchard, who had arrived in Penmadoc seventeen months ago without any emotional reserves of any kind had, under stress, built up an invisible reserve that was capable of facing facts whatever they were. But before I could adjust to this entirely new situation I had to know, beyond a shadow of doubt, that I was not third man to a brother and sister team but fall guy to man and wife. To Mr. and Mrs. Giuseppe Beppolini, no less. Beppo, the ex-con and Mrs. Beppo, alias Lickerish Lil the Wanton Wop. Strategically, perhaps, it didn't matter all that much but I had to know precisely what I was up against and I thought I could see a way to find out in the few minutes left to me. In fact, I thought I could see two ways and, given time and opportunity, I would explore both. After that I could improvise as I went along. I had two strong suits. One was the key and the other was the knowledge supplied by a discarded envelope. They were smart but they could have been smarter. They could have kept up the act a little longer, until they had possession of the key. And they could have exercised that much more care in feeding the fire.

I went out into the passage and listened at the cellar door. Everything was quiet down there and so it was at the foot of the stairs. They had not had a chance to compare notes and I didn't intend giving them one. I shot the bolt of the cellar door and slipped out into the yard through the scullery. Proof of a kind might be inside that van but when I eased open the door, and shone my pocket torch into the interior, there was nothing inside except my grip and one suitcase fastened with a strap.

It was a very bulky suitcase, about twice as large as either of them should have taken along on a trip like this. You couldn't run very far with a suitcase as large as that. It would slow you down all the way from Penmadoc to Puerto Rico and apart from its size it was distinctive.

I didn't think the suitcase could tell me much but I was wrong. When I tested the catches the brass tongues snapped back and I had the strap undone in a moment. It contained nothing but clothes, all neatly folded, her clothes on top, his clothes underneath. I wouldn't have thought he was that much of a gentleman but perhaps she had done the packing. I shut the case, refastened the strap and closed the door of the van with the same great care I had exercised outside Evan's bedroom.

I went back into the house, unfastened the bolt of the cellar door and listened at the foot of the stairs again. I thought she was in the bathroom but I had to be certain. I called up, "Sure you won't have a drink?" and she called urgently from the bathroom, "I'll be down in five minutes. Wait there for Beppo!" What I had in mind wouldn't take long. I slipped off my shoes and went up, testing each stair for creaks.

At that moment she flushed the pan, an old trick of mine I recalled as I tiptoed into her bedroom. I didn't have to stay more than a minute. Her small attaché case lay on the bed, half filled with toilette accessories and a pink nightdress but under the nightdress was the buff file. It had two pockets, one inside each cover. The right side contained a sheaf of papers and a book of traveler's checks but I only glanced at these. In the left flap was the passport. I grabbed it and crept out again, the rush of the cistern refilling itself covering my retreat. Not for the first time I thanked God for the old-fashioned plumbing on our side of Station Road.

I hadn't been gone more than a minute and there was still no sign of Beppo. I flicked through the passport and it confirmed everything I wanted to know. Their photographs, bad ones, were stuck one below the other. His age was given as thirty-seven, hers as twenty-six, and although their places of birth were respectively set down as Bastia and Los Angeles, and their joint profession as restaurateurs, most of the other information they had given me had been as phony as the brother and sister story. They had been living in Britain since 1925, before that in Ostend, and before that Marseilles. Mr. and Mrs. Beppolini were great travelers. Their British citizenship dated from 1928, the year they had arrived in Penmadoc.

It was while I was turning the blank pages that a small envelope fell out, the kind of mini-envelope my father issued to his pupils for church missionary collections at school. This one was stamped with the letters "LMS" but the letters, in this case, did not stand for London Missionary Society. Inside I found two first-class rail tickets from Chester to Greenock. The date stamp showed they had been issued a few days ago.

The tickets interested me more than the passport. Greenock wasn't on my itinerary and it hadn't been on Beppo's. It was a longish way from Holyhead and even farther from Harwich, his proposed port of embarkation. I sat holding them in my hand, asking myself what I knew about Greenock. It was near Glasgow. It was a shipbuilding town and a port. That clicked. Perhaps Mr. and Mrs. Beppolini were more sophisticated than Beppo and Delphine. They liked to travel first class with natty luggage. They liked the long way round and this prompted yet another thought. Perhaps Uncle Berni, until this moment allegedly awaiting us in Queenstown, Eire, had changed from Irish whiskey to Scotch? Perhaps he preferred passengers he could identify to one vouched for by relatives?

Suddenly I had too much proof, more than I knew what to do with, and it took another few minutes for the alternatives to harden. There were, as I saw it, three. I could improvise until they made a move one way or the other. I could confront them when we assembled here in a few minutes' time. Or I could backtrack, walk out across that yard, pay another call on Evan for the purpose of re-switching keys and leave them with nothing to show for our all-round effort but two false keys and a damn great hole in their next-door neighbor's cellar. I still had the ace and it couldn't be taken from me without force and force meant outcry.

It wasn't as difficult a decision to make as it sounds, at least, it didn't seem so at the time. Confrontation had never come easily to me but waiting for something to happen always had. As for backtracking, that amounted to abject surrender and behind that surrender months of uncertainty, wondering what move they might make with access to the washroom, a key that opened the outside grille, and the key to the safe. It wasn't simply that I knew myself incapable of living under that amount of stress. It was more to do with the kind of person I had become since graduating from pen pusher to thief. Trying, and to some degree succeeding, to detach her from the picture and view it objectively I realized that this was the only thing of the slightest importance I had ever attempted, the only occasion in the whole of my life that I had put nerve, brains and personality to the test. If I gave up without a fight I was back where I started, a sixteen-year-old boy arriving his first day at Caddie's in his new suit and falling over himself to change blotting paper and fill inkwells; or a young man of twenty-three staring down on Penmadoc on All Fool's Day and accepting the fact that, from here on, he was a goldfish looking out from the inside of a bowl. It never occurred to me that there might be other, more conventional opportunities of justifying myself in the years ahead. You can indulge in those sort of dreams when you're waiting around for someone to ring a bell for you but not when you have strayed as far off the rails as I had in those last few months. Do that and you get to know your limitations and I knew mine well enough to understand it was now or never for Charlie Pritchard. If I threw in the towel now I would slip back into the slow current that took me down the years to the presentation clock, and that was at best. At worst I would sweat out the rest of my life in fear, but fear without the prospect of a reward. So I went back to my original intention. I would play the hand until every card was on the table. I would stick with them wherever they went, be it Greenock, Gravesend or Guadeloupe. They had been riding on my back a long time now and it was time to change places. Charlie wouldn't stay home quietly after all. He was going places with Mr. and Mrs. Giuseppe Beppolini for as long as it pleased him to travel in convoy.

As I say it was a fairly easy decision to make for Charlie, discounting his retirement pension, had damn all to lose.

2

They arrived almost together, Delphine in a smart blue two-piece that announced she had no intention of scrambling through holes into a bank vault, Beppo in filthy overalls, with brickdust in his hair and the eyes of a man who badly needed a drink. I poured him one and he emptied it down his throat without so much as a greeting. Delphine looked at him and then me. Then, with the air of an uncertain hostess hoping to start a polite conversation, she said, "He's got it, Beppo. Did you cope all right?" He nodded and then he too looked confused so that I wondered if he had surfaced with the expectation of her having gone some way toward getting me up to date. Finally, after another questioning glance at her, he growled, "Let me see that key, Bub," but I said, "Looking at it won't help, Beppo," and when he stood there, holding his empty glass and staring at me with baffled eyes, "It's twenty after midnight. If you're through why the hell don't we go after the safe?"

They looked at one another yet again. I thought he was trying to convey to her that I should be told before we went another step but if this was so she thought otherwise and, having made up her mind, was explicit. "Get on with it," she said suddenly, "we've got about four and a half hours before daylight."

They would, I believe, have given a great deal then to confer in private but there was no way of achieving this. It would have been very different, I thought, if they had known I had their passport and railway tickets in my pocket but it was obvious that she must have closed her attaché case without checking. She was holding it now, together with her raincoat. "We've got to be out of here by one-thirty at the latest," she said, "so that gives you just over the hour."

"It won't take us that long," I said, standing aside for Beppo to lead the way.

From then on it was action all the way. Any doubts he had

about my participation in the raid were shelved, at least temporarily. From here we moved and spoke on terms of equality, neither of us having the least idea how the situation would develop but each independently resolved to give the actual job absolute priority. I have a feeling, and it persists even now, that his intentions were based upon the size of the take but this is no more than a guess. Removed from her he shed a good deal of his menace. He was still truculent and taciturn but in a more guileless and less ponderous way. Perhaps it was the absence of that vacuous grin. He could switch it off when his mind was occupied.

At the foot of the cellar steps he picked up two canvas bags, each the size of a rucksack. He gave me one and we went through their grating with him in the lead. The stink in Cook's cellar had moderated. It might have been due to a current of fresh air from his hole.

I followed him through the enlarged second grating and into the shaft. At the bend he flashed his torch upward and the beam revealed a jagged hole as wide as a man's shoulders immediately right of the exposed pier. The mortar between the bricks had been chipped away but they were still stacked one upon the other to act as a support. The concrete skin of the washroom was slightly thicker than I had predicted, maybe a couple of inches above the hard core.

He laid aside his rucksack and asked me to hold the torch while he rummaged in a recess of the shaft for what looked like a kit bag. He told me to hold it open level with his knees while he loosened a few more chunks of hard core and pieces of concrete that fell into the bag. The hole was now large enough to scramble through and I steadied his legs while he hoisted himself up. I passed up the bags, he gave me a hand and we were inside the washroom. It was a good deal more straightforward than I had anticipated in my most optimistic moments.

There were no windows down here so we could use our torches freely. We could, for that matter, have switched on the light but I warned him against this. Somewhere above us was an air vent and I wasn't sure where it surfaced. Powell and his wife sometimes stayed up until after midnight. I had seen lights in their flat several times when I checked on the Cook windows before entering the yard. For all I knew they could have seen a reflection from one of their rooms at the front.

We moved round to the grille at the foot of the stairs and he took the key from his overall pocket. I shone the beam of the torch on the keyhole and the grille swung open as easily as it did every morning. Then I produced Evan's key and I heard him hiss with satisfaction when that gate opened. We each withdrew our keys and returned them to our respective pockets.

I could sense his excitement and was the more astonished by it because I didn't feel much, just a pulsating glow of the kind that accompanies a stiff drink on an empty stomach, a pleasurable sensation that warmed and enlarged me and gave me a very real sense of achievement. I had the impression that my outward serenity disconcerted him. He didn't know quite what to make of it and neither, for that matter, did I.

He had the safe key out before we had crossed the strong-room but this one gave us a little trouble. It more than half turned and then grated but the check didn't seem to bother him. He withdrew it, tucked his torch under his arm, and took what looked like a square cake of soap from his overall pocket. Then he fiddled for a moment, like a man chafing cold hands, and after that he put whatever he was holding away and reinserted the key, bending forward from the waist and cocking an ear for the tumblers. I had seen crooks do that in any number of films. It looked far more improbable in front of our safe.

Whatever form of lubrication he had applied seemed to work. This time the key turned and when he laid hold of the heavy door it swung outwards so that we could stand back and play our torches onto the shelves. He said, "Take over now, I'll hold the bags," and I gave him my rucksack and went to work at once, beginning with the float tray at the bottom.

The notes were in paper-banded bundles of one hundred and I ladled out fifteen hundred in ones and fourteen hundred in bulkier bundles of new ten shilling notes. That was a good start, only a hundred short of three thousand. We left the fivers in their heavy clip at the back of the tray. For me at least the temptation was easy to resist.

Then I moved up to the third tray, bypassing the documents section and the vertical space alongside where the silver sacks were stored. Here were the three tin boxes I handled almost every day and the money in them represented the Thursday-to-Saturday deposits of regular customers. The notes were girdled by rubber bands, sometimes in fifties and sometimes in blocks of two hundred but, for the most part, in hundred-pound packs. It was impossible to keep an accurate count as I passed them over my shoulder to Beppo but by the time the tins were empty I estimated there was about nineteen thousand in the rucksacks, give or take a thousand or two. There was another tin on the top shelf that I knew contained fivers from an earlier float so I ignored it, but when he wanted proof of this I took it down and opened it. He flashed his torch on the notes and said, glumly, "You sure they keep serials of these? You certain about that?" I wasn't going to start an argument with him down there so all I said was, "We're doing damn well so far, Beppo. Take them along if you like but you might as well put a call through to the police and gripe to them about it." He accepted this as final and handed me the tin. I put it back and closed the safe door, leaving him to hump both bags across the vault and round the buttress to the washroom.

He was breathing hard and it wasn't from the weight he was carrying. He was sweating too and the gleam of moisture on his forehead increased my feeling of superiority over him. I knew then the approximate line I would take as soon as we rejoined Delphine in the café. They could mind the cash and I would take care of the passport and tickets, but he didn't seem in any hurry to get out of that vault. He set the bags down beside the hole and wiped his forehead with his sleeve.

"How much we got?" he asked.

"Upwards of twenty thousand," I said. "There was two

thousand nine hundred in the float and over seventeen thousand in the tins."

He looked surprised. "You mean you can't say exactly?"

"No, I can't. I might work in a bank but mental arithmetic has never been my strong point. I can tell you as soon as we lay it out upstairs."

"Without counting?"

Somehow I hadn't realized he was that stupid. "By counting the bundles," I said, "and for God's sake let's get going."

He didn't make a move even then so I went down through the hole ahead of him and that, as it turned out, was the luckiest move I made that night because it meant I kept ahead of him all the way back to The Rainbow cellar steps. At the hole itself, and at each grating, he handed me the rucksacks before sliding through feet first but he picked them up again as soon as he was standing upright and I made no claim on mine. As long as he had both hands occupied he couldn't put them to any other use and it was no part of my plan to tempt him. Once we were above ground, and within easy screaming distance of the Cook family, the price of physical violence on his part would be prohibitive. I wasn't sure what would happen when we reassembled in the living room. Maybe, with the money in hand, they might continue to stall, hoping to lose me later on. Ideally we could arrive at the Chester barrier before they discovered I had charge of their passport and railway tickets.

In this way, with me three strides ahead of him, we regained the cellar steps. The light switch was at the top and we had turned it off on the way down. I had my foot on the first step when I stopped, my stomach contracting for the first time since I had stood on the threshold of Evan's bedroom. At first I thought my imagination was playing tricks with me but then I realized it wasn't. There was no doubt about it. The honkytonk was playing "Carolina Moon"!

Being far more sturdily built than me, Beppo had a little trouble squeezing through The Rainbow grating where no bricks had been removed, so that I heard the sound before he did. Thinking Delphine must be mad or drunk, I began to run up the stairs and was two-thirds of the way up when the door opened and the cellar light went on to reveal Delphine standing in the opening. Her voice, very level and controlled, came down to me.

"Stay where you are, Charlee! You too, honey!"

I glanced over my shoulder and saw lover-boy standing on the second step. He was holding a bag in each hand and blinking up at the naked bulb. It occurred to me that his slight deafness had prevented him from hearing the honkytonk. From here the music was not anything like as harsh as it was in the café but it was loud enough. I shouted, "For God's sake, turn that bloody thing off! Do you want to rouse the entire bloody neighborhood?"

She looked past me at the still blinking Beppo. "The little bastard is on to us," she said. "He's got our passport and tickets in his pocket."

It had never occurred to me that she would open the attaché case after we had gone downstairs. Trapped below ground, with that damned honkytonk masking any noise of a quarrel or struggle, was no place for a showdown. I said, trying to keep the quaver from my voice, "If you want them you'll have to take them by force. I told you once I didn't give a damn what happened to me if this goes wrong. I'm not staying and I'm not letting you bastards go without me. I haven't got a passport so I'm sticking with you at least as far as the boat. I'll make my own deal with your uncle."

Suddenly her poise deserted her. She came down two steps until she was within touching distance of me.

"You bloody little fool," she screamed, "there *isn't* any uncle and there isn't any boat! We're going by liner, we booked our passage weeks ago!"

I had known for a long time now that I was being double-crossed but not to the point of being thrown aside like a pair of old boots. I just stood there gaping up at her until, hearing his foot scrape, I instinctively swung round and saw that he was no longer holding the bags but a short-barreled gun.

My immediate reaction was not fear so much as amazement.

In all the months of association with them I had never once thought of him owning a gun. Guns belonged in a world of boys' magazines and films, along with men who cruised about in sedan cars and cowboys on horses. Granted we had been playing a bizarre game down here, with our false keys and tunneling and sleeping tablets, but to me at least it was still rooted in reality. It didn't involve shooting people and burying them in cellars.

I turned back to her in a kind of dazed panic and at that moment he fired. He hadn't the slightest intention of hitting me. That first shot, aimed wide, was intended to produce their passport and tickets as the price of my life. I suppose that was how they thought of me, a sniveling little nobody who, quite unpredictably, had got between them and their carefully worked out plan, someone who could easily be scared and fobbed off with a hundred or so and discarded when the time for the shareout arrived.

They had reckoned, however, without the instinct for survival that prompts the most unlikely people to take the daring course. With the boom of that gunshot ringing in my ears I acted in blind panic. Convinced that the next shot would kill me and unable, because she was still blocking my path, to escape from the cellar, I whirled round a third time and jumped straight down on him.

In shooting, or immediately after, he had run halfway up the steps and was now only two stairs below me so that my knees struck him squarely in the chest and we both rolled the length of the stairs with me uppermost and cushioned by his bulk. I didn't really hear the second shot, fired in the act of falling. It registered as a far-off pop, like the backfire of a distant exhaust. I was far too occupied breaking my fall and in this I had more luck than I deserved. My outstretched hand caught and held the iron rail that ran down the outside of the staircase, and in falling my knees drove down on his chest so that I slewed round and rolled sideways, without anything worse than a heavy jolt as my right shoulder struck the terminal knob of the rail. In a flash I was on my feet again and looking down at him. He lay sprawled on his back, his head on one of the rucksacks, his heels resting on the lowest step.

I knew at once that he was dead. I read this not only in his stillness but in the grotesque angle of his head in relation to his shoulders, and the knowledge that my leap had been instrumental in killing him hit me in the pit of the stomach within the instant so that I grabbed for the banister rail, keeled over, and was sick on the spot. The sour smell of vomit mingled with the reek of gunpowder and for what must have been a couple of minutes I hung there, supported by one hand, retching like a landsman in a gale and incapable of doing anything other than empty my stomach. Then, feeling weak and dazed, I hauled myself upright and glanced up the steps. The light bulb was swinging in the draft from the open door and immediately below it was what looked like a bundle of clothes piled on the last two steps before floor level.

It seemed strange to me that she should have fainted. She wasn't the kind of woman one associated with Victorian vapors, especially tonight, when she had been so purposeful after that first show of nervousness when she had admitted me to the premises. I wiped my mouth with my handkerchief and went slowly up the stairs, averting my eyes from the sprawling figure of Beppo. Then, in the combined light of the cellar and the passage bulb, I saw that she hadn't fainted. The passage light, falling directly on her face through the half-open door, revealed a small, bluish hole in the center of her throat just below the Adam's apple and as I stared down at her she twitched and then lay still. She was as dead as Beppo. His second shot, fired inadvertently at the moment of impact, had either struck her directly or, more probably, ricocheted from the arched ceiling and penetrated her throat.

Chapter Fifteen

The body wasn't as repugnant to me as Beppo's. I could look down at it with a kind of wonder, noting the ordinariness of her expression, and the almost casual spread of her limbs as though, on her way down the steps, she had stumbled and fallen but without hurting herself. Her eyes were wide open and in them was just the faintest hint of surprise. Her complexion, always so pale, looked waxen in the light of the unshaded bulb, as though she had been dead for hours. I stooped down and put my hand under her heart but it was no more than a conventional gesture. There was absolutely no doubt in my mind and if I had needed proof I could have found it in the wound. A narrow trickle of blood ran diagonally from throat to collarbone and was already beginning to clot. The bullet must have traveled upwards at an angle of more than fifty degrees and had almost certainly lodged itself in the back of her skull. I was half inclined to turn her over and see whether it had emerged but suddenly I felt sick again and was unable to do it. I stumbled past her and closed the cellar door, making straight for the cupboard in the living room and gulping down several mouthfuls of brandy from the bottle. It made me cough and gasp but it checked the nausea sufficiently for me to cross to the fireplace and stand with my weight resting on my hands spread the full width of the mantelshelf. I remained like that for what seemed to me a long time without any attempt to come to grips with the situation. It had changed too quickly. I wasn't living in the same world anymore. There wasn't a single landmark, apart from the brandy bottle, that I recognized and this was because something odd seemed to have happened to my vision. What little I could see distinctly I saw from a distorted angle. Things that were vertical seemed horizontal, and everything in the room was bathed in a light that pulsated with colors, red, blue, purple and pink. I took off my glasses and attempted to polish them on the end of my tie, but with or without glasses I was unable to adjust to the new dimensions of the room. It seemed to me larger and higher than I remembered and nothing in it obeyed the law of gravity. The furniture, with outlines blurred, hovered above the ground and every piece was washed by the succession of strong colors. Finally, with a deliberate heave, I pushed myself away from the fireplace, groped my way to the window and pulled aside the curtain. The night air, reaching me through a narrow aperture in the top sash, was like balm. I gulped down great mouthfuls of it and gradually my vision began to clear although, to compensate for this, there began a prolonged roaring in my ears that was as stunning as the sound of the Bettws-y-Coed falls that day Ida took me on the charabanc trip.

I stood there not thinking at all of Beppo and Delphine and all that money in the cellar. Neither did I give a thought to my situation, or what it was likely to lead to at any moment. When the knocking began I wasn't really thinking of anything except the pleasure of fresh air entering my lungs and that nonstop roaring in my ears.

I became conscious of the knocking the moment I realized the honkytonk had stopped playing, and the honkytonk was my first handhold back to reality. I couldn't have said when it stopped, or whether it had been jangling away while I stood looking down at Delphine, but suddenly I was aware of stillness outside my own head and then, gentle but insistent, a soft rat-tat-tat from somewhere in the yard outside.

I associated the sound with help. It didn't matter to me who was rapping out there, whether it was a passerby, Gwyn-the-Boots, or a squad of detectives with a Black Maria ready to burst in and whisk me off to police headquarters. Whoever was rapping had to be human, someone who could share with me the knowledge of what lay at the top of the cellar steps and what lay at the bottom. I dragged myself into the scullery and out into the yard where the rapping continued at spaced intervals. I called, "Wait, wait! Don't go away!" and steered a blundering progress round the van until I was facing the door cut in the double gates. The rapping stopped while I fumbled with the catch but my fingers were like a string of wet sausages and it was very difficult to turn the knob that operated the lock. In the end I found my torch and shone it on the catch and then I was able to twist it so that the door opened by pressure from outside. A tall woman in a red mackintosh stood there, the beam of my torch striking her substantial bust. I moved the torch an inch or so and a hand went up to screen her face. It was Ida's.

I wasn't surprised to see her standing there. I don't think I would have been surprised if it had been Evan or Gladys or my father. I had reached a point where nothing was capable of adding to my state of shock. I had just seen a small, familiar room expand into a chamber the size of a cinema, its tables and chairs floating clear of the carpet. I stepped aside to give her access to the yard, watching as she closed the door and placed her back against it. I heard her say, in a low voice, "What *is* it, Charlie? *What's happened?*" but before I could answer she reached out, took my torch, extinguished it and pushed me backward in the general direction of the light that was flooding half the yard from the uncurtained window of the living room.

It wasn't until I was standing in the pool of light that I got my bearings and led the way into the scullery. She was on my heels and when we were inside she shut the door and pushed past me into the passage where she stopped, as though undecided which way to go. I saw her eye fall on the cellar door and my heart gave a leap. I ran past her saying, "Not in there! The other way, *that* way!" and I almost dragged her along the short passage and into the living room where she at once broke free to cross the room and pull the curtains. Then she took a long, steady look at me.

"What's happened, Charlie? Take your time but tell me. You're in trouble, aren't you? You're in bad trouble. I knew you were, even before I got here."

I didn't answer so she looked across at the brandy bottle that stood in the middle of the table. She picked up the tumbler Beppo had used and poured a drink, carrying it over to the sideboard.

"Drink that," she said. "You look as if you've had more than enough but drink it. Nobody knows I'm here and nobody saw me come in."

This did have the power to surprise me. I had seen her as the vanguard of half Penmadoc, headed by the police, the Cook family, and anyone else who had been roused by the honkytonk, the shots, the crash of Beppo rolling backwards down the stairs and the glare of light from the window. I raised the glass to my lips and swallowed.

"Right," she said, seeing the effect the drink was having on me, "start talking and begin with what's in there, behind the door in the passage."

"They are," I said.

"That Italian girl and her brother?"

"He isn't her brother, they're man and wife. They might even be both."

This information, which would have intrigued almost anyone in Penmadoc, produced no effect at all upon her.

"What the hell have they got to do with you? And why are you here in this awful state, at this time of night?"

I had been wondering that myself until the second shot of brandy went to work on me. Ida represented sanity and as long as she remained I was at least in touch with the world outside The Rainbow café. I said, "You won't go away, Ida?"

"No," she said patiently, "I won't go away, Charlie. Just tell me and don't waste any more time about it."

"We broke into the bank."

She looked at me then like a person who hears something or sees something outside the range of their senses.

"*Caddie's* bank? *Our* bank?" and when I nodded, "You mean . . . you and those Eyeties?"

234

"They're dead," I said, "both of them," and because, like a small flame being snuffed out, compassion left her eyes, "*I* didn't kill them! He broke his neck on the stairs when I rushed him and his gun went off hitting her. He was trying to kill me but he killed her instead."

She said, in little above a whisper, "Give me that glass," and I gave it to her and watched her pour almost three fingers. She didn't stop to add soda but drank it down like a toper. It brought a high flush to her cheeks and all her freckles were wiped out.

She said, "You're mad, Charlie. You're *all* mad. You must be. You *have* to be!" and then, as to herself, "I said trouble but I never thought..." She left the sentence unfinished but her lips continued to move as though at any moment she would begin to scream. Finally she regained control of herself, cleared her throat, and stood up. Squaring her shoulders she walked swiftly out into the passage and I heard her open the cellar door. She was back again in less than a minute and this time she did not look at me but shut the door and carefully rechecked the curtains.

"Is the money in those two bags, Charlie?"

"Yes."

"How much?"

It seemed an irrelevant question but I answered it. "I don't know exactly, about twenty thousand, I think."

"How—how the hell did you go about it?"

"We dug a tunnel from Cook's cellar into the bank washroom. I got impressions of two keys and took the other one from Evan's ring."

"You mean, *tonight*? You took Dadda's key *tonight*?"

"Yes."

"But how was that possible? ... The slightest noise ..."

"I gave them both sleeping tablets. I crushed them up and dropped the powder in their cocoa."

"When? *When?*"

"What does it matter when? About ten."

She considered this, and perhaps a number of other factors before saying, "How on earth did you think you could get

away with it? That's what I don't understand—how did you
... I mean ... how could you possibly persuade yourself it
could be done?"

"We did get away with it. It all worked as we planned. But
then I found out they were going off without me and things
began to get out of hand."

"Where were you planning to go? After I mean?"

"Mexico and then America, she said her uncle had a boat.
We were going to Ireland first but ..."

"Shut up a minute. Shut up and let me think."

We stopped talking. The room had returned to its normal
size. Gradually the furniture sorted itself out and settled down
on the floor. The roaring in my ears didn't stop but it receded.

"It's ... it's like a nightmare," she said, finally. "I can't believe it's happening at all. Tell me how—what *happened* exactly, after you'd got the money?"

I told her in detail. That part of it was becoming clearer
every moment. She didn't take her eyes off me all the time I
was talking and when I had finished she said, "You don't think
of yourself as having killed either of them? Don't waste time
thinking up a lot of silly excuses, just tell me that one thing."

"No, I don't," I said, "it was them or me. If I could have got
out of the cellar when he brought out the gun I would have
run, without thinking of the money. But he fired straight up
at me. He was crazy. He didn't even give me the chance to
hand him the bloody passport. He just fired, so I jumped down
on him. I don't really know why. It seemed the only thing to
do at the time."

She believed this, every last word of it. I could see that in
the way she looked at me and the way she nodded while I was
still talking.

"Don't say anything for a minute, Charlie. Let me think
again. There's a way out of this. There has to be, but I've got
to think."

I let her think. The prospect of being caught with two
bodies and twenty thousand pounds on my hands still hadn't
caught up with me. I could think back as far as the body of
Delphine on the stairs, and the bundle at the foot of the steps,

236

but I was unequal to the task of wrenching my mind beyond range of the cellar. Presently she said, "Were you that much in love with the woman?" and I replied, "I thought I was when I began it."

"Were you lovers?"

"Yes, several times."

She compressed her lips, one of the few tricks she had inherited from her father. Then, with a glance at her wristwatch, she said, "It's ten past two. We've got about two and a half hours. With luck a little more but not much more."

"What are you going to do?"

"Clear up," she said briefly. "Get rid of them and the money."

"You mean put the money back?"

"No, there isn't time to do that. Who has the keys?"

"He's got the two we made and I've still got Evan's."

"Give it to me."

I gave it to her and she put it in her handbag.

"That van outside. Can you drive it?"

"Yes."

She looked doubtful. "You know how to drive a car? I've never seen you drive one."

"I used to drive a Ford van at my last branch. A chap there taught me."

The prospect of hauling those bodies out of the cellar and carting them away brought me part way out of my state of shock. I was beginning to thaw a little, not appreciably so but about as far as the knuckle and toe joints. I said, "Suppose we got them out, where could we take them?"

"We'll have to think of somewhere."

"But we couldn't do it without noise. The Cooks would turn on their lights and look down in the yard."

"We'll have to chance that."

I forced my mind to look into the future, at least as far as daylight. "Wouldn't it be easier to go down to the police station and tell them exactly how it happened?"

"No," she said, sharply, "it wouldn't be easier at all. It would be disastrous."

"But you believe me, I mean, about how they came to be killed?"

"I believe you, but nobody else would. You're alive and they're dead."

"Surely to God nobody would imagine I could have killed them? Deliberately, I mean?"

"Nobody would imagine you got impressions and helped them to break into the bank but you did."

"But couldn't we just—just *go?*"

She had been standing the far side of the table holding the empty glass. Now she slammed it down so violently that it was a miracle it held together.

"For crying out loud, Charlie, use your head! *Think!* You must have done a whole lot of clever thinking before you got yourself into a situation like this, so do it again, do it *now!* Somebody killed them and they'll start looking for a third person the minute they find them. It might be different if only one of them was dead but they're both dead and who could have killed them? Is a trained detective going to believe they killed each other? That he shot her and she pushed him backwards down a flight of steps before she died?" She broke off suddenly and put a hand to her mouth. I could see her strong teeth tugging at the seam of her glove. "They're sure to question you anyway and if I knew you were mooning after her everyone else in town will have known it. When a thing like this happens they put everyone through third degree and who else among the bank staff practically lived in that sleazy café across the passage? Who else sat there night after night, mentally undressing that woman? You're their first choice. Surely you can see that?"

My brain was clearing very rapidly now. "They won't suspect me any more than anyone else," I said, "probably a lot less. I never laid hold of Powell's grille key for more than a moment or two when we brought up the cash, and I never handled Evan's key until tonight. As for the safe key, even the junior uses that every other day, and as for knowing them, there was the row."

"What row?"

"We staged a big row in public. I complained of their food and Beppo threw me out in front of witnesses."

She perked up immediately. "How long ago was that?"

"Months ago, when we first started talking about it."

"And since?"

"I only came here after dark and always made certain nobody saw me. They gave me a key to that gate to let myself in."

"You've still got it?"

I gave it to her and she put it in her handbag without looking at it. "Then there's a chance," she said, "just a chance."

It struck me then, and for the first time since I had opened the door to her, that her presence was a more improbable twist than anything that had occurred that night.

"How do you happen to be here? How did you trace me?"

She made one of Evan's little chopping motions and because it was so characteristic of him it had the power to divert my thoughts for a few seconds, so that I pictured her as a small, plump child, watching him in one of his testy moods and then practicing the gesture in front of a mirror.

"That'll keep," she said, "it's not important. Have you worn those gloves all the time you've been here?"

I told her I had worn them since going downstairs to get Evan's key ring.

"The real professional," she sneered, "but we can't waste time talking, not another second." She crossed to the door and threw it open. When I didn't move she said, quietly, "I can't do it alone, Charlie. It's your only chance, and it's not much of a chance at that."

I still didn't move. "I could help move her but I don't think I could touch him," I said, but she replied, in the same unequivocal voice, "You've got no option, Charlie. It's that or hang."

The word had an immediate effect, amplifying the roaring in my ears again as though it was part of a defensive barrier against the formal words of a black-capped judge, the merciless questions of a prosecutor and, ultimately, the creak of the drop lever. I knew about these things. I was an avid reader of

Sunday newspapers. But until she said "hang" they had no more relevance to me and my situation than the crimes of Crippen and Jack the Ripper. The word stripped away the cocoon I had spun around me and I made a low sound that told her she had administered the right stimulant. I stood up very shakily and when I reached out to steady myself on the mantelshelf she came back and poured the last of the brandy in the glass, handing it to me but saying nothing. It was no more than an inch or so in the bottom of the tumbler but it worked. When I had swallowed it she walked in front of me as far as the cellar door. The light was still burning, the bulb swinging in the draft. Nothing had changed on the staircase. Delphine still lay on the top steps as though she had stumbled, and in a patch of shadow thrown by the arch I could just see Beppo's upturned soles and an arm flung out at a wide angle.

She bent down, grasped Delphine under the armpits and pulled her into the brighter light thrown by the passage bulb. As she did this the head fell forward and I saw, to my intense relief, that the back of the head was undamaged. The bullet must have been of exceptionally small caliber not to penetrate right through.

Ida said, "Take her heels," and I lifted them. One of her shoes fell off but Ida said, "Leave it!" and we carried her into the scullery and set her down near the door. With a kind of stupefaction I watched Ida put the door mat under her head and wondered why she did it. Much later I realized it had been a precaution against further bleeding but she wasn't finished even then. She knelt beside her, picked up the limp hand and felt for a pulse. Then she straightened up, brushed past me and led the way back to the cellar. She didn't have to order me to follow. I wouldn't have been parted from her at that moment.*

To carry Beppo up the full length of the stair, along the length of the passage and lay him beside Delphine was a far more difficult task. Not only did he weigh more but he had bled freely from a cut on the temple in the few seconds before he died. The blood might have been a serious complication had it not been for the fact that the wound came in direct contact with the tough fibers of the rucksack. We noticed this as she shone my torch on him and it checked her. She said, briefly, "We'll have to do something about that, Charlie. We can't risk our clothes being stained. Don't look, I'll do it."

I had no idea what she was going to do but I turned aside and waited until she said, "You'll have to help me heave him round, I can't do that by myself."

When I looked again I saw what she had done. She had pulled the half-filled rucksack over his head and fastened the cords round his throat. Trussed up like that he lost all resemblance to a human being. He looked like a masked dummy and the sight of him was too much for me. I started retching again.

She didn't protest but I heard her breathing hard and when I turned again I saw that she had managed to heave him in a half-circle so that he was now propped against the lower steps. She said, "Take his shoulders, you won't have to look at him that way," and I scrambled over him and half lifted him, backing slowly up the steps and dragging him with me.

We made miserably slow progress. I knew there were only thirteen steps to that staircase but we might have been hauling him up several flights. We moved about two inches with each heave, me tugging, her pushing, but the tremendous physical effort required was a kind of buffer between consciousness of what I was doing and the terrible repulsion I had felt for him at floor level. It was easier going when we reached the passage. Here we managed to lift him clear of the floor and get him more than halfway to the scullery. Then Ida said, "I won't be a minute," and returned to the cellar. I was too dizzy and breathless to ask why but stood leaning on the wall of the passage. Finding the distempered surface cool to the touch I faced it, pressing my forehead to the wall. It was this action, I think, that prevented me from fainting. Then she was beside me again. In one hand she had the other rucksack and in the other a small, automatic pistol. She held the pistol out before dropping it into the rucksack. After that she retrieved Delphine's shoe and added it to the contents. Whoever found that rucksack was going to have more than one puzzle to solve.

I felt appreciably better now and the improvement may have been the result of fatalism on my part. In the interval of waiting for Ida I had moved some distance toward accepting her verdict. It was, as she had stated, this or nothing. We had come so far and we might as well go all the way. I even began to give part of my mind to where we could take them if, by some miracle, we got clear of the premises, and my first thought was the beach but then I had what promised to be a better idea. I suppose, by now, I was more than half drunk. Beppo and Ida had had one drink apiece but in three tots I had accounted for the rest of the bottle, and that in a matter of an hour. By the time we had dragged him as far as the scullery it was twenty minutes past three. We had, at best, another hour's darkness.

She took off her cotton gloves and washed her hands at the scullery sink and at her advice I did the same, although I couldn't see any traces of blood on me. She said, "Put your gloves on again and go out and see if everything's quiet out there," and when I hesitated, "all right, you stay here," but this didn't suit me at all. With both of them lying at my feet there seemed nowhere to stand in the little room.

I opened the door and looked out. Everything was quiet except for some distant shunting down at the goods yard. The night was cloudy and smelled of rain. The Cook windows were still dark and I thought, enviously, "My God, that family can sleep!" and wondered if I would ever sleep again.

When I returned to the scullery Ida was standing over them, her hands on her hips. She said, coolly, "Have you thought of anywhere? Someplace they might not be found for a bit? It can't be far, not more than a mile or so."

The vague location that had half suggested itself when I was in the passage resolved itself into something precise. "They've been excavating our side of the Craigwen plantation," I said. "There's a pit there and they've already started filling in. There are workmen's tools around and the nearest house is nearly a hundred yards away."

"It'll have to do," she said, "but it's too near home for my liking. Come on."

Even at the time I marveled at her self-possession.

We took Delphine first and Ida, holding her feet, somehow contrived to open the van doors without setting her down. We eased her in gently, elbowing the traveling case to one side. Then we went back for him and bundled him into the rear of the van with less ceremony, but that was because it called for a far greater effort. I was going to close the doors then but she stopped me and went back into the house. In the dim light that reached the scullery from the passage I could see her beckoning so I left the van doors open and rejoined her.

"You must have had hand luggage," she said, "where is it?"

I told her it was already in the van alongside theirs and she gave a long, gasping sigh. It was the only sign of weakness she had exhibited since I had told her what lay behind the cellar door. She said, thoughtfully, "You're sure there's nothing else here? Nothing that could link you to them in any way?"

"I can't think of anything," I said, "except the drawings."

"What drawings?"

"The tracings I made of the two keys."

"You didn't sign them, did you?"

It was the nearest thing to a joke cracked in the house that night.

"He was going to send them to Head Office if I didn't go along, but all that was a long time ago. He's either destroyed them or has them on him."

She considered this and finally discarded it.

"Drawings couldn't prove a thing," she said, "and anyone would assume they were his. You didn't write to her at any time?"

"Never. When I wanted to discuss anything I always called."

"Did she write to you?"

"Twice but I burned the letters."

"Maybe you're not such a bloody fool after all," she said, and went into the passage. A moment later the lights in passage and living room went out and when she stood beside me again I sensed rather than saw that she was carrying the second rucksack containing, besides money, the gun and shoe.

"Those gates," she said, with her hand on the door, "will they open easily?"

I told her Beppo had arranged to keep them oiled and also that he had made a number of dummy runs on successive Saturday nights with the object of getting the Cook family accustomed to hearing the van come and go in the small hours.

"You seem to have thought of everything," she said and there was bitterness in her voice. "Now listen," she went on, "when we go out make straight for the van but don't start it. Get in from the near side, leave the door open and slide over. That way we'll only have one door to close. I'll open the gates first and then go to the bottom of the alley. We'll drive round by the station. Down there a van won't attract attention. All the paper vans and milk lorries use that yard early in the morning. Drive down the alley, past the station, then straight up Station Road. And I hope to God you can drive as well as you can tell lies, Charlie."

Before she unlatched the scullery door she had another thought. She picked up the mat on which Delphine's head had rested, rolled it up and stuffed it into the rucksack.

It wasn't until that moment that the full extent of her involvement was brought home to me and with it a deep sense of shame. Until then she had been someone I could think of as a friend qualified to give me a whole series of repugnant orders but now, as I saw her stand with one hand on the latch and the other holding the bulging rucksack, the nature of her complicity beat in my head like a bell. I jogged her elbow, saying, "Wait, Ida!" and when she turned, irritably, "Go on home. I can manage from here."

"I don't think you can, Charlie."

She sounded more tired than desperate, too tired to argue about something that had no bearing on the situation but then, bracing herself, she added, "You'll muff it. You muff everything in the end. Just do as I say, and remember, we haven't a minute to waste!" Then she went out, circling the van and approaching the gates from its near side.

I followed, watching the uncertain flicker of the torch as she bent to draw the ground-level bolts of each gate. They swung open almost soundlessly and she passed out into the alley, turning right toward the station. I moved round to the near side and slid across to the driving seat. I had familiarized myself with the dashboard more than a fortnight before. Even then I must have anticipated some kind of last-minute hitch regarding the journey to Chester.

She seemed to be away a long time. Quiet reigned there, except for the far-off clang of shunting and the sough of a moist wind, the certain promise of rain in Penmadoc. I sat thinking of nothing. It was the only thing to do with the kind of load I had aboard, and the plywood partition at my back made this possible. Then I saw her shadow pass the brick pillar of the right-hand gate and a moment later she was beside me, the rucksack balanced on her knees.

"No one about," she whispered, "just a few lights over at the station, and a parked lorry or two. Start her up and get out of here."

I pulled the starter loop and the engine caught first time. I groped my way into the third gear gate and pushed the accelerator. The van lurched and I heard her hiss, "Lights!" They came on without me being conscious of touching the switch and only just in time because my off side mudguard was within an inch of the pillar. Then I got the feel of the vehicle and was able to ease her round and point her down toward the station end of the alley, but before I moved down the incline I depressed the clutch and applied the clumsy handbrake.

"What about the gates?"

"Damn the gates. Get on with it. For God's sake, get on with it!"

We went down the narrow alley at about ten miles an hour and out into the wide station approach. No one was around.

Apart from the glimmer of yellow light over by the goods yard the place looked dead. I remembered then it was Sunday morning and the thought comforted me a little.

I swung hard right at the bottom of Station Road, passing the bank and the café and turning right again into the main road. There wasn't a soul about and I wondered, considering the time, if Gwyn-the-Boots wasn't pushing his luck with the widow. At the junction of Craigwen Terrace I turned left. I was still in third gear and she took the incline easily. The houses on both sides of the road were dark and when the gradient increased the lights were reflected in a greenhouse set back behind a border fence. In less than three minutes after passing the station we were at the "Y" junction of the terrace and the plantation.

I saw in the beam of the headlights that the council work-men had made considerable progress since I was last here. The excavation that had been started opposite the last gate in the terrace was now filled in and the canvas hut housing tools had been shifted higher up the slope, where a wound ran diagonally across the hillside passing within yards of one of the great clumps of rhododendrons. I turned right here and stopped with the wheels still resting on the made-up surface of the old road. We were within about ten yards of the hut. She said, "Back up a little and turn off the lights," and when I told her I might get bogged down on that loose surface she snapped, "Do as I say! Back as far as you can, then turn off the lights!"

I lunged around until I found the reversing gate and eased the van back until I felt its bumper jar against the low bank. Then I turned out the lights. My fingers were so wet that they slipped on the Bakelite surface of the switch.

As soon as I got out I saw that she was more perceptive than me. The workmen had been filling in the new approach road as they advanced and using their own track to dump loads of rubble and cinders by lorry. I remembered then that I had read about the project in the local paper. The Council was doing two jobs in one, transporting slag from an un-sightly tip down near the corporation housing site, to here, where hard core was badly needed on the steeply sloping lip of the estate. The tippers were evidently a day or so ahead of the diggers because there was a pyramid of rubble about five yards from the back of the van. Beyond that, and only a couple of yards beyond it, was the shallow end of the broad trench they were filling. At our end it was about two feet deep but descended steeply where the half-bricks and cinders tailed off. The torch showed us that, a few yards ahead, the excavation was about five feet in depth. She inspected it in silence crunching across the gritty surface beyond the pyramid. She didn't seem to need any advice and by now I was content to leave everything to her.

"We're dead lucky," she said, "they're filling in here every day and that stuff behind you is loose and easy to shift. Wait here a minute."

She went up the bank to the canvas hut and I saw her fiddle with the fastenings. Behind her, over toward the Chester road, I could see the sky lightening in contrast to the solid darkness in the direction of the mountains. We had no more than twenty minutes before it would be half-light but for the first time since I had looked up the cellar steps and seen Delphine at the top, I began to hope.

She came back carrying a couple of squat, broad-bladed shovels and stood them carefully against the side of the trench. I was getting used to the deliberation she was able to bring to our ghoulish work and, to some extent, was adapting to it myself for I saw it as something that involved us equally. I could think of those sprawling figures in the van as stages beyond which both Ida and I had to travel if we were to survive. Perhaps it was this tacit admission of near-helplessness, of being trapped together in a whole string of incongruous circumstances, that mitigated the horror of what we were about to do. I don't know if she was aware of this but I know that I was. To hump both those two bodies from the van to the crest of the track was an almost casual act compared with shifting them from cellar to scullery a little over an hour before. In that brief interval of time my susceptibilities had coarsened in that I felt neither guilt nor repugnance, just an overriding fear that even now something else would go wrong.

She made sure that it did not. We scraped a hole in the loose cinders at the point opposite where she had put the shovels, and when the grave was about eighteen inches deep we laid them side by side, with the spare rucksack between them and the suitcase in the deepest part of the depression. Then, without pause, we shoveled earth, hard core and cinders on top of them, taking the first layers from our own heap but adding fresh shovelfuls from the adjacent pyramid. Once or twice our shovels struck a tin can or a fragment of old iron that gave out a clink but we made no attempt to work soundlessly. Speed was all that mattered. Without exchanging a word we shoveled for perhaps fifteen minutes and when we had finished neither of us could have said precisely where they lay, only that it was a point about halfway between the lip of the trench near the van and the line of raw earth marking the deepest point of the excavation. When, by common consent, we paused, the sky in the east was pearl gray, shot through with blue-black trailers of cloud. As I took the shovel from her and carried them both across to the shed the first spatter of rain fell.

When we were sitting together in the van I spoke for the first time since she had told me to wait in the trench while she fetched the tools. I said, "Maybe it's not enough earth. "We could come back tomorrow night," but she said, "I couldn't, Charlie."

Suddenly and inexplicably the leadership passed to me. I knew then that she was used up and that I would have to ditch the van alone. I said, taking her hand, "You get out just beyond home. I'll leave the van in that place the tin-plate lorries use weekends, in Melbourne Grove. I'll be about twenty minutes." She made no reply so I gave her my house key. It was the third key I had given her that evening and it reminded her of something I had forgotten.

"We've still got to get the grille key back on Dadda's ring."

"That's not urgent," I said, "there's a dummy key just like it on his chain."

"Come in the back way," she said, "I'll leave the kitchen door unlocked."

I coasted down the incline without starting the engine and braked gently about three houses beyond St. Ninian's. She got out and disappeared at once in the grayness.

There still wasn't anyone abroad in the main road although it was now coming up to a quarter to five. The rain held back the dawn although I was now driving directly into it. Thankfully, and without passing a soul or a single lighted window, I turned right into Melbourne Grove below the tin-plate works. A large building lot scheduled for development was used as a temporary parking place for a variety of vehicles, by no means all of them belonging to the works owning the site. There were several tradesmen's vans and one or two private cars in there. I drove in, took my bag and left the van in the farthest corner. Then I went up the lane along under the factory wall to a point where the path rejoined the edge of the Craigwen estate. From here it was only five minutes' walk to the top of Craigwen Terrace.

She was sitting hunched over the kitchen table sipping tea when I let myself in. She didn't look up but remained propped by her elbows, staring down at the saucer.

"Wipe your feet," she said, "mine were covered with that cindery stuff."

I went out again and brushed my shoes with Gladys's yard broom. Already the thing was beginning to recede at a fantastic speed. It might have happened a month ago and that month, I knew, would soon extend to a year. This was the only way either of us could live with it.

She poured tea for me, black and strong, the way Gladys always brewed it. I told her where I had left the van and that I hadn't seen anybody. She said, shrugging this information aside, "Tell me something, Charlie. Do you feel this was meant to happen? Or something like it?"

I told her I had had that feeling all the time we were digging. "It's odd," she said, "because that's the real reason why I came. You never guessed why I went I suppose?"

"Because I wouldn't take that job."

"No," she said, "that wasn't the reason. I was more than two months pregnant."

I think this made a more profound impact on me than anything that had happened since I had walked out of that house with Evan's key six hours before. It explained more than her impulsive flight, her long silences, and her insistence on coming home expressed in that one letter she had written. In some way it had a direct bearing on her miraculous reappearance at the gate of The Rainbow yard.

I said, after a long pause, "You could have told me. It would have made all the difference."

"Would it?" She looked at me across the table, a wan, exhausted woman, with all her natural jocundity drained from her. "I don't think it would, Charlie. It might have stopped you doing a crazy thing like this but it wouldn't have made any difference to us. All that would have happened was that you would have taken to your heels instead of me, and who was I to gripe? I was the one who began it and I wasn't going to help load Dadda's shotgun."

"The child," I said, "what happened? Where is it?"

" 'It' is adopted," she said, "I arranged that before it was born, six weeks ago. I wasn't sure it was the right thing to do then but I'm sure enough now. I wouldn't wish you and me as parents on anyone, would you?"

"What was it, Ida?"

"A boy," she said, "but after tonight don't talk about it. Don't even mention it. From here on we've got enough to cope with."

"I still can't understand how you came to turn up at that moment."

"Premonition was part of it, but not much. Mostly it was a matter of putting things together and seeing what they looked like."

"*What* things?"

"All kinds of things. Those nightly trips to The Rainbow to gloat over that girl. The frantic letter about your not being here if I came this weekend. You'll have to explain that, Boyo.

Tried to phone you at your father's school I did and he was interested to learn he was retiring and getting a presentation. Then I got to thinking, 'Why should he be so keen to stop me now? He hasn't a clue about the baby but he's damned scared of something.' You find that surprising? It isn't, you know. Can't hold a man in your arms without learning something about him, Charlie. Not even half a man like you."

"It still doesn't explain how you came to be knocking on that gate in the middle of the night."

"Like I said, it was a lot of little things and there's a pattern they made for me. I decided to come home, anyway. I thought you ought to hear about the baby now that it was off your hands. Fair is fair, Charlie. I'm not such a bad liar either. I was out of work and down to a shilling, over and above my train fare. I got in on the eleven twenty-five, let myself in with the key I still had and crept up to your room. Like old times it was, except that you weren't there and some of your things were gone. I sat on your bed thinking. 'They all go,' I said to myself, 'first Wally, then Waring and now Charlie,' but in your case I couldn't understand where or why or how. I knew you hadn't been gone very long. You forgot to rinse out the cocoa cups. You even left that for me to do. This too, one more clue you won't have to sweat about."

She snapped open her handbag and took out the dummy key I had slipped on Evan's ring.

"*You* switched them while I was dumping the van?"

"It wasn't difficult. They're still snoring their heads off and likely to be for hours. Maybe that's the least you could do, Charlie. Evan is going to need all the sleep he can get, poor little basket."

She got up and crossed to the sink to empty the teapot. "The rest is chance. I had a feeling you might have gone to London to find me. That was a laugh, wasn't it? So I went back to the station to check trains and found there hadn't been once since late afternoon. That made it Liverpool, the blue water idea you had, remember? I was trudging past The Rainbow when that music started up. I don't know why it told me you were there but it did and that made me mad, as mad as I've ever been with any man."

"Why, Ida?"

"Why not? I'd just ditched your kid and had fourpence in my purse. You still had money to spend on stargazing. It's all right, I'm not mad anymore."

There was nothing to say. To thank her for doing so much and risking so much to get me out of that awful jam, even temporarily, would have been an insult but as I watched her washing the tea things, and going through the motions of a woman performing an ordinary routine job in a kitchen, I thought of all the bloody nonsense people write and most people think about romance and love and the rituals of mating. Nearly everyone puts all the emphasis on bed so that other factors never get a show. To listen to them no one would imagine love had any connection with loyalty and courage and self-sacrifice of the kind she had in such abundance.

"Where do we go from here, Ida?"

"To bed. Where else? There's nothing more we can do. The rest depends on whether you can keep your nerve and go right on lying, no matter what."

"There's those keys I gave you and their passport and tickets."

"We'll have all day tomorrow to cross the 't's,'" she said, "but just in case give me the passport and tickets. I daresay you think you won't sleep but you will. It'll be this time next week you'll need some of those tablets. Me too, I wouldn't wonder."

I helped her dry the tea things and we went up together, she to her old room above the kitchen, me up the second flight to recommune with Wally and Waring. I undressed without much hope but Ida was right. I slept like a dead man. I didn't even dream.

Chapter Sixteen

1

I don't think any of us could look back on more than a blurred picture of that Sunday. It began for me about midday when Ida slouched in with a cup of tea and told me that Gladys was still in bed but Evan had been stumbling around for about an hour, wondering what had hit him. He finally put it down to a couple of restless nights, plus his spade work in the garden the previous afternoon. He would probably have worried about it more if Ida's presence hadn't surprised and pleased him and when she told him she was home for good he was almost himself again by teatime. Gladys never really woke up. She came down for lunch and had another nap before tea but that only increased her drowsiness. She put it down to something she had eaten and none of us bothered to argue with her.

After tea Ida and I went along the front and over the headland. The tide was in so we stood a while throwing pebbles and in between we threw the two keys into twenty feet of water beyond the breakwater. In a shallow cave a mile or so along the beach we made a driftwood fire and burned the passport and tickets, poking among the embers until the last traces were gone. On the way back we passed the open gates of The Rainbow yard. Everything looked normal and we said "Good evening" to Mr. and Mrs. Cook, Junior, on their way home from Chapel. Neither of them looked as though they had spent a disturbed night.

As we turned into the main road I said, "Let's get married,

Ida. Let's get married right away and tell your people we intend doing it, as soon as we get in."

She didn't seem outraged or even surprised by the proposal but rather as though she had expected it.

"Any special reason," she said, "apart from the law about a wife not being able to give evidence against a husband? That shouldn't bother you, I'd be in the dock as an accessory."

I accepted this as my due. "I can manage so long as you're there," I said, "but I couldn't cope alone anymore."

"How about me," she said, "you think I could?"

We walked on in silence as far as the corner of Craigwen Terrace. I didn't think I had the slightest right to bring pressure on her, and waited. She said, finally, "You got any kind of feeling for me, Charlie? Besides gratitude?"

I thought hard about this. I would never lie to her again, not if it cost me my life. I said, "You used to say 'No strings,' Ida, whenever we made the most of our opportunities and I went along with that then."

"You don't any longer?"

"No. We didn't have anything much then but we have now. We've got each other, and I've got by far the best of the bargain, but that's all we've got."

"We'll get married if you want to, Charlie."

We reached the gate of St. Ninian's and as we turned in we caught each other looking up the incline to the green slopes of the Craigwen estate. Within a couple of hundred yards of where we stood two people who had walked and talked less than twenty-four hours ago lay under about three feet of rubble, and our main hope of a future rested in the probability that the Council steamroller would seal them in first thing Monday morning. She knew what I was thinking and laid her hand on my arm. She said, "There's an old proverb, Charlie—'Take what you want and pay for it'—but those who do like to owe as long as possible. They got what was coming to them and that's the way you'll have to start thinking of it. It's the only way. Otherwise you might as well pack it in from here."

"Right now I feel like doing that, Ida."

"No," she said, emphatically, "because if you did you wouldn't be long discovering the law claimed a damned sight more than you owe."

"Is that why you're ready to stick it out with me, Ida?"

"That and selfish reasons," she said and suddenly smiled. "Truth is I always did have a bit of a yen for you, Charlie. Maybe because I always liked little men. Tell me just one thing, before we face up to the gush."

"Well?"

"In the end you went along because you had to, but in the beginning, *why*? Was it because you thought it was the one way you'd ever amount to anything?"

"That was the main reason when you boil it down."

"Then it wasn't really because of her?"

"Not once it stopped being a game."

"What was she like in bed, Charlie?"

I could answer this without lying. "Not nearly as good as you, Ida."

"I can believe that," she said, "the pretty ones nearly always take a man for granted. Anyway, what the hell can you expect of a woman who uses her fanny as a burglar's jemmy?"

We went in and found Evan alone listening to the news, and told him of our decision. He was so delighted that he hugged her and nearly wrung my hand off before rushing upstairs to rouse the still somnolent Gladys. It was good to be able to give him that much pleasure before the roof fell in on him. I never saw him smile again.

2

We went down to the bank side by side just before nine on Monday, father-in-law and son-in-law elect, walking head-on into a cyclone.

Signs of it were apparent even as we passed the shuttered Rainbow. The bank doors were wide open to the public an hour before time, and as Evan broke into a run Powell came dashing down the stairs from his flat with his wife at his heels.

255

His face was the color of junket and when he saw Evan he nearly fell on him, but the words that poured from his lips made no kind of sense. He just hung there, gibbering like a frenzied baboon. Then Porsen reeled out, just as if he was drunk, and because Evan was cluttered with Powell he made for me and did a kind of tap dance on the pavement. He too had difficulty in passing the news but after a minute or two I understood him to say, "Clean through the place! Bloody great hole, bloody great hole . . . !"

Soon people were beginning to collect on the pavement and a growing crowd edged the four of us over the threshold. Inside was Gregg, the junior, perched on a stool behind the barrier and looking exactly like a waxwork. His eyebrows seemed to have climbed halfway up his forehead.

By now Evan was beginning to get a glimmering of what had happened but it hadn't sunk in and neither did it until we descended the stairs in a body and stared at the hole in the washroom floor. We were not alone. Powell had lost his head completely and had forgotten to close the outside doors so that when we looked round there were at least twenty passersby standing around and more coming all the time. That was the first time in my life I admired Evan. Rage at seeing his bank invaded as well as robbed rose in his throat and emerged as a scream of indignation. The onlookers received the full blast of his displeasure.

"Get out of here!" he shrieked. "Get out at once, do you hear! I'll have every one of you arrested! You hear me? Arrested!"

This threat had an immediate effect. The tide of people flowing down the stairs suddenly reversed and began to flow through the bank and out into the street where it collided with Sergeant Roberts on his way in. Roberts had no idea what had occurred but had been attracted by the eddy of people outside the bank, and his presence soon restored some semblance of order. In about five minutes we had disposed of the sensation-seekers, slammed the doors and put the chain up. Apart from the sergeant, the only unauthorized person left behind was Powell's wife and she had fainted. Powell, trying to administer a glass of water, dropped it, and from then on everyone who passed the barrier had to scrunch over splintered glass.

Evan weathered it better than I thought he would. In some ways, considering the magnitude of the shock, he was superb. He showed Sergeant Roberts the phone to get through to the CID and then issued orders to all of us not to touch a thing until the fingerprint men had arrived. To the dithering Powell he administered a testy rebuke.

"In God's name, pull yourself together man!" he said and then, seeing the sagging Mrs. Powell, "Get her out of here, and don't let anybody in while you're doing it. Go with him, Pritchard, and hold the door!"

I was glad of something to do and helped Powell unlock and propel his wife out onto the porch where she could return to her flat. It was like throwing someone to the wolves, and I heard later that a dozen or more people gained access to their bedroom on the pretext of helping her upstairs. Powell didn't accompany her. He came back fumbling in all his pockets like a man in a fever to get his braces undone, and I wondered what he could be doing until I saw him lay his keys on the counter.

"They're all there," he shouted, "they haven't been out of my keeping for a second! What about yours, Rhys-Jones? What about yours?"

Evan took out his key ring just as the sergeant came out of the office. Roberts was a quiet, ponderous man and I could tell by the fruitiness of his voice that he was beginning to enjoy himself.

"Someone will be along in a couple of minutes, Mr. Rhys-Jones," he said. "The inspector wants to know if you've checked the cash yet?"

"Good God, of course I haven't," said Evan, "how could I until we get the grilles and the safe open?"

"Then you'd better do it right away. Leave the youngsters up here to let our fellows in. I'll come down with you to make sure you don't touch anything."

"For God's sake, man, how can I open the grilles without

257

touching anything?" snarled Evan, transferring his rage and dismay to the policeman.

"We must make up our minds to do the very best we can," said Roberts. He sounded just like a Sunday school teacher coaching pupils for a local Eisteddfod.

They all three went down and I was left upstairs with Porsen and the junior, now slowly emerging from his daze and beginning to give a running commentary on what was happening outside.

"It's stopped all the traffic," he announced, "the crowd is right across the road."

"I'll stop your bloody traffic if you don't come away from that window," said Porsen, and I thought he was already beginning to show extreme nervousness. He lit a cigarette and let it go out. When I struck another match for him he looked helplessly at me, his eyes rolling like a heifer's. "This *is* a do," he said, "we'll all be mixed up in this, mark my words, the whole damned lot of us."

"I don't see why," I said, "it must be obvious we didn't blast our way into our own bank. How could we?"

"Why you damned fool," he said, "who's talking about blasting? If the money's gone they must have had keys. There's not a mark on those grilles or the safe as far as I could see. They must have got impressions. Three separate impressions!"

I was going to ask him more about the hole and where he thought it led but at that moment the junior shouted, "Here come the coppers! They're trying to get through the crowd!" and he rushed round the barrier to slip the chain and open the door. Porsen forestalled him, uttering dire warnings against a second invasion but there was no fear of this. The inspector had posted two constables in the porch and a third in the road to keep the traffic moving. I saw through a chink in the window blind that the one in the road was Gwyn wearing civvies but without a collar and tie, as though he had been hauled out of bed an hour or so after he had climbed into it. He looked, I thought, worried and harassed. He was probably wondering if anyone was likely to ask where he had been during the crucial hours of Saturday night.

The inspector and the CID sergeant marched in, their boots scrunching on the remains of the smashed tumbler. The inspector was new to the district, a courteous, fresh-faced man who was already popular in the area. The CID sergeant I hadn't seen before. He was an Englishman and Penmadoc shared his services with a larger town farther along the coast. His narrow face and iris-blue eyes registered with me at once. The inspector was flustered but he wasn't. He reminded me of a young sheriff in a Western, pledged to rid the town of crime and shooting it out if he had to. Porsen took them both downstairs and listening at the top I heard the grilles swing back and, a moment later, the soft *clunk* of the safe door.

I had anticipated that, by now, I would be wanting to grab my hat and run but I can't say that I was more than mildly scared, possibly because I was so absorbed watching everybody's reactions. It was a curious feeling, like being the one member of an audience who had seen the film before and waiting for everybody else in the cinema to hold on to their seats as climax succeeded climax. I didn't think about Beppo or Delphine but just the bank and in this way I got my money's worth. There were even times when I wanted to chuckle and other times when it seemed to me quite ludicrous that so many adults could work themselves into such a blather over a hole in a washroom floor and the possible loss of a few bundles of treasury notes. For the money, as money, had ceased to have any meaning for me. How could it be otherwise when some of it had been used to soak up Beppo's blood and all of it was lying under a pile of rubbish on the crest of Craigwen estate?

After about five minutes Powell came rushing up the stairs. He looked like the last survivor of a shipwreck or a train smash going in search of help, and at once disappeared into Evan's office where I heard him gabbling into the telephone. He was almost certainly phoning headquarters in Cardiff and it gave me a certain amount of satisfaction to contemplate the stark incredulity with which the news would be received down there.

Before he had finished Evan came up with the sergeant.

259

He looked stunned and his legs seemed to move independently of his body. Already I felt more sorry for him than for any of them, finding it easy to remember his good points and forget his tendency to fuss, nag and bully. He had gone to work that morning looking so chipper and expansive but now he looked sick and drawn. I made him and the sergeant some coffee. It helped to ease my conscience a mite. He said, stirring the cup and addressing no one in particular, "Everything but the high denomination notes. *Everything.* Nearly twenty thousand pounds. I can't begin to think . . ." but then, like a charging bull, the inspector came up and behind him Porsen, both red in the face. The inspector dashed past us and let himself out where he immediately conferred with the two constables standing on guard. I saw one of them shoot off up the incline, followed by a section of the gawpers. Porsen, almost incoherent with excitement, said, "That hole! It leads to Cook's cellars . . . it can't be Cook . . . it *can't* be!" and Evan, choking into his coffee, said, "*What's that?* What's that you're saying?"

Porsen repeated what he had said about the tunnel so Evan, who couldn't keep still, rushed down again to have yet another look at the washroom floor. I wondered if he would insist on scrambling through and discovering where the hole led and it occurred to me that if he did we might have a case of apoplexy on our hands in less than five minutes.

Then the CID man came hammering at the outside door and the sergeant let him in. He was coated with brickdust and I realized he had been through as far as The Rainbow but he didn't say anything. He just asked for the phone and when Porsen showed him where it was he shut the door on us.

Sergeant Roberts called me and Porsen over and began to pump us for information. Who was on holiday among the staff? What were the names and addresses of the cleaners? Had any of them independent access to the premises, and so on. He wasn't grilling us but just building up a background. When we told him about Griffiths he sent the junior to fetch him and then Evan came up again shaking his head and muttering half-finished sentences like, "Can't believe it . . .

doesn't make sense . . ." as he pottered mindlessly to and fro about the premises. It wasn't until the inspector returned via the main door that he made a tremendous effort to pull himself together and ask if the Cook family had been interviewed. The inspector said, "Someone is there now, Mr. Rhys-Jones, but I don't think they're involved. That hole led back to the café and neither of those Italians can be found. I've just been right through their place. Most of their clothes have gone and their van too. Do you know anything at all about them? Were they customers of yours?"

Evan said they weren't and that he knew nothing whatever about them except that they were Catholics and had been there more than a year.

"Two years plus," Porsen said, unwisely I thought, for the inspector said, quickly, "You know about them, Mr. Porsen?"

"Everyone in town knew them. All the scruff in Penmadoc were regulars there. Pritchard used to go there, didn't you, Pritchard?"

"Yes," I said, "one time I went there quite a lot."

"You stopped going for some reason?"

"Yes, I found a tack in a sandwich and broke a tooth on it, but when I complained they accused me of trying to play a confidence trick on them and threw me out in the street."

"Did you complain to anyone about them?"

"No," I said, "I didn't want a fuss. There were witnesses of the incident from the tin-plate works but they all thought it was screamingly funny. I was going to take it up with the Council's Public Health Officer but then I realized there would be a lot of unpleasant publicity and I would have had to go to court."

"Apart from that the man was a rough customer," added Porsen helpfully.

"When was all this?" he wanted to know, and I told him it was months ago, round about Whitsuntide, and that I had never been there since.

"Have you been there recently, Mr. Porsen?"

It was his first carefully-aimed question and it made Porsen flush.

"I've dropped in for coffee now and again. Once a fortnight or so."

"Can you describe these people?"

"Any of your constables could do that better than I could," he said, sounding truculent, but the inspector took his point and said mildly, "Good, we'll go into all that but I shall expect all of you to help us in any way you can."

"Naturally," said Porsen. I thought he had got off to a bad start.

I began to realize then that Ida's advice concerning the disposal of the bodies had been very sound indeed. If a break-in caused this kind of upheaval what might have happened to all of us if the CID man had found Beppo dead at the bottom of the stairway and Delphine shot through the throat at the top? I wondered gloomily if he had found any bloodstains but it seemed unlikely as yet. They would go over every inch of the vault and the café but there was no special reason why they should scrutinize the cellar beyond the shaft. They would probably be more interested in Beppo's workshop on the top story. As to fingerprints, I thanked my stars that I had worn gloves during the entire operation and that Ida had too. They wouldn't check hers, of course, but I knew it wouldn't be long before they got around to taking ours, if only to match them with any that showed on the grilles and safe door.

The bank was closed for business, and even if we had been allowed to open we couldn't have operated. Apart from the silver and copper, there was nothing smaller than a five-pound note on the premises. Neither Evan nor I went home for lunch, he because his presence was needed all the time, me because I didn't want to be the one to break the news to Gladys. The police set up temporary headquarters in Evan's office and the phone was permanently in use. Two reporters turned up and were shown the door but the local man succeeded in pumping some information out of young Gregg and made a killing with the London dailies.

By early afternoon the place was crawling with police. A CID superintendent arrived from Chester and spent an hour in the vault. They dusted the grilles, the safe, and the whole area round the hole for fingerprints, taking any number of photographs there and in the café. They got in touch with the tin-plate works and a number of Rainbow customers moved in on the act, giving lurid descriptions of Beppo and Delphine that later found their way into all the papers. Reporters began to congregate in increasing numbers but they weren't allowed access to the bank and we were all expressly forbidden to talk to them. This didn't stop them getting interviews outside, and filling in gaps with fairly accurate speculation. One could sense the thing growing, like a balloon stretched to alarming dimensions, and it seemed to me, practically a prisoner on the premises, that the terrible tensions must soon result in an explosion of some kind. My fears were justified. It came about four o'clock, just after the staff had been fingerprinted.

Powell, by then, had regained control of himself but Evan was beginning to wilt and Porsen was very edgy. None of them could object to having their prints taken, to be matched against those found in the vault, but when the messy business was done Porsen, out of police hearing, expressed his view on the futility of the check.

"Anyone breaking into that vault would have had the sense to wear gloves," he growled, "and what about all those idiots who followed us down from the street when we first found it this morning?"

Powell, sensitive to having left the door open, resented this and told Porsen to hold his tongue but Evan, glad of a chance to turn on somebody, reminded Powell of his hysterical display that had led to the invasion. Powell's frayed nerves were unequal to this and the hatred between the two men flared up at once.

"I never have been satisfied that the security here was adequate!" he said. "I'm surprised that something like this hasn't happened before under the kind of direction that existed!"

For a moment I thought Evan was going to fling himself on the cashier.

"How *dare* you say that? How *dare* you?" he screamed,

263

jumping up and down. "You, who held three keys to my one!"

Powell chose to accept this as an accusation that he was some kind of an accessory.

"Are you suggesting *I* had anything to do with it?" he roared, "because if you are I shall resort to law! *You* heard him, Porsen! You heard what he said!"

"I only spoke the truth!" said Evan, not in the least intimidated, "you had the custody of the bank and you were here on the premises when it happened. Furthermore, you have consistently undermined my authority ever since I came here and perhaps it won't come as a surprise to you that I've already put that on paper and sent it to Head Office!"

This was more than Powell could take. Shouting, "You pot-bellied little hypocrite . . . !" he flung himself on Evan and all the poisonous undercurrents of the last few years found a moment's outlet in that one burst of primitive energy. He ripped Evan's collar loose and then seized him by the ears with the apparent intention of smashing his face down on the counter, but Porsen jumped on Powell's back and I dived to floor level and came up between them so that when the local inspector ran from the office he found the four of us locked in a scrum and shouting at the top of our voices. He bellowed, "*Gentlemen*! For God's sake!" and seized Evan and Powell by the shoulders, thrusting them apart with a single, resolute heave. Then the sergeant came out and between them some kind of order was restored, but not before both Evan and Powell had babbled incoherently about their respective keys and Porsen, his own nerve badly shaken by the incident, had declared, "I'm going home! No one can keep me here cooped up like a suspect. I had nothing to do with their bloody keys and I'm sick to death of them all! It's been hell here, Inspector, sheer hell I can tell you!"

Out of the corner of my eye I saw the local CID man leaning against the frame of the office door and appraising the scene with his expressionless blue eyes and it seemed to me, at that moment, that here was one man who was seeing more than was good for us. For the first time that day I found myself face to face with fear, the confrontation expressing itself in a shudder that I tried to conceal by pressing my body hard against the ledger counter.

The inspector said, more reasonably, "Come now, this won't help at all. Let me be frank. For my part nobody here is suspected of anything worse than carelessness. Naturally you're all under considerable strain but this kind of behavior, why it's downright childish and does nobody any credit."

It occurred to me that if someone in authority had said that to them a few months ago there wouldn't have been a robbery to investigate and two people wouldn't be lying under the cinder track on Craigwen ridge.

The inspector turned on his heel and addressed the watching CID sergeant.

"Where is your chief now?" he asked and the sergeant said the superintendent was taking statements from the Cook family. "Very well," the inspector said, "you can begin your own interviews while he's at it. We'll take individual statements in writing tomorrow but let's clear the ground right away."

"One at a time, sir?" He sounded, I thought, like an underling charged with the not unwelcome duty of beginning a string of executions.

"One at a time," said the inspector grimly, "we don't want another free-for-all."

3

It was then about four-thirty and we went into the office in order of seniority. I found the period of waiting intolerable and was glad when Griffiths rejoined us, and told us this had helped him to make up his mind to break with Caddie's and start training as a solicitor. It gave us something else to think about and in any case I was glad for him. The promise of escape from that place gave him the power of detachment that had been denied us for so long. He was encouraging too, in his ability to put the situation in perspective. "I daresay it all seems terribly important right now," he said, "but in a week or two it won't. Somebody will blow up the Albert

Memorial or impersonate the Prince of Wales and even people around here will refer to this as 'the time the Eyeties had a bash at Caddie's.'" I'm sure Griffiths had no idea how much comfort that single remark brought to me, reminding me as it did that, whatever else happened, nobody could arrest the passage of time.

Powell came out and Griffiths went in but they didn't detain him long. Then it was Porsen's turn and after that mine. I braced myself to meet the steady gaze of the CID sergeant, telling myself that if I could bluff him I could bluff anyone. He asked a few routine questions about my access to the keys and was clearly satisfied but then, with what I thought too casual a tone, he said, "You lodge with the manager, don't you, Mr. Pritchard?"

"Yes," I said, "and I'm engaged to his daughter."

"Really? Mr. Rhys-Jones didn't mention that."

"There's no reason why he should. It's nothing to do with the bank."

"No." And then, "You've been here about eighteen months, haven't you?"

"That's right."

"Like it?"

I decided I could afford to be truthful in this sector.

"No," I said, "and none of them do. There's far too much unnecessary friction; you saw what happened. Mr. Rhys-Jones and Mr. Powell don't get on at all."

"How about you? With the others, I mean?"

"I get on with Griffiths but Porsen and I never have liked one another, mostly because Mr. Powell sided with Porsen and Mr. Rhys-Jones with me."

"You've always got along with the manager?"

"No, sergeant, only lately."

"Since you got engaged to his daughter?"

"It made a difference, naturally."

He pondered this before saying, carefully, "That Italian girl next door but one, how friendly was Porsen with her? It won't go any further than me."

I didn't like Porsen but I wasn't going to link him to Delphine in a way the sergeant half hoped I would.

"He wasn't friendly in that sense at all," I said, "he'd tried his luck with her, the same as most young chaps in Penmadoc, but he didn't get anywhere. Nobody did."

"She was that attractive?" It was curious, I thought, how he spoke of her in the past tense.

"Yes," I said, "she was the kind of girl anyone would look at twice and then again."

"You included, notwithstanding the manager's daughter?"

"Well, up to the time they threw me out, yes . . . I went there quite often until then."

"Fine," he said, standing up, "now send the junior in and after that you can all go home." He smiled. "Been rather a day, hasn't it?"

"I wouldn't care to go through it again," I said, and went out of there feeling that he still had something in reserve.

Evan was already home when I arrived and had told Gladys the news. By the time I got there she had recovered from the shock and words streamed from her like water over a dam. I had had more than enough for one day and my new status as prospective son-in-law gave me the authority I needed.

"Look, Gladys," I said, taking a line Evan should have taken on his honeymoon, "do us all a big favor and pipe down. We've both had a hell of a day and it's going to start all over again tomorrow and the day after that. For God's sake, give Dadda a break and read all about it in the newspapers."

She took this meekly enough and Evan shot me a tired, appreciative glance. All she said was, "Well, I hope they catch those dreadful people and put them in prison for the rest of their wicked lives!" and after that, despite the brooding presence of Evan, she proceeded to dispose of a very hearty tea. Nothing had the power to destroy Gladys's appetite or keep her awake at night.

On Ida's advice Evan went round to his doctor after the

meal and asked for something to tranquilize his mind. It was
ironic, I thought, that he should resort to sleeping drafts now
but the mixture helped him through the week and I would
have taken a dose myself from his bottle if Ida hadn't called
me aside and insisted on a walk. On the way along the front
and over the dunes west of the town I told her everything I
could remember about what had occurred during the day and
she said there was nothing to worry about so far. The prospect of them finding an old fingerprint of mine in the café
was remote, she thought, and she had taken care to wipe the
sink, taps, draining board and soap dish after we had washed
our hands.

"I daresay they'll find stains in the van when they locate
it," she said, "but that won't lead them anywhere. They'll almost certainly concentrate on catching the Italians at a port
and a bloodstain or two could mean anything or nothing.
They could have cut themselves digging or climbing in and
out that hole. The real trouble, of course, will be how they
got the impressions and Caddie's people will go to work on
that tomorrow. Our strong card is the age of the locks down
there. Before you came in Dadda said they hadn't been
changed or altered in any way since the branch opened. Is it
possible to make keys by measuring keyholes?"

"I'm hanged if I know," I said, "Beppo was the key expert.
If it is we're more or less home and dry, aren't we? So long
as nobody starts digging on Craigwen ridge."

"I'll tell you something, Charlie," she said pensively, "I
don't think they'll ever find them."

I must have looked amazed for she went on, "We were
incredibly lucky. If we'd put them anywhere else it would
have been a matter of days, possibly hours, but I went up
there this afternoon and the Council roller was working fifty
yards beyond the tool hut. That part of the trench is now
filled in to ground level and there's a machine starting to tar-
mac nearer the road. It isn't as if it's ordinary surface-laying
either. Down in the town the road is always coming up again
for one reason or another, drains, gas, water, telephones, but

up there it's a scheduled park now and no one can ever build on it. That was a condition of the gift."

I digested this and it brought me a degree of comfort. More and more I began to realize how much I owed to her initiative. I said, "I wouldn't have had a hope in hell if you hadn't shown up when you did, Ida. I don't think I'd have had the guts or the gumption to take some of the money and run."

"Wherever you ran they would have found you," she said. "Your one chance from the start, Boyo, was to stay put and stick to your story. You do that, not only for your own sake but for mine."

"Is there anything we overlooked that we can put right while there's still time?"

"There was," she said, "but it's taken care of. Our gloves for a start. I burned them in the stove this morning. Then I got rid of your slacks and windcheater and my mac. There were traces of blood on all three."

"Did you burn those too?"

"No, I couldn't do that with Mam around. I made a parcel of them, together with our shoes, and took it up to Windgates, the far side of the moor. In a patch of wood there I cut everything up and stuffed the pieces down rabbit holes at places some distance apart. Then I buried the shoes in mud at the edge of the pond. A real waste of money it was, more than ten pounds just thrown away. But people have been hanged for less."

We walked on in silence for a while and then I said, "You must wish to God you'd never met me, Ida. Deep down you must hate the sight of me."

"The funny thing is," she said, "I don't, Charlie. In a twisted kind of way I think more of you than I did when I went away. I wouldn't, if you had blood on your hands, but you haven't, not really. Quite apart from the gun you had no choice at all after he threatened to turn those drawings in."

"But how about getting to the point of giving him drawings?"

"I still think that was mad but you don't owe loyalty to

Caddie's. Nobody does. Or to any organization like Caddie's."

"All right, but you've seen what it's done to Evan and to people like Powell too. It'll ruin them all, won't it?"

She lifted her big shoulders. "Depends how you look at it. So they'll be moved on, or even turned loose a year or so earlier than they would have been. That means Dadda would be free to unwind and potter about. Nobody who knows him will believe he had anything to do with it. At first people will feel sorry for him and then they'll forget. They never would have done that if we'd left those bodies where they were, they would have pointed him out wherever he went for the rest of his life. That's the difference between bank robbery and murder. One is a bit of a lark but the other . . ."

"So you did it for him as much as me?"

"I did it because it had to be done."

We left it there and went home along the lower road that passed Melbourne Grove. Someone was half asleep. The green van was still in the corner where I had left it.

Chapter Seventeen

1

The bank remained closed for the rest of the week, business transferring to one of the Big Five under an emergency agreement Caddie's had in the event of a fire or similar calamity. That didn't mean, however, that we were left to our own devices. We had to be on call to make statements and answer questions during regulation working hours and each of us had to give an undertaking not to leave the area.

The second day, Tuesday, was relatively uneventful as far as I was concerned. Two of Caddie's directors appeared, one of them my ginger-haired friend, but they were not much concerned with juniors and did not even bother to question Porsen or Griffiths. They gave Evan and Powell a thorough going over, however, and Powell looked ashen when he came out. We heard later he had offered his resignation but it had been refused. For the meantime, like Evan, he was suspended from duty with pay, subject to further inquiries, and Evan told me the inquiries were likely to take a long time unless the police caught up with the Italians.

The hunt for them was now mounted on a national scale. We read in the papers about checks at all the ports and at places like Croydon Air Terminal, and every paper in Fleet Street carried detailed descriptions of "a man and a girl wanted to assist police in their enquiries concerning the N. Wales Bank Robbery." That was how it was referred to now but one or two of the zanier papers played up the tunnel approach and called it "The Penmadoc Mole-Robbery."

Young Mrs. Cook had a nervous breakdown and went into a nursing home. That left Edgar Cook free to carry on his *affaire* with the redhead above ground, providing he had the time. Personally I doubt if he did. The police were always popping in there and it was through the local sergeant that I discovered Mrs. Cook had heard noises in the yard during the small hours, had wakened her husband and asked him to investigate but he had refused to get out of bed, reminding her that the Italian often drove his van in and out long after midnight on Saturdays and Sundays.

I think it was this that gave the police the idea that they were dealing with a team of experienced burglars and efforts were made to link the break-in with other and relatively minor unsolved crimes in the area. One paper said Scotland Yard had been called in and had asked the help of the French police after Beppo had been spotted on the Riviera. Another reported that Delphine had been seen at Rio de Janeiro, but the global chase, if one was actually mounted, didn't concern us. We were on the spot permanently and the local police never ceased asking us questions and cross-checking the statements each of us made.

Porsen began to crack first. He was actually looking forward to his rural posting now and said he couldn't get out of the place quickly enough. On the other hand Griffiths, who quietly refused to be intimidated by anyone, kept his temper and one day surprised everybody by producing his solicitor uncle who told the CID inspector to his face that he considered the police were subjecting the staff to unreasonable duress and harassment. This seemed to work as far as Griffiths was concerned. From here on he faded out and Caddie's hardly saw the going of him.

By Thursday of that week inquiries began to make a pattern. Having disposed, as they thought, of any possibility of a criminal link between any one of us and The Rainbow pair, the probe in this particular field shifted to the younger element among the tin-plate workers, some of whom were known to be skilled or semi-skilled mechanics, capable of making keys. In the meantime, working on a theory based upon carelessness, relentless inquiries about key custody were directed at us and an almost minute by minute work-back of the system was built up, mainly by Brownlow, the local CID sergeant, who was always mooching about, sometimes in the bank and sometimes in the café. For some reason I was always more aware of him than of any of the others.

The key routine went like this. First, we all had access to the safe key and it was accepted that any one of us could have been careless enough to leave it around long enough for someone to make an impression. Secondly, we all, at one time or another, had handled Powell's grille key but it was reckoned impossible that anyone other than Powell could have held it long enough to serve any other purpose than open the outer grille in the presence of Powell or Evan or both. Thirdly, none of us, including Powell, ever handled Evan's grille key, except when the manager's annual holiday had required a general post, Powell taking the manager's key and giving Griffiths custody of his own. Luckily for Griffiths Evan hadn't taken a holiday for nearly two years so the changeover hadn't been made during the period I was on the staff. Not that any one person so much as hinted that any of us had connived at making an impression, or causing one to be made. The implication was that one or more of us had, in some unguarded moment, laid them down somewhere, on the counter perhaps, in the café, or even at home, where a watchful professional had taken swift advantage of an opportunity.

Attempting, with some success, to disprove this theory, we acted out a lengthy charade involving the opening and shutting of the vault in the presence of the police, and later that day Evan took the inspector home and showed him exactly what he did with the key at night. Powell produced an even better alibi. He proved that his keys were deposited in a concealed wall safe every night and produced his wife to witness the fact that at no time had that safe been disturbed. Then Powell questioned the age of the locks and the comparative simplicity of their pattern, and it was this that led to an alternative supposition, one hinted at by Ida concerning the possibility of making false keys by an expert study of the type of locks involved.

On Friday of that week a locksmith was introduced onto the premises by Caddie's directors. He was a refreshingly blunt character from Manchester, who told the police in our presence that he would have expected to find the safe in a museum and that any enterprising burglar could assess its type of lock merely by looking at it and then come up with a key that, subject to adjustments, would open the safe as easily as the key we held. This rattled the directors and they asked for an opinion on the grilles. It was scarcely more encouraging. The locksmith said that a skilled man, who really understood his business, could make keys for both grates providing he had the time and opportunity to study them at close quarters and carry out certain preliminary tests with the kind of apparatus a man like that would have at his disposal.

This theory, of course, hinged on the date the tunnel was completed and the police, who were now getting desperate, began to adapt the facts to fit the theory, assuming that Beppo and his confederates had been popping in and out the washroom like rabbits.

By the following Monday, when this theory was well established, we were all more or less off the hook and it began to appear as if Caddie's system and not their staff was under review. The only one who did not subscribe to the new theory was Brownlow, the blue-eyed CID sergeant. He told his inspector that it was nonsense and a close examination of the material found round the hole would prove as much. In his view the washroom had only been entered once, the night of the robbery. When asked to establish an alternative means of entry, however, he admitted he couldn't and contented himself by saying that there was an unknown factor in the case and no real progress could be made until they got a lead on a confederate with some knowledge of engineering. Only the qualification brought me any comfort. It seemed to indicate that he thought an accomplice could be found among the tin-plate men.

I learned all this by keeping my eyes and ears open, and also by comparing notes with Gwyn, whose conscience was troubling him these days. It was not necessary for him to explain why but after we had discussed the break-in several times he did, converting the confession into a plea. He said, when we met by chance in the main road one lunch hour, "You ever told my gaffer we were at school together, Boyo?"

"No," I said, "why should I?"

He looked very relieved. "Then don't, Boyo," he said, "and I don't have to ask you to stand by a pal if they ask how I put in some of the time nights, do I now?"

Since he put it like this I saw no reason why I shouldn't ask him where he was on that particular Saturday night. Who knew but the information might not come in handy when I needed it? I said, "Didn't you see anything in the least unusual on that night, Gwyn?"

"Not a thing," he admitted, "quiet as a graveyard, it was," and then, reluctantly, "fact is, Boyo, I was up the far end of town until round about four. They would have finished by then, I reckon."

"With that widow?"

He winced. Maybe he had been hoping I'd forgotten his confidences. "Well, part of the time," he said, "I got back this end just as it was getting light. Damn it, I passed that bloody bank of yours as it was striking half-four!" He was lying, even to me, but nevertheless I couldn't have missed him by more than a few minutes when I was dumping the van and the thought of how close it had been made me shudder.

"Well, I shan't say anything," I reassured him. "We're all in enough trouble as it is. They seem to think we've been leaving bank keys in all the local telephone kiosks. What do you think, Gwyn? About how it was done, I mean?"

"I don't," he said, "only the CID thinks in our outfit and they get a better rate of pay for doing it, Boyo!"

He strolled off and I could see by the jauntiness of his stride that I had taken some of the weight off his mind.

By the middle part of the second week police pressure had been relaxed, particularly after someone located the van. They were incredibly slow getting round to this. I suppose it never occurred to them to search so near home and it was driven off to Chester for various tests. That didn't bother me much. I had been particularly careful about fingerprints in that respect and I thought the vehicle would make the identification of the chief suspects that much more certain.

When the blow fell on us it was not from the CID but Cadwallader's and was administered by no less a person than Sir Adrian Lloyd-Jenkins, OBE, the Chairman of the Board of Directors.

I had never seen Sir Adrian in the flesh although photographs of him presiding at banquets and other functions had often appeared in the bank journal. He paid us a visit on Friday, nearly a fortnight after the break-in and we were all assembled in the bank like a troop of schoolchildren chivvied in front of a visiting inspector.

He was a big, florid man with an outwardly courteous manner but inside he was proofed steel. The carroty director introduced him, rather like Gabriel might pray silence for God, and in booming tones from which the Welsh accent had been carefully extracted half-a-century ago, Sir Adrian described the robbery to us as if it was our first acquaintance with it.

"I need hardly say that nothing of this nature has ever come within the orbit of our organization before," he went on, having disposed of the preamble. "Other banks, yes—fortunately very rarely I might say—but Cadwallader's, *never*! We take it very much to heart. *You* take it to heart! No specific blame lies anywhere I am informed but we cannot blind ourselves to the fact that it happened. A person or persons burrowed their way into these premises, opened the vault and safe, and made off with a little under twenty thousand pounds. That money has not yet been recovered and the person or persons responsible have not yet been apprehended." He made it sound as though, in addition to robbery, the crime of lese majesty had been committed, along with the desecration of an altar.

He continued, "Under these circumstances, of course, certain routine procedures must be put into practice, as by all undertakings responsible for the custody of large sums of money. As I say, this has never happened to us before, but provision was made for it in standard procedures, as for any other contingency. The rule is there and, much as it distresses me, I am obliged to apply it. The staff will be dispersed among other branches and an entirely new staff brought in to replace it. Disturbance allowances will be paid up to the sum of thirty pounds per unit. That, gentlemen, I insisted upon, and in the meantime, in order that personal arrangements may be made, everyone will get a month's paid leave dating from September fifth."

There was a stir at this and he waited for it to subside. Then he went on, "As regards the manager, Mr. Rhys-Jones, with whom I would like to take the opportunity of expressing my sincere sympathy, an alternative presents itself."

Everyone looked at Evan who sat right under the speaker. He remained utterly motionless, his round head seemingly balanced on hunched shoulders, a pink and gray football resting on the back of a chair. "Mr. Rhys-Jones has been with us for over forty years, during which period he has rendered loyal and faithful service. He is now within three years of the optional retirement date. My directors have asked me to give him the ... er ... the choice of retiring now, if only to avoid what would be, I cannot but feel, the acute embarrassment of taking charge of a branch elsewhere. As to the remaining members of the staff, Mr. Powell, together with Mr. Griffiths, have submitted their resignations but that of Mr. Powell, I am happy to say, has been withdrawn. Mr. Griffiths has decided upon a new career and I am sure all of us wish him success and happiness. Are there any questions?"

A question came from an entirely unexpected quarter. The

sunken head of Evan raised itself as he hoisted his tubby frame upright. His voice, I thought, was unnaturally pitched, as though he was addressing Sir Adrian through a long, thin tube.

"Am I to understand, Sir Adrian, that as a result of this I am being asked to retire while my chief cashier is being given another post?"

Somebody coughed and the slight interruption gave the chairman a moment to brace himself against the deadly directness of the query.

"You are being given an *option*, Mr. Rhys-Jones. I thought I made that clear."

"What kind of an option is that?"

This released general tension. I thought I heard Powell exclaim and Porsen giggle.

The other director rose to intervene. "Sir Adrian was explicit . . ." but Evan made one of his famous chopping motions. It was marvelous to see it work on a director. "I *know* all that," he said, his accent thickening as he proceeded, "I'm not deaf, I got *yers*, man! He's asking me to resign but he's letting Powell stay on. That means I take the full responsibility and Powell goes off sniggering. But he was here at the time, and he holds three keys to my one. I would have lived on the premises if I'd been given the chance but nobody gave me that chance. When I came yer first I wanted that flat badly but he clung to it . . ."

"Mr. Rhys-Jones, this really isn't serving any purpose . . ." protested Sir Adrian, half-rising in his seat.

"You asked for questions," went on Evan, quite unabashed, "and here's another I want answered. Over forty years' service I've given this bank and now, when something like this happens, I get my marching orders and a man who is more to blame than me gets promotion! That's not all either, though it's bad enough. What about the people down in Cardiff who are supposed to be responsible for the fabric? Are they being asked to retire? Those locks down there are out of date. You've seen the police report, same as I have. What about the directors who draw dividends for making sure things like this

278

can't happen? Do *they* get retired early? Are *you* going to step down, sir?"

His voice had been growing louder all the time and he finished on a note that rang through the building. He was absolutely splendid. I wanted to get up and cheer, particularly when I saw Sir Adrian's heavy features turn purple, but nobody got an opportunity to answer his questions for suddenly Evan kicked the chair away from him, snapped his fingers in the air, and marched toward the street door. He had some trouble with the chain and it delayed him long enough for some of us to cluster round him as he fumbled with it, but as everyone was talking at once I didn't hear any individual remark. Then he was across the threshold and some of us, among whom Sir Adrian and his fellow director were not included, followed him out onto the pavement but here he shook us off like a mastiff shedding fleas, and stumped up the incline at a brisk pace, disappearing round the corner into the main road. I would have followed him had I not assumed he was going home where I could join him as soon as I had checked on the result of his extraordinary outburst.

There wasn't that much reaction. They were ruffled but not shamed, as I would have expected them to be. By the time we had reassembled inside and closed the door Sir Adrian had himself in hand.

"That was *most* unfortunate," he said, "unfortunate and quite uncalled for! Clearly Mr. Rhys-Jones is not himself, and I suppose one can make allowances for that in the circumstances."

"It only underlines what was indicated in the preliminary report, Sir Adrian," said ferret-face, to which the chairman replied, vaguely, "Quite so, quite so!" Then, as though realizing that anything that followed would be an anticlimax, he dismissed us and Powell, all smiles now, went snuffling round the directors like a dog who had found two bitches in season.

Griffiths said, as we went out, "Good for Evan! If he hadn't said it, I would. Provided I'd had the guts!"

Porsen said, "That bastard Powell! He's fixed himself but it never occurred to him to put in a word for me."

I let that go, I was anxious to get after Evan, but when I arrived at St. Ninian's a few minutes later he wasn't there so I gave Gladys and Ida a brief account of what had occurred. Gladys was deeply shocked. "But that was mad," she said, "that was crazy of him! Forty years, and he has to throw it all away like that! I'll give him a rare piece of my mind when he comes in, you see if I don't."

"You'll do no such thing," Ida said, "I'm proud of him and I never was when he played safe. You leave him alone, d'you hear? He's got enough to put up with, besides your nagging."

To my surprise Gladys accepted this with no more than a rumble of protest. The events of the last week or two had undermined her belief in her infallibility.

When we were alone Ida said, "Where do you suppose he's gone, Charlie?"

"To get tight I wouldn't wonder," I said, thinking how much I would like to do the same myself but she said, thoughtfully, "I'm worried about him. Outwardly he's borne up pretty well but inwardly he's taken a terrific pounding. I never put much value on his little world but it can't be funny seeing it fall to pieces in a fortnight!"

I noticed then that it was coming on to blow, the way it sometimes did in Penmadoc in mid-September. A southwesterly was building up over the mountains and its gusts rattled the window frames. "I suppose it's no use looking for him," she said, but I said we could try the chapel, his doctor's, and the homes of one or two of his cronies among the deacons. She said this was better than hanging about, so we made the rounds, without the least result.

By seven o'clock it was blowing a full gale, with the wind whooping along the streets in seventy-mile-an-hour gusts and rain falling in torrents. We arrived home dripping wet and had something to eat. Gladys had gone to lie down and as it got wilder and darker outside Ida began to get more and more anxious. There was absolutely nothing we could do and not much we could talk about with Gladys in the house. We sat there getting gloomier and gloomier and around ten there was a faint chinking sound from the hall, and we both got up and ran out to be struck by a terrific blast of wind that came straight through the open front door.

I switched on the hall light and there he was, crouching on all fours like a dog that had wandered in out of the rain. He was plastered in both senses. Every garment he was wearing was wet and muddied and his thin gray hair was sticking to his forehead. His collar was loose, one shoe was missing and his round face, ordinarily so pink and glowing, was the color of a ripe plum, as though a huge port-wine mark had spread across his jowls and neck. We were so shocked by his appearance that we stood there staring down at him while the wind charged into the house and set everything rattling and banging. Then Ida, without a word, helped him to his feet and as he stood upright I saw his key ring hanging the full length of its chain. He must have found his way home by instinct and fallen forward in the act of opening the door.

We got him up to his room and sent Gladys to prepare hot water bottles while we peeled off his clothes and gave him a good rub down. He was as helpless as a baby and a good deal more passive. He babbled a lot of nonsense but he didn't say anything coherent and we never did discover where he had passed the afternoon and evening. Gladys gazed down at him as he lay in bed snorting and grunting but could find no words to express her amazement and indignation. Her world was falling apart as rapidly as his, for Evan had been a pillar of the Temperance movement ever since she had known him.

His color had returned to normal by morning but his breathing was labored and we called in the doctor about midday. We said he had been caught in last night's storm but didn't add that he had been on a terrific bender. We didn't have to, the room stank like a four-ale bar, and the doctor told us he had a severe chill and was running a temperature. The next day, Sunday, he diagnosed double pneumonia and advised us to let him shift the patient to hospital. Ida wasn't keen on this but the doctor and I persuaded her to agree and he went off by ambulance that same afternoon.

My posting was due any day and there was still almost a fortnight left of the leave Sir Adrian had announced. I rang the hospital every morning and evening and the sister described his condition as "poorly," whatever that meant, but when we all three called there on the first visiting day we were shocked at his appearance. He could talk but only in a whisper. In bed he looked smaller and older and I got the impression even then he was dying, but I hadn't the courage to tell Ida what I thought and Gladys was no good at all in this kind of crisis. She seemed to resent him falling ill at a time when he should be around to sustain her. By then the robbery had dropped out of the front pages of the newspapers but there were still occasional references to "clues" and "sightings of the Italian gang" on the inside pages. The police didn't bother us and neither, for that matter, did the bank.

Early one morning they sent for us and the matron waylaid us in the waiting room, taking me aside and telling me that Evan was critically ill and asking me to break the news to Gladys. I let Ida do that and went in to see him first. They had shifted him into an isolation ward and I saw at once that he was unlikely to last the day. Gray stubble sprouted on his faded cheeks and his brown eyes were vacant although he was able to recognize me. What could you say to a man in that condition? Especially when you were mainly responsible for it?

I made the only gesture that occurred to me, lifting his hand and pressing it. That touched him and his pursy little mouth twitched. Assembling what few resources he had left he said, in a whisper, "You and Ida—*when?*"

"As soon as you're up and out of here, Evan," I said. It was the first time I had ever addressed him by his Christian name. After a longish pause he made another effort. "That Lloyd-Jenkins fellow," he wheezed, slowly and carefully, "been wanting to say something like that to him all my life." It was as good a way as any, I thought, to sever a lifelong connection with Caddie's, particularly an alliance as one-sided as his had been, all give on Evan's part, all take on theirs. At that precise moment I rejoiced in what I had done to them but wished with all my heart that it could have been achieved without hurting him. I went out and Gladys and Ida went in. That same night, just after eleven o'clock, he died, without saying another word to anyone. Ida had assured me I had no blood on my hands but I didn't believe her anymore.

3

As soon as I notified Caddie's they gave me another week's leave to clear up but this time it was unpaid. That was typical. Somehow or other they had to begin recouping the missing twenty thousand. Three days later they saved another pound or two by failing to send a wreath or an official representative to the funeral, but Griffiths and Porsen turned up, and so did a number of people who had no connection with him but had met him in the papers over the last three weeks.

It was a still September afternoon and half Penmadoc enjoyed the outing. Ida said, on the way home, "I hate this place, I've always hated it! Let's hope to God you get a city posting." I hoped so too and wondered what had become of my determination to escape the clammy embrace of Caddie's, and then, suddenly, I knew. Watching Evan stand up to those directors I had unconsciously made up my mind to stay on and do battle with them and now, I felt, I owed it to him to do just that. I could never hope to beat them but my continued presence among them, a man who had walked off with nearly twenty thousand pounds of their money and hadn't been caught, was a kind of lifelong sneer at an organization capable of taking people like Evan and Powell and Porsen and me and shaping them into parasites who fed one upon another, becoming less than human in the process.

We drove straight from the cemetery to the station, Gladys having decided to spend a week or two in Anglesey with her sister who had attended the funeral. After we had seen her off Ida and I walked home. She said, "You'll be gone in less than a fortnight, Charlie. Do you suppose Mam would be shocked if we got married at a registry office before you went?"

"She'd probably be relieved," I said, "but she wouldn't admit it. Can it be done that easily?"

"By special license," she said. "We'll talk about it in the morning."

It was curious how Evan's death brought us even closer together than our brief partnership in crime. I had thought she might want to walk out on me on a plea that I was responsible for killing him but she must have buried prejudices of that kind along with Beppo and Delphine. In fact, I began to sense that she now had as great a need of me as I had of her, perhaps because a normal, civilized person can't carry that weight of guilt alone and faces a straight choice of dropping it or sharing it with someone. I told her about Evan's final query concerning us and she said it made sense. He had always felt slightly ashamed of having a lumpish daughter nobody was anxious to marry and had, in addition, old-fashioned notions about a single woman being unequipped to fend for herself when she was past her youth. His inner feelings concerning Caddie's, she said, were even more basic. Buried deep down in him was the near-extinct ghost of Celtic independence that had been trying to get out for half a century.

Then, as we turned into the terrace from the main road, we saw him leaning against the gatepillar of St. Ninian's in the act of lighting his pipe. Brownlow, the CID sergeant, negligently poised for the kill.

My heart didn't stop at my boots. It plummeted through the pavement and out of sight. She sensed my terror and tried to counter it by gripping my forearm, nodding pleasantly in the direction of the lounging figure, and muttering, without turning her head, "Stay with it, Boyo! The only way they can get you now is through your own big mouth!" Then she quickened her step, almost dragging me along and said, by way of a greeting, "Hullo, Mr. Brownlow. Charlie and I have just come from the funeral. Won't you come in and have a cup of tea?"

Although he was the professional she had the most self-possession. A flicker of uncertainty ruffled his impersonal gaze and he said, touching his hat, "I'm sorry, Miss Rhys-Jones, I ... er ... knew about your loss, of course, but I didn't realize today was ..."

"It doesn't matter a bit," she said, almost too cheerfully, "Mam's not here, we've just packed her off to Anglesey for a rest and change."

He hesitated a moment longer but she held the gate open. "There were just one or two odds and ends I thought Mr. Pritchard might be able to clear up," he said, and she replied, "I'm sure he'd be glad to, wouldn't you, Charlie?" I don't recall what I said but whatever it was it was noncommittal.

"I'll put the kettle on," she said, and to me, "Show Mr. Brownlow into the front room, Charlie. I won't be a minute."

I didn't have her kind of confidence in myself. The journey over the threshold and into Gladys's fusty little parlor was like a rehearsal for that eight o'clock walk I had read about in the Sunday newspapers.

I made the effort, however, and pulled up the blinds that Gladys had lowered in obedience to terrace-house protocol. We sat facing one another over the patchwork rug, with Gladys's two pop-eyed Staffordshire dogs for company. He puffed contentedly at his pipe.

"Sad about Mr. Rhys-Jones," he began and when I agreed, "sudden too." The late afternoon sun fell on his narrow face and once again his expressionless eyes reminded me of the underside of iris petals.

I said, "I suppose you also heard they more or less gave him the push after forty years. That's a bank for you. They wouldn't get away with that if we had a decent union."

"They'd try," he said, sympathetically I thought. Then in the same restrained tone, "About your association with those Rainbow people, Mr. Pritchard, you ... er ... forgot something. I don't think it was deliberate. But you forgot something I think is important."

He was a talented cross-examiner. His golden rule was never to betray how much or how little he knew. I realized

I was turning the color of cheese but I couldn't do a thing about that. I remembered Ida's warning about the big mouth, however, and it limited my response to a single word. The word was, "Well?"

He had been hoping for more than that but when he realized he wasn't going to get it he went on, "There was a bit of a rough and tumble there getting on for nine months ago. Round about New Year, it was. You were involved, I believe."

So he had dug as deeply as that and it seemed to me he had reached danger level. I said, cautiously, "There were often squabbles over one thing or another when I used to go there. The tin-plate men didn't come in until closing time at the pubs and sometimes they were half tight, particularly on Fridays."

"This was a Friday."

I made a pretense of thinking but I don't think it fooled him. It would take a lot more than that to fool Brownlow.

"I remember now," I said, "I'd completely forgotten."

"Good. Tell me about it."

"One of the tin-plate workers tried to grab the girl."

"Yes?"

"I hit him over the head with a vinegar bottle."

"Wasn't that an extraordinary thing to do?"

"I don't think so. He was fighting drunk and his pals were pretty well as bad."

"How many were there?"

"I don't remember, four or five maybe."

He occupied the next ten seconds packing his pipe and the exercise gave him a paternal air. Then he said, "You against four or five? And all of them bigger than you. *Why* exactly?"

I took my time answering. The truth wouldn't do at all but then, neither would a deliberate lie.

"For two reasons now I come to think about it. One was obvious, he was mauling the woman and she objected very strongly. The brother was there but he was down the far end of the shop and behind the coffee machine. He was also a bit deaf."

"I see. And the other reason?"

"That particular chap always had it in for me."

"Trevor Thomas? The one you hit?"

"I don't know his name. He was a big, lumbering lout, and a bully with it."

"You mean he had provoked you in some way before that evening?"

"He and others. One of them tripped me up when I was walking back from the counter carrying a coffee so that I went sprawling and spilled it. That kind of thing. Those chaps always try and take it out of white collar men. They think of us all as sissies and I was fed up with it. I didn't stop to think what I was doing. If I had I daresay I wouldn't have had the guts to crown him. Once the fighting started the brother chipped in and kicked them all out."

"Did they thank you for rescuing the lady in distress?"

"The brother did but it didn't stop them both turning on me a month or two later when I found a tack in my sandwich."

"Ah, yes, that was when you stopped going there."

"That's right."

He was silent, puffing away at his pipe and looking into the clouds of tobacco as though he still had hopes of finding the truth there.

"I wish you had remembered that," he said at last but I parried this easily enough.

"Look here, Sergeant," I said, "I've been as upset by all this as everyone else. It's a wonder any of us remembered anything at all clearly, much less something that happened getting on for a year ago."

I thought he might go then but he didn't. I could hear Ida rattling teacups in the kitchen and a moment later she appeared with a tray and set it down.

"Well?" she said, in that party voice of hers, "Has Charlie been able to help you?"

"We've run down another cul-de-sac, Miss Rhys-Jones," he said, adding, as he took his tea and stirred it, "this is extremely kind of you, particularly at a time like this. You weren't in the town when the robbery took place, were you?"

It was put as an innocent question but she wasn't fooled either.

287

"As a matter of fact I was," she said, "just about. I got in that very night rather late. I came on the eleven-twenty, from London. I wasn't expected until the weekend after but I had my key. They were all asleep so I surprised them in the morning."

"You must have passed The Rainbow on the way up Station Road."

"I expect I did," said Ida, "I generally come that way. Is that tea too strong, Mr. Brownlow?"

"No, it's just right," he said and drank it up. "No more, thank you, that was very nice. You didn't see or hear anything unusual going on there, I suppose? Lights, or that organ playing?"

"As far as I can remember the café was closed," Ida said, "but I couldn't swear to it."

He sat musing while we sipped our tea. Mine tasted like scalding vinegar. Then, extracting his wallet, he probed carefully in its folds and produced an envelope. I was absolutely certain that it contained my sketches of the keys, the ones we had assumed were either destroyed or buried with Beppo but when he opened the flap it wasn't to extract sheets of drawing paper but a faded newsclipping three columns wide.

"I came across this turning things over at The Rainbow," he said. "It was in a bureau, with a few other papers, bills and things. I thought it might amuse you. Your Christian name *is* Charles, isn't it?"

I took the cutting and smoothed it out on my knee. I didn't have to read the caption. It was the photograph of the suburban wife looking over the gateway of "Mon Repos" or "Chez Nous" appealing to Charlie to come home and face them. I hoped I looked blank and I hoped he didn't notice my shaking hands. He stood up, suddenly, "Keep it as a souvenir," he said, "it doesn't come in the category of evidence I'm afraid."

It was lucky Ida was there to show him out. My knees would have buckled if I had tried to stand. I heard him thank her again and then his step on the path. Ida came back and looked at the cutting.

"Where does this fit in?" she said, and her voice had lost its hostess ring.

"It all started from that."

She studied it again, finally folding it carefully and putting it behind the mantelshelf clock.

"Does he know anything? Is he keeping something up his sleeve or has he shot his bolt?"

"He's got a hunch," I said, "and it'll torment him for the rest of his life. But he knows it's a hunch and can never grow into anything more."

"What does that mean, exactly? That he'll continue to keep an eye on you, wherever you are?"

"For a bit. For a year or so maybe but there's only one way that hunch could lead anywhere."

"If they started digging up at Craigwen?"

"No, not even then. If we started spending money in excess of what he knows we earn."

"Then he's got a hell of a long wait ahead of him," she said and went out into the kitchen with the loaded tray.

My posting came through on the last day of the month. It was for a steel town in the south, one of our biggest branches where, I imagine, Caddie's hoped I would be absorbed and lost, a stray survivor of the Penmadoc disaster where the bank's prestige took such a beating. It didn't work out like this but that is another story.

Ida and I were married by special license a couple of days before I moved south, a discreet and what Gladys thought of as a furtive ceremony. We had two witnesses, the cleaning woman and Griffiths, who somehow heard about it and appeared to offer his services. By that time Powell had gone and so had Porsen and a fresh staff had been brought in, but not before there had been considerable activity below ground. The ponderous old safe was hauled out and sold for scrap and modern combination locks were fitted to the grilles.

In the early hours of the morning I was due to go I woke up and, sensing Ida was awake, made what I believe was our last reference ever to the child conceived in this narrow, comfortless house. I said, "Did you ever meet the people who adopted him, Ida?" and she said no, this wasn't allowed to happen, and all she knew was that they were approved as suitable by the authorities.

Then she said, "Whoever they are, Charlie, they're a damned sight more 'suitable' than either of us," and I said that this was undeniable. Nothing more was said at the time but I think it was about then we made up our minds independently not to have any more children.

We were, as it turned out, a good deal happier than we deserved, at least, than I deserved. Right from the start it was a good marriage and when Ida and her mother moved south to join me, and we shared a bungalow bought with Evan's insurance money, I even grew attached to Gladys in the way one adapts to a dog that makes a lot of noise but has no sense. Ida tolerated her too and we got along well enough, particularly in later years when the dust had settled. She died early in the war, peevishly demanding chocolates, sugar, butter and everything else that was fattening and rationed.

As time went on Ida and I found it increasingly difficult to regard the Penmadoc affair as something that had actually occurred, at least to us. By some devious method of reasoning we were able to slot it into the mental bracket one reserves for disasters with which one was once marginally associated, a train or air smash on a journey you meant to take but somehow didn't, a blitz that killed people you knew but left you with a few bruises and a bad fright. We almost never referred to it and when we did it was indirectly. After the first year or two we even stopped dreaming about it and waking up in a sweat to seek comfort in one another.

And yet, in another way, it had long-term effects and was also of indirect benefit to the lower grades of Cadwallader's staff. I learned through the grapevine that Evan's outburst had had repercussions at the highest level. Sir Adrian, the chairman, was given what we should now call the golden hand-

shake and the ferrety little director who, all unknowingly, had
made a contribution to my participation, was kicked upstairs.
At the summit he plucked a knighthood out of electronics.
Security was given a face-lift in all branches and pay and conditions slowly improved until the inevitable happened and we
were absorbed into one of the Big Five. By then I was a chief
cashier and I like to think a much better one than Powell, at
least as far as my dealings with juniors were concerned. I
heard of him from time to time until he retired and went back
to Chester in the final year of the war.

He was luckier than Porsen. Porsen's passion for the internal
combustion engine led him to enlist in the Armoured Corps
in 1940, where he soon got a commission. When I heard about
this I used to fancy him strutting about the parade ground
and workshops, with his fat arse sticking out and his eye
assessing the possibilities of the ATS girls. I did him a grave
injustice. He was decorated for gallantry at El Alamein and
later fried alive when his tank was knocked out on the Mareth
line.

I kept in touch with Griffiths for a long time. Maybe we had
more in common than we knew for, as he prospered, he became more and more prominent in Welsh Nationalist circles
and was even rumored to be involved in an attempt to blow
up a dam in Carmarthenshire. It was curious, I thought, that
a six-man branch of a conservative institution like Caddie's
should number two desperadoes among its staff.

Gwyn-the-Boots kept his small secret as successfully as I
kept my big one. Years later, while on holiday in the Barmouth
area, we met him and I was surprised to find him a civilian.
He made an oblique reference to that terrible Saturday night,
edging me out of earshot of Ida and confessing, with a broad
grin, that he had married the little widow from the guest
house after discovering that she had enough money to enable
him to leave the force and set up as a hotelier in Cornwall.

"It only proves," he said, by way of a valediction, "that it
pays to advertise, Boyo! Been around in her time had our
Mavis, but she settled for me in the end and it couldn't have

been on account of my pay and prospects, could it now?" I was glad for him and for myself, too. I didn't want Gwyn on my conscience as well as Evan.

I evaded war service on health grounds but staff shortage greatly accelerated my promotion. By 1948 I had my own branch and could start worrying about security. I hung on until I was within a year of retiring age and then left on an almost maximum pension. That same year Ida began to show signs of the heart defect that had killed her mother more than twenty years earlier. She tried to get her weight down but she had her mother's appetite and it wasn't easy. She had a couple of bad attacks and after the last one came to terms with the inevitable. The day I fetched her from the hospital, with a bag full of pills and a long list of instructions about what to eat and what not to eat, she made one of her rare references to that part of our past we had buried on the crest of the Craig-wen estate. "Charlie," she said, "we've both had a damned sight more luck than we could expect so why complain? That Saturday night up in Penmadoc I didn't think either of us would see forty and here I am nudging seventy!" Then she started doing what she liked and eating what she liked and three months later, one sultry afternoon when I was working in the garden, she collapsed. With a neighbor's help I got her indoors and the neighbor phoned for the doctor. I could see that she wanted to say something and bent over her. She was in considerable pain but she managed a wry smile. "Well, Charlie," she said in a whisper, "we made it." Seconds later she was dead.

In a way I died the same day but I don't mean this in the conventional sense. There was a bond between us which was that much stronger than exists between most couples who have managed to adjust to all the hidden pressures of marriage. What I mean is that after Ida went the secret didn't seem all that important and as to survival I stopped giving a damn one way or the other. I was lonely and desolate but in another and less logical way the tension under which I had lived for so long relaxed so that for the first time I could contemplate a return to Penmadoc, not to live (although that in fact is what happened) but to browse around a bit and strike some sort of bargain with myself. This had nothing to do with the criminal's traditional return to the scene of the crime but everything to do with all I remembered and admired about Ida.

For some time I resisted this tug as irrational but in the end, some weeks after her death, I packed a bag and drove north to find the old place more changed and enlarged than any other town I remembered.

It seemed that at last Penmadoc had found its muddled destiny and evolved into a great sprawling, bustling labyrinth linked to older, more successful resorts east and west of the bay. The only thing that hadn't changed much was Station Road. The bank was still a bank, and Cook's was still a draper's, although now a multiple concern. More surprising still was the fact that The Rainbow was still a café, but there the similarity ended. The new place had a chromium front, had been enlarged upward and from front to back, and was obviously doing a roaring trade. It was called The Pan Handle and had a trendy, transatlantic air. Its menu card offered hot dogs and three-decker Danish sandwiches, served from a glittering snack bar that was fitted with a long row of perches that looked like mushrooms.

I went in and bought a coffee for old times' sake but there wasn't a thing about the place, architecturally or atmospherically, that was recognizable. The music was piped and seemed to dribble from gilded cornices as if the musicians had been walled in at ceiling-level and were trying to bring their plight to somebody's notice. The clientele were mostly young girls wearing false eyelashes and miniskirts an inch or so shorter than flappers wore when I bought my first coffee there. Their escorts wore their hair on the shoulder and sported clothes that nobody would have remarked on thirty years ago if it had been the day of the annual carnival.

When I went up the hill I discovered new roads carved out of the long gardens of the big detached houses behind the main highway and I had some trouble locating Craigwen Terrace. The house was still there but it looked far less sober than I recalled. It was painted red and cream, and bathing towels flapped from the sills of first-floor windows.

I stood looking at it a long time feeling old, tired and defeated. I had lived in a lot of houses in my time but this was the only one that had made an impact on me. Just to see it brought Ida so much closer and I spared a thought for the child conceived in that cheerless room at the back, a child I had never seen and never would see. I realized, with a sense of shock, that he would be getting on for forty now. I moved on, climbing the hill to the edge of the enlarged plantation that crowned the southern slope of the Craigwen estate. "Take what you want," Ida's old proverb had said, "and pay for it." That day the price seemed prohibitive, even though the bill had never been settled.

Then, with considerable interest but no sense of shock, I saw what they were doing up there. A huge bulldozer was gnawing its way into the bank that divided the branch road from a row of empty flowerbeds on either side of a curving asphalt path. The asphalt had already been split and seamed by pneumatic drills. On each side of the track were deep cuts in the soil, flanked by mounds of freshly-turned earth. Close by was a big white board bearing the name of a local building contractor and under it stood a man in dungarees directing the machine. After watching for a few minutes I strolled over and asked him what was happening.

"Car park," he said, "Council contract. Time enough, too. Can't move for cars down in the town. Not too bad now but in August the five seafront parks fill up by midday. This will take another five hundred."

"But it's a long way from the front, isn't it?"

He looked at me as if I was someone who had ridden penny-farthings. "So what? They'll have to drive here and walk down, won't they? Another year or two and cars won't be allowed inside any town boundary." He turned away, shouting to the operator, "Swing left, Roddy! Over left! We're level this side!"

I watched for another five minutes. At a guess the jaws of the bulldozer were about forty yards short of the spot where the bones of Beppo and Delphine lay some five feet below ground. To keep them company there was around twenty thousand pounds in treasury notes, providing they hadn't moldered inside the rucksacks. There was also an automatic pistol, a shoe, a doormat and a trunk full of neatly-packed clothes.

After that I couldn't keep away. I was there or thereabouts every morning, marking their progress by the advance of roped-off sectors indicated by white posts driven into the ground. I was spellbound by the lumbering lurches of the bulldozer, the methodical raking back of the soil and boulders it shifted, and the steady extension of a vast rectangle of level ground into the hillside. Higher up pneumatic drills were at work on the old paths and the din they made was deafening. Nobody noticed me. Everyone was too absorbed in the job.

It happened about eleven o'clock on a windless overcast morning in late July. I was standing well back on the summit of Craigwen Terrace when I saw the bulldozer falter at the top of a fresh mound. The operator, perched high on the machine, began to shout and gesticulate and then everybody began to run, converging on a point immediately below the grab. I tried to make myself join them but I couldn't. Perhaps it was squeamishness or, more probably, the instinct of self-preservation reasserting itself. I walked home, back to the flat I had rented, and poured myself a stiff drink.

It was on every front page the next morning but before that there was a summary on the TV news. "Grisly find at Penmadoc. Bulldozer turns up two skeletons and what seems to be the remains of a fortune in treasury notes." A double inquest was promised. Detectives were already at work on the mystery.

I wondered. Thirty-eight years is a longish time and twenty thousand pounds was still a big sum of money to me, but not much compared with the two and a half million the train robbers had taken.

They would find the bullet, no doubt, and match it with the gun. Forensic and ballistic science had made great strides since 1930. I knew because I had continued to take an interest in such things. They might even check on the numbers of some of the notes but even if that was possible it would take time. Two bodies, one shot through the head and the other with a broken neck. A gun, a large suitcase, a doormat, and two rotting rucksacks stuffed with the shredded fragments of treasury notes. All that and what they might or might not find among personal effects that had resisted time. Was it enough? And if so where would it point them? Was it true that the police never closed a file on an unsolved case?

It was one of those stories that lingered. BBC and news-papermen descended on the town in far greater numbers than they had in 1930. Penmadoc, approaching its seasonal peak, reveled in the free publicity, but it was more than a week before I read a report linking the exhumation with the raid on Caddie's bank all those years ago. Somebody must have done a lot of digging. The sudden death of Evan was recalled and although the writer did not accuse him of complicity he let it be implied, so that I was glad Gladys and Ida were beyond reach. I wondered then about the persistent CID sergeant, Brownlow, the man with the hunch. Was he still living? If so, he would be in his eighties. Porsen was dead and Powell, more than twenty years my senior, almost certainly so. Griffiths and the junior, Gregg, I didn't know about but it seemed no time to start looking them up. I did what I had done for nearly four decades. I sat tight and waited.

The inquest was held and fully reported but although speculation in the witness box was rife nobody called could positively identify the bones as those of the two Italians who had once kept a café in Station Road. It remained an assumption and the coroner returned an open verdict. It seemed they couldn't even be absolutely certain as to how either of them had died. I could only suppose that the bones had been crushed by the earth-moving machines and that the small caliber bullet that had killed Delphine had been overlooked.

It wasn't easy to sit it out, but it was much easier than it would have been if Ida had been alive. The days passed and interest began to wane. Nobody got in touch with me from the bank. No representative called on me from a Sunday news-paper offering me money for an exclusive story. Maybe they couldn't trace me. Maybe I was right about the change in public outlook. Murders were two a penny now and twenty thousand was reckoned a modest haul in terms of current rob-beries. The car park they were gouging out of the hill would cost twice that amount but even that wasn't all. In the last thirty-eight years the value of human life had been debased. Hitler and his successors had seen to that.

4

The doctor was fairly frank. I had half expected him to brush aside my demand for truth, in spite of my insisting that I had important personal obligations to fulfill. He said, pursing his lips in a way that reminded me of poor old Evan trying to refuse a Welsh-speaking customer an overdraft, "Never easy to be specific, Mr. Pritchard. Depends so much on diet, on treatment, on all kinds of things," and when I pressed him to be specific, "with care as long as two or three years."

"Leading what you chaps call 'a normal life'?"

"No, Mr. Pritchard. That way six months, maybe a little longer."

"Will there be more pain? More than brought me here?"

"We can do something about that, Mr. Pritchard. If you'll take my advice you'll come into hospital straightaway. We're breaking new ground every day in your field."

There was irony in this metaphor but I had to enjoy it in private.

"When I've done what I've got to do," I said and he walked with me to the door, a tall, rawboned Scot, who took himself and his profession seriously. I didn't look over my shoulder but I sensed he was following my progress down the road and wondering, incuriously, what kind of personal matters could take priority over a suspended death sentence.

I started writing that same night and it surprised me to dis-cover, in a matter of hours, that I could bring objectivity and a steadiness of vision to the task. I had never written more than the odd letter and even then found it difficult to cover both sides of a page, but this was like a long browse through an album of faded photographs I had not realized, up to that time, that I possessed. Before long it became the most absorbing job I had ever tackled and I stuck at it day by day and week by week, reminding myself that it didn't matter now whether a knock on the door, or an innocent-sounding summons by letter, would interrupt it.

By the New Year it was almost complete but revision took me into the spring, when I was living on tablets and having difficulty in fighting off the doctor's repeated demands to go into hospital. By then, of course, he was curious, and so was the local solicitor to whom I gave instructions regarding the disposal of the typescript. But doctors and lawyers are obliged to exercise a great deal more discretion than policemen when dealing with enigmatic characters.

It was almost done when the lease of the flat I had rented ran out and the owners wanted it back for the summer. May was always a pleasant month in Penmadoc. The sky over the mountains was washed clean and sometimes the sun played on the bay for a week at a time without once having to go into hiding behind the streamers of cloud that were such a feature of that place all the year round. I packed my few things and was at a loss to know where to go other than the hospital that I meant to avoid if I could. Then I had an idea and walked slowly along the main road and up the gentle slope of Craigwen Terrace until I came to the narrow house that I still thought of as St. Ninian's.

The seasonal rush had not begun and the cheerful bright-eyed Welshwoman who answered my ring said I could have a room if I didn't mind the smell of paint and the presence of ladders and trestles all over the landings. "We're doing over," she said, apologetically, "we generally do this time of the year. If you get a decorator in it wipes out half the season's profits." The front rooms were in disarray, she added, but I could have a room at the back. I said this would do, wondering whether it would be mine or Ida's. It was mine and I might have known. Whatever else my story lacked it had shape.

The steep staircases cost me an effort but she was patient and carried my bag. When we got to the room I had to sit down and she looked at me sympathetically. She was an amiable and rather pretty woman, with the dark hair and fresh complexion of the North Walesian.

"You're about done," she said, and feeling some kind of explanation was necessary I told her I had been ill and was convalescing. She said, maternally, "Then take it easy and I'll fetch you a nice cup of tea." Like the British all over the world she believed a nice cup of tea was the final solution to every human problem, from a headache to a bombardment.

I heard her go clattering down the stairs calling to her husband to say she had let number seven, and then I forgot about her and looked about me, renewing my once hostile association with the ghosts of Wally, the consumptive, and Mr. Waring the traveler in pickles, both lovers of my wife Ida. I didn't feel the same vague hostility for them. We were all pals together in this little room, Wally, Mr. Waring, Ida, Evan, Gladys and me. And close at hand, within call as it were, stood Beppo, Powell, Porsen, Griffiths, Gwyn-the-Boots and the girl I had once thought of as a Renaissance Madonna but who turned out to be a trollop with a personality more difficult to recall at this distance than any of them. Then, as I heard the clatter of cup and saucer on the stairs, I remembered the introduction card Delphine had handed me at the very beginning of our partnership. "Come home, Charlie, and face them!" Well, Charlie was home all right, but he wouldn't be facing them after all. They would have to make what they could of the mountain of scribble they found among his effects.